THE EMPRESS GAME

EXILE'S THRONE

Also available from Rhonda Mason and Titan Books

THE EMPRESS GAME
CLOAK OF WAR

THE EMPRESS GAME
EXILE'S THRONE

RHONDA MASON

TITAN BOOKS

The Empress Game: Exile's Throne
Print edition ISBN: 9781783299454
Electronic edition ISBN: 9781783299461

Published by Titan Books
A division of Titan Publishing Group Ltd
144 Southwark Street, London SE1 0UP

First edition: August 2018
10 9 8 7 6 5 4 3 2 1

A CIP catalogue record for this title is available from the British Library.

Printed and bound in Great Britain by CPI Group (UK) Ltd.

What did you think of this book? We love to hear from our readers. Please email
us at: readerfeedback@titanemail.com, or write to us at the above address.

To receive advance information, news, competitions, and exclusive offers online,
please sign up for the Titan newsletter on our website: www.titanbooks.com

To the three most wonderful women in the world—
my mother Beverly and my sisters Rosemary and Andrea.

Thank you for your unconditional love, I would be lost without you.

AUTHOR'S NOTE

The character Wetham, who debuts in this novel, is named in honor of a special friend of mine—Matthew Thomas.

I only write about heroes. Matthew *is* a hero, facing a great many struggles in his daily life. "Meeting" Matthew through letters has enriched my life, and I wanted to show my appreciation in a way near and dear to my heart—character naming.

THE EMPRESS GAME

EXILE'S THRONE

1

THE *YARI*, CENTER OF THE MINE FIELD, IMPERIAL SPACE

Vayne Reinumon finished his final push-up with a groan of agony. Shoulders burning, core quivering, he collapsed on the deck of his cabin on board the *Yari*—Ordoch's ancient warship. Exertion had opened his Eustachian tubes and the roaring white noise of the room's mild air currents wrapped him in isolation; no one asking how he was, no one burdening him with their concern, no one waiting for him to self-destruct.

You don't look well, my dear Vayne.

No one but his ghosts.

The voice alone stoked his simmering rage. It was the voice of the *kin'shaa* Dolan—the Wyrd Worlds' most prolific intellectual sadist.

Dolan, who had murdered Vayne's family and abducted him from his homeworld of Ordoch. Dolan, who had torn his soul and his sanity apart through five years of torturous mind-control experiments.

Dolan, who should be dead.

He is dead.

"Perhaps," Dolan said, appearing in the center of Vayne's cabin. "*Then again, perhaps not.*" The apparition took a seat

11

at the cabin's lone desk and then smoothed his lilac robes around his diminutive frame.

Holy—

Vayne shut his eyes. Wasn't it enough that a demented part of him had imagined Dolan whispering in his mind for months? Now he'd graduated to full-blown visual hallucinations? Saliva flooded his mouth as nausea struck.

For five years Vayne had known that every time Dolan visited his cell or called him to the "playroom," he would be warped further, another piece of himself torn away. Mere months of freedom couldn't undo the unconscious conditioning, nor erase the sick, despairing fear that Dolan's presence inspired.

This isn't real!

He focused on his body, on what he could feel with his other four senses. He stank of sweat. His limbs trembled with exhaustion from a long workout. He was thirsty. *Those* sensations were real, not this hallucination.

Satisfied that he'd talked himself down from the edge of madness—again—Vayne opened his eyes.

Dolan remained.

Would he never outrun this demon?

Dolan smirked. "*Not today.*"

Vayne pushed himself to his feet. The hallucination was so convincing that for a split second he was back in his cell, powerless.

And that really pissed him off.

"You're dead," he snapped. "I killed you."

"*Technically your ro'haar, Kayla, killed me.*" Dolan's smirk stretched into a smile, eyes twinkling. "*And wasn't she glorious while doing it? You merely pulverized my corpse afterward.*"

Vayne's fingers curled into fists at the way Dolan purred Kayla's name.

"*Touchy today, aren't we?*" Dolan sounded so pleased that Vayne took a step in the figment's direction, fists curling tighter.

And now what? Was he going to strangle a specter?

Dolan laughed, a deep, intensely satisfied sound. A sound that brought with it so many mortifying memories.

"I love that you're trying to reason this out," Dolan said. *"I'm dead, I'm a specter, I'm your psyche torturing you..."*

All of the above.

Time to put an end to this nonsense. Vayne focused all of his awareness on Dolan's image, willing it away. The *kin'shaa* merely sat there, one eyebrow slightly raised, waiting.

Bastard.

Vayne tried again, straining with the effort. He was one of the strongest psionics alive. He could defeat any telepathic attack, could bend lesser minds to his will if he chose. It was inconceivable that he couldn't order a figment of his own imagination away.

"Am I just a figment, though?"

And there it was—the crack. The breach in the hull of his surety. Had Dolan done something to him, somehow embedded a form of his consciousness into Vayne's brain?

Scans done on all of the Ordochian POWs back on Falanar said no.

Dolan chuckled. *"You're going to rely on primitive imperial tech for an answer?"* He chuckled again. *"How quaint."*

He could check again, use the *Yari*'s equipment... which was just as primitive, being five hundred years out of date. Damnit.

"The equipment in my laboratory could have confirmed your fears. A pity you destroyed it."

Not possible. Vayne had won. Tia'tan and her people had traveled all the way to the Sakien Empire from the Wyrd World Ilmena on the rumor that Dolan might be holding Ordochian POWs. Tia'tan had joined forces with his *ro'haar* Kayla—his twin sister, bodyguard, and closest friend in the universe—and Kayla's friends in the Imperial Diplomatic Corps to rescue Vayne, his older sister Natali, and their uncle Ghirhad. Kayla had stabbed Dolan in the throat with the *kin'shaa*'s own torture implement in the process, giving Dolan a violent death that was the bare minimum of what he deserved.

Death would never be enough to counter the wounds Dolan had inflicted on Vayne and his family, but it should have at least ensured an end to the mental torture.

"*And yet*," Dolan said, "*here I am*."

Vayne squared to face Dolan straight on. At this point, what did it matter? Talking to a hallucination or ignoring it, he was still messed up enough to be seeing a dead man in his cabin, so he might as well get it over with. "What do you want?"

Dolan leaned back in his chair and rested an elbow on the molychromium surface of the desk. The shimmering pink-gold metal, so precious to Ordoch in current times, made up the bulk of the *Yari*. He toyed with a figurine of the Monmoth Tower that rested there, a keepsake of a long-dead crew member, relic from a life that ended over five hundred years ago.

"*I want what I've always wanted: to see how deep you'll go, to see how far I can push you. You have depths in that heart of yours that even I haven't plumbed—yet*." Dolan rose, set the figurine down, and crossed to stand by the door.

A faint *whoosh*, then a *click* sounded, but Vayne ignored it.

"*You've so much untapped potential for darkness that even in five years I couldn't access it all*."

The words, so close to his own fears, turned his sweat to frost. Vayne tightened his fists.

"*Vayne?*" Dolan took a step toward him. Another. His arm reached out.

Vayne backed up until his calves hit his bunk.

"*You are mine, Vayne,*" the voice whispered in his head. "*You always will be.*" Dolan's slim hand reached for him and there was nowhere to go.

"*Natali's been summoning you.*" Dolan's lips moved as he spoke, but the voice was odd, higher than the *kin'shaa*'s. Then it slipped lower. "*You remember Natali,*" Dolan's voice purred in his mind. "*What fun we had with your sister…*"

Vayne's answering growl of rage shook the room. A hand closed on his upper arm and he lashed out, flinging Dolan against the door with telekinetic force. Dolan impacted with a satisfying grunt as the wind rushed from his lungs. Lavender eyes blinked wide. The fact that their color was all wrong didn't penetrate Vayne's fury. The hurt was still too fresh. The humiliation. The disgust.

He launched himself at Dolan, leading with his left forearm, planning to pin the man to the door by his throat.

The strike never landed.

Instead, Vayne felt his arm caught at the wrist and twisted. Dolan spun him around with amazing quickness. The momentum carried him face first into the door and stars exploded in one eye when his cheek struck the molychromium. Behind him, Dolan wrenched his left arm into his back, sending pain screaming through his shoulder and pinning him in place. He struck with his free elbow but Dolan blocked, then trapped that arm to the door, his fingers around Vayne's wrist like a manacle.

What the frutt? Dolan never fought. Actually, Dolan never came to them without his psionic shield active, now that he thought about it...

Harsh breaths sounded in his ear, and Dolan's body pressed against his with each hard-fought lungful of air.

Only it wasn't Dolan. It couldn't be. Not unless he had grown by a dozen centimeters as a ghost.

"I don't want to hurt you." Tia'tan's voice. Her grip on his wrists cut off circulation to his hands and her feet were planted inside of his, making it impossible for him to move.

Reality slammed into him, along with a bone-deep shame. Why couldn't it have been Uncle Ghirhad who found him, or even his older sister Natali? They'd been tortured alongside him, had their own nightmares of Dolan, their own secrets to keep. They would both pretend they hadn't found him talking to a dead man.

But no, it had to be Tia'tan, his... well, not quite friend—he wasn't really capable of that. She was, though, the one ally whose opinion had begun to matter to him, so naturally she'd be the one he would attack in a hallucination-fueled rage.

Vayne closed his eyes, resting his throbbing cheek against the metal door, trying to erase the last few minutes of time.

"You okay?" she asked quietly. When he gave her a stiff nod she released him and stepped back.

"I'm not crazy," he said without turning around. He couldn't bear to see her thoughts written on her face.

She didn't respond. And really, what could she even say to that?

He forced himself to turn around. Dolan was gone. Tia'tan stood tall in the center of the room, her vibrant energy filling the space. Judging by the salt at her brow, the sweat stains on her tank top and the mid-thigh bruise revealed by her shorts, Tia'tan had spent her afternoon sparring. But while she looked like the glowing picture of health, strong inside and out, he felt like he was breaking down.

I'm not crazy, he wanted to say again, but that would only cement it.

Tia'tan swept her long lavender bangs to one side and tucked them behind her ear, politely looking away, giving him a moment to get his shit together.

An echo of Dolan's laughter floated through his head and Vayne shoved it down deep inside.

"What was that all about?" she finally asked.

How long had she been in his cabin; what had she actually seen? "You surprised me, that's all."

Despite her calm demeanor, Tia'tan's lavender eyes were full of concern—concern and something else he couldn't name. Caution? Distaste? Dolan's mind games had destroyed his ability to identify and trust emotions in others.

She studied him for another moment. Was she worried he might snap, or certain that he already had?

"Natali's been comming you. I buzzed your door several times before entering."

"My mind was elsewhere." *For frutt's sake, say what you came to and leave me alone.*

"When I walked in… it wasn't me you saw, was it?"

All he wanted was quiet, peace. Solitude to go insane with no one watching.

"If you want to talk…"

Vayne shook his head. "I'm fine. Why are you here?"

Tia'tan pursed her lips, clearly debating pushing the issue further, but the moment passed. She rubbed the back of her head, fluffing her short bob haircut. "Kayla and the imperials have arrived and are holding position outside of the Mine Field. Your sisters want to have a conference before Kayla attempts Corinth's plan of taking a hyperstream straight into the heart of the field. I knew you wouldn't want to miss it."

His tension ebbed. Finally. Kayla was almost here. Everything would be better once he had his *ro'haar* back and they could combine their strengths. She might even be able to talk sense into Natali.

That is, *if* she and her imperial friends survived the journey to the Middle of Nowhere. The Mine Field was filled with the wreckage of a war long lost by both sides. It stretched in a void between the farthest Sovereign Planet and the closest Protectorate Planet. A freak exception to kinetic laws drew all of the hyperspace streams in the area through the point, and the same energy anomaly caused disruptions in hyperspace such that fifty percent of ships dropped stream there. Popping out of stream midfield was usually a death sentence. If you didn't wreck your ship on all the debris, the rooks got you. Vayne had seen them himself and he still couldn't say what a rook actually was. An ancient mechanical sentry? A ship flown by pirates? An alien species from another dimension? All he knew for certain was that they were gigantic and could tear a ship apart in minutes.

"Come on," Tia'tan said. "Natali's setting the conference up now." She gestured toward the door but didn't touch him, careful to give him space.

She cared enough to come looking for him, knowing he would want to speak with Kayla before the last leg of her journey. Not only that, Tia'tan took his insane behavior in her stride, making allowances for what he'd been through. What about him warranted such kindness?

"*Women are such suckers for wounded animals, aren't they?*" Dolan whispered in his mind.

Vayne fled his cabin.

17

THE *LORIUS*, IMPERIAL SPACE

The *Lorius* slumbered like a space-born glacier on the outer reaches of the Mine Field. The custom-built luxury starcruiser opalesced white-blue-purple as fuon fibers within the hull's thermal protection system caught the starlight. The Vrise-class hyperstream drive was cold, the ship peaceful. Who would guess that such a rare beauty hosted the Sakien Empire's most wanted fugitives?

Anyone watching the news vids, Kayla thought sourly. They incessantly aired the manufactured story of her "stealing" the ship with the help of Malkor Rua and his octet. Thankfully, the octet knew how to disguise the ship, as well as change out its supposedly tamper-proof transponder for a dummy version. They'd made the journey without incident, the changes making them indistinguishable from any of a number of rich imperials with the credit capital to buy a luxury starcruiser of this size.

Kayla Reinumon, exiled Wyrd Princess, Empress Game winner and *ro'haar* to Vayne and Corinth, shifted her position in her allegedly stolen bed. In truth, the emperor-apparent, Prince Ardin, had willingly given his one-of-a-kind starcruiser to Kayla, Malkor, and the remnants of Malkor's octet to aid their getaway. And perhaps to apologize for his wife Isonde's perfidy.

Kayla refused to think back on Isonde. There was enough to worry about looking forward. Soon she would be reunited with her family, with Vayne, especially with Vayne. *Il'haar* and *ro'haar* had yet to determine how one's five years in captivity and the other's in hiding had affected their bond. More than that, Kayla couldn't deny her sense of dread at discovering just how much the loss of her psi powers would hurt their bond.

She pulled the silken covers higher, careful not to tweak her damaged arm, and then curled toward the naked man asleep beside her.

Malkor Rua.

Her Malkor.

She hooked her leg over his hip to pull herself even closer. She felt his skin, his heartbeat, his breath. Smelled the scent of his hair, his body, and the aftermath of their lovemaking. Malkor cradled her in his sleep, and it was the most natural thing in the universe.

She loved him. If she could fuse their souls together, she would.

But that was the problem, wasn't it? Her soul was essentially fused to Vayne's. That bond, twin to twin, *ro'haar* to *il'haar*, was supposed to fulfill her, complete her. And she had a second, less intense though no less important, bond with her younger brother Corinth, to whom she'd been acting *ro'haar* for the past five years. As a *ro'haar*, she shouldn't want any more than that.

Il'haars and *ro'haars* never married. Each twin took lovers to satisfy their physical needs, but they never bonded with anyone romantically. A strong romantic attachment of that kind on either side would draw their focus away from the twin bond. It just wasn't done. Even when it came to having heirs, the *il'haar* chose a partner based on their superior genetics and psionic ability to have a child with. That woman might be the heirs' mother, but she did not rule.

Yet here she was with Malkor. She had found romance, had found love, which, now tasted, she did not want to give up.

The two weeks since their escape from the imperial homeworld had been the best two weeks of her life. She hadn't known happiness like this existed. Contentment, surely; satisfaction with her skills as a bodyguard and the ease of knowing her *il'haars* were safe, absolutely. But happiness? Now that they were together, truly together, she finally understood.

While the rest of the octet—which now consisted of five members—took turns flying the ship, Kayla and Malkor took turns exploring each other. Her life had been a nightmare since the empire captured her homeworld, what with living in hiding, protecting her younger brother, fighting in the Blood

Pit on the slum side of Altair Tri… not to mention being pulled into Isonde's schemes. And it was no secret that once they reached their destination, the center of the Mine Field, chaos would claim her life again.

But here, for two weeks, she didn't have to hide. She didn't have to fight, didn't have to plot or scheme or run. The only thing she wanted to do, the only thing she did, was spend time with her love. These were two weeks out of time, and they meant everything to her.

Considering she was joining the war to retake her homeworld of Ordoch from the Sakien Empire, they were probably her last two happy weeks, as well.

Malkor's lashes lifted. He peered at her with sleepy green eyes whose corners crinkled at the first glimpse of her face.

"Hi," he said, his arms tightening around her, bringing their bodies flush.

"Hi, yourself."

"Have you been watching me sleep again?"

She kissed him in answer, and that kiss led to another, and another. Kayla forced him to his back and stretched her length out atop him, longing to get closer, to feel every centimeter of skin against skin. Malkor wrapped one arm around her waist and threaded his other hand into her long blue hair, cupping the back of her head and holding her there so she couldn't pull back from their kiss.

As if she would.

Kayla moved against him with an almost fatalistic need. She hadn't known herself to be capable of such hunger, such desire, until Malkor. Malkor responded with a low growl and shifted his grip to her hips, fingertips digging into her flesh.

Did he taste the desperation in her kiss? The fear of losing him? Did she taste just a hint of desperation in return? Malkor was no fool. Although he had secured a place in her heart despite her protection of Corinth, he must have given some thought to what it would mean to Kayla to have Vayne truly back in her life.

20

They had arrived at the edge of the Mine Field the night before. And as soon as Natali contacted them, the cocoon they had wrapped themselves in would be sundered. They would belong to their destinies from then on.

There might never be another moment like this one.

Kayla braced herself on Malkor's shoulders and rose above him, ignoring the complaint in her healing arm. His hands gripped her tighter, urged her faster, and she knew he felt it too, these last precious moments slipping away.

Less than an hour later, while they lay replete in a sweaty tangle of limbs, their holiday ended, Rigger, Malkor's tech specialist, broke in with a comm:

"Natali's called in—it's time to talk plans."

Kayla could practically hear the sigh they both refused to make. Malkor rolled over to touch the comm. "On our way."

They scrubbed down quickly, donned fresh clothes, and entered the bridge of the *Lorius* to be greeted by game faces all around.

Rigger was at comms and Hekkar, Malkor's second in command and close friend, sat at the weapon controls—which didn't surprise Kayla in the least. Of the octet members, he was always the most serious, the most prepared for a negative outcome. He was also the member of the octet who had disapproved of her relationship with Malkor from the start. She'd won him over with her dedication and fervor to free Malkor when he'd been taken prisoner. Now she and Hekkar had a special bond as the two people who cared the most for Malkor's welfare.

Beside Hekkar stood Trinan and Vid, the main muscle of the octet and holders of a special place in Kayla's heart. They had taken her younger brother Corinth under their wing as if he were their own son, while Kayla had been busy with the many intrigues of the Empress Game. Indeed, Vid had almost given his life to save Corinth. Kayla wouldn't hesitate to do the same for either of them.

The last person in the room was the medic Toble, not actually a member of the octet. Toble was a long-standing friend of theirs, probably to his regret. He had been dragged into every clandestine mission the octet ran, whenever they needed unreported medical attention. That included treating Kayla when she'd taken Isonde's identity during the Empress Game, saving Isonde from her deathly coma (with Prince Ardin's help), and operating on Kayla's right arm when Siño had nearly destroyed it. The wound was still tender, but thanks to Toble's expertise Kayla had had a chance to recover full use of the limb. Without that she might as well be dead, for all the good she'd be as a *ro'haar* to her brothers.

Missing from the octet were Janeen, who had betrayed them, Aronse, who couldn't afford to run rogue because she had an extended family to support, and Gio, whose gambling addiction had forced him to become a puppet to the octet's enemies. Janeen had been killed, and Gio and Aronse had stayed on Falanar and denounced Malkor to save themselves.

Malkor reached to take her hand, but Kayla sidled away, pretending not to notice his gesture as she stepped toward the massive vidscreen the bridge boasted. Their blissful time as a couple—and her reprieve from her many duties—had ended. She felt a heavy weight as the mantle of *ro'haar*, Wyrd rebel, and Ordochian princess settled on her once more.

If Malkor was surprised by her sudden distance, she had no idea, for she didn't look back to acknowledge it.

The communications console beeped and Rigger checked the input. "Natali and the others are waiting to speak to us."

Malkor nodded, and everyone on the bridge activated their aural translator implants and turned to face the vidscreen as it lit up. Though she'd seen it a few times before, Kayla still couldn't believe she was looking at the actual control room from the actual *Yari*.

Instead, she focused on what she could believe: the people in the room. Her older sister Natali—who had been *ro'haar* to her own twin Erebus before he died under Dolan's years of torture—stood front and center. Everyone aboard the *Yari* looked to Natali, and seemed to be waiting for her to speak.

Kayla and Natali had trained together growing up, but they'd never been close. Natali and Erebus were Ordoch's heirs, destined to rule, and that had set them apart from their siblings. Beyond that, Natali had a natural coldness and superiority about her. She never asked for help, she never asked for quarter, and she never asked for comfort. All the Ordochian *ro'haars*, twinned and untwinned alike, knew that Natali was the best. Kayla had lived with a mix of awe and fear of her older sister as a child.

There was something immovable in Natali's gaze now, as she stood in command of the ancient battleship, that put Kayla on alert.

"Sister. You look well," Natali said crisply in Ordochian.

Kayla stood just a little taller. It took an effort not to drop her gaze under Natali's intense aquamarine stare. "You seem improved," Kayla said. *But not by much*. The last time Kayla had seen her sister, Natali had been free from Dolan's prison for mere hours. Now she had more meat on her and a less vacant stare, but her pale blue ponytail looked tight enough to rip hair out at the roots and her features were practically immobile. She seemed more… herself. More solid, more fierce. But also more brittle, like a breath of solar wind might crumble all that ferocity in pieces.

Kayla had never seen her sister's strength so mixed with vulnerability, though she doubted anyone else in the room noticed anything other than the perfect confidence she projected. Only Kayla, who had known Natali before the Dolan years, recognized what was underneath, and somehow, that made her sister seem all the stronger, because for Natali to command them as she did now spoke to her steadfastness to do what must be done.

"No time to waste recouping." She glanced at Kayla's damaged arm. Kayla unconsciously shifted her stance to hide the weakness from sight.

"I'll be fine."

"Good. The Reinumons can show no weakness. You've always been exceptionally strong, we'll need your strength in the months ahead."

Kayla nodded, unwilling to let her sister see how greatly the compliment affected her. Natali's expression was unreadable as she took a step backward. "Our brother is eager to see you."

Kayla's pulse quickened. She looked beyond her sister and saw the *Yari*'s master, Captain Janus, who now went by her informal first name, Ida. Beside her were Abenifluis Strokar—Benny—the *Yari*'s main gunner and now Ida's second in command, Navigations First Officer Navriel Entar—Ariel—and the ship's physicist, Tanet. The collection of greenish-blue hair proclaimed their age. Over generations, the natural hair color of modern Ordochians had shifted from the ancient green-blue to the fully blue spectrum.

Noar stood on the other side of the room. His lilac hair color proclaimed him a citizen of the Wyrd World Ilmena. He had come with Tia'tan and a group of Ilmenans to free Kayla's family from Dolan's clutches, and she would be forever grateful. Then the doors on screen opened, and everyone turned to look.

Tia'tan entered first and took up position beside Noar, apparently unfazed by the attention, and then, finally, behind Tia'tan came Vayne, who hesitated in the doorway when he saw everyone staring at him. He had a hunted look, and Kayla's heart went out to him. As much as she was thrilled to see him alive and safe, it hurt to see him in any distress.

"Vayne," Kayla called out. "I'm here."

Vayne met her gaze through the vidscreen and seemed to draw strength from their connection. His shoulders relaxed the tiniest bit. "Good to see you," he said, giving her a ghost of a smile.

Vayne stepped forward and positioned himself halfway between Tia'tan and Natali as if trying to keep equal distance from both.

Odd. Kayla knew he and Natali disagreed on using the *Yari*'s massive weapons systems in the Ordochian War, but surely he felt more comfortable with their sister than an Ilmenan. She wanted to ask. She wanted to speak, but they stood on opposite bridges surrounded by too many people who weren't each other. Twin conversation would have to wait.

"Where's Corinth?" she asked.

"Same place he's been since we arrived—the engine room, working on the hyperstream drive. He'd sleep there if I let him," Vayne said with humor.

"Are you making sure he's getting enough to eat?" Vid asked.

Noar nodded. "I'm keeping an eye on him."

The Ilmenan was? Not Vayne? Kayla looked a question at her brother but he broke eye contact.

"Greetings to the agents as well," Natali said, glancing at the members of the octet for the first time. "Senior Agent Rua, you have my thanks and the thanks of my family for the part your octet played in our rescue from captivity." She inclined her head to Malkor.

"It is our honor," he replied.

"Thank you also for aiding Kayla in her journey to this point. We will always be grateful."

Most people might say they were in Malkor's debt, but for Natali, who knew the role IDC had played in the Ordochian coup, the scales would never tip in that direction.

"Good luck in your travels back to the empire."

"Back?" Malkor asked. The one-word question seemed to increase the tension on both ships.

Natali paused before answering. "I assume you have a rendezvous with a ship to take you and your octet back to your homeworld. Kayla is more than capable of flying an imperial ship alone." She made the *Lorius* sound as complex as a bathtub toy.

"There is no way—" Malkor started, but Kayla cut him off with a hand on his arm.

She widened her stance, squaring off against Natali. "The octet is coming with me." Their blue gazes locked. On the periphery, Vayne frowned at her words.

"I appreciate what've they done, but imperials have no place on this ship."

"We're here to help," Rigger said. The look Natali shot her prevented Rigger from elaborating. Trinan and Vid straightened and Kayla recognized the prelude to their battle stances.

Over on the *Yari*, Captain Janus looked like she might say something, but Natali didn't give her a chance. Her eyes narrowed. "Your place is with your family and your people now, sister. There is no room in your future for distractions."

Kayla didn't even have to think about her response, though she was loath to oppose her sister. "You're wrong."

Natali's chin lowered a fraction. A defensive move, one declaring she was ready to fight. "As heir to the Ordoch throne, I order—"

"I said no. The octet stays with me."

The moment dragged on as Natali, backed into a corner she hadn't seen coming, debated her response. Her final verdict was harsh. "Imperials are not welcome on this ship, and if you will not part with them, it follows that you cannot board either."

Captain Janus definitely looked disturbed now, but she held her peace.

Kayla took a step closer to the vidscreen, ignoring the flash of guilt at her betrayal. "I recognize that you are Ordoch's sovereign now, but your title can't stop me from seeing my *il'haars*." Kayla looked to Vayne, letting him know that she meant the words. She would not abandon him again. "My whole purpose is to free the people of Ordoch, and everyone on this ship shares that goal. The octet and I will execute Noar and Corinth's crazy plan of flying straight into the Mine Field, and if we survive, we will *all* be joining you."

She switched her attention to the captain. "Captain Janus, the docking mechanisms on the *Lorius* are significantly different than Ordochian design. I doubt we'll be able to form a seal."

"Is no problem! Dockings have umbilical, many many, will shunt you through the space." She smiled. "Eager we have been for arrival of yours."

Natali remained silent and everyone held their breath. If glacial ice could smolder, her gaze would burn, despite the control she had over her expression. "We'll speak soon, sister." She left the room without another word, taking the tension with her.

It seemed as if everyone on both sides of the vidscreen relaxed once she had gone.

"Okay, Noar, Tanet. Let's talk about this hyperstream vector you propose." Kayla forced a smile. "Promise it won't land us in the middle of the field and kill us all?"

Noar returned the smile and made a wobbly motion with his hand.

Vid chuckled. "That's about how our luck runs, huh, boss?"

"Sure seems that way these days," Malkor answered.

2

FALANAR CITY, FALANAR, IMPERIAL SPACE

After a decade of intricate political schemes and maneuvers, Isonde Veriley—princess of the Sovereign Planet Piran, empress-apparent of the Sakien Empire—had earned her seat on the Council of Seven. *And they'll have to pry my dead body out of it if they want it back.* The prestigious chambers of the Council of Seven claimed a place of pride within Falanar's imperial palace. Few had ever entered, despite the centuries passing. Fewer still had sat at the great oblong table in the center, claiming one of the precious seven votes that decided the ultimate fate of the Sakien Empire.

Seated at the table now, Isonde glanced at the chronometer embedded in the wall. How could it be late afternoon already? There was so much more to do. Always more. Already today, she'd held meetings with two members of the Sovereign Council and several members of the Protectorate Council, trying to further her agenda of helping all planets in the empire infected with the Tetratock nanovirus.

Precious moments passed as Sovereign Council member Elivar Bellst argued—again—in favor of a plan to pull humanitarian support from some of the Protectorate Planets— where it was needed most—to focus on Sovereign Planet Wei-lu-Wei. The first outbreak of the Tetratock nanovirus on a Sovereign Planet had rocked the empire, and priorities were shifting once again. Apparently, the Sovereign Council was ready to let the Protectorate Planets be eaten alive in order to save one of their own. Knowing Bellst would formally make this proposal today, Isonde had come with arguments prepared against him, but with the chronometer counting down, it seemed she'd be forced to wait until tomorrow's session. The last thing she wanted was for the other council members to have a night to ponder the merits of a plan that would let thousands, if not millions, of people die.

Another few minutes of this and I'm going to cut him off, etiquette rules or not. If the Protectorate Council member, who looked to be at a fine boil, didn't beat her to it.

In truth, Isonde was well aware that delaying an abandonment of the Protectorate Planets to focus resources on Sovereign Planets would make no difference. The TNV was spreading exponentially now. The nanotech had been designed as a weapon, supposedly one with containment protocols, but once unleashed the TNV quickly mutated, evolving past those protocols and learning to replicate itself biologically. The virus ate a person from the inside out, consuming the body to make more of itself.

Once it had devoured Velezed—the Protectorate Planet on which it originated—and escaped to space inside unwitting travelers, there was no hope of containing it. The only thing that could save the empire now was a cure.

Something her people seemed incapable of discovering.

The Council of Seven's recent decision to double-down on their military occupation of the Wyrd World Ordoch was completely asinine. If they didn't reverse that vote and start negotiating with the Ordochians—who had the advanced knowledge needed to create a cure—there would be nothing left of the empire to save.

Suddenly, in the middle of one of Bellst's long-winded sentences, the emperor himself interrupted with a bang of his gavel. As adjudicator of the Council of Seven, he had that right, but all heads at the table jerked up in surprise. "As it is time to close today's session, this item will have to be tabled until tomorrow."

"Request for tomorrow's opening proposal," Isonde said immediately. All eyes now turned her way. Perhaps, as newest member of the Council of Seven, she was supposed to be deferential. *Never in my life*. And she wouldn't start now. She'd worked too hard, sacrificed too much, to waste a single second.

Emperor-Apparent Prince Ardin offered her a tiny nod of approval. She might have ruined forever her chance at marital bliss, but at least they were united in their determination to do what was best for the people of the empire—all of the people, not just the privileged ones.

"Granted," the emperor said. "Now, one last bit of administrative business before we close. In light of this council's decision to increase our military presence on Ordoch"—a decision that still horrified Isonde—"I've decided that we'll benefit from the biweekly presence of an advisor from the Imperial Army.

Outsiders having access to the deliberations of the highest authority in the empire? Especially the Imperial Army, whose leaders seemed diametrically opposed to everything she was trying to accomplish? "Absolutely not," Isonde said, five angry responses echoing hers. Only the empress seemed unsurprised—likely complicit.

The emperor held up a hand. "It's already been decided."

"Without a vote?" the Protectorate member asked in a choked voice. "Outrageous!"

"It is well within my right as adjudicator, I assure you."

We'll see about that. Isonde made a mental note to get her aides scouring the council's articles of incorporation this evening.

The emperor commed the secretary in the outer council chambers with a request before turning his attention back to them. "The representative has already been agreed upon."

"That should have been the right of the council," Ardin said, his voice stiff with the same anger she felt.

The doors opened, cutting off debate, and General Elmain Wickham entered. *Not surprising.* He'd been a main author of Operation Redouble, which the Council of Seven had approved on that fateful day two weeks ago. He moved out of the way and a second figure entered.

Foreboding settled in Isonde's stomach with the density of a neutron star. In the doorway stood Senior Commander Jersain Vega of the Imperial Diplomatic Corps.

What the—?

Wickham made the appropriate formal greeting to the emperor and the council, as Jersain, expression neutral, edged slightly in front of him. Wickham spoke, seemingly unaware of Jersain's subtle move: "In light of our changing needs *vis-à-vis* the empire's plans for Ordoch, I have decided that a new head of the Ordoch occupation is needed. The army has appointed Senior Commander Vega."

Only years of diplomatic training kept Isonde from falling out of her chair. The army granting the IDC authority over them? Since their inceptions, the two organizations had never done anything besides butt heads over jurisdiction. What was going on here?

Vega in charge of the occupation meant any negotiation with Ordoch would have to be done through her, and there was no chance her terms would align with the ones Isonde had in mind.

Looks like my plate just got a lot fuller.

And time was still counting down against her.

Even with a headache brewing, Jersain Vega had a spring in her step as she left the council chamber in search of Agira. The consternation on Princess Isonde's face after the emperor's announcement was too delightful. *Uppity bitch.* Isonde had been climbing her way up the empire's political ladder since birth, so sure of her ultimate triumph. No doubt she had wet dreams about unofficially ruling the Council of Seven. *Sorry,*

Isonde, there's only room for one woman at the top.

Jersain intended to be that one. Let the others claim their council seats. She had something better than all of their exalted positions combined: the Influencer. Jersain allowed herself a smile as she strode down the ornate corridors of the imperial palace. With Dolan's mind control device in her possession, nothing was out of reach.

Now she just had to master her stolen psi powers and learn to operate it herself.

Jersain pushed that concern off for another day and entered the lounge where Agira waited. Agira had been allowed into the palace as Jersain's assistant, but of course she wasn't admitted to the council chamber. The Wyrd stood as Jersain arrived, a tentative smile on her face, clearly hoping for approval. An unexpected feeling bloomed in Jersain's chest: the need to reassure. Looking upon Agira, she realized that even if things had not gone to plan, she would have moderated her disappointment to avoid crushing the thrall.

"Excellent work, Agira. I never would have gotten that appointment to the Council of Seven without you."

Agira beamed. "The first of many great things to come for you." There was no pride in her voice, only happiness. She looked eager to cross the room and embrace Jersain in congratulation, but she was too well trained to do that in any public space.

Such a good thrall.

Even riding high on triumph and the momentary defeat of her enemies, Jersain felt the pounding in her head. The headache promised to be brutal, and she'd only used her psi powers to follow Agira's work with the Influencer. Agira, on the other hand, had had to interface with the incredibly complex machine for hours, constantly adjusting her delicate control over the emperor so that he wouldn't second-guess his decision to appoint Wickham, and by extension Jersain, to positions of power.

"You must be exhausted," Jersain said, wending past two

gaudily brocaded chairs and a luxeglass table to reach Agira. "Rest a moment before we leave." She took her arm and led her to a more comfortable moleskin sofa.

"Only a moment or two; I won't keep us long." Agira sank down into the sofa, slumping against the back without her usual grace. Jersain had felt her struggle with the Influencer, sensed the strain building in her mind while she worked on the emperor. Agira would need a quiet night of rest at home, which Jersain, sitting here listening to Agira's breathing and feeling her unwind as they sat close, suddenly desired as well.

Agira possessed only moderate psionic abilities. With the powers that Dolan had ripped from Vayne to grant to Jersain, she was actually the stronger psionic. She still needed to master complete control of her power, but she'd advanced by leaps and bounds in the last few weeks, surpassing Agira in brute strength, if not finesse.

She let her gaze drift over her slave. Dolan had brought her with him when he fled the Wyrd World Ilmena all those years ago. He'd already broken her will during his experiments on his own people, and instilled in her the permanent mind-control order of living to please Dolan. Dolan had transferred Agira's loyalty from himself to Jersain at her demand. Since he'd arrived on Falanar, Jersain had been his ally, a necessary evil—the Wyrd was a sociopath. She had personally overseen the capture of Wyrds in the Ordochian coup, providing a way for him to regain his psionic abilities.

It was the very least of what he owed her. *And Agira is better off with me.*

Agira's eyes fluttered closed, exhaustion written in every line of her face. Dolan had commented once, "I'd call her plain; then again, I'm the diplomatic type." *More like the asshole type.* His cosmetic changes to her hair and eye color didn't help. A synth color appliqué faded Agira's hair to ash blonde and her irises had been darkened to blue-gray. Jersain much preferred their natural color, a matching shade of heather. A pity her identity as a Wyrd must be kept secret.

She was something of a wren—small in stature, drab, with an impressively beakish nose—and Jersain would have ruled her out as a lover if not for what she offered beyond looks. Initially, Agira had been no more than a servant, invaluable for reading the thoughts and intentions of others and passing that info on to Jersain in real time. In addition she was Jersain's full-time tutor in the psionic arts. Thanks to the mind control, Jersain's goals were her goals, Jersain's successes her successes. They shared the same frustrations, disappointments, schemes and risks. It was only natural that they'd grown close.

It was time they left the palace, but Jersain hesitated to disturb her. Agira had a generous heart, she had discovered. A strong sense of empathy, a quiet way of understanding others perfectly. She also lacked ambition for herself: she was more interested in the needs of those around her. To Dolan, those qualities made her the perfect thrall. It had been all too easy for him to bend her natural tendencies into a permanent demand focused on one person.

For Jersain, those qualities made Agira the perfect confidante. Somehow they had shifted from a master–servant dynamic into something more like partners without Jersain realizing it. The connection almost felt genuine.

Was it weakness to care? It was certainly unnecessary, yet there it was.

No soft feelings for a thrall would get in the way of the ruthlessness she'd need to accomplish her goals. As much as she enjoyed Agira, they could never be equals, because Jersain's goal was to have no equal. She closed her eyes and summoned the psi powers Agira was helping her master. Slowly, carefully, she reached out, touched the part of her thrall's mind that Dolan had taught her to, twisted it as Agira herself had been teaching her. She felt the dim resistance that all minds, even the most pliant, reflexively raised against control by another, and easily clamped it down.

::Agira, kneel before me.::

Agira's lids rose slowly, and it took her a moment to focus.

Jersain kept the clamp tight in her mind, making resistance impossible. Her thrall blinked as her exhausted thoughts registered the command, and when understanding hit, she shifted off of the sofa and fell to her knees on the floor.

Jersain held her there, supplicant, inferior, head bowed and hands cupped before her in a bowl, symbolically offering herself, and through the psi link Jersain felt the strength of the thrall bond, how willing—no—eager Agira was to please her master, and after today's meeting of the council, Jersain's imagination filled with images of that blissful day when she would be able to command any person at all to fall at her feet.

And it made a corner of Jersain's mouth rise to think of that person being Princess Isonde Veriley.

THE *YARI*, MINE FIELD

The hyperspace jump went as planned—miraculously, in Kayla's opinion—and the *Lorius* arrived without incident in the center of the Mine Field. There were a few oaths uttered when the hyperstream deposited them dangerously close to the *Yari* and set every proximity warning klaxon to life at full volume, but still, they were alive.

The ancient battleship filled the entire vidscreen, edge to edge, so massive in scale that they couldn't see it all. Kayla released the crash harness of the seat she'd been strapped into for the short jump. "I feel like an ant looking up at a skyscraper." The octet remained speechless. Even their largest deep-space vessels were toys compared to the *Yari*.

A loud "Whoop!" came from the comms, breaking the silence. "It worked!" Captain Janus called from the other ship. "You gain permission mine to come aboard. *Yari* out."

Everyone disentangled themselves from their seats. Kayla looked at Malkor, then at the others. "Are you ready for this?"

"Ready?" Vid asked. "We're imperial IDC agents about to

board a Wyrd battleship crewed by people lost in time for five hundred years."

"Not to mention the empire and the Wyrds are about to be at war," Trinan chimed in.

"Don't remind me," Malkor said.

Vid shook his head. "How could we possibly be ready?"

Seated at the nav console, Rigger said, "Kayla, *you* don't even look ready for this."

True. She knew the physical measurements of the *Yari*, remembered that it was built on an unprecedented scale, but to see it live, to float next to it while it loomed...

Captain Janus hailed them again. "Shuttle launching now is Ariel, you to receive. Also, young Corinth says you to be hurrying." The words pushed all thoughts of historic ships out of Kayla's head. Her *il'haars* were close, finally. She'd physically ached to be away from Corinth. And Vayne? She'd had precious few days to spend with him after his rescue, before he and the Ilmenans had fled Falanar. At this point she'd do an untethered spacewalk if that was what it took to get to them.

Everyone gathered their gear, and Trinan powered the ship's systems down to dormant. Kayla was already waiting impatiently outside the shuttle bay by the time the octet members arrived.

Toble asked, "Who is this 'Ariel' again? I am trying to keep all the names and nationalities of those on board straight."

"Navigations First Officer Navriel Entar," Trinan and Vid answered simultaneously.

"Unofficially third in charge, after Captain Janus and First Weapons Officer Abenifluis Strokar, according to Vayne's report on the situation," Rigger added from where she stood near the bay doors, monitoring Ariel's arrival.

Toble raised both brows, earning a laugh from Malkor. "Facilitating meetings between multinationals with different agendas, sometimes in hostile territories, who may or may not be at war, is pretty much the IDC's mission."

"Don't worry, doc," Vid said, "we do this sort of thing all the time."

Kayla hadn't needed the reminder, but she welcomed it. "I apologize for the less-than-friendly welcome you're about to receive."

"That's nothing new, either," Hekkar said, shifting the weight of his pack on his back. "But hey, we won you over, didn't we?"

"After we kidnapped her," Vid reminded him.

"And my *il'haar*," she said.

"See? We'll have them eating out of our hands by morning."

Kayla couldn't help but smile. The unlikeliest of allies, now her closest friends. "Thank you all. I couldn't—" She cut herself off before her voice could tremble.

Malkor clapped her on the shoulder. "Don't go getting emotional on us. We'll start thinking you've been replaced by a doppelgänger."

"Who says she hasn't?" Hekkar quipped.

"One that fights that well?" Vid shook his head. "Not likely."

The team filed into the shuttle bay to greet her. Ariel gave Kayla a socially correct bow and a polite, if tepid, smile. "Ida to be eager to see you, Princess Kayla." The others she acknowledged with a single nod before turning and walking back into her shuttle.

Beside Kayla, Vid leaned close. "Friendly, eh?"

She didn't have the heart to tell him their reception was about to get worse.

The shuttle docked smoothly into its berth on the *Yari*. As soon as they entered the bare-bones construction of the ship's interior, Corinth's voice sounded in her head.

::Kayla! We're up in the large observatory; Ariel will show you the way!::

She couldn't reply without her psi powers, but it didn't matter because she felt Corinth brushing at the edge of her mind, seeking permission to enter her head. As Ariel led them through a series of maglifts and cylindrical corridors, Kayla sorted her thoughts into compartments, locking things away, before she lowered her outer shields and let Corinth in. Even though it went against the grain to be that vulnerable to anyone and ran counter to all her *ro'haar* training, she did it for Corinth. With Vayne, such a thing would have been as natural to her as breathing.

Corinth rushed in like an overeager puppy, filling near to bursting and sending an instant ache to her forehead.

Easy. She didn't have a psi voice to speak with, but in her mind this way Corinth could read her surface thoughts. *Hasn't Vayne taught you better by now?* The rebuke lacked bite. Corinth had been her sole family for five years—he could do no wrong in her eyes.

::Sorry. I've been working with Noar. Wait until you see all I've learned! We did this thing where you levitate a glass full of water and you can't spill a single drop...:: He regaled her with his psionic exploits all the way to the observation deck.

"Welcome you are to the *Yari*," Captain Janus said as soon as they entered. With her thigh-length sea-green braid streaming over one shoulder and her confident smile, she looked exactly as Kayla remembered her from the history vids. "Being, of course, the ship most magnificent."

"It's surreal to meet you, Captain," Kayla said, accepting her enthusiastic handshake.

The captain laughed. "So they are telling me. Please, you will call Ida. And my second—" she gestured to the stocky man beside her. "You will call Benny. Too few we are for formal."

Benny bowed without smiling, his intense aqua gaze scrutinizing what was left of the octet. Kayla made the introductions and the temperature in the room dipped a degree or two.

Corinth broke through the awkward moment by coming forward to wrap Kayla in a hug. ::You made it. I knew our plan would work.::

Something internal that had been out of joint for weeks realigned itself as she held onto him. *Nothing as inconsequential*

38

as the physics of space travel was going to stop me.

He swirled inside her head, his version of a mental hug. ::Wait until you see the rest of the ship! And the hyperstream drive we're working on—it's amazing!::

Ida and Benny made way and Kayla got a look at the rest of the room's inhabitants. The sight of Natali, Uncle Ghirhad and Vayne hit her square in the chest. *My family.* Her emotions rose up in a tumult, and through their mental link, Corinth pulsed with love and support.

::We aren't alone anymore.:: He released her from his hug and dashed over to greet the octet almost as enthusiastically as he had greeted her—Trinan and Vid especially.

Her gaze locked on Vayne, and it was all she could do not to knock everyone out of her way to reach him. She even took a few steps toward him before faltering. Protocol, there was protocol to observe. It was right to greet her sister first, as Ordoch's exiled sovereign. And perhaps it was best to save greeting Vayne for last, since she'd have no interest in anyone after that.

Natali approached, saving Kayla from a misstep. "It is very good to have you back with us, sister." Her brief smile dispelled the earlier tension between them. "Back where you belong."

The rightness of being reunited with her Ordochian family—permanently, this time—overwhelmed Kayla. She surprised them both by giving Natali a fierce squeeze.

Her sister stiffened.

Kayla released her immediately, remembering too late that Natali's torture at Dolan's hands had changed more than her sister's attitude about her responsibilities as heir to the throne. "I'm sorry." She backed away to give Natali space as the room went silent. "I didn't think."

What should she say? Kayla looked to where Vayne stood, hoping for a sign of what she should do, but he gazed fiercely the floor.

Natali took a breath, a second, slowly relaxing.

"I'm sorry," Kayla repeated, meaning something entirely different this time.

Natali shook her head. "No, I apologize. It has just been some time." Some time since what, she didn't say. Her pale blue eyes scanned Kayla's face, took in her attire—kris daggers strapped to each thigh, flat-heeled boots for sure footing, tunic slit on each side to allow for maximum movement, and belt holding an ion pistol at the small of her back. She nodded in approval.

::It is good to be with another *ro'haar* again. There is so much the others don't understand, such as duty, sacrifice, and making the hard choices.:: The kinship in Natali's mind voice connected them in a way the hug hadn't. Kayla completely agreed, even if the sentiment might have offended the others.

She had an affinity with the octet, whose creed was much aligned with hers, but only another *ro'haar* could truly understand how far she would go to protect what was left of her family.

Kayla's mind was still filled with Corinth, and she loved the happiness that bubbled over from him through their link. Nevertheless, she would have gently squeezed him out in order to speak mind to mind with Natali, had her sister given any indication that she would welcome the connection.

No such indication came from the ever-reserved Natali.

Uncle Ghirhad, apparently unable to contain his greeting a nanosecond longer, broke into the moment, joining them to give Kayla a boisterous hug.

"You are looking so well, my dear. The picture of health," he said, still hugging. In contrast, he looked much diminished from how she remembered him. "It is wonderful that you're here. I'm delighted, absolutely delighted." If she didn't surpass him in height and muscle mass, Kayla imagined he'd be twirling her in the air. Uncle Ghirhad hadn't been particularly effusive before the coup, and this overwhelming show of excitement seemed out of character. Then again, Corinth hadn't been mute before Dolan tore their family apart, and she hadn't been psionically dead.

So much had changed.

Unsure how to deal with this new side of Ghirhad, and

unable to break away, she said the only thing that came to mind: "Uncle, can I reintroduce you to my friends, who rescued all of us from exile?" At last he released her, but not without a kiss on the cheek. She braced herself for any number of reactions.

"That would be splendid. Absolutely splendid." His smile grew, which hadn't seemed possible. "I am thrilled to be in their company again, these heroes. Especially as they have done so much for us." He stood on tiptoe to kiss her cheek, then headed straight toward Malkor without waiting for her to lead. The octet would understand his greeting, thanks to their translator implants, but would not be able to reply. Uncle Ghirhad didn't seem to mind one bit, shaking hands enthusiastically and clapping each of them on the elbow, as shoulders were out of reach for him.

At last she was able to greet her *il'haar*.

Corinth respectfully withdrew from her mind as she crossed the room to where Vayne, Tia'tan, and Noar stood beside the observation windows. Kayla nodded vaguely to the Ilmenans, then everyone in the room faded from her awareness.

In the brief vidchats they'd had the last few weeks, Vayne had seemed edgy and tense. Now, standing face to face, his eyes held a measure of peace.

::*Ro'haar*.:: His mind voice expressed a dozen emotions that found an answer in her. He reached mentally for her and Kayla responded, eager to connect. She reached, and…

… found only the hole in her mind where her powers should be.

Disappointment flashed through him and into her before he could stop it, and hit like a whip strike. She scrabbled at the void, clawing with mental fingernails at the edges, searching for any way past the black glass that separated her from her powers.

For one millisecond they had both forgotten her handicap, making reality all the harsher.

The moment passed as Vayne sent a flood of emotion that was welcome and love and joy and reunion all in one.

In her heart, she knew peace. *I am home.*

* * *

It took Kayla a minute to become aware of a presence at her elbow, despite that presence being her shadow for the last five years.

Corinth.

Standing beside her and giving Vayne, the brother he idolized, an uncharacteristically serious look. Vayne looked back, just as serious, and Kayla itched to know what was passing between them. She was stuck between wanting to speak with Vayne alone, and not wanting to hurt Corinth's feelings by asking him to leave them.

Corinth saved her from the choice by walking away, closer to the huge viewports as if studying the Mine Field.

By unspoken agreement, Kayla and Vayne headed to the back corner of the room and settled in chairs. He brushed against her mind, asking permission, and Kayla paused before letting him in. She quickly boxed away her feelings for Malkor and set them behind a deeper mental wall, feeling guilty even as she did it. In the past she wouldn't have considered hiding something from her twin—yet another lovely part of Dolan's legacy.

Vayne slipped into her mind gently. His essence filled her and he drank her in, and the moment felt so right, it was as if half of her soul had finally returned to her.

It was right, but it wasn't perfect. The ghost of her missing powers lurked between them, and though he shared much of himself, she sensed that he held back as well.

::Things will be as they were before,:: he said. ::We just need some time.:: He sent a wave of confidence through with the words that swept Kayla along. How could it not, when she wanted so badly to believe.

Kayla let out a breath it felt like she'd been holding since Vayne fled Falanar with Tia'tan months ago. It wasn't until this moment, sitting here with him close enough to touch, that she finally believed she'd see him again.

::I'm so glad you're here.::

How have you been?

They spent time in silence getting reacquainted, then Vayne sent memories of the events on the *Yari* in the past few weeks. He attached an intellectual and emotional commentary to each still or moving image that gave her a much more complete understanding of events than an oral report ever could.

She saw the rooks chasing Tia'tan's ship through the Mine Field, saw the same ship self-destruct thanks to Itsy, a *stepa at es* who was still at war with Ilmena in her mind. Kayla felt the horror of coming upon Itsy's cell, and Vayne's fury that Captain Janus and the others had knowingly endangered him by keeping information hidden. Gintoc almost killing Corinth accidentally when he was trying to protect him, Vayne, full of guilt for killing Gintoc. The grief of Tia'tan and Noar over the deaths of their teammates, Ida, Larsa and the others grieving for Gintoc and Itsy.

She felt the frustration of hours upon hours of debate with Tia'tan, Natali, and the others over whether they should abandon the *Yari*, if the ship was worth fixing, if they should step through the Tear to Ordoch, and the biggest: should the PD—the ship's superweapon, dubbed the Planetary Destroyer—be used in the war to secure Ordoch's freedom.

Interspersed throughout were grueling workouts, unending runs through the ship, mid-sleep cycle pushup sessions, and on and on. She felt exhausted herself as she experienced Vayne's punishing routine to keep himself centered on the physical rather than trapped inside his own mind.

It was a *ro'haar*'s preferred way of dealing with difficult emotions—avoidance.

Vayne mentally chuckled. ::True, but it works. I wish you'd taught me it years ago.::

Hey, being an il'haar *is all* about *staying inside your mind and avoiding distractions.*

A memory not her own flashed in her mind: Incarceration at Dolan's laboratory. Natali, urging Vayne on as they worked out together side by side, in a fierce bid for sanity amidst the chaos their world had become.

It vanished as soon as she became aware of it, and she felt Vayne pull back from her.

He looked away. ::That was a long time ago.:: She could practically hear him slamming mental doors shut. Kayla didn't protest. If memories of his time with Dolan were too fresh to share, she respected that.

::What have you been up to while all this craziness on the *Yari* has been going down?::

She slammed a mental door of her own, reinforcing the box that held memories of her time spent with Malkor.

Most of the time I impersonated Isonde, and that was about as fun as you'd imagine. She dredged up a few minutes of memory from one of the Sovereign Council meetings, until Vayne held up his hands.

::No more, please.::

Told you it was fun. I thought fleeing Falanar as an interstellar criminal would have been exciting, but... Kayla showed him her memories of lying in the medical pod on Ardin's starcruiser while she recovered from her battle with the biocybe, then, once she was out of bed, more healing time, long sessions with Toble while he poked and prodded the massive wound on her arm to check its healing progress, wearing regen cuffs to bed, coolant cells at other times to keep the inflammation down, then there was rehabilitating her arm muscles...

::Wow, you really hit the fun lottery, didn't you?::

Most of the time she'd spent with Malkor, happier than she'd ever been in her life, but he didn't need to know that. It would be so much easier to keep parts of herself private if she didn't have to let him fully into her head in order to communicate mentally. He would have less access and she could choose to be as forthcoming as she wanted to, the way all Wyrds handled private communication.

She needed her damn psi powers back.

::You thought that so loudly I heard it with my actual ears.::

He grinned, having regained some of his former good humor. ::It was so classically Kayla.::

What, to be so frustrated I'm swearing?

::Exactly.:: He chuckled and she joined in. The carefree moment was precious beyond words.

When it passed, she felt the loss of her psi powers—and the connection that came with them—that much stronger.

Vayne shifted forward in his seat, making certain he held her gaze. ::The loss isn't permanent. You know that.::

She frowned. *Why, because Dolan said so?*

His lips tightened when she mentioned Dolan, but he powered on. ::We both saw the pristine scans of your brain. Dolan was a great many terrible things, but he was scrupulously honest about what he called his "research." If he says it's possible to reconnect with your powers, it's going to happen.::

I've been trying for five years. Her protest was half-hearted, though, because his words aligned with her own secret hope.

::You have not had me to help you for five years. Now that we are back together, *il'haar* and *ro'haar*, all will be well.::

In this moment, she could almost believe it.

Malkor breathed a sigh of relief when Kayla's garrulous uncle finally wound down his effusive greeting and wandered out of the room. In someone else the enthusiasm would have been faked, but Ghirhad seemed genuinely thrilled to meet them.

It was a little eerie.

That left him face to face with Ida and Benny once more. Something in the captain's eyes told him the welcome party was over. *Ah, the glamorous life of an IDC agent.* Travel the galaxy and meet new people everywhere who dislike you on sight. The way Benny stood next to the captain, tense, with watchful eyes, illustrated that he was as much here to protect her as he was to greet the newcomers.

At Ida's prompting, Benny handed Malkor a collection of lanyards with RFID chips for his team, who had moved off to the side of the room, out of the way.

"Always to be worn," Benny said. "Allowing access to floors and rooms permitted."

If he hadn't been warned about the crew's ancient form of the Ordochian language, Malkor would assume his aural translator implant was malfunctioning.

"Is calibrated to our bullpups, also. Might save you from the friendly fire by registering on the weapon."

Might? Well that was comforting.

With that the two crew members left, leaving Malkor standing alone. Natali followed them out, on the way making brief eye contact to acknowledge his existence, but that was it. Kayla and Vayne were ensconced in chairs at the far end of the room, deep in discussion. It would be some time before he saw her again.

He rejoined his team and the Ilmenans came to greet them and get reacquainted.

"It's quite a relief to see you here," Noar said in Imperial Common. He smiled. "I had some doubts about our plan."

Rigger shook his hand. "Thank you for not elaborating on them beforehand."

"Otherwise we'd have hightailed it out of here and headed for the beaches of Yallahs," Vid added, and Trinan nodded in agreement.

With the exception of Corinth and Kayla, Tia'tan and Noar were Malkor's favorite people on board. Their help had been invaluable in the Ordochians' rescue.

"Since the not-so-welcome wagon has left," Tia'tan said, "how about we show you around?"

A few months ago, Malkor could never have conceived that Ilmenans would become his only willing allies. "We'd appreciate that."

"Please don't take offense, but I'm going to return to the engine room," Noar said. "Larsa is installing a large piece of the engine casing today and she needs help with the heavy lifting."

Malkor sized Noar up, who couldn't be taller than a meter

and a half. Noar chuckled and shook his head. Malkor caught something about "non-psionics" as the Wyrd left.

Tia'tan grinned. "You're in a whole new league now, agents. Come, I'll show you the ship."

She led them down the corridor to the maglift, held her RFID tag to the door to unlock it, and ushered them in. It was a tight fit. "You won't be able to access most of the floors." A diagram of the ship showed a mind-boggling number of levels. Tia'tan keyed in several of them and the screen flashed an angry red at each one. A command came up, but Malkor couldn't read Ordochian and his aural translator wasn't any help.

"Kayla warned us about that." The restriction didn't sit well with him or his team, even if it was for safety reasons.

They traveled to one of Tia'tan's allowed levels and stepped out into another rawboned corridor. Struts ribbed the wall at regular intervals and no bulkheads covered the glittering, rose-gold molychromium surface. Thankfully, a planked walkway had been laid down the center or else they'd be stepping over a strut every ten meters.

Tia'tan stopped at a door identical to the hundred they'd already passed. "I think this is you, Agent Rua. Try your ID tag."

"Malkor, please. My career as an IDC agent died a spectacular death." His tag worked, revealing a small, sparse private cabin fit for a military vessel.

Tia'tan went through the rooms, getting each of Malkor's octet members to their bunks. Malkor met her in the corridor as his team unloaded their gear. "Which way are you and the others situated? I know Kayla will want to have Vayne and Corinth on either side of her, even if that means some rearranging."

Tia'tan looked embarrassed. "Um, Kayla will be located with her family and the rest of the Wyrds, two decks up."

Malkor let his silence indicate what he thought of that move.

"It's not as though Ida and Natali expect you to murder us in our beds at night."

"Isn't it, though? Why else quarantine the imperials down

here?" *That really burns my space fuel.* It was one thing to say that he was used to an unfriendly welcome as an IDC inside the empire. The IDC had unlimited jurisdiction and were often called in to make unwelcome changes to local governments. But to be unwelcome here, when they had proven their loyalty to Kayla, her family, and their cause, time and again...? Malkor ground his teeth.

An awkward moment passed in silence. Finally Tia'tan brushed past it. "Let me show you where the commissary is, and then I'll take you to the engine room to see the hyperspace drive."

"I'd prefer to see my octet outfitted with plasma bullpups first thing. Who knows how many *stepa at es* are loose on the ship, and I won't have my team facing such a threat unarmed." The octet was trained in hand-to-hand combat and marksmanship with an ion pistol—which meant absolutely nothing against a shielded psionic. Rigger, Hekkar, and the others were no better than bait walking the corridors without a plasma weapon capable of penetrating a psi shield.

"The captain confirmed that thirteen crew members were unaccounted for," Tia'tan said, then corrected herself. "Twelve, now that Itsy has been killed." Her voice took on an edge at the mention of Itsy—who, suffering dementia, had killed two of Tia'tan's people. "Some or all of those twelve may be dead, since the brain damage from faulty cryopods seems degenerative. We've searched as best we can, but it's a massive ship and there are only a handful of us. We haven't found anyone."

"No bodies either, though." Which meant Malkor counted twelve hostiles on the ship his team now called home.

"Ida insists they are harmless. In her words, 'Hide mostly. Burrow, carve out dens in the walls. Stockpile.'"

That sounded exactly like soldiers trapped behind enemy lines, living in fear of capture, waiting for their moment. It was what they would do when they felt their moment for action had come that set him on edge.

"Is this level secure?" He sure as frutt wasn't bunking his people here otherwise.

Tia'tan nodded. "The maglifts only open if you have those RFID badges, same with the cabin doors. One of us is always in the control room, monitoring vidfeeds and the like."

It would have to do, for the moment. First things first, though. "Let's get those bullpups."

"We'll have to speak to the captain."

"I won't take no for an answer."

Tia'tan nodded approvingly. "Good."

Vayne normally avoided the commissary any time he thought it might be inhabited. Tonight, though, as he headed there side by side with Kayla, he didn't give the coming meal a second thought.

He'd spent so many years thinking she was dead, or worse— that she had abandoned him. With their future together stretching out before them now that she was here, for the first time in a long time Vayne felt a quiet ember of optimism.

But things were not perfect. Her psi powers were lost, for one thing. For another, she had witnessed a part of his torture at Dolan's hands, and even without psi powers, she sensed his continued suffering under PTSD. With their psi bond severed, the healing they needed to give each other would be... more difficult.

"You're doing it again," he said, when from the corner of his eye he saw Kayla glance at him.

"Ha!" she laughed at herself. "Busted. I have the overwhelming urge to poke you just to reassure myself you're real."

He returned her smile. "I promise not to vanish in a puff of smoke if you promise the same."

"Done."

While the scrutiny of the others made his skin crawl, her concern was comfortable and familiar. *Ro'haars* and *il'haars* were alert to any distress in their other half; were always ready to help.

They arrived at the commissary to find it full, and despite Kayla at his side, he hesitated on the threshold when all eyes focused on him. She entered first, screening him from scrutiny while he gathered himself. Just one more way she protected him. After a moment, conversations interrupted by their arrival continued and the awkwardness passed.

A buffet was laid out on the counter, the fresh food courtesy of Cinni's final visit. They helped themselves, and he followed Kayla's lead as she led them to where her IDC agent and his second in command sat talking with Tia'tan and Noar. Uncle Ghirhad was having a lively discussion with Ida and Benny at another table, and as usual, Natali sat alone, working through correspondence from Ordoch.

Kayla laid a hand on Malkor's shoulder as she passed, pausing no longer than a second before choosing one of two seats left between the IDC group and the Wyrds. Still, that one second of contact conveyed a wealth of emotion.

Why, my dear Vayne, Dolan whispered in his mind. *Jealous?*

Vayne tamped down the voice and sat beside her, next to Tia'tan. The instant Tia'tan looked his way, eyes full of concern, the events of this morning flooded back.

Her voice—*I don't want to hurt you*. His face, slammed against his door as she subdued him. If he could have fled the commissary without making an even bigger ass of himself, he would have done it.

Tia'tan gave him a smile and he dropped his eyes to his plate. Shame killed his appetite, but he shoveled the food in anyway. The sooner done, the sooner gone.

::It's forgotten.:: Tia'tan's quiet psi voice entered his mind, along with a brush of reassurance.

Forgotten? Not for him. Never for him.

The IDC agents were speaking to each other, the guttural sound of whatever imperial language they spoke at odds with the fluid accents of ancient Ordochian coming from Ida and Benny. Vayne listened to Malkor speak, as much for distraction as for curiosity. The man used the same phonemes over and over; what did they have, like, five consonants in their alphabet? When Kayla replied in the same harsh tones, Vayne's skin crawled.

She lived in hiding in the empire for years, he reminded himself. Learning to speak it like a native would have solidified her cover. Still, the knowledge chafed.

Of course her lover would enjoy it...

Still silently eating while the others conversed, Vayne studied Malkor. Kayla dominated any room she entered on Ordoch, being among the tallest women, but Malkor topped her by at least fifteen centimeters. His form was hulking and brutish. With the aggressive set of his shoulders and the square jaw, he looked ready to erupt into violence in a millisecond. And, he sat much, much too close to Kayla for Vayne's comfort.

Not that she couldn't kick the man's ass, if it came to that.

It was worrisome that Malkor had brought his octet with him to follow after Kayla. It would be that much harder to get rid of him, once Kayla's freak fascination with the man wore off.

Kayla caught the disgusted look on Vayne's face and broke off speaking. What was he thinking? Damn her broken psi powers. They could have had entire conversations in seconds with thoughts and emotions, if only she weren't so damaged. She arched a brow in silent question, all she could do at the moment, and Vayne merely shook his head in response.

To be discussed later, or not at all?

"How is the construction of the hyperstream drive coming on?" Malkor asked Noar. He spoke in Imperial Common, which Tia'tan and her team had learned before journeying to Falanar for the Empress Game. Vayne, Natali, and their uncle had no such knowledge, she'd learned today. They'd had little use for it while Dolan kept them locked up like animals. Malkor and the octet could understand at least modern Ordochian with their translator implants; she'd have to shuttle back to the *Lorius* to grab more translator bots for her family.

Something Natali and Vayne would just love.

"The last structural beam is in place," Noar replied. "According to Larsa, it's time for a long series of stress tests on the entire thing. If it can't hold, there's no point in continuing with the finer elements of the drive."

Kayla nodded. "Makes sense."

"The resulting vibrations from the tests could rock much of the ship." He thought for a moment. "That's assuming something doesn't break loose and tear the engine room open like a can opener."

"You're not exactly filling me with confidence."

Neither did the look on his face—it was far too cautious for her liking.

"Well, with the hodgepodge of parts we have available to us, I'd say the odds are... thirty to seventy."

"A thirty percent chance of success?" Malkor asked.

"Thirty percent chance it blows to pieces."

"And two percent chance of total annihilation," Tia'tan quipped, grinning.

With my ro'haars *on board?* Kayla ground her teeth. "Not even remotely funny."

"Do not be despairing," Captain Janus called from the other table. She grinned. "*Yari* sustaining through five hundred years of life, she will be sustaining through this. No fear of odds, you can be trusting me." Clearly, the captain was one hundred percent confident in her statement. "And Benny to agree!" Ida clapped her second in command on the shoulder, and her cheerful attitude spurred even the cautious Benny to smile.

Kayla liked the positive attitude, but she was quickly learning that Ida was positive about almost everything. Her natural state, or a slightly manic euphoria brought on by too many years in a cryopod?

"Captain," Malkor said when the discussion of the ship's soundness had ended, "my octet and I need to be outfitted with plasma weapons right away. I understand they're currently locked against our RFIDs."

Someone—Tia'tan?—must have translated Malkor's words for Ida telepathically, because the captain's good humor dimmed. She turned her gaze to Malkor, acknowledging him for the first time since the conversation started, but did not immediately reply. If the less than pleased expression on her second in command's face was any indication, he was giving her a mind-full about his thoughts on that request.

"Having your own weapons, I see," Ida said, gesturing to the ion pistol on Malkor's hip.

"Which can be ineffective against a psi shield, if the Wyrd is focused."

Hekkar added, "As you well know, captain."

Kayla held her tongue as the tension kicked up a notch. If Malkor was to have any position of respect on this ship, he needed to win a confrontation with the crew directly, without her facilitating it.

Ida squared off against the imperials, seeming to evaluate each in a harsh light. With access to bullpups, the octet could— if they suddenly went homicidal—take out Ida and her team.

Ida finally said, "I to think on it."

Malkor shook his head. "I will not have my people ineffectively armed against the threat your *stepa at es* present."

Ida's face darkened—clearly now was not the time to bring up her deranged crew members.

"Ariel is in the command room, correct?" Malkor asked.

"She is."

"Please contact her at this time and have weapons permissions added to my team's RFIDs. We will each claim one bullpup, and I assure you," he said with total conviction, "that my agents will die before allowing them to fall into the hands of the *stepa*."

Another silent conversation between Ida and Benny, Kayla was certain. Ida remained silent for so long that Kayla nearly jumped in to support Malkor's request. It galled her to see him treated so suspiciously.

At last Ida nodded once. "It is done." She immediately left the table and the commissary, followed by Benny.

Tia'tan blew out a breath. "Wasn't that fun?" She gave Malkor and Hekkar a grin. "Your first victory among us: well done."

Kayla decided it was time to switch topics. "As far as the hyperstream drive construction is concerned—isn't it all academic, considering that we don't have the fuel to power such a massive engine?"

"The *Radiant* has the fuel," Tia'tan said, looking a little grim.

"The *Radiant* would be here by now if it had survived arrival in the Mine Field." Noar's voice was gentle, but he didn't sugar-coat the truth. No one but Tia'tan held out hope of the Ilmenan fuel carrier miraculously appearing.

"There's no way the rebels on Ordoch can procure the vast amounts needed," Noar continued.

"Could we get some from an imperial world?" Malkor asked.

Kayla shook her head. "Different fuels. Wyrd hyperstream drives are powered alternatively."

The reality of their situation, and the overwhelming odds they faced, lay like a pall across the room. In the depressing quiet, Vayne stood up, the plate in his hand still half full. Kayla stood automatically, a *ro'haar* tuned to her *il'haar*'s movements. They might be mid-conversation with a group of friends, but if Vayne felt he needed to leave, it was time to go.

Malkor looked first to Vayne, then up at her. He arched a brow as if to say, *Seriously? You have to go at this exact moment?*

"You can fill me in later," she said. She dumped her plate into the reclamator and followed Vayne through the door without looking back.

3

FALANAR CITY

Seated in the sun parlor attached to her apartments at the imperial palace, Isonde sipped her guqu tea, ignoring the rest of her breakfast entirely. It wasn't the food that made her nauseated—it was the morning's news vids.

It wasn't much past dawn, but even in the pale morning the stained-plascrystal window lit up, painting oceans of light across the floor. Piece after tiny piece of translucent plascrystal was placed in a silver setting to depict Falanar's tropical sea in living detail. The masterwork craft, so intricate that she couldn't appreciate the true genius of it, usually soothed her nerves. Not so, today.

She irritably tapped the toe of her slipper against the table leg and took another sip of tea. The bellbirds nesting in the orangery chirped their joy at waking to another day, but their sound couldn't drown the voices of the reporters on the vidscreen.

The words UPSET IN THE COUNCIL OF SEVEN SENDS EMPRESS-APPARENT FLEEING scrolled across the bottom, while Eloy—easily her least favorite talking head on the political beat—managed to make footage of Isonde leaving the palace last evening look like a crisis.

Even she had to admit that she looked like she'd been drinking battery acid. That would teach her to school her expression more carefully anytime she was out of doors.

"Utter bullshit," she muttered at the news vid. That piece of propaganda had apparently been fabricated since last night's reports. "And where is the speculation about why Vega was chosen, when she isn't officially on the IDC leadership team?" Not to mention the furious reactions of everyone *else* on the council that wasn't in on the emperor's plans.

The tea tasted as flat as her mood, and she set it aside. She would have to do some serious damage control, considering that she'd gone from being labeled "most progressive" member of the council to the pettiest in a single day.

The gentle *schnick* of the conservatory door closing caught her attention a moment before Ardin's voice reached her.

"Why are you still watching this nonsense?"

His unexpected presence caught her off guard. In the wordless cold war between them, she had claimed the conservatory as her personal sanctuary; he had yet to violate her unspoken claim.

If she thought his presence here this morning signified a thawing in their relationship—which had been in a deep freeze since she publicly denounced Malkor in order to retain her seat on the council—the brittleness of his tone quickly disabused her of the notion.

"Aren't there more constructive things you could be doing?" His gaze took in her dishabille. She'd come straight from bed, after throwing on a robe and grabbing some files, not bothering to put herself together yet. In contrast, he looked as neat as a soldier on the parade ground. In a brief moment of pettiness, she hated him for the advantage.

Ardin didn't take a seat at the table, instead preferring to stand and loom over her from his greater height. She refused to be challenged by this.

"How can you not watch it?" she countered. "What is more important to our cause right now than this sabotage of my—and by association, your—image? The journalists have undermined my legitimacy as a council member in less than twenty-four hours."

"Oh, I don't know, maybe I'm too focused on the rising sentiment that the time has come to force the Wyrds to create a TNV cure for us by releasing the plague on Ordoch?"

"*What?*"

He approached the table and reached past her to take possession of the controller, and then switched to a different newsfeed, this one out of Wei-lu-Wei.

The onscreen reporter stood amid a mass of agitated people, each covered in a hodgepodge of protective medical gear. The demonstrators wore everything from respirator masks to organoplastic surgical gowns and underwater dive helmets—anything to keep themselves safe from the rapid spread of the

TNV across their planet. The reporter herself was clothed from head to toe in a suit of tissue-thin, copper-colored metal, one of the only known barriers to the virus. Only her eyes were visible through a tiny slice of glass, and adding even that slim weakness was a huge risk.

The crowd around her posed a significant threat as well. She'd be lucky to make it out of there without being attacked, beaten, and robbed of the precious suit.

Her voice came across clearly despite the cacophony, piped as it was from her mouthpiece.

"I'm here in Ngyehn Square in Wei-lu-Wei's sovereign city, Itzu-Feng. With me are thousands of people who have come out in support of the Alliance for Justice, once considered a radical group, and their call to release the TNV on the Wyrd World Ordoch. The Alliance hopes that such an extreme action will finally force Ordochian scientists to formulate a cure."

She raised the microphone she held and angled it toward the fierce woman beside her.

"Fa Han, what do you think of the Alliance's plan?"

"It's no more than the Wyrds deserve. They have the technology to help us and they've refused, staying safe on their world while our people continue to die by the millions."

"What do you say to people who claim it would be an act of terrorism?"

"We've been too nice to them. If we want to save our empire, it's time to give them a taste of what we've been suffering."

The woman went on to list all that she and her friends and neighbors had lost since the TNV outbreak on Wei-lu-Wei. Ardin shut down the vidscreen.

"'Too nice?'" Isonde couldn't believe it. "We invade their world, murder their rulers, set up an occupation, and foist problems of our own on to them as if they had some obligation to help us, and we've been 'too nice?'"

"People are desperate," Ardin said.

"We were desperate for years before the occupation was even agreed upon. Now that the Sovereign Planets have finally been infected, we're ready to become terrorists?"

"Don't get fired up at me: I never said I supported those extremists." He moved closer, but still didn't sit. "I came here to write a joint statement condemning this sentiment, which we'll discuss during the press conference I called for eight."

The Council of Seven didn't meet until ten today, which meant she had packed her morning schedule full with meetings. Isonde was due to meet with Raorin in an hour, then with Commander Parrel, Malkor's former superior officer, directly afterward. She needed intel on Vega, and Parrel would be her source, since he did claim to be collecting evidence of Vega's activities, with the long-term goal of bringing her down. If she could reschedule with Raorin, then…

"That's the scheming look I know so well." Ardin's words lacked bite. There might have even been a hint of admiration in his tone.

"Ardin…"

He shook his head. The apology she wanted to offer, for betraying Malkor, betraying *him*, by condemning Malkor as a traitor in order to solidify her own political future, hung unspoken in the air. He shook his head again, rejecting it.

"I can't do this right now, Isonde." But he did pull out the second chair and sit at her table. "Let's get this statement hammered out."

She gave him a smile. Maybe things *were* beginning to thaw. "I'm also expecting to hear from Malkor. Vega didn't get herself invited to council proceedings by chance. I need to know every piece of Dolan's data that they turned over to her in exchange for Malkor's release."

"Agreed. I know they had a plan to sabotage it somehow, but I fear it didn't go as planned. If Vega can use the Influencer to control members of the council…" He didn't have to elaborate on how worthless their votes would be in that case.

4

Malkor finished his dinner and then took his plate to the reclamator. The conversation had definitely lost momentum after Vayne and Kayla's abrupt departure. It wasn't that he expected Vayne to act like a normal, well-adjusted person who hadn't been a tortured POW for five years. Any weirdness on his part could be excused, probably for the rest of his life. But Malkor *had* assumed Kayla would act as she always had, and not fall into Vayne's mode of behavior.

Don't be an asshole, he told himself. She'd been back with her brother for all of one day. Things would even out.

"It's time for me to go to bed, according to *Yari* ship time," Tia'tan announced.

"I want to check on Larsa's progress first." Noar's mind had clearly turned back to the problem of the hyperstream drive.

Malkor looked at Hekkar, who shrugged. A bit early to sleep according to the schedule they had adopted on the *Lorius*. Might as well check in with Rigger to get the status on their mobile comms network, and then he'd like to do a little reconnoitering.

He selected a bullpup from the rack by the door, as did Hekkar. Ida might consider these levels secure, but he wasn't going to take any chances. Tia'tan and Noar took bullpups as well. The engine room sat many levels below the secure levels.

After familiarizing himself with the controls, Malkor caught up with Tia'tan in the corridor.

"I'll walk with you down to your level," Tia'tan said. "I'm sure you can find it, but I could use a little exercise before bed."

Noar headed off in another direction, and the three of them continued to the maglift farther down the corridor. Malkor reached out and rasped his fingers against the slightly gritty molychromium surface. Everything about the *Yari* was so alien to him. There were the complink systems, programmed entirely in Ordochian. His translation implant was useless in that case. He couldn't even access the general comms without help, and had to memorize which buttons on the lift corresponded to which level in order to use the thing. He wore the entire ship like an ill-fitting uniform.

The lift doors opened on the level that held his octet's quarters. Malkor led the way left out of the lift. He remembered that much at least, written Ordochian be damned.

As they started down the corridor, movement at the far end caught his eye.

Rigger? No, the woman wore a black jumpsuit, not the T-shirt, pants, and boots combo that his agents favored. She had her head down, and shoulder-length teal hair screened her face. Another crew member? Larsa? He hadn't met the engineer yet.

The woman glanced up at that moment and, catching sight of them, froze. Beside him, Tia'tan did the same.

"*Stepa!*" Tia'tan's shout spurred him to action. He raised his weapon, but before he could brace the bullpup against his shoulder the *stepa at es* flung out her arm, and a force hit him like a hovercar to the chest, knocking the breath from him. Boot heels squealed across the decking as she forced all three of them backward. Malkor gritted his teeth and strained against the telekinetic hold without success. The bullpup lay trapped against his chest.

Tia'tan growled. Her fingers formed talons and she clawed free of the invisible force. She stopped dead—just as Malkor slammed into a support brace at a bend in the corridor. Pain exploded, white hot, in his back.

Frutting psionics.

Tia'tan slashed her hand downward in a knife strike and the pressure vanished. He fell to his knees, gasping out a cough.

"You guys okay?" Tia'tan called. The *stepa* woman was already out of sight, having sprinted back the way she'd come. Tia'tan was up on her toes and about to follow.

He choked out a "yes," as did Hekkar, and Tia'tan took off after the woman. Malkor felt like the greenest recruit, being caught unprepared on a ship with known hostiles. *Secure, my ass.* He staggered to his feet, wincing at the pain in his spine and shoulders. Hekkar, still upright, had fared better than he had.

"Grab Trinan and Vid and go secure the engine room. And tell Rigger to get our damn mobile comms network up."

"On it."

Malkor readied his bullpup and ran after Tia'tan. He'd be damned if he was going to be taken by surprise again. Tia'tan must have alerted someone telepathically because the ship's klaxon blared to life and Ida barked orders over the comms system.

He caught up with Tia'tan after a series of turns in the corridor, but only because she had stopped in the center of an intersection. The corridors branched off in three directions.

::I'm heading left.:: Tia'tan's voice sounded in his mind. Malkor motioned silently to the right, and they took off in opposite directions.

His corridor quickly dead-ended at a lift, which wasn't in operation—he'd chosen wrong. He doubled back at a sprint and took the third choice, but after a few hundred meters it became clear that if she had gone this way, he'd lost her. No footfalls sounded ahead of him when he slowed, nothing to indicate her presence.

::Anything?::

"Nothing down either way," he called as he headed back to the intersection. What the frutt? How had she disappeared so quickly? He met up with Tia'tan, both breathing hard. She looked as frustrated as he felt.

Malkor scanned the ceiling. "Tell me we have security cams on this deck."

"On these levels, yes, because they're officers' quarters, but not on all of them. The cams hadn't been installed on lower-priority decks before launch, and the units were lost when that cargo hold got ripped out of the ship." She uttered a curse in Ordochian. "Let's get to the control room, I'll find the vid footage myself if I have to."

Tia'tan started toward the closest lift at a jogging pace, clearly unwilling to waste time by walking.

I like this woman. He caught up, adrenaline still pumping through him. He wanted an update from his team, and he *needed* confirmation that Kayla was okay. *Damn ship and its damn Ordochian comms system.* He must have muttered some of his thoughts out loud because Tia'tan shot him a glance.

"Kayla's safe, no *stepa* were spotted on our level. She's guarding Corinth's cabin."

His mobile comm chirped. *Finally.*

"We're up, boss," was Rigger's message.

"Good. I'm swinging by your room, then we're going to the control room."

He opened a group channel to the octet. "No one travels solo. Plasma weapons activated at all times—new protocol going forward."

The control room was massive. Considering the size and complexity of the ship, Malkor supposed it was to scale. It seemed like every surface was covered in complinks, consoles, and indicator lights. An immense vidscreen covered the entire front wall. Several persons tall and wider than back-to-back hovercars, it made for an amazing view of the Mine Field. Ida sat in what had to be the captain's chair, Ariel at one console and Tanet—the ship's remaining physicist—at another.

Malkor was way too keyed up to sit, and judging by Tia'tan's ready stance, she felt the same.

The vidscreen image segmented and the Mine Field disappeared, replaced by multiple security feeds. Ariel queued up the lift they'd entered Malkor's cabin level at and reversed the time until they came into view, walking backward toward it.

"There," Tia'tan said. "Start it."

On screen, they walked out of sight again.

"Coverage being minimal." Ariel switched views. "*Yari* being not completed, leaving little time for these things." There was no footage of the actual encounter. *Least secure "secured" level ever.* Ariel hunted until she came up with a view of the four-way intersection. The *stepa at es* woman flew through at a sprint, hooking a left before disappearing. Ariel switched feeds again.

At last she found an angle that showed Tia'tan running down the same corridor, but the *stepa* woman was nowhere to be found.

"Reverse it," Malkor said. "Two minutes prior to Tia'tan's appearance."

Still nothing. How in the void had the woman vanished? "Play it again."

A second play-thru produced the same results. A third, though... "Wait," he said, pointing to the uppermost edge of the screen. "There. Is that a boot?"

Ariel reversed and retimed the sequence. Sure enough, a boot and part of a lower leg, bent at the knee and kneeling on the floor, appeared on screen for a few seconds. Ariel slowed it down, and the leg seemed to crawl *into* the wall of the corridor.

"What's there?" he asked, but Ariel was ahead of him, calling up various ship schematics. Floor plans, elevations, assembly drawings, component drawings. Fire suppression systems, heating, cooling and ventilation systems...

Ariel called out the ventilation schematic and dismissed the others, overlaying its diagrams on the structural drawings. Sure enough, a ventilation shaft ended in a grate at the *stepa at es*'s egress point.

Ida frowned. "That is most wrong. That level being secure."

"Obviously not," he answered. Great, at least one insane person knew her way around the ship better than the captain did. This just got better and better. They scanned previous footage to see her enter from the same location.

"They to grow bolder," Benny said, standing beside the captain's chair. He was stiff with controlled agitation. "Encroaching onto our levels." His hands were clasped behind his back, one hand grabbing one wrist, while the other hand balled tightly.

Ariel froze the feed when the *stepa at es* stood and began to stride down the hall.

Benny sucked in a gasp. "It is not to be."

The look he exchanged with Ida sent Malkor's instincts to even higher alert. "Who is it?"

The captain called on Ariel to zoom in. On the vidscreen, the woman's face came into focus. Her teal hair hung loose to her shoulders. A bit ragged, but not completely unkempt, like the others they'd come across. Her fingernails were neither ripped off nor bitten to the quick, and her expression held wary intelligence, not the glaze of madness. She looked nothing like the pitiful creature he'd seen on the footage of the *stepa* who had blown up Tia'tan's ship a few weeks ago. What did that make her: less or more dangerous?

Ida muttered something too low for his translator to catch.

"Captain…" Benny seemed to be waiting for her to confirm something.

It took a minute—two—but she finally nodded. "That is Science Officer Fengrathen."

Malkor caught the unease in her tone. "Is that significant? More so than knowing another *stepa* is still alive?"

"She isn't *stepa*. Not officially." Ida's hand flashed over the console beside her command chair. Another window opened on the vidscreen and the personnel file for one Major Cicara Fengrathen loaded. Tia'tan translated the pertinent details to him silently. Her military ID showed a face full of determination, and several commendations were listed in her service record. Beneath her name, her status was listed as CRYOGENIC HIBERNATION.

After her status, stamped in bold red letters, were the words REANIMATION NOT ADVISED. MOST PROBABLE RESULT: DEATH. SEQUENCE LOCKED BY CAPTAIN JANUS.

Apparently Major Fengrathen should be sealed in cryopod F-621, in cryochamber 13-2.

The image of Fengrathen skulking around put lie to that. "Let me guess," Malkor said. "All of the stasis chambers are 'secured.'"

Ariel called up an image of what he assumed was the interior of chamber 13-2. All was as still as a graveyard. Row after row of luminous silver pods filled the screen. Now that he knew these ancient cryopods were never meant for long-term use, the chamber looked more like a morgue than a sanctuary from time.

Everyone stared at the screen, breathless, waiting for something—anything—to happen.

Nothing. They could as easily be watching a still image as a moving vid.

"This is where Fengrathen should be?" It was hard to believe she'd be anywhere else.

Ariel brought up what seemed to be logs. "All three hundred pods in the chamber are sealed and active, captain."

"Wait," Kayla said, pointing to the lower right of the image. "Is that—are those children in the pods?"

Three of them, it looked like. Damn, they weren't too much older than Corinth.

"Is wartime," Ida said with a shrug. "Anyone can serve."

"Is this feed current?" Tia'tan asked.

When Ariel checked the data and scowled, Malkor knew the answer before she spoke.

"It's from"—her gaze cut to Ida for a nanosecond—"months ago."

What the frutt is going on here?

An hour after Fengrathen's appearance, Kayla and Vayne remained where they had been since the klaxon first went off: in the corridor on the officers' quarters level, guarding Corinth's cabin.

Thank the stars he's been sleeping, Kayla thought. She'd rushed to find Corinth when the alarm sounded, Vayne at her side. Corinth had taken a rare break from the engine rebuild to sleep, for which she was grateful. The HVAC vents in each of the cabins were too small for a person to travel through.

That didn't mean the level was secure, though. Not by a long shot. One of the ventilation grates not far from Corinth's cabin was a definite problem. Kayla would have judged it as too small, also, and it looked to be in perfect condition. A close inspection showed that some of the bolts had been removed. If she gripped the grate and manipulated it just so, the cover would rotate upward to allow access.

Not for long.

The lift doors opened at the far end and Rigger stepped out, carrying two laser welding torches. Kayla and Vayne went to meet her.

"We're welding the ventilation grates in place, even the ones that haven't been breached yet," Rigger said, handing a torch to each of them. Vayne took his silently, unable to understand the Imperial Common and unwilling to ask for a translation.

"Noar, Larsa, and Trinan are securing the hyperstream engine room," Rigger continued. "Tia'tan and Vid are securing the commissary level while Malkor, Hekkar, Benny, and the captain clear the levels above and below command level."

"Who is watching the control room?" Kayla asked. That was a top priority, obviously, but a dozen other crucial locations came to mind, including the ship's non-drive engines, which powered daily functions such as life support and gravity; the shuttle bays, which provided the only means to reach the *Lorius*; not to mention the ordinance storage.

"Ariel and Tanet guard the control room, Toble is standing by for medical emergencies, and Corinth and your uncle are locked in their cabins on this level." Rigger grimaced. "We're spread too thin as it is."

Kayla nodded. "Agreed. And there's only so much we can do tonight." She translated the plan to Vayne.

"I'm on board with your imperials' plan," he said, speaking directly to her even though Rigger's translator made it easy for her to understand him. "Let's get this done."

"Thanks for the torches, Rigger. Once this level is secure, have the octet move their belongings to this level. I'll handle the captain; we'll get crew cabins unlocked for you."

Rigger nodded. "Got your mobile comm?"

"Always. Keep us informed."

"Will do." Rigger gave her a two-finger salute and headed back to the lift.

It only took Kayla a minute to figure out how to operate the laser torch. There was safety gear too: glasses with clear lenses and specialist gloves. She handed Vayne a pair of each.

"Apparently, gas emissions aren't a worry," she said, switching to Ordochian.

"I'm certainly not a welding expert, but I have some concerns over using equipment with safety precautions that are five hundred years out of date."

Kayla chuckled, pulling on her own gloves. "I'll take a little radiation over a homicidal psionic any day."

The joke didn't get a response from Vayne. In fact, he looked just as darkly intense as he had all day, the one exception being his smile when she first arrived on the *Yari*. An edgy energy hung about him, never allowing him peace, never allowing *her* peace. What should she do? She and Vayne had always shared the same sense of sarcastic humor. Even in the worst situations they made each other laugh. Now, though, it was as if the action had been wiped from his memory.

Kayla suddenly didn't know how to reach her *il'haar*. Their bond felt broken, unrepairable, and that could be fatal for both of them. Should she push? He'd only barely been freed from capture. Maybe his mental state was exactly where it should be. Or maybe his imprisonment had been so brutal, he'd never come back to himself. The thought left her cold.

The only thing she knew to do in this moment was handle the task ahead of her.

She hefted the torch in her left hand, careful to keep the strain off of her still sore right arm. "Do you want to start at this end and I'll begin at the other?"

Vayne glanced from her to the torch, to the length of corridor stretching out behind her. He shook his head. "It'll go faster together."

It seemed to her it would go about the same, or slower, even, if they got in each other's way. But she would prefer to keep her *il'haar* in sight, and his determined expression said he felt the same. They fell in step without another word, footfalls synched as they strode down the corridor to the far end. The effortless pairing beat back some of her fears. Perhaps things were not as strained as they seemed. Maybe she—

"This way I can protect you." Vayne's words cut through her. Not, 'so we can protect each other.' No. So *he* could protect *her*.

Again her disability separated them.

"I can take care of myself." But she couldn't. Not against a psionic with enough sanity left—or pure instincts—to attack telekinetically.

Vayne didn't voice anything further. He didn't have to. She was handicapped in the eyes of her people. It was only that she'd lived so long among imperials, she'd forgotten how damaged she was.

They arrived at the corridor's end and inspected the vents there. The one on her side remained sealed, all sixteen bolts firmly tightened. Vayne's, though... A single bolt remained in the upper left corner as a pivot point.

Her brothers had been sleeping unsecured for how long? Blood rage surged, fueled by fear. They could have been killed, both of them. They had left Falanar supposedly safe with the Ilmenans and instead she could have lost them forever.

Vayne laid a hand on her shoulder. "We'll fix it." The heavy glove grounded her, bringing her back to the moment.

Her *il'haars* were safe, or would be, once they secured this level. Still, it took an effort to release her anger—anger at the captain for allowing the *stepa at es* to run free, at the *stepa* for existing in the first place, at the circumstances that endangered her brothers. She gripped her torch tight and began counting her breathing, timing it to slow her down.

She was here now, and she would keep them safe.

Vayne knelt in front of the compromised vent, fired up his torch, and began welding the grate to the corridor wall. Kayla, emotions under control again, did the same on her side. The torch had its own light spectrum filter built in, and the gloves shielded her from any residual heat. Acrid gases escaping from the molten molychromium penetrated the corridor as they worked.

::Are you almost done, Kay?:: Corinth asked. He brushed against her mind, asking for entrance. Kayla took a second to lock away all her fears about his safety, the reality of their situation, the extent of the dangers they faced, and the heartbreaking rift between her and Vayne. When her mind was serene, at least on the surface, she lowered her outer mental shields and allowed Corinth to slip into her mind so that he could hear her thought voice.

::I need to get back to the engine room.::

You're supposed to be resting, she answered.

::With all that's going on?::

At least try.

::Did you really have to lock me in here? After you decided I was safe?::

You're safe because *I locked you in there.*

::I don't want to sleep, I can help.:: His restlessness bled through the link to her. He was excited by the danger, wanted to be part of it.

Kids.

::I am not a kid!::

You most certainly are. You might as well resign yourself to sleeping. Securing these few levels is going to take most of the night, and you're not going anywhere until it's finished.

::But—::

Il'haars do not argue with their ro'haars *when it comes to safety, mister.*

He was quiet a moment. She felt the subtle shift in him, a vague mix of disappointment, disgruntlement, and dismay.

::You're not my *ro'haar* anymore, are you? You're Vayne's now.::

Her heart broke for the loss in his psi voice, the loneliness.

No one will ever take me away from you. I am your ro'haar *for life.* But she knew her twin needed her so much more right now. All her energies were focused on Vayne, and it was a challenge to shield that truth from Corinth.

Plus you have the octet. You know they all love you. He was still so young, so in need of a place to belong. *Sleep now and let me work. I'll wake you when it's safe to go back to the engine room.*

His mental sigh came through loud and clear. ::All right, Kay. And... Be careful.::

He slipped away, but not before she felt his frustration at being locked in, at the weak state of his psi powers. He wanted to be the one protecting her, instead of Vayne, and it chafed him to admit, even to himself, that he couldn't.

He was growing up too quickly.

Kayla finished with her grate and thumbed off the torch. Corinth had passed the awareness on to her of Vayne holding a psi shield around them. "You're going to wear yourself out if you keep the shield up all night," she said to Vayne.

He finished welding his grate shut, and then stood. "Just a precaution." Despite the "just," it was clear he was in deadly earnest.

"Save it for when the trouble starts." She might not have her psionic sense, but she knew her *il'haar* well enough to know he'd been shielding her the entire time—probably since Fengrathen was first sighted. "When I'll really need it."

"Yes, ma'am."

She also knew Vayne well enough to know that he wouldn't risk her safety, despite her orders. The shielding was his way of expressing love. She could only hope that he understood the plasma bullpup she had slung over her shoulder was her answer in kind.

Vayne's expression changed, something dark clouding his features as he withdrew inside himself.

"Hey," she said. "Where are you going?"

"We've more vents to seal," he answered. He started walking down the corridor and she automatically fell into step beside him.

"That's not what I meant, and you know it." He didn't deny it—admission enough that he had pulled away from her mentally. These things between them, the losses and experiences of five years apart, ate her up.

They stopped in front of the next vent, she staring at him, he avoiding eye contact. She took it as a good sign that he at least hadn't turned away.

"Talk to me, Vayne." She pushed her protective glasses up on her head, and after a moment he did the same.

Still he refused to look at her. She held her ground, unrelenting, demanding a response.

"What is there to say?" he finally asked.

"Besides the obvious?"

He shook his head once, hard—a sharp refusal.

"We're going to have to talk about it some time."

"I said no," he snapped, turning to face her. His free hand clenched until his knuckles turned white, as if he could physically force the subject away.

"If you won't talk about what you went through, at least tell me how you're feeling." Based on his current expression, "tortured" came to mind. She'd seen caged animals looking less confrontational.

She left the subject of his imprisonment behind for the moment. "Why is Noar handling Corinth's psionic training?"

"I've been busy."

"And Noar hasn't, with his work on the engines?"

Vayne set his torch down, then crossed his arms in front of

his chest, bulky gloves making an excellent shield.

"I gather that Noar is a strong psionic, but there's no way he compares to your power or finesse."

Kayla set her own torch down. He *knew* it had been her express wish that he handle Corinth's training. She'd said as much in the safehouse after they'd killed Dolan. "He hero worships you, Vayne."

"Not anymore. Now he hero worships you. I think the kid wants to be a *ro'haar* when he grows up."

The kid. Years ago, Corinth had been Vayne's shadow whenever his twin was busy training with the other *ro'haars*. He'd spent hours of every day in silent awe of his older brother, so close he apparently made Vayne claustrophobic at times, and now Corinth was just "the kid" to Vayne?

"Is five years such an eternity?"

Vayne's aqua gaze, so intense, so chaotic, pinned her in place. "Those five years are a void beyond your imaginings." His voice was pure emotion.

She wanted to reach out, to bridge the chasm between them in any way possible. "I'm trying to understand."

"You never will." Such finality. Would those years forever separate them?

He held himself stiffly but vibrated energy, as if his experiences were trying to burst through his skin and it was all he could do to lock them inside.

"Vayne..."

"Don't." His arms tightened around his chest.

Everything was so frutted up.

It wasn't in her to give up, though. She would fight her way back, she would fight *him* to regain their connection. She wasn't sure she could live without it.

"What about you?" Vayne challenged. "You haven't said a word about your years in hiding, your life as an imperial citizen."

Because it is too painful to tell you I moved on without you. That I lived free while you died a little more each day.

Still, it was a fair accusation. "What do you want to know?"

"The octet leader." The words came too quickly—this had clearly been on his mind.

Her face flashed hot. "Malkor? What about him?" And why did she already feel defensive?

"Your relationship. Do you really care for him?" It was clear from his tone that he thought such a thing impossible.

"I—I love him," she forced herself to say, the words awkward in the face of Vayne's obvious disapproval. "I do." And she did, more than she ever thought herself capable of. So why did she feel almost embarrassed at the admission?

Vayne turned away. "They're going to need help securing the path from the commissary to the engine room. Most of that section isn't powered and the lifts are down." He knelt by the grate and took up his torch. "Let's get this done."

Kayla knelt beside him and started welding from the opposite corner.

She'd meet him in the middle.

5

Midnight in Ordoch's capital. Mishe lay on his side, body aching, wrapped in the embrace of Symina Aretes, major general of the Imperial Army and division leader of the imperial troops stationed in Vankir. She slept hard, but even in sleep she gathered him close as if he were precious to her.

And why not? He was hers. Her kept man, though she preferred to call him her boy. Compared to a strong imperial military woman, his size was diminutive. His features were finer, more delicately wrought then those of the average imperial male, and he looked younger than his age—a fact that made whoring himself to the imperials that much easier.

All for the sake of the rebellion, he thought cynically. At least he'd slept his way to the top of the occupation forces. And over the years, he'd gathered valuable intel from soldiers who had no idea how to shield their thoughts from him. The number of secrets he could glean from a well-sated man or woman in the afterglow was staggering.

Now he was Major General Aretes's "boy"—part frutt toy, part cherished confidant. One of those parts was valuable; one eroded his soul. Prostituting himself night after night to one anonymous face after the other he could handle—barely. But this permanent arrangement, pretending to form an attachment...

Is this how you felt, Cinni, once you executed your mother? Did it eat at you night after night, until you thought you would go mad from it, until the scream building inside you threatened to burst free and never stop?

No way to know, now. Cinni—his best friend—had been dead for weeks. She'd taken her own life in a drug-infused storm of self-loathing and despair. She hadn't been pressured into executing her mother. She'd volunteered for the job, knowing that with her knowledge and skillset she had the highest chance of success. In the same way no one had asked Mishe to whore for the rebellion. He had simply known that while he wasn't soldier material, his youth, diminutive size, and exquisite Wyrd looks made him the perfect sex worker for the imperials. The problem wasn't the whoring—sex work was a valued and protected vocation on Ordoch. No one really gave a damn who slept with who, and society recognized that sex drove everyone. The shame came from servicing his enemy.

It was his price for freedom. Now all he had to do was survive paying it.

Symina finally relinquished her hold on him and rolled over, still asleep. It wouldn't last long. Her softer side came out once her lust had been exhausted. Even unconscious, she would want to snuggle close.

Time to move.

His aching body protested as he rose from the bed and dressed. The muscles of his shoulders stung from the extreme extension she'd employed in her bondage play. He had rope burns on his wrists and ankles—she loved to watch him struggle futilely to free himself—and welts on his thighs and buttocks from her work with a paddle and her beloved riding crop.

If pain got him off, if games of submission and domination fueled his fire, Symina would be the perfect lover. She was generous, inventive, and tireless, always demanding more from him, and giving more in return. They'd passed out after their last round of sex, but if Mishe stuck around, Symina would care for him in the morning. She'd rub salve into his welts, use a medstick on his tender, rope-burned skin, and draw a hot bath for his aching body to soak in.

Somewhere out there a submissive was missing the time of their life.

Staring down at her sleep-softened features, Mishe felt only one thing: the need to shove a stylus through her eye and straight into her brain. He didn't give a damn about her sexual proclivities, and it wasn't her fault he faked his way through it all. But he sure as frutt hated the living shit out of her for her continuing role in the subjugation of his planet. Her death couldn't come soon enough.

And it was going to come by his hands.

Mishe pushed tantalizing thoughts of revenge out of his mind, grabbed his credentials, and left the sleeping quarters. The credentials were his right as Symina's kept boy. He'd convinced her of his need to visit his "family" beyond the fortifications that ringed the capital city, and she'd gifted him with an ID that allowed him to come and go freely from Vankir.

The fact that his "family" was a band of rebels who plotted her demise didn't need to be mentioned.

It was an arduous trip to the main rebel base, located in the defunct manufacturing subcity of Estraden. The imperials had destroyed public and industrial transportation systems throughout the heavily populated northern and central regions of the planet's main continent. The airbus routes were closed. Summoning stations for the autopilot cab network were no longer connected to the linkhub. Magrails. Freighters. Public waterway craft—all grounded.

Once he passed through the gate in the wall that shielded Vankir City proper, Mishe started with a good old-fashioned run through the remnants of Vankir's suburban areas, his muscles loosening as he went. Eventually he made it to the dilapidated shed where he hid his two-cycle, and ghosted through the abandoned populace subcity, across the environmentally unrecoverable flats—destroyed by a now outlawed fuel refinement process—and into the bombed-out manufacturing subcity.

The guards on duty at the Factory, as the rebels affectionately called the base, recognized him on sight and gave the all-clear for him to enter. All the soldiers on guard duty knew him. In fact, everyone in the base knew of him and the few other whores working the imperials. No one had given him shit about it, since his work as a spy was so valuable, but no one bothered to befriend him, either. People who accidentally met his gaze looked away. The only peace he found, now that Cinni was gone, was with his direct superior, Aarush.

Aarush understood what Mishe went through, understood why he had chosen whoring as his way to fight the war. Aarush valued his efforts. He'd named Mishe and the other sex workers in the rebellion "intelligence agents."

A title that did little to appease Mishe's demons.

Thankfully, tonight he had information to report.

There just aren't enough hours in the night, Wetham Inia, de facto head of the Ordochian rebellion, thought to himself. The time lurked somewhere near the o-two-hundred hour, and silence reigned in the bowels of the Factory.

There were pros and cons to being the leader of the entire freedom movement. On one hand, it allowed him to organize and orchestrate the rebellion in the most efficient and effective manner for the greatest chance of success. On the other, it meant the only time he had to himself was when his lieutenants and soldiers slept. Even then, this current uninterrupted two-hour stretch was a luxury.

Time he probably should have spent sleeping.

Instead, he sat in a storage locker on the lowest underground level of the manufactory-turned-rebel base. He'd affectionately dubbed the storage locker his "study." It was large, ten meters on each side, and had been mostly emptied of the crates of manufacturing chemicals it had held at one time. Two large crates formed a table on the right side of the room, and a stack remained in the far corner, atop which extra lamps had been placed. The last random one sat beside his armchair as an end table. Richly woven rugs, heirlooms from his family's estate, covered the poured concrete floor. Unmatching chairs of varying degrees of comfort stood here and there, and shelving had been dragged in from other storage lockers to create a bookshelf that dominated the rear and left walls. Row after row after row of books rested on the shelves in their canvas pouches, tightly tucked against one another. Wetham had left the overhead utility lighting off, leaving the room in a cozy glow from the assorted lamps.

It was so far down from his existence as a son of one of Vankir's greatest families that his previous life felt like a fantasy. Some days, he mused, he liked his new life better, despite living in hiding and poverty while waging a near impossible war.

Wetham glanced at the chronometer again, fighting the urge to sleep because he was greedy for more research time. He had a complink and stacks of datapads in the room, but with the planet-wide linkhub first destroyed and then rebuilt—and controlled—entirely by the imperials, it was incredibly hard to get access to information these days. Luckily for him, he much preferred researching from books directly. As a professor, he had a long history with them. Some of the books he had brought with him from his university library in Vankir City; some from his private collection. Most, though, had been stolen one by one from the now defunct city libraries.

Time to get back to it, while I still have time.

Wetham selected a faded crimson book sleeve from the stack atop the end table—his latest acquisition. The tied cord gave way as he undid the knot, and he upended the bag to slide the book out. Thoreson's *Winning the Unwinnable War: How Separatists Turned the Tide of Ordoch's Final Civil Conflict*; the life's work of an obscure, self-taught military historian largely ignored by the academic community. Wetham had been trying to get his hands on a printing of it even before the occupation.

As he used his thumbnail to pry the first paper-thin organoplastic sheet from the rest, someone knocked. Of course. His schedule was almost as full now as it had been as an overworked professor.

No use in ignoring it, someone else would just come in their place. "Enter."

Aarush, Wetham's favorite lieutenant, hobbled in, awkward on what had to be a stolen set of crutches. The medics would never have released him. Clearly, Wetham was looking at a fugitive.

Aarush wore an oversized set of pajamas, and the right pant leg trailed empty on the ground. That foot was long gone, thanks to an explosion on their last raid—a raid based on bad intel that had turned into a trap. Aarush had escaped with his life, but the blast had burned through the skin of his arm and obliterated the right half of his face. Bandages still swathed him, each showing fluid stains from wound weeping.

Wetham shot to his feet, his treasured book falling to the floor. "What the stars are you doing out of bed?"

Aarush ignored him, brow furrowed as he hobbled farther into the room, angling for a chair. His face was a mix of pain and determination.

Wetham swore under his breath and rushed to move a seat closer to him. Aarush dropped into it with a huffed "Thanks."

"What an idiotic move." Wetham glowered at him. "The medic insisted on bed rest for at least another month, as you well know. Which imbecile gave you clothing—he's going on latrine duty."

Aarush managed a weak smile. "I stole them. It *is* o-two-thirty, you know."

"Do I need to put a guard on one of my own officers in the infirmary?"

"I'd still be up and about and you know it." Aarush held the crutches in his good hand and lowered them to the rug beside his chair. Even that small effort seemed to pain him.

Wetham narrowed his gaze. "You aren't taking the pain blockers, are you." It wasn't even a question.

"They make me foggy. I can barely see or hear anyone speaking to me, never mind trying to hold multiple details in my head." He brushed his blue-black hair off his forehead with his unbandaged hand. "And that's only when I manage to stay conscious."

Wetham opened his mouth, ready to blast Aarush for the insane health risks, but from the way Aarush tensed, he knew the subject had closed. *Damn idiot!* But the curse came with concern for one of his closest friends since the rebellion began.

"So, what do you have for me?" he asked instead.

Aarush shifted in his chair, easing this way and that in what appeared to be a futile attempt at comfort. He finally gave up. "Mishe, the intelligence agent who managed to gain the trust of Major General Aretes, returned with intel."

That was certainly worth being disturbed for. Any insight from the woman on the second tier of command of the entire occupation was worth good credits. It wasn't worth rousing Aarush from his infirmary bed, however...

"What has he learned?"

Aarush shifted slightly, but froze on a wince. "It seems the imperials are still unaware of the survival of the remaining Reinumon family. As of right now, they believe Kayla to be the only Reinumon in existence, thanks to Empress-Apparent Isonde's revelation of her identity. Current imperial intel assumes she has gone to ground on an imperial outworld, along with her IDC traitors."

"So they've no notion the Reinumon heirs are headed here?"

Aarush held himself too stiffly to shake his head, but there was a gleam of satisfaction in his remaining working eye. "They believe Kayla doesn't even have the capabilities to return to Wyrd Space. They think she'll limit her efforts at freeing Ordoch to working on the empire from the inside."

"And meanwhile, we have the exiled family coming home. As rallying points, Kayla, Vayne, and especially Natali will be immeasurably helpful to us." Citizens would flock to the rebellion, bolstered by the return of the royal family. The imperials would soon find themselves facing a much larger opposition than they'd prepared for.

"As the rightful rulers, you mean," Aarush said, breaking into the plans Wetham was already making.

"Pardon?"

"You said 'rallying points.'" Aarush could only frown with the left side of his face, but frown he definitely did. "You mean the exiled rulers are going to take their rightful place at the head of the rebellion, right?"

The wording made Wetham's skin crawl. Rightful? By what right, exactly? As members of the strongest psionic family, ruling by dint of an outdated political system defunct these last five years? And what of his right, as the current leader of their fractured populace?

"Something like that," he murmured, unwilling to argue about it now. The time for that would come later. "The imperials' continued ignorance will help us immensely."

Aarush left that alone.

"And what of the empire's so-called Operation Redouble? Are the occupation leaders here still keeping that info to themselves?"

It took Aarush a moment to reply, the furrow of his remaining brow hinting at the struggle to withstand the pain he must be in. He was slightly short of breath when he finally spoke. "Apparently yes, at least until they know exactly what reinforcements they'll be getting. No sense in reporting one thing and then having the troops' hopes crushed if the numbers don't come through."

Especially since Mishe's last report confirmed that morale among the occupation troops was continuing to fall to new lows. A blow like that could have real consequences for the continued occupation. All rebel intelligence agents reported the same: imperial soldiers hadn't expected to be here this long. They missed their homes and loved ones desperately. Being the oppressive force on a populace whose only crime was indifference about the TNV spread was taking a heavy toll on the soldiers' mental health.

Grumbling had started in the dark corners of taverns.

Wetham used every available intelligence asset he had to fan sparks of mutiny within the imperial army.

"There's more, though," Aarush said, "and I'm not sure if it's good or bad news." He caught his breath, wincing as though trying to ride out a new wave of pain. Wetham could only wait and watch helplessly as Aarush struggled.

"You need to be back in the infirmary." Fury welled in Wetham's chest. The imperials had done this. This and so much more. *I will drive those dogs from Ordoch, and slaughter as many as I have to to make that happen.*

For tonight, though, his friend needed him. "You are going back to the infirmary *now*."

Aarush managed a nod. "I'm not quite as ready as I thought I was."

"Nicely understated." When Aarush tried to reach for the crutches, Wetham stopped him. "Don't even think about it."

He reached to the infirmary with his psi powers, shouting in the mind of the sleeping medic on duty until the woman woke and jumped from her chair. She was out the door with a stretcher and an aide in under a minute.

Looking at the sheen of sweat on Aarush's face and the tightness to his lips, Wetham hesitated to push his energy any farther. But... he had to know.

"What was the rest of the news?" He hated himself for pushing, but damnit, they were at war.

"The empire's named a new head of the occupation, an IDC agent, and—" Aarush paused, taking another tight breath before continuing. "And Major General Aretes is apparently uneasy about the agents' plans for us. Very uneasy."

Definitely not good news.

6

As was his custom, Vayne hit the communal showers on their resecured level in the dead of night to avoid running into anyone. That small freedom—the choice to shower when he wished—still felt like a luxury. Dolan hadn't controlled their *every* move in captivity, but he could control *any* move he wanted, at any time, and that threat had hung over every choice Vayne made while a prisoner. Now, he sometimes felt like showering five times in a row just to prove that he could.

He leaned hard on his arm, palm against the wall in the tiny shower slot, head bowed as water sluiced down. The water's burn on his skin and the glory of regained freedoms eased the stiffness inside him. He put both palms on the wall and surrendered to the feeling.

Steam. The scent of soap. And blessed, blessed privacy.

All too soon the shower beeped and began to cool by rapid degrees—the ship's warning that he approached the end of his water allotment. Vayne soaped up, rinsed, and called it quits before things got unpleasant.

Towel wrapped around his waist, he padded barefoot to the sink where his toothbrush and clothes waited. He rubbed one gritty eye, lack of sleep catching up. At least he and Kayla had secured this level. He would crash for a few hours after this. A long day of investigating the extent of the latest *stepa* threat lay before them all in the morning.

Vayne brushed his teeth, spat, and rinsed his mouth. He gave his hair—overgrown now and well past his chin—a cursory finger combing. His reflection in the mirror looked every bit as rough as he felt. Just as he was gathering up his hair and securing it away from his face, someone entered.

An image appeared beyond his shoulder in the mirror and he froze. His mind took the details in even as his instincts triggered an irrational fight or flight response.

Long legs. Barely there shorts. Tank top. Lavender hair.

Tia'tan.

Fantastic. The only person he'd rather see less was Natali, and at least he could count on his sister leaving without a word.

He dropped his hands to grip the sink's edge. Tia'tan remained poised on the threshold. She had a towel in one hand, clearly having come for a shower herself. She could have nodded politely and moved on. Instead her gaze held his in the glass. Could she see the adrenaline spike, the drive to flee from her? Did she see the man he pretended to be, or the wounded animal he so clearly still was?

"Don't do that," she said, taking a step into the room while holding his gaze. The word trapped him in place as she took another step.

Don't what, Tia'tan? Hallucinate and attack you again?

"That," she said, as if she'd heard his thoughts. She pointed at him in the reflection. "That right there. I know what you're thinking—don't put that on me."

"Excuse me?"

"That shame I see screaming across your face." She continued to advance, her voice as determined as her steps. "I don't judge you. Condemn you. Yet when you look at me, that's what you're seeing."

He turned to face her, expecting her to stop. She kept coming.

"You're imagining things," he said.

Three paces away. Two. He resisted the urge to push her back telekinetically.

"You're the one seeing things that aren't there," she countered. "What do you imagine? That I think you're a monster? That I fear you?" She hit the truth head on, a blow that split a crack in the shield he surrounded himself with. "Does it seem like I fear you?"

She stepped inside the circle of his reach and demanded, "Look at me."

He could do nothing else. He followed the lines of her body with his eyes. Her tone was serious but her posture was easy. Her strong, sculpted shoulders were down, her arms loose at her sides. The tank top revealed that her core was relaxed: she wasn't coiled, ready to spring an attack, and, more importantly, she wasn't braced for a blow.

"I am your friend, Vayne. Stop imagining I think the worst of you."

How could he, when he thought the worst of himself? "The other day..."

"You had a bad moment."

"I *attacked* you," he bit out. It burned to say it out loud. Damn her for cornering him like this. And where the frutt were his clothes? He was entirely too vulnerable to her wearing nothing but a towel.

"Maybe I shouldn't have barged in to your room without permission."

He spied his clothes on the bench to his right, out of reach. And he didn't dare move, not pinned as he was with the sink at his back and Tia'tan so near that he might touch her if he did.

"Then don't, next time," he said.

One of her lavender brows arched, as if gauging his seriousness.

"Why did you?" *Don't answer.* Why had he even asked?

She seemed surprised by the question. "I was concerned when you didn't answer."

Concerned. The word irked him. A woman he admired

thought him a child that needed tending. "Concerned that I had done something?" he asked, his tone bitter.

"Concerned *for* you. This ship isn't exactly a safe haven." Her lips quirked in a brief smile. "I probably will do it again."

"And what happens next time?" Dolan's ghost hadn't bothered him since Kayla had arrived, but he didn't feel confident that was the end of things.

She shrugged. "I'll handle it."

"You'll handle it?" he growled, leaning in. So close he could feel her body heat, smell the residual fumes from the welding she'd done tonight. Too close. "This conversation is over."

She didn't give a centimeter. "No, it isn't. You don't have to pretend your captivity didn't happen, not with me."

That was exactly what he planned to do.

"I know terrible things happened to you, Vayne. It's okay to acknowledge it."

He stared her down. She was the only person to mention his torture since he'd been freed, and he couldn't tell if he hated or admired her for daring to.

Tia'tan lifted her hand and pressed two fingers firmly against a twisted scar just below his left collar bone. "*This* happened."

Her fingers contacted like the shock of ice, staying there, burning him. He hissed at the contact, going rigid in surprise.

"This happened," she said again, softly this time. She held him prisoner with two fingers and an intense gaze.

Gods, she was touching him. Actually touching him. Skin to bare skin.

Because she wants to. No mind control, no compulsion. *She chose to touch me*.

Frutt. He was making more of this than it was. What was her point, again?

He cleared his throat. "How do you know this wound happened... then?"

"The skin isn't weathered." Her touch became more gentle, the rest of her fingers joining the first two as she traced the ridge of scar tissue. "Plus, it looks like it was healed with shitty imperial medical tech." She grinned.

His mind whirled—so many chaotic thoughts—and his psi powers roared up in response. Their strength was unbelievable.

He reached out and sensed her latent psi ability—moderate, nothing compared to the force he had since last regrowing the connection. Even if she prepared for it, fought him, he could fling her across the room. Slam her into the far wall. Drive her and her disturbing words away from him.

How could she grin at him like he wasn't dangerous?

Gods, those fingers. So delicate. He wanted to crush every bone in her hand, force her to understand.

He wanted to…

She turned serious again, seemingly oblivious to the war raging within him. Her fingers stilled.

He wanted to…

… gently flatten her palm to his skin, increase their contact and the exquisite pain of it. Slide her hand downward. Would she let him?

Why force her when you can convince her she wants to? a voice whispered in his mind.

He could, too. Her shields were loose tonight, and thinning with each silent moment passing between them. With his skill he could slip in undetected, gently plant a seed…

I've taught you so much in the last five years, my dear Vayne.

He was frutting sick. *I have to get out of here.* He wrapped one hand around her wrist as gently as he could, tightly controlling himself to keep from pushing away and alerting her to his struggle. If she ever knew what he had thought…

"Tia—" he began, but laughter and the guttural accents of Imperial Common interrupted the words he couldn't even say.

She pulled away and he let go just as the hulking figures of the two largest octet members came into view. Vid and Trinan—maybe?—entered with fingers intertwined and shared smiles, still laughing over whatever joke one of them had made. If they thought it odd to see Tia'tan less than a meter from him when he wore nothing but a towel, they didn't indicate it. The agents merely nodded politely and headed toward the bank of showers.

Vayne felt dirty in a way a shower could never fix.

He gathered up his clothes, then forced himself to meet Tia'tan's gaze. If he stormed out the way he longed to, she'd only be more *concerned*, and that would lead to another painful confrontation like this one.

"I'll think about what you said," he managed, and walked out with his best appearance of calm.

Deep inside, a familiar voice chuckled with satisfaction.

A few hours later, fortified by a brief interval of sleep, Kayla gathered with the others outside cryochamber 13-2. It had taken most of the night to ensure the necessary levels were secured to her and Natali's *ro'haar* standards. She was satisfied that they could eat, sleep, build the new drive, and fly the ship in relative safety.

Now it was time to crack the mystery of how Gunnery Sergeant Fengrathen had been awakened. The captain was here, along with Benny and Ariel. Ida had specifically requested that Toble come. He might be an imperial, but he was the only medic on the ship. Natali was here of course. Kayla and Malkor, with *il'haars* and octet members to protect, had come to see for themselves what fresh mess of a situation they'd brought their people into. Kayla especially refused to be left out of any decision-making process from here on out, not when Vayne and Corinth's lives were at risk.

With the exception of Toble, everyone was armed with bullpups. Ida might be captain of this ship, but she'd lost control of these lower levels long ago.

Ariel entered the unlock code and Ida verified it for the system. The door to the cryochambers slid open without a sound, unleashing the most horrific smell Kayla had ever encountered.

Bile rose in her throat and she unconsciously took a step back as if that would save her from the scent. Natali stood tall, holding down her gorge with supreme effort. Ida gagged and Ariel covered her mouth. Only Toble seemed unaffected—probably used to this kind of thing.

Kayla cautiously stepped into the huge chamber, even while her nose was telling her brain that this was not a safe place to be.

Everyone spread out to secure the entry and confirm the absence of hostiles at present. It took Kayla a few seconds to fully comprehend what she was seeing.

There were dozens of open pods, their organoplastic lids retracted. Several of these were empty, but more disturbing were the pods that held the corpses of crew members who had not survived reanimation. The bodies were in various stages of decomposition, with distorted faces, bloated abdomens, skin slippage, and in some extreme cases, desiccation.

Still other corpses lay face down on the ground, legs and arms contorted, having survived reanimation only to die mere meters from their cryopods. The chamber had become a field of death.

Ida, Benny, and Ariel were frozen, the horror Kayla felt reflected in their expressions. Indeed, everyone stood rigid, the horror of it all trapping them and making moving forward with an investigation nearly impossible.

Toble broke the quiet, and perhaps, as the medic among them, he was the only one who could have without giving offense. "We're going to need biological containment gear."

A short time later, everyone was suited up and Toble made the first—rather unnecessary, given the condition of the corpse—pronouncement of death. Once fully geared, Ariel went to the room's complink console, intent on discovering how the crew had been awakened without the system being alerted. Benny and Ida, each with a datapad listing the crew manifest, went among the dead to identify them.

Kayla and Malkor would help prepare the bodies for space burial once Toble had determined cause of death as best he could, but for now they hefted the plasma torches they'd brought and set about sealing the ventilation grates in the room. Ida was adamant that none of her remaining crew members be vulnerable to the *stepa at es*.

With the number of cryochambers the Yari *possesses, this is going to be a long day.*

Much later in the afternoon the last cryochamber was declared undisturbed and the final tally given.

Twenty-seven dead and eight missing, Kayla reported to Vayne, knowing he could hear her thoughts. Beside her, Malkor reported the same to his team via mobile comm.

::That many?:: Vayne replied. He could have shielded himself and simply read her mind, but instead he let his surprise, frustration, and impatience come through with his words. Either the openness was so instinctual with his *ro'haar*, or he didn't feel the need to guard against her. Whatever the reason, she was grateful for the intimacy. ::How could the crew be so careless?::

Kayla glanced at Captain Janus, thankful the woman couldn't hear Vayne. The captain stood with her back to everyone, still as a statue, one hand resting on the cover of a sealed hibernation pod, her gaze locked on the pod's occupant. *There is no reason to suspect the* stepa *capable of anything like this, or that they'd even be interested in waking other members of the crew.*

::Well they have, and we're the ones who are going to pay for it.:: Anger joined his other emotions.

We don't know that the eight that walked out of here are still alive. Based on the condition of the bodies left in the two chambers that have been disturbed, whoever opened the pods did it over a period of a few weeks.

::Only two chambers?::

When the first crew members died, they must have assumed that things were faulty in that one chamber and tried a second. No need to try any more when they got the same results.

::Even with a seventy percent mortality rate upon reviving,

they continued to open pods, huh?::

Kayla sighed. *So it seems.* Why take the risk, just to wake a few more people? What were they planning? *It's possible the missing crew members are still sane and not hostile.*

::Or they could be sane *and* hostile, which is even worse than the *stepa at es* we are already dealing with.::

Hostile at who, though? The Ilmenans on board? The crew? Was there a division in the ranks over how life on the Yari *should continue?* They wouldn't get any further by speculating amongst themselves.

How is your day coming? she asked instead.

Immediately she felt him raise a barrier, even without her psi powers. The emotions coming through shifted and dampened, as if being more tightly controlled.

::We're doing well, almost done installing the RFID readers on all the lifts on the non-secure floors.::

We. Vayne and Tia'tan. Working as a unit when Kayla, as his *ro'haar*, should have been the one with him. But she couldn't be in two places at once. And Tia'tan still had full possession of her psi powers, in addition to being a skilled fighter. Perhaps Vayne was safer with her. Kayla buried the thought before Vayne could read it.

No one could keep Vayne as safe as she could. No one would ever be as in tune as she was, or as dedicated. Tia'tan might be a fine fighter, but wasn't as skilled. And certainly not as hyperaware, as hypervigilant as Kayla was. Tia'tan hadn't survived five years on the slum side of Altair Tri. She hadn't fought off men larger than her, intent on rape and murder. Hadn't defeated opponent after opponent in the Blood Pit. She hadn't lived on death's edge like Kayla had.

And frutt Tia'tan's psi powers, anyway. Kayla trusted Vayne to keep himself—and his *ro'haar*—safe in that regard. *Il'haars* were born for that, and Vayne was one of the best.

::This situation is totally frutted. No matter what we do, it's not safe on the *Yari*, not while crazy people have the run of the ship.::

Vayne—

::You know I'm right. Now that we have the *Lorius*, we should at least be sleeping there.::

And abandon the Yari *to the* stepa?

He didn't speak, but the emotions he sent through answered the question of how little he cared about that.

Malkor had finished checking in with his team, and now cocked a brow in her direction.

We'll meet up after you and Tia'tan are finished; there's a lot for all of us to discuss, Vayne agreed, but the tone, conveyed in emotions, left her little hope that he'd change his mind.

Fantastic. Her *il'haar* wanted to go to Ilmena and escape everything, her sovereign ruler demanded they stay with the *Yari* until it could catch a hyperstream out of here, and her lover needed her to accompany him to Ordoch to convince her people to finally make a cure for the TNV, despite five years of occupation.

Things weren't complicated at all.

7

sonde did her best to smile at the man on the vidscreen, when inside she was screaming. Aich Nias was a member of the Protectorate Council and someone she'd hoped never to have to deal with. He was a hotheaded, domineering, outspoken councilor who tended to speak first and think afterward, and now, he would be her replacement on the Council of Seven.

"I'm very pleased to appoint you as my representative on the council while I am in absentia." By which she meant, "I'd rather drink coolant than let you anywhere near my seat." She smiled harder and gritted her teeth.

Aich beamed with satisfaction. "I am happy to accept, and gratified by your faith in me." By which he meant, "I hope you die en route to Ordoch so that I might have this seat permanently."

She ended the comm with a few more polite words, before she could renege on her end of the deal and tell him what she thought of his abilities as a councilor of any sort.

"Stars, that was painful," she said to Ardin, who had sat silently throughout the exchange as it took place in their state room. Less than two full days had passed since Vega had been granted authority over the occupation, and Isonde and Ardin's counteroffensive was nearly finished.

"It was all I could do to keep my mouth shut," Ardin agreed. "Are we really doing this?"

Isonde sighed. She really wanted to kick her hoverchair and hurl something across the room, but she didn't have time for petty antics—she never did. So she remained seated and calm.

The previous night they'd spoken with Malkor, who'd confirmed that *if* the octet's plan to sabotage the data they had exchanged for Malkor's life had failed, then Vega knew everything there was to know about the Influencer—including how to operate it. That's assuming that her claim of having Dolan's third incarnation of the Influencer—made to Hekkar while they'd been negotiating for Malkor's release a month ago—were true.

Isonde fully believed the woman, now, though it hadn't been confirmed. How else could she have been named the new military leader of the occupation?

If she knew enough about the Influencer to control the Council of Seven, she likely knew exactly how to harvest psionic powers from the Wyrds and bestow them on anyone she wanted. All she needed was a ready supply of Wyrds...

Which was no doubt the driving force behind Vega taking control of Operation Redouble. If she controlled Ordoch, she would be unstoppable.

This morning's bid had to work. If Ardin and Isonde didn't get to the planet and start negotiating a treaty with the Wyrds before Vega arrived with the fleet of reinforcements, there would be no treaty at all.

Which could mean no TNV cure... Ever.

She checked the chronometer: only a half-hour until the Council of Seven convened for the morning. They'd really cut this backroom deal close.

Ardin tipped his chair backward slightly, folding his hands behind his head. "I really hope Vega isn't planning on setting up shop as a peddler of psionic powers."

"But..."

He grimaced. "But I know she'd use any capital of any type

to gain power in the empire. The council members will agree to anything she proposes if it means they can get their hands on the coveted advantage of the Wyrds."

"True. I doubt she even has curing the TNV on her agenda." By contrast, Isonde would trade all of her political currency to save her people from the plague, even if she was destroyed in the process.

"I'm betting she does. If she can come back with a cure, she'll be the biggest war hero the empire's ever seen, which sets her up even more nicely to take over." He stood and straightened his tunic. "Time for council."

"I need to check in with Raorin quick, I'll be ready in five."

Ardin headed for the door, but paused before he reached it. He looked at her, tilting his head while he considered. "You know, I think you might be the most brilliant political mind of our generation."

She chuckled. "One of them, anyway."

"I'm serious. We heard from Malkor less than twelve hours ago. In that time you've researched the Articles of Incorporation of the council, figured out a solution, and brokered deals with both the Sovereign and Protectorate council representatives."

"To be fair, you brokered the deal with the Sovereign councilors. I just got the Protectorate member on board with our plan. We did it together."

"But it was your plan." He considered her, and she held her breath. She was acutely aware of the tension between them, the hurt and disappointment she'd caused him by falling in with Vega and denouncing Malkor in order to save her seat on the council. She felt herself on the edge of her seat, wondering with hope and trepidation what he might have to say.

No one but Ardin could make her feel this way. She'd loved him as a friend her whole life, and romantically these last few years, but never in the way he deserved. It was a truth she hadn't recognized until she'd lost his esteem—something she had previously thought of as immutable.

He smiled momentarily. A genuine smile, and that gave her

hope. "You really are brilliant," he said, then left the room.

As a compliment from a husband to a wife it might not be romantic, but to her, it was everything.

Isonde took her seat at the table in the chambers of the Council of Seven, Ardin beside her. In a more sentimental moment, she might have reached out and squeezed his hand briefly for support at such a crucial time in their careers. Instead, she raised a brow as if to say "Ready?" and he nodded.

He leaned in. "Let's do this," he murmured, the thing Malkor had said to them a thousand times over the years, and would have said again in this moment. She couldn't help but smile.

The emperor called the session to order and turned it over to the Salamander of Biddan, Jobu, who was one of two Sovereign Council representatives who made up the Council of Seven.

Jobu surprised the emperor and empress—but no one else—by abdicating his right to announce the first item to be debated and voted on by the council to the woman seated beside him, who in turn abdicated her right to the man beside her, Protectorate Council member Ino Ig Catan.

He opened his mouth to speak but the emperor interrupted him. "What, exactly, is going on?" He skewered the two who had declined their turns—which never, ever happened—with a fierce glare. Isonde felt a smug satisfaction to be one up on the emperor, who was a strong supporter of Vega. "This is highly irregular." He looked at the empress for support, but she merely shrugged. She, who always fell in line with whatever the emperor wanted, seemed for once curious at the proceedings.

"Irregular, perhaps," Ino said, "but well within our rights. And with that I abdicate my opening bid to the next speaker, the Empress-Apparent." He inclined his head to Isonde. "You have the floor."

By now the emperor's face was red with suppressed agitation, and he glared at her. She merely smiled. His son might have been his greatest opponent at the table in previous years, but that was before she'd gained her seat. Emperor Rengal had never met an opponent like her before.

"Thank you, Ino." She inclined her head to him. "Ardin and I will gladly make the first proposal, as it is a joint proposal between us."

The empress arched a brow, very intrigued. She leaned back in her chair as if settling in for a show, just as the emperor opened his mouth to object.

Isonde breezed on before he could. "With the stated purpose of Operation Redouble to be to apply increased pressure on Ordoch with the expected outcome of a full capitulation to our demand—request—that they manufacture a cure for the TNV, it's come to our attention that we've left out one crucial part of the plan: treaty negotiators.

"Ardin and I propose that we be elected as the official treaty negotiators for the empire, and volunteer to travel to Ordoch immediately."

The emperor frowned but held his peace, as was required until she opened the topic up for debate.

"We realize this is unorthodox," Ardin said, taking up the proposal, "but in light of Senior Commander Vega—who is not a member of the military—being appointed as head of the occupation, this is an unorthodox time. The Articles of Incorporation for the Council of Seven allow for the appointment of one or more of its members as treaty negotiators in times of great immediacy, when someone with the highest authority needs to be there to see that a treaty is drawn up and ratified with utmost speed.

"Considering the overwhelming spread of the TNV and the sheer number of its victims, I think we can all agree that Operation Redouble needs to conclude as swiftly as possible. Isonde and I have the authority to draw up such a treaty, and can have it to the Council for Ratification immediately, without waiting for another negotiator to have to go through proper channels."

"There is precedent for such a decision," Isonde said. "The council appointed two of its members as treaty negotiators during the annexation of the first Protectorate Planet, and again when the Altair System was annexed in totality." Thankfully. While she and Ardin might technically be able to do what they were proposing based on the articles, it was a lot harder to argue with precedent than it was with a legal technicality.

"We understand that what we're proposing would disrupt the Council of Seven's day-to-day functioning, since we would be out of communication while traveling to Wyrd Space, and for most of the time once we reach the planet. We would therefore temporarily abdicate our seats on the council, appointing one member of the Protectorate Council and one member of the Sovereign Council, which is the order in which our seats were to be filled in the case of our death."

At least in this case, as it was a temporary measure, she and Ardin had the right to choose who would take over their seats. She would have chosen a primate before she would have chosen Aich Nias, but agreeing to his appointment secured Ino's vote in favor of her proposal. Both Sovereign Council representatives agreed to vote in their favor as well, should Ardin put forth Archon Raorin as his replacement.

Which was crucial, as the emperor—and thus the empress— were sure to vote against Isonde and Ardin having any more influence over the outcome of the Wyrd occupation than they already did. If at least two of the three who pledged their support voted their way, they would have their victory.

She looked into the eyes of all three councilors and knew that it was a done deal. They practically salivated at the thought of having another member of their respective councils on the all-powerful Council of Seven.

Isonde sat back in her chair as they opened the floor to debate and the emperor began his argument against the motion. It would be a short, one-person debate, and when the others had no objections, they'd vote and she and Ardin could be on their way.

Good thing they had an ally in Senior IDC Commander Parrel. With almost limitless funds—thanks to the Council of Seven's recent funding bill for the IDC—and access to cutting-edge technology most of the empire hadn't even heard of yet, she and Ardin would be on board the fastest ship known to imperial minds as soon as the vote concluded.

Her smug moment didn't last long, though, when she remembered that the score was something like Bad Guys 2, Good Guys 1. She was counting the days to Vega's defeat—even if that wasn't a certainty yet.

8

THE *YARI*, MINE FIELD, IMPERIAL SPACE

It was late evening, *Yari* ship time, when Kayla, Malkor, Tia'tan, Noar, Vayne, and Natali gathered in the commissary. Kayla's body was completely confused between the ship-to-ship time difference and the length-of-day difference; a standard day on Ordoch lasted longer than a standard imperial day. At some point her body and mind would sync again, but for now she felt out of sorts.

No one else seemed to be faring any better, though that was more likely due to the day's revelations. Dinner was eaten in silence. Malkor, Kayla, and Natali sat on one side of the long rectangular table, with Vayne, Tia'tan, and Noar seated on the bench opposite. Despite images of dead *Yari* crew members floating around in Kayla's mind, she managed to pack away a few calories out of necessity. Hauling bodies was heavy work, and who knew what might be asked of her next. No good *ro'haar* would allow herself to get fatigued due to hunger. Malkor and Natali, also fresh from packing corpses into coffin cases, managed the same.

It wasn't until the meal was done and they were all sipping the remains of their beverages that anyone decided to speak.

"I'll say it—the situation with the *stepa* is messed up."

Malkor's deep voice perfectly elucidated her thoughts. "We have no idea of the number of unaccounted-for crew members, and if those remaining are sane or not."

She caught a brief look of distaste on Vayne's face, quickly hidden. He fished something out of the pocket of his trousers and positioned the device in his ear. The translator bot. *Finally*. Even knowing Malkor would be at dinner, he'd not put it in before? That brought a frown of her own.

"There's no indication that any of the missing crew members are hostile," Natali said.

"No indication?" Noar challenged. "What do you call blowing up our ship?"

"None of the *sane* members of the missing crew, then."

Tia'tan set down the coffee she'd been sipping. "Are any of the crew sane? Truly?"

"The captain, Benny, Ariel, Tanet, and Larsa are fine," Natali said, as if she could assure it.

"Gintoc was 'fine,' until he killed Luliana and Joffar," Tia'tan countered.

"It could be said that it was your people who triggered his break."

Tia'tan drew a sharp breath and Kayla felt the explosion coming from a kilometer away. But seated beside Tia'tan, Vayne laid a hand on her arm just as she opened her mouth to blast Natali. Her sister had immediately glanced away from Tia'tan when Vayne moved, and she now spoke to the tabletop. "I apologize."

In the resounding silence that followed it was clear Vayne, Tia'tan, and Noar were having a discussion. Neither of the Ilmenans spoke to accept the apology.

They should, Kayla thought to herself. As heir to Ordoch with her twin brother, Natali had always been tightly focused, goal driven, and a bit unrelenting—none of which left her much time to be concerned with the feelings of others.

And that was years ago, when they'd all still been happy, healthy adults.

These days Kayla herself could barely stop to consider Malkor's feelings when in pursuit of an objective. For Natali, who had been tortured for five years and was now responsible for the fate of a world at war, to apologize…

"It's been a long day," Kayla said, a sentiment that excused most sins. She was in sympathy with both women—Tia'tan had only recently lost two friends—and was too wound up to sort through that at present. "I dislike not having a clear idea of numbers, but the captain is in no position to discuss it tonight."

"Has she said how many crew members had been revived prior to this?" Malkor asked the room at large. "Once the ship had awoken her?"

Natali sat forward to answer him, and Kayla breathed a silent sigh of relief. At least one family member didn't seem determined to ignore Malkor's existence. "A total of seventy-three people survived the initial revival. Of that number, some had been successfully locked up when it became clear that their minds were deteriorating. Others wandered off, never to be seen again, but Ida was vague on how far gone all of those crew members had been."

"Are we talking about sane members of the crew going AWOL?" Malkor asked, raising a brow.

Natali nodded. "Seems that way."

"Tired of the military life, or were there disagreements among the crew about how things should be handled?"

"I couldn't pin the captain down on it."

"Neither could I," Vayne offered, though not to Natali directly. "And the rest of the crew just said, 'Ask the captain,' whenever I brought up the topic."

Tia'tan agreed as well.

Information that none of them had shared before Kayla arrived. But then again, she hadn't asked. *Who am I kidding?* She would have come even if Vayne had told her the ship had been overrun and set on fire. Especially in that case, with her *il'haars* on board.

Not that they were all that far from being overrun now…

Malkor looked at each person gathered at the table, herself included. "And none of you think we should abandon ship?"

"Hey, I'm with you," Vayne said, surprising the stars out of everyone. "We should take your ship to Ilmena."

"You mean Ordoch. I'd prefer to take the *Lorius*, as well, but we'd never make it past the barricade. I hate to say this, but the Tear—"

Vayne cut him off rudely. "How could you think joining a rebellion on an occupied planet any safer than this?"

::I thought you said he was intelligent.::

Kayla glared at her twin, longing for the power to answer such an insulting comment directly.

"Better open terrain than trapped in a bottle."

"No one's leaving," Natali said, capturing everyone's attention. "The crew can't possibly hope to hold the ship alone if the *stepa* organize intelligently against them. And Ordoch needs the *Yari*'s firepower against the empire—ground forces aren't enough."

"Ilmena agrees," Noar said. "Though *not* with the use of *Yari*'s planetary destroyer."

The room erupted with opinions on that. Kayla sensed that this was well-trod ground between them all. She held up a hand to cut through the noise. "We can debate the ethics or insanity of using the PD til the stars burn out, but without fuel and a drive, it's all theoretical. I stand with Natali—we need to further secure the ship." Natali was right that the *Yari* would be invaluable in the effort to free Ordoch. Kayla still hoped for a peaceful resolution—a cure for the TNV should be everyone's focus, not a protracted war—and having the might of the *Yari* behind them would give Ordoch the best chance at that.

"We've got a much bigger problem with the *stepa* than Ida led us to believe," Vayne said. He detailed what had been done so far to secure vital areas of the ship, and what they'd accomplished since Itsy's spectacularly successful attack.

Kayla instantly tuned him out when Corinth spoke in her mind.

::Kay?:: Uncertainty hit her, all his. ::I need you.::

She shot to her feet, simultaneously grabbing her mobile comm, which Rigger had tied into the ship's system. "What's happened, Corinth? Where are you?" Everyone else froze.

::Nothing. It's just… I just need you.:: Fear, embarrassment.

A nightmare, then. She breathed a silent prayer of relief that was all it was. "I'll be right there." Five years of habit to run when Corinth needed her had her turning for the door instinctively, but her mind righted her, gaze shooting to Vayne.

How could she leave one *il'haar* to comfort another? Was her first loyalty to Vayne or to Corinth? The surge of adrenaline Corinth's voice had caused demanded she *do something*, but her heart held her still. Vayne was her twin, but he was strong, well trained, and Corinth was still so young, so vulnerable.

Malkor was on his feet beside her. "I'll go." He understood her struggle perfectly, even without words.

She shook her head. "It's night terrors. They're very real to him—he'll need me."

"I promised Corinth, when I rescued him from Janeen all those weeks ago, that I would always be there for him." Malkor smiled gently. "Let me do this."

A wave of gratitude, relief at no longer being alone, left her speechless for a second. Malkor, so in tune with her, correctly inferred her agreement.

As soon as the IDC agent left the commissary, Vayne pulled the imperial translator bot from his ear and returned it to his pocket. Seeing the look of relief on Kayla's face when Malkor offered to help, the way her posture relaxed as she retook her seat, made Vayne realize just what an asshole he was.

Il'haars looked out for their *ro'haars*. They made their *ro'haar*'s life easier if they could. The partnership worked both ways. Kayla would give her life for him, and he hadn't the decency to think of the position he put her in by sitting mute while she struggled to decide who needed her more.

Me, he'd wanted to shout. *I need you more. You're* my *ro'haar.*

While Corinth needed Kayla the way a child needed his mother for comfort.

Yup. I'm an asshole.

He wanted to apologize to Kayla. He should have offered to go with her, not put her in the position of having to choose. Corinth was his brother, too. What kind of monster had he become, to resent his sister for caring for a child?

Kayla smiled at him the tiniest bit, inclined her head as if she understood and accepted him just as he was. He felt even worse. *Who have you made me into, Dolan?* his mind cried for the millionth time. *Are you pleased with what I've become?*

Clear as a bell, as if Dolan stood at his shoulder and whispered in his ear, the words came.

Simply delighted, my dear Vayne.

Kayla and the others outlined a plan for securing the *Yari* against hostile takeover from within. It was lengthy, and would of course require the captain's approval, so they agreed to sleep on it for a few hours. Kayla woke feeling no more optimistic about the *Yari*'s chance of flying than she had yesterday, but she wouldn't abandon ship until Natali gave the order.

That meant giving Larsa time to complete the hyperstream drive, which meant securing the *Yari.* Wetham, the man apparently in charge of Ordoch's rebellion to date, reported that recruitment had risen sharply among their people with the news that original members of the Reinumon family were returning to Ordoch. The rebellion needed time to train new forces, to expand their control. Ilmena needed time to finish the rebuild of their ancient battleships, not to mention time to hopefully create a prototype cure for the TNV.

All of which annoyed the frutt out of Kayla.

She'd done nothing *but* wait for the last five years. Now she had a purpose beyond mere survival. She was reunited with her family, soon to be reunited with her people, and every cell in her body screamed that it was time to *act*.

Instead, she gritted her teeth and bowed to the wisdom of waiting—for now.

Noar, Larsa, and Corinth remained working on the drive, and someone was always on guard in the command center—usually either Ariel, Benny, Tanet, or the captain, who knew the most about the ship's complex systems.

That left everyone else free to perform the thousands of tasks needed to ensure their control of the ship. They worked in two-person teams, a more vulnerable nonpsionic paired with a Wyrd, not just for extra protection, but for the ability to read the ship's Ordochian labeling system.

Kayla's first instinct—to hunt down the *stepa* in a deck-by-deck search—just wasn't feasible. The *stepa* knew the layout of the ship and its various maintenance tubes and HVAC systems. If Kayla did manage to find a lair on one of the myriad decks, the *stepa* could just disappear into the very walls of the ship, hiding and relocating, leading them on a never-ending chase.

Instead, she had to content herself with playing defense—for now. There were a million essential areas of the ship—they couldn't hope to secure them all.

Time to get to work.

Everyone carried their RFID badges with them, and new scanners were added to chambers containing the life support systems for the levels in question: a medical station, the nearest shuttle bay, power relay hubs, and so on. In addition, keypads were added and each person was issued an alpha-numeric code that changed every day. These precautions, coupled with the welding of the access grilles, meant that entry by conventional means, at least, should be near impossible for the *stepa*.

Kayla wouldn't feel comfortable unless every vital level of the ship was thus secured, but they didn't have the manpower or resources for that. At first, she'd found some comfort in the knowledge that a large part of the lower ship wasn't powered. Without life-support and artificial gravity, it was unlikely the *stepa* ever went there.

According to Vayne, the ship's damage was the result of two things: whatever massive cataclysm had torn them out of time and space, and early battles with the rooks in the Mine Field. Apparently, the creatures—or were they enemy ships? No one seemed to know—had inflicted significant damage to the hull before the *Yari* had established its current defensive perimeter.

Kayla's relief evaporated when the crew discovered that several extravehicular mobility units—spacesuits—had been stolen from one of the depots. It had been the work of a day for one of the teams to gather the remaining EMUs from the unsecured but still powered levels and relocate them to several of the empty crew cabins on their living level.

A day that was needed for hundreds of other tasks.

The first challenging job had fallen to Natali: convincing Captain Janus to permanently seal the doors of the cryochambers. The pods themselves would remain powered, but no one would be able to access the rooms again without cutting through the triple-thick walls. They couldn't afford men to guard each of the chambers, and the risk that whoever had awoken the unauthorized crew members would continue to do so was too great.

With so many crucial tasks to complete on board the *Yari*, it was inevitable that there were arguments over which to prioritize, and where best to use manpower. Number one on everyone's list, however, was collecting every last weapon they could find. Not only to keep the weapons out of the hands of the *stepa*, but to supply armaments for the rebels on Ordoch. A daunting task on a battleship as well stocked as the *Yari*, and seemingly impossible when the reality of just how many decks were unpowered hit them.

And so it was, three days later, that Kayla found herself in a stygian, unpowered corridor on a lower level with only Vayne for company. At least they'd been able to power the freight maglift with a portable generator in order to reach the deck. Encased in somewhat unwieldy EMUs, they'd pushed off from the maglift doors with their feet and sailed through the air of the corridor where the artificial gravity was out.

Every time she made a course correction using one of the wall struts, the power pack attached to her utility belt via an umbilical bumped into her. Vayne fared better, using his psi powers for adjustment, and he bobbled here and there as his attention was fixed on telekinetically maneuvering two large hovercarts down the corridor ahead of them. The dual beams of light from the lamps attached to their suits bounced erratically around the corridor with each movement they made.

"I'm starting to get trippy," Kayla said through her helmet comm.

Vayne huffed a laugh. "After more than a dozen hours of this and zero food, I'm starting to get nauseated. Benny and Vid can do the dark-walking tomorrow." The datapad embedded in the arm of his suit lit up as he accessed the schematics again. "The armory should be just ahead."

She and Vayne were collecting armaments on the lower levels and moving them up to the powered section of the ship. It had to be done in small batches, and rather than having to remove and replace their suits, they stayed in the unpowered section while Benny and Vid, the other half of their four-person team, took possession of the weapons at the lowest powered level and moved them to various holding rooms on the secured areas. All across the ship, the others did the same thing.

"We're lucky the *Lorius* was well stocked with EMUs," Kayla said. "No way Vid or Trinan would fit in one of the *Yari*'s EMUs." She stopped in front of the door marked ARMORY 22-5 and yanked the mobile power pack into position in front of its access panel.

"At least those big shoulders are good for something," Vayne said.

She let the remark pass without comment—too exhausted to combat his prejudice at the moment—and engaged her magnetized tether to hold herself in place against the wall. Vayne set about releasing the power pack's connections from their storage space in the case while she pried the face off the access panel, a routine they'd perfected by now. They had the unit linked to the door's power mainline in no time. Vayne switched on the pack, she entered the unlock sequence, and the heavy-duty armory doors groaned open.

He led the way, moving the hovercarts into the center of the large room and securing them to the floor with magnetic locks. Kayla scanned the armory's contents. Like the small weapons caches found on each level, this armory had a supply of bullpups and hand weapons racked and easily available. The *Yari*'s molychromium skeleton could withstand several direct shots from these smaller plasma weapons if a firefight broke out on board. The ion pistols were also safe, but the larger plasma weapons, and all projectile weapons, were crated away in large armories like these, and usable for land-based combat only.

Who knew if the *stepa* would remember that fact...

"This is the last one today," she said, watching Vayne's sluggish movements as he set about releasing the clamps holding the first of the giant crates. Truth be told, she was more fatigued than she wanted to admit. Maneuvering in EMUs wasn't exactly easy, and her body was feeling the lack of fuel. "No skipping lunch tomorrow," she added. Even if it did take up precious time. He didn't argue.

While Vayne floated the first crate to the cart, she turned her attention to the smaller weapons that were easily accessible in the racks. Their packaging cartons had been collapsed to the thickness of a datapad and stored in a compartment at the back of the armory. It was the work of seconds to pop them open and restore their rigid shape. She began packing the weapons away while Vayne did the heavy lifting. With this large an armory, it would take them several trips on the freight maglift to empty the room.

She glanced up from her work and caught the tightness of Vayne's lips as he directed another crate through the air with his psi powers.

"You're wearing yourself down too much."

"It's quicker to move them this way."

"Maybe, but it's not entirely necessary." In the zero-g environment, she could just as easily remove a heavy crate from its moorings and push it into place on the cart, securing it with a magnetic clamp. "It's not worth you exhausting yourself over."

He never paused. "We can switch tomorrow."

Her packing carton started to float away and she snatched it back. She opened her mouth to argue, then shut it. Vayne wasn't Corinth. He was an adult; he knew his limits. And even if it pained her to watch her twin suffer in any small way, after all he'd been through, she wouldn't bring it up again.

It was well into evening ship time when they guided their loaded carts down the corridor for the final trip to the maglift. They arrived only to find that the lift wasn't waiting for them, as it had been all the other times.

Kayla jabbed the button to call the lift. No response. The message LIFT LOCKED displayed on the console screen. She blinked stupidly at it for a second, having been on autopilot for the last few hours of repetitious work.

"Vid?" She commed the upper level where Benny and Vid worked. "Are you guys still offloading that last shipment?"

No way they could be. All they had to do was pull the fully loaded hovercarts out of the lift, slide the previously emptied carts in, and send them down for Kayla and Vayne to fill.

"What are you talking about?" Vid sounded confused. "We sent the lift back after the last batch, about ninety minutes ago."

Ninety minutes? "We sent crates up no more than forty minutes ago."

All of a sudden the lift spun to life, the car dropping floors on a faint hum as the console tracked its descent.

"Frutt." Kayla hadn't brought a weapon—she wouldn't have been able to fire it with the bulky EMU gloves. Which meant she was as toothless as she was defenseless, and only the void knew what was coming for them.

Suddenly everything was in motion, including her.

Vayne manipulated the hovercarts, pushing them to the front as he dragged Kayla backward and down behind the carts. In the space of three heartbeats, and without moving a muscle, he had them as safely situated as it was possible to be in the zero-g corridor.

I'm going to frutting murder you all. Kayla thought for the millionth time of the imperial soldiers who had attacked her world and somehow caused her to lose her psi powers five years ago. The soldiers who had made her so useless now.

The maglift eased to a stop on their level, and the doors opened to reveal...

Nothing.

The weapons were gone, and the thieves along with them.

9

"The weapons are just gone?" Natali sounded incredulous, and Malkor couldn't blame her. It seemed absurd that dozens of weapons crates could vanish in the space of forty-five minutes, especially with Vid involved, one of Malkor's most watchful agents.

Observation deck one remained silent in the wake of Natali's question, despite being full of people. She paced in front of the massive bank of floor-to-ceiling viewports. She had to be as tired as anyone there, but her bearing was upright and regal to the point of stiffness. Her pale blue hair was pulled back in a ponytail nearly as severe as her frown.

Every eye in the room was on her, and Malkor was in no doubt that he was looking at the next leader of Ordoch—even in exile.

Captain Janus stood to one side of the viewports, head high, hands clasped behind her back in an "at ease, but still ready" pose. Benny stood beside her in a similar stance. Malkor had found it hard to believe that the captain, master of her ship for five hundred years, had agreed to fall under Natali's command. That is, until he had seen Natali in her element. She'd come a long way from the glassy-eyed POW rescued from captivity just months earlier. There was so much of Kayla in her—

they shared the same fierce determination, tireless drive, and physical prowess. They both burned with the need to free their people, but where Kayla was fiery in her passion, Natali's scald seemed to come from a core temperature of absolute zero, and something about that put him off.

Or maybe it was just the look of disapproval Natali had given Kayla when she reported the missing weapons that he disliked.

Right now Kayla sat beside her twin on one of the few benches the observation deck boasted. They were both still in the liquid-cooled ventilation suits worn under spacesuits, having come straight from the lower levels. Tia'tan sat on Vayne's other side.

Malkor stood a few meters away, one booted foot on a bench because he was too unsettled to sit. Likewise, Vid and Rigger had kept on their feet.

"And you don't know which level they stopped at?" Natali didn't need to specify who "they" were.

"We couldn't search the levels via maglift," Kayla said. "Not safely, at least."

Malkor chimed in. "Riding the lift to each floor and opening the doors would have been asking for a faceful of plasma shot."

"With no working cameras on those levels," Vayne said, "it's impossible to tell where the *stepa* took the weapons, or how many were involved."

Natali nodded. "And so now the *stepa* are armed against us."

"Heavily armed," Kayla added. She especially would be feeling the weight of that truth.

Vid spoke for the first time since entering the room. "We need more people."

"Not more of your people," Natali said so quickly that distaste had to be her automatic reaction when faced with imperials.

"Fine, then what of your people?" Vid shot back just as quickly. "If we want to hold the *Yari*, we'll need help from Ordoch."

Malkor agreed. Moving armaments and stored food resources to the levels they could secure was a temporary solution at best. Without knowing the *stepa*'s objectives or

114

plans, they couldn't prepare, never mind go on the offensive.

"Have you asked the rebel leader for more troops?"

Natali stopped pacing and faced Vid head-on. "I do not need to ask. By all accounts Wetham did a fine job while I was incarcerated, but *I am* the rebel leader, now. They are my troops."

Silence reigned for a second time.

Natali, Malkor mused, had a way of inspiring that.

Vayne finally spoke. "If we're intent on salvaging the *Yari*"—and his tone implied he thought that was a bad idea—"then we need to stop thinking of the *stepa* as crazy." He turned his attention to the captain. "It took coordination and planning to steal those weapons—people working in a team and under a time constraint. This wasn't the act of a group of brain-damaged zombies."

"I not to call them zombies," Ida said, her lips tight. "But troubles after reanimation their brains are having."

"*Some* of them are having troubles. And Gintoc certainly did. But you're not." Vayne gestured to Benny. "Neither are you, or Ariel, Larsa, or Tanet. It stands to reason that if your brains came through unscathed, theirs could have, too."

"We not to have segregated crew being healthy, Vayne. Only being a last resort." It was clear the captain resented this line of thinking. Ida claimed she and her crew had quarantined Itsy, along with others, as they became irrational. Locked them in crew cabins for their own good. Once Itsy escaped, Vayne and Tia'tan had discovered that the other cabins were empty as well.

"Well, someone thought they were sane enough to free them."

"Or someone being insane enough to think so."

Malkor broke in before things could become heated. "Neither of which we can determine at present, though I concur with Vayne's assessment that at least some of the *stepa* are with it enough to plan the recent events." He held up a hand to forestall whatever reply the captain had. "The crucial question is: how in the void did they know *where* we were working at each moment. It is not possible to have happened upon those weapons by accident."

"They could be monitoring comms," Tia'tan said, but she didn't sound convinced that was the whole of it.

"Maybe, but to pinpoint with such accuracy..." It was an uncomfortable thought. Perhaps they should have bypassed the *Yari* and gone right to Ordoch. Crazy people running loose on the ship was bad enough. But well-armed crazy people—or not so crazy, as the case may be—with access to inside intel? The risks might outweigh the benefits.

"Captain." Larsa entered the observation deck just then, interrupting. Her gray jumpsuit was liberally stained, crusty in more than one spot from some kind of solvent or epoxy. Her short, blue-green hair was mussed and she wore a look of defeat. Corinth trailed in despondently after her.

"I can't do it," she said without preamble. "I'm not being sure it can be possible."

Natali stopped her pacing dead. "The hyperstream drive?"

"Aye. It being a right muddled mess." She shook her head in disgust.

::Gintoc's plans are hard to decipher.:: Malkor heard what he recognized as Corinth's voice in his head, and the others must have as well. ::He wrote a lot in a shorthand, which is tough enough. Additionally, his schematics keep changing— we think due to the insanity that was creeping in.::

"And being modern parts that rebels bringing us, mixed with old..." The look she gave the captain spoke of her frustration. "I am not thinking it possible. At least not with five-hundred-year-old expertise mine."

If the stolen weapons infuriated Natali, this news threatened to send her into orbit. "It has to be done. What if you had help? An engineer from Ordoch?"

"I not to be knowing," but Larsa looked like she did, and it looked like the answer was still no. "Rebels not having access to parts being top of the line, or even compatible at times."

"I'll speak to them, we'll get better parts. Anything you need." Natali switched from shock to action in seconds. "And

I'll get you an engine expert." She sounded utterly confident, no hesitation. Her gaze locked onto Kayla and Vayne. "It's time the ruling family had a sit down with Wetham and his lieutenants."

Hours later, Kayla shifted her position on the tiny bunk in Malkor's cabin. It was the middle of the night and they were tangled limb for limb in a jumble. Her healing arm throbbed dully and her foot was asleep, but every ache was worth it for the warmth that filled her heart. If she could spend every night with him like this for the rest of their lives, she would count herself blessed.

Though, with the way things are shaping up on the Yari, *that might not be all that long.*

The dark thought intruded on her bliss. By the chronometer's dim glow, she traced Malkor's features with her gaze. Every line and plane was dear to her, every scar familiar. That she might lose him, when they'd only just begun their lives together, was too painful to contemplate.

"I can feel you staring at me," he said without opening his eyes, his lips curving into a grin.

She kissed his brow. "I wasn't staring."

"Liar." He disentangled his hand and cupped her face to kiss her properly. Sleepy kisses in the dark that spoke of love. It was a long moment before they came up for air.

"What has you awake and worrying at this hour?"

"Who says I was worrying?" She threaded her fingers through his and turned his hand so that it lay against her chest.

"The day you stop worrying is the day you stop breathing."

A true, if depressing, statement. The life of a *ro'haar.*

"I dislike the idea of staying aboard the *Yari.*"

"You and me both. Not that the octet can't handle themselves in dangerous situations, but I'm not keen on putting their lives on the line if it's not absolutely necessary."

She smiled. "Trinan and Vid would tell you to stop babying them."

"As if you're any better with Corinth and Vayne."

"Fair."

"At least they have the added protection of psi powers."

"Shields are no defense against a plasma blast."

"I'm not talking about that. The way Fengrathen threw us against the wall like dolls—even unarmed, she could have killed us with little effort. Do you have any idea what an advantage telekinetic powers are in a fight?"

Did she ever, now that she might be fighting psionics instead of just imperials.

He shifted to pull her closer. "Sorry, but you know what I mean."

"Moving to Ordoch might not be any safer: we'll be at the same disadvantage."

"But we wouldn't be locked in a molychromium can ripe with opportunities for explosive decompression."

"I don't see that we have another option. You heard from Ardin, the empire sent the first wave of battleships from Operation Redouble. We won't win the rebellion without a way to threaten those ships, no matter how many boots we have on the ground."

"Ilmena's ships?"

Kayla sighed. "Tia'tan doesn't think they're as far along in repairs as they're claiming. They'd been junkyarded, left to corrode away on one of Ilmena's moons." The same was true for Ordoch's ships, once interplanetary conflicts between the Wyrds became a thing of the past. They were entirely too costly to maintain, especially when they were never needed generation after generation. Once the military was forced out of power on Ordoch, the battleships reached the end of their lifespan.

"There's no telling when Ilmena's ships will be ready," she said, "and it's crucial that we stop the empire before they establish new military bases on Ordoch." Or else they would have a long and protracted war that could destroy her world whether they won or not.

"Are the *Yari*'s offensive capabilities really that powerful? At five hundred years old?"

"Wyrd tech will always be superior," she answered quickly. Too quickly? Was that reality, or the imaginings of a smug race who thought themselves superior? "I don't actually know," she was forced to admit. "Once we secure the *Yari* from the *stepa*—"

"If."

"*Once* we secure it," she insisted, "we'll go over the exact weapons spec with Benny and compare them to what you know of the imperial arsenal. The *Yari* was the most confidential project in our planet's history. Very little detail was released to the public, and then only in carefully scripted propaganda vids."

Her jaw cracked with a yawn before she could stop it, and Malkor yawned in sympathy. "You need to sleep if you're going to present a 'royal face' to the rebellion leaders in the morning."

"Ugh." Just the idea of presenting herself as a member of the "royal family" made her feel pompous. So much had changed in the last five years.

"There will be plenty of time for worrying tomorrow. And the day after that. And the day after that..."

She lightly slapped his shoulder. "I get it." With some difficulty she managed to roll over without falling off the bunk. She snuggled back into Malkor's warm body and did her best to turn off her worries.

For the next few hours, at least.

Vayne lay on his back in his bunk and stared at the dark ceiling of his quarters. Middle of the night and he was alone with his thoughts—not a good place to be.

It had been decided that he, Natali, Kayla, and Uncle Ghirhad would travel through the Tear, which opened underground on Ordoch near the main rebel base, to meet with Wetham and his lieutenants. Initially, Natali included Corinth in the party, wanting the full might of the Reinumon family represented. Kayla had refused this, and when Corinth argued, Kayla shot Natali so severe a look that their sister ordered him to stay on the *Yari*, ending the debate.

Vayne had also argued, but in the opposite direction. The Tear was a risk only an idiot would take. The thing twinkled like a long-distance star, its brilliance and size fluctuating with no discernible pattern. Cinni, the girl assigned to travel through the Tear with new parts for the ship—who had subsequently blasted her head off in a drug-fueled fit of depression and remorse—told him it hadn't done that initially. And that it was getting worse. The Tear could close at any minute, taking them to Ordoch without a way back, or, more likely, disintegrating them.

However, Natali had decided it was important for the Reinumon family to make a formal appearance on Ordoch, not only to reinforce their commitment to the rebellion, but to inspire the troops. And when Natali had looked directly at him, when she had said *I need you to do this*, every horrible act he had done to her under Dolan's control rose up between them—every betrayal, every violation—and he could do nothing but agree.

She'd never said the words "you owe me," and she never would. She didn't need to, they both knew it. Every breath of pain she took was in some way his fault. The final breaking of her will had been at his hands, even if Dolan's machine drove his mind. He could never repay her.

Never.

::But Kay!::

Standing in one of the many shuttle bays aboard the *Yari*, Kayla gave Corinth a quelling look as he argued—for the hundredth time—that he should be allowed to travel to Ordoch.

::I'm a Reinumon, too.::

"Of course you are. But we have plenty of Reinumons attending already, so there's no need for you to take the risk."

::You're letting Vayne go.::

She glanced to where her twin stood, speaking quietly with Tia'tan while they both geared up in ventilation suits. That he was here surprised the shit out of her. He'd made his feelings quite clear about traveling to war-torn Ordoch by any means, never mind through the Tear.

Natali had commanded it, and an uncomfortable silence had fallen over the two of them. That thing they did, of looking at each other but never quite making eye contact, somehow convinced him, and he nodded without a word. Kayla didn't need psi powers to feel the war inside him when he did.

"Vayne is an adult and can make his own choices. For now, I'm still the boss of you." She ruffled his hair in an attempt at light-heartedness but he pushed her hand away.

::I'm not a child, Kay.::

Oh, but you are, in so many ways still. Thankfully, Corinth wasn't in her mind this time. He looked pretty belligerent, though, so she tried a different line of reasoning. "You promised Trinan and Vid that you'd take a break from helping Larsa in the engine room and get some exercise with them. You don't want to disappoint them, do you?"

::But—::

She held up a hand, cutting off the protest. "You'll go to Ordoch soon enough, just not today. All right?"

He gave her a sulky nod and she resisted the urge to roll her eyes.

Teenagers.

She blinked. When had he reached that stage? It felt like he'd been a child only moments ago.

"Make sure you stick close with Trinan and Vid today." She hated to leave him on the dubious safety of the ship, but she couldn't ask for better bodyguards. The agents treated him as if he were their son.

::You already said that.:: Even his mind voice was petulant.

Let the guys deal with him today, she thought, a little thankfully.

She donned her own ventilation suit, checking that the liquid cooling lines were in place and the electronic life-support sensors functioned properly. Even for such a short spacewalk—from the shuttle to the Tear—no one took chances. Corinth helped her climb into the EMU she'd practically been living in this past week. Malkor, Vid, and Trinan arrived in the shuttle bay just as she popped her head through the neck ring.

Corinth struggled to maintain his attitude problem even as his eyes lit up at the sight of the agents. Excitement won out, and he waved at them just like the happy kid he'd become since leaving exile on Altair Tri.

"You, sir, are late for training," Vid boomed out in mock chastisement. They might be overprotective, but they never treated him like a kid. Which was probably why Corinth had loved them from the beginning.

"Today is self-defense day, so we'd better get cracking," Trinan added.

::Gotta go, Kay! Good luck.:: And then he was jogging out the door.

Malkor approached and then picked up her helmet. She eyed him. "Tell me you're not going to be sulky about being left behind as well. I've had all I can take from Corinth already." Natali had made it very clear the night before that imperials were not invited on this trip. She'd been polite about it, but Natali's version of polite was always a little clipped.

Malkor shook his head. "Just came to see you off." He looked like he might say more, but Ariel announced that her preflight check was done and Kayla's family all began piling into the shuttle. Malkor handed her the helmet. "Don't get sheared in half by that temporal anomaly, okay?"

She smiled. "No promises."

The trip through the Tear, for all the danger it posed, was entirely uneventful. Kayla, Vayne, Natali, and Uncle Ghirhad emerged unscathed on the other side, arriving in the darkly lit chamber the Tear had carved for itself in Ordoch's bedrock.

Kayla breathed a sigh of relief.

A short male Ordochian awaited their arrival on the edge of the room. Once everyone had popped the seal on their helmets and removed them, the man bowed and introduced himself as Mishe. He was quite possibly the most beautiful young man she'd ever seen, with hair and eyes the color of a tropical sea, and the kind of delicate, classic features Ordochians had celebrated in statuary for hundreds of generations.

Suddenly she was staggered by so great an emotion that she couldn't breathe. The pleasure-pain bloomed in her chest and squeezed out all other sensation.

It happened, it finally happened.

She reached out and Vayne's hand met hers halfway, clasping hard. His emotions swirled within her, identical.

Natali, a sheen of tears in her ice-blue eyes, whispered the words echoing through them all:

"We're home."

Mishe led them to a chamber where they could doff their EMUs and change into the clothes they'd brought. For Natali and Kayla, that meant weapons as well. Kris and an ion pistol for Kayla, a telescoping baton and NX-12 plasma handgun for Natali. Armed with high and low tech, as any good *ro'haar* should be. A weapon designed to fight other Wyrds seemed in poor taste to Kayla, but she certainly hadn't wasted any breath trying to convince Natali to carry an imperial weapon.

Kayla and Vayne followed behind Natali and an unusually subdued Uncle Ghirhad, as Mishe led them through the tunnels and up to what he said was the main rebel base. Surprisingly, the base was located outside of Vankir City, which Kayla was used to thinking of as an industrial wasteland. Then again, an abandoned and defunct manufacturing facility, one of hundreds in the zone, made the perfect space to hide out.

Though she'd never been there, the facility was immediately dear to her simply by being Ordochian. The architecture, the building materials—even the lighting—were as foreign to the empire as they were familiar to her.

Her imaginings of what it might be like to return to Ordoch

after five years in exile couldn't come close to the poignant reality of the moment. She shook her head to clear it. There would be time for sentiment later. Now, it was time to plan a rebellion.

Mishe finally brought them to a sealed door and keyed in a code for entry. The locks released with a whoosh and they were ushered in. Mishe announced them with a solemnity and deference Kayla hadn't heard since before the coup. The four people waiting in the room bowed as one, all of which had her feeling more than a little uncomfortable. The things she'd done to survive the last five years, to keep Corinth safe, they were not the kind of things that inspired people to bow to you. The reminder of the schism between her former life and her current existence made her feel dirty.

Vayne seemed equally uncomfortable, avoiding eye contact with everyone. Natali, by contrast, looked regal as she confined her response to an acknowledging nod.

The man in front, who Kayla recognized as Wetham from prior comm calls, opened his mouth to speak, but before he could, Uncle Ghirhad was across the room, introducing himself jovially and shaking hands with enough force to rattle teeth.

Now everyone in the room looked as uncomfortable as Kayla, Uncle Ghirhad excluded.

"Thank you all for coming," Wetham finally managed, once he had introduced his three lieutenants.

"Of course," Natali said, as if she'd been doing them a favor rather than exactly what she wanted. She and Kayla had agreed it would be good to tour the base, as well as meet some of the rebels in person and hopefully inflame their patriotism.

Wetham was a slender man of indeterminate middle age. He hailed from the Liamets, a lesser-known family that had fallen to the bottom of the noble hierarchy as the psi powers of its members weakened with each successive generation. Kayla hadn't heard of him before the coup. Now, with his confident stance and direct, piercing gaze, Wetham would have fitted in among the royals attending the Empress Game. His demeanor alone left no doubt that he was the person who had pulled together the scattered pockets of dissidents in a cohesive resistance. With the help of his lieutenants, he'd implemented a command structure, organized supply runs and recruitment drives, planned strategic military operations, and infiltrated the imperial troops with several well-placed spies.

More than the entire royal family combined had done for Ordoch in the last five years.

Really, *they* should be bowing to *him*.

Wetham and Natali engaged in the polite jockeying for position—disguised as small talk—that all world leaders engaged in upon meeting one another. Kayla had had no taste for it before the coup, and had certainly had her fill of it during her time as Isonde. Vayne stood rigidly beside her. Now that the emotional homecoming moment had passed, he looked as displeased to be here, in the middle of a war zone, as she expected.

"Let's get down to business," Wetham said, taking charge of things. It seemed that neither he nor Natali had reached a mutually agreed upon hierarchy of power. Or at least, agreed upon by Natali.

Wetham motioned for everyone to take a seat at the round table in the center of the room. "As far as the situation on the *Yari* is concerned, I absolutely agree with you that more forces are necessary if we are to assure control of the vessel."

"Thank you," Natali said. "I recognize that our rebellion is undermanned, and that every soldier is needed on Ordoch. I do not make the request for troops lightly."

Wetham shifted his gaze to Kayla. "You've made some friends among the empire, have you not?"

Everyone stared at her. With the gaze of her rightful ruler on her, of the rebellion's leader and lieutenants, even her *il'haar*, it felt like treason to admit that she had befriended—and even liked—some of the enemy.

She forced herself to speak, and there was no way to deny it. "I have."

"Are there no more sympathizers you could call on? As Natali said, I need every rebel soldier on Ordoch. Perhaps this

Agent Malkor has people he could call on?"

"No. There will be no more aid from that quarter." Not unless Ardin and Isonde could magically reverse the Council of Seven's decision to double-down on the Ordochian occupation.

Natali shook her head as well. "The *Yari*'s existence must be kept from the imperials. It is in Imperial Space after all, and though it is nearly impossible to access, it is still highly vulnerable at this point. We'll have to rely on our own people." She focused her gaze on Wetham. "How many will you be sending?"

Natali's question, phrased such that her demand was assumed to be met, was so typical of her, so familiar from childhood, that Kayla almost smiled.

::Same light touch as always.:: Vayne spoke into her mind, and she heard amusement there.

Wetham's face showed nothing of his thoughts. "I can spare... ten people."

"Twenty," Natali countered.

"Knowledge of the *Yari* and the existence of the Tear are closely guarded secrets here as well. We can't afford to lose such an advantage as the *Yari* to the empire. Few have the clearance to be part of such a team."

"But our people *do* know we're alive, correct?" she asked.

One of the lieutenants spoke up. "We spread word among the rebellion, but have hopefully avoided the imperial forces present from hearing it."

Vayne spoke up. "So if no one knows about the *Yari* and our attempts to fix this supposedly glorious battleship, what do they think we've been doing?"

Wetham shrugged. "You have been housed at an undisclosed location for your own safety."

"Hiding?" Vayne sounded incredulous. "We're risking our asses on an ancient ship filled with crazy people plotting our demise and you told them we were sitting safe and sound while they fought for Ordoch? Unbelievable."

"They must be really impressed by us," Kayla muttered, less than pleased herself.

"As I said, the security—"

Natali waved away the rest of Wetham's sentence. "We understand." She shot her siblings a quelling look before continuing. "For security on the *Yari*, we could make do with fifteen people. Assuming they're well trained, of course."

Fifteen would double their number, and go a long way toward easing Kayla's mind about Corinth and Vayne's safety.

Wetham acquiesced without further argument. "They will be ready by the end of the day. As for your other request..." He gestured to one of his lieutenants. "Anita worked up a list of the three best hyperstream drive scientists in terms of design and construction."

The lieutenant retrieved a few sheets of reprintable paraffin paper from her binder. Natali arched a brow at the outdated medium and Anita flushed. "Our access to tech is somewhat limited. These you can take with you." She handed the papers to Natali, still looking embarrassed. Wetham might look at ease with the fabled Reinumon heirs, but it was clear his lieutenants were still in awe.

"Great foresight," Kayla said, and offered a smile. Their attitude was making her skin crawl. Well, they *had* all come back from supposed death, but... seriously.

Anita seemed to regain her confidence. "Fedee and Jordon are the leading structural engineers, and Mesa tops the field in fuel sublimation and injection systems. Unfortunately, they all live in technological cities heavily occupied by the empire. The empire is hot to get our more sophisticated hyperstream design integrated with their current one. Mesa refused to help them adapt our fuel-injection processes to their inferior fuel source, so she's in lockdown. And while Fedee and Jordon aren't technically prisoners, they're living in Chun'sa, and that city's under a dusk til dawn curfew. Access to it is by permit only."

Fantastic. Though not surprising. One couldn't hope to hold a planet while all the brightest minds ran free.

Anita said, "There are a lot of other scientists on this list, but in my opinion one of these three will give us the best

127

shot of completing the *Yari*'s drive."

"Confer with your engineer to see whom she prefers," Wetham said.

"We'll take all of them." Natali's statement hushed the room. The lieutenants looked to Wetham, who seemed to be debating the best reply. "With respect, that's just not possible."

"Make it possible," she countered. "Why did you give me three names if it cannot be done?"

"To offer you options, ma'am," Anita said. "You or the ship's engineer have a much better idea of which type of help is needed. I wanted to give you the best choices available."

Another of the lieutenants—Kayla had already forgotten his name—jumped in. "We reasoned that we might, *might*, be able to spring one of these three. As soon as we did, however, the empire would know we were after hyperstream scientists and all of the others would be locked down tight."

Natali switched her gaze to the lieutenant, who seemed to wilt a little under her stare. "So take them simultaneously."

"We don't have the kind of covert operatives or intelligence resources to pull that off."

"I don't care how you do it, just get me those three scientists. ASAP." Natali's lips tightened the slightest bit, a sure sign of her frustration to anyone who knew her well. "We're not building hovercarts, for void's sake. If the *Yari* is ever going to fly again, never mind in time to help us drive out the empire, then I need the very best people on that engine." She looked at each person in the room in turn as she spoke. "This is the rebellion's number one priority, is that clear?"

Again the lieutenants waited for Wetham's lead.

The balance of power certainly had not been settled yet.

"It might be possible," he finally said, "but I'll need some of your imperials." He didn't look at Kayla as he spoke, but she answered anyway.

"Absolutely not," she burst out at the same time as Natali said, "That's acceptable."

Wetham nodded as if it had already been decided. "The

commander of one of the imperial bases has come over to our side. He's agreed to give them falsified papers as members of his staff. Your imperials should be able to move about freely after that."

"They're wanted fugitives," Kayla nearly shouted.

"Deep in the heart of the empire, maybe." The rebel leaders seemed unconcerned. "But it's not like the soldiers here have access to the daily news back home. And they're certainly not going to be recognized on sight."

"He's right," Natali agreed. "They speak whatever language that is without an accent, which none of us can manage. Plus they have the look, they know the rules…"

Kayla had plenty to say to that, but wouldn't do so in front of others. She leaned close to her sister and bit out, "A word." She stood without waiting for Natali's response, and bowed slightly to Wetham. "Please excuse us a moment." Kayla was out the room before anyone could stop her.

A moment later Natali, followed by Vayne, joined her in the corridor. As the door shut behind them, Kayla could hear Uncle Ghirhad excitedly take up the conversation with the rebels.

She checked to make sure the corridor was empty before speaking. "You are *not* offering Malkor and the octet as bargaining chips."

Natali eyed her, probably trying to assess how flexible Kayla was on this point. "I am merely offering their services. They came here to help, didn't they?"

"They're helping on the *Yari*."

"Not as much as a psionic would, not when our enemy is Wyrd."

Kayla ground her teeth. Vayne stayed silent, but she could practically hear the two of them thinking, *They can't do anything better than a psionic can.* And on some level, they were right.

She said, "I'm not asking Malkor or the octet to come here and be surrounded by people who view them as the enemy."

"They *are* the enemy," Vayne said quietly. The words hit like a betrayal.

"The octet rescued you. Both of you."

Natali inclined her head to acknowledge that fact. "And I thank them for that. But we wouldn't need rescuing if their people hadn't taken our planet over and taken us prisoner in the first place."

"Dolan—"

"Dolan didn't act alone. And by Malkor's own admission he was part of the team that came to Ordoch."

"The IDC knew nothing of the army's plan for the coup. Malkor was on Ordoch as part of a diplomatic mission only."

Vayne intervened. "We can have that argument later. For now, I think Wetham's plan makes sense."

"We don't even know what the plan is, not really." And how much did she trust Wetham, or the imperial commander supposedly in his pocket?

"Aren't they trained for this sort of thing?" Natali asked.

Kayla nodded. Skills or not, though, she wasn't about to sign Malkor up for a mission—any mission—on Ordoch. "I don't want them here."

Both of her siblings blinked, surprised.

"Then why…?" Vayne asked.

"On Ordoch, I mean. Not…" Kayla blew out a frustrated breath. "Not without me."

Natali got it first. "To vouch for them, you mean."

Which was ridiculous. They were good, loyal people, who had left everything they'd known behind to come and fight for Ordoch's freedom. If they said they were on the rebels' side, then that should be the end of it.

Only it wasn't.

Their word, the word of IDC agents, wouldn't have been worth shit to Kayla half a year ago, before she'd gotten to know them. She would have attacked them on sight if it wasn't imperative that she keep her cover as a pit whore.

And who's to say the rebels wouldn't do exactly that?

"I just don't think it's a good idea," Kayla finished lamely. She could handle the stress of the octet being on a mission.

What she couldn't handle was one of her own people killing them just for being born in the empire. To any rebel who didn't know them, Malkor and the octet would be just be six more occupation soldiers who needed killing.

"Well," Natali said. "This really is the best use for them." Her word choice said it all. To her, they were simply tools.

Vayne laid a comforting hand on Kayla's shoulder. "They're adults, Kayla. Let them decide for themselves."

Which meant Malkor and the octet were coming to Ordoch.

10

With Natali committed to requesting Malkor's aid, and Wetham committed to delivering fifteen rebels to the *Yari*, the meeting turned toward less contentious topics.

Not that things are pleasant, Kayla thought. It was clear that Natali intended to take control of the rebellion, and just as clear that Wetham would allow nothing of the sort. Natali politely demanded to be brought up to speed on all aspects of operations: troop numbers, weapons status, how they were provisioned, where their spies were embedded, et cetera.

Wetham tried to take a "you don't need to worry about the details" approach, and was quickly overridden. *Ro'haars* were intense even when relaxing. Natali? She took it to the next level, and Wetham clearly wasn't used to that.

He caught on quickly, though, and Kayla had to admire the way he held his own as Natali peppered him with questions.

For her part, Kayla found the details of managing an entire rebellion nearly overwhelming. She was a bodyguard through and through, never a leader of men. Point her at a problem, pull the trigger, and she would fire. She was a weapon, not a politician, and she liked it that way. Natali was welcome to it all.

The meeting finally wrapped and Wetham led them on

a tour of the base. The building was massive and mostly underground. Whatever they had once manufactured here must have had an explosive element because the base was built to withstand immense blasts.

The ground level and above had been left in their derelict state in order to perpetuate the imperial assumption that the building was abandoned. Below, the base hummed with activity. Rebels from every part of the planet filled the gray plascrete corridors near to bursting. Supplies were stockpiled in every available space until they reached the ceiling. Whole manufacturing bays were filled with row upon row of bedrolls, the sea of fabric parted only by the slimmest walkable paths.

Wetham told them about another base, farther away from the direct conflict, where families lived together in more of a tent city setup, while here on the front lines it was a soldier's lifestyle for the rebels. No one wanted their families living in a city that was the center of the imperial occupation, especially considering it was going to become a battleground when the rebellion finally made its ultimate move to retake the planet.

They visited the makeshift infirmary and met another of Wetham's lieutenants, a brutally injured man by the name of Aarush. In another time, his injuries would be an ordeal, but quickly overcome. His amputated foot would have been grown and reattached within days, the same for his badly burned skin. Nerve regeneration would follow, and from there it was only a matter of recovering from the procedures and undergoing physical therapy.

As Kayla gazed at the limited medical technologies available in the crowded premises, she knew that Aarush's story would be drastically different. Yet another crime the empire should be punished for. The situation was all the more frustrating because Wetham had told them on their way to the infirmary that he considered Aarush an irreplaceable asset to the rebellion.

In a moment of unexpected tenderness, Natali sat by Aarush's bedside. She expressed sorrow for the wounds he suffered and thanked him for his service to their people.

Aarush's face flushed and he looked away, his body stiffening. Even with half his face swathed in bandages, Kayla could tell Natali's awareness of his condition bothered him. Natali must have sensed it, too. Her voice regained its brusque tone. She began to grill him on his near-fatal mission; on what went wrong, where improvements could be made. She asked his opinion on what the rebellion needed to do in order to retake their planet, what their weaknesses were in terms of combat training and missions ops—his area of expertise.

By the time they were ready to leave the infirmary, Aarush's one remaining eye shone with purpose, his voice was strong, and he seemed much more a soldier than a victim. Something must have passed between them telepathically because Natali paused, then gave him a firm nod before striding out the door.

They traveled more corridors, stopping to inspect weapons depots and even vehicle storage. At last they ended their tour in what Kayla was convinced was the only open space in the entire building. All the derelict manufacturing equipment had been pushed to the edges of the large room, leaving patches of floor space, which were dedicated to martial training. Her people had no standing army and only minimal police forces on the main continent. Most of the rebels would know nothing of fighting, neither with weapons nor hand to hand, making their forces completely inadequate for a rebellion.

Whoever had a hand in setting up the training exercises, Kayla liked immensely. This, here, was something she could finally do, somewhere her skills would be invaluable. Leave the plotting and planning to Natali and Wetham. She and the octet could make a great contribution here. *And the octet would be safe, once they were known around the base.*

For now, the room was packed to capacity with rebels. A crowd filled the open floor space, people sitting on the training equipment, and even climbing on the manufacturing skeletons to get a view of the Reinumons as they entered.

Vayne hesitated on the threshold when he saw the crowd.

::What the frutt is this?:: he said in her mind, his voice more growl than actual words.

Kayla dropped back to stand beside him. "I think Natali intends to make a speech."

::And put us on display.:: His emotions rolled into her: anger, embarrassment, even fear, all carried on an insistent need to flee.

Shielded by Uncle Ghirhad and Wetham as they made their entrance, she gripped Vayne's forearm and met his eyes. "Nothing is going to happen to you here." She injected as much reassurance as she could into her voice. She couldn't lower her mental defenses to let him inside her head—not surrounded as they were by so many psionics—so she silently tried to convey both her conviction that they were safe here, and the promise that she would protect him if any threat should arise.

Even without a shared connection, he seemed to sense her message. He didn't relax, but the thrumming need to flee eased somewhat, to where they could enter the massive room together. She didn't like being on display any more than he did, didn't like the feel of so many expectant, hopeful gazes on her. But, she supported her sister, and so she went to stand beside the workbench that Natali had climbed up on to use as a makeshift dais.

Kayla had to admit that Natali looked every millimeter the returning hero, ready to lead her people. She stood tall and proud, shoulders back, chin lifted slightly, her gaze scanning the crowd as she patiently waited for quiet. She was honed sharp as a knife's edge. In her gold bodysuit, utility belt, and weapons, Natali looked ready to run her own martial drills at that moment.

The room held its breath as people waited to see what she would say.

"My name is Natali Reinumon. I have finally returned to our homeworld to reclaim my rightful place as Ordoch's *en'shaar*."

Well, at least she didn't mince words.

::She's calling herself the *en'shaar*?:: Vayne said in Kayla's mind. ::I wonder how well that'll play.::

Kayla wondered the same. *En'shaar* was the term for the ruling *ro'haar–il'haar* bonded pair. It had been generations since anyone had ruled alone, and they certainly hadn't claimed that title when they did.

Murmurs among the crowd seemed to echo her misgivings, but Natali merely waited for the disturbance to settle down.

"I have been told that it was assumed every last Reinumon had been killed in the imperial coup, but as you can see, that is not the case. I present to you my sister and brother, Kayla and Vayne, and my uncle, Ghirhad Reinumon. Our youngest brother, Corinth, also lives.

"You have all suffered great losses in the last five years. You have fought and sacrificed for the resistance in the hopes that we will reclaim our homeworld from these imperial dogs, and we thank you, from the bottom of our hearts." Natali paused, and bowed deeply toward the people. Kayla, touched by the gesture, followed suit, as did Vayne and their uncle.

When Natali finally rose, the crowd was doubly intent on her words.

"We have not cowered in safety and left you to fight alone. I came here today to share with you, in my own words, where we have been these last five years.

"In the confusion of the coup, Vayne, Ghirhad and I, along with several other members of our family and staff, were taken prisoner by the imperials. This was done at the behest of Dolan, a Wyrd traitor who had defected to the empire after his exile from Ilmena. He had been working with them for more than a decade, trading the secrets of superior Wyrd technology in exchange for the power and resources to conduct certain experiments."

Natali drew a deep breath, as if steadying herself to continue.

"I cannot begin to describe the thousands of ways he tortured us, experimented on us, violated us."

Vayne went rigid. His face screwed into a sort of rictus that belied a deep pain. Kayla's heart ached for him, for Natali, for all of them, and that ache expressed itself as a throbbing, burning need to extract vengeance. Vayne was correct—Dolan's death had been entirely too quick.

"Among the many things we endured was a process by which Dolan ripped our psi powers from our minds and grafted them onto his own. He repeated this process over and over. Each time our powers grew back, he harvested us again, and it was this brutal procedure, when combined with all the rest, that slowly killed us.

"The first of us to die was our father. He fought the hardest initially, and Dolan killed him to make a statement. Even though I knew it was futile, I held on to the hope that one day I might somehow make my escape. That hope diminished each day as one by one we fell. My mother. My two aunts. And at last, my beloved twin, Erebus." Natali's voice choked as she said his name and she had to stop. Tears shimmered in her eyes. She bowed her head and turned her face slightly away from the crowd.

Kayla couldn't stand it any longer. She broke from the line and approached Natali. "You don't have to do this," she said in a soft voice. *Please don't do this*, she wanted to say. *You're killing my* ro'haar *and I can't bear it.*

"I owe it to them," Natali said just as softly. Still, those in the front heard her words, and passed it to their neighbors, who passed it to theirs, until everyone in the room knew. Of all that Natali had said, these few words seemed to affect the crowd the most.

When she had her emotions under control, she continued. "I lost track of time after Erebus's death—I can't tell you what happened in those dark days. Somehow I survived, but it seems impossible to me even now. Finally, miraculously, we were rescued. My siblings," she gestured to Kayla and Vayne, "killed Dolan, and all at once I was free." She let that word linger in the air, as if she still couldn't quite wrap her mind around the idea.

"As I escaped exile, I thought to myself, 'It's over, it's really over.' But then I learned the truth: the imperial coup attempt had not been thwarted, and my people, *our* people, live under the rule of those bastards. And so I have come home—we have come home—to fight."

Cheering broke out, clapping, even boot stomping. Shouts of "We're with you!" and "Ordoch!" echoed off the walls.

"We've come to fight not only for our freedom, but for our very lives. Dolan's tortuous experiments had a purpose. He was not just a sadist. He betrayed our people on the most basic level. After learning how to steal our psi powers in a way that would allow them to regenerate, he developed a technique for grafting the powers onto the inferior mind of an imperial. He freely gave this technology to the empire.

"That means they're not satisfied with just our planet, they want our minds. The emperor and his council have launched a second invasion wave. They're coming to enslave us, to lock us up in farms and harvest our powers over and over."

Natali stopped and looked hard at the crowd, connecting with them on this vital point. "You might make it through the first procedure. You might last months, even years. But in the end, none of us will survive. And what then? Will they move on to Ilmena? We need to stop them here. Now. Not just for us, but for all Wyrds.

"I promise you this: I will fight until my very last breath. I will give everything I have, everything I am, to free Ordoch, and I will not rest until the only imperials left on our world are dead or dying."

The cheers that erupted rose up as if from one throat. One heart crying a promise of battle, a need for justice. It roared off the walls, shook the ceiling. Fists pumped the air. Feet stomped. Kayla's heart soared with the sound, her own blood singing for violence. She was up on her toes, ready to fight, ready to defend her people, ready to be fully Wyrd once again and shed the dust of the last five years.

And then she remembered Malkor.

Vayne felt uncomfortable on the walk back through the base. The cheering rang through his head and he couldn't get it out.

Hundreds of people cheering, shouting their names, applauding; as if they'd done *anything* yet—all they'd really done was survive five years of torture and then arrive on their doorstep.

Kayla, walking at his side, looked disturbed, though whether she shared his same feelings or was just worried about the fate of her lover, he couldn't say.

By contrast, Natali was in her element. She led the way through the corridors, every nanometer the prodigal daughter returned triumphant. He would have hated her for it if she didn't look so frutting... alive. The air around her practically shimmered with her force of personality. Her eyes shone like sunlight reflecting off of ice and she actually smiled. Natali. Smiling. He hadn't seen her smile in years, and the sight filled him with happiness and deep sadness simultaneously.

Walking beside Natali, Wetham looked somewhat less pleased than the rest of the rebel forces.

Not quite the homecoming of the heirs you were expecting, eh?

Wetham had clearly never met Natali, if he thought she was going to abdicate her throne for any reason less than death. But their inevitable power struggle could wait for another day.

The trip back through the Tear was blissfully uneventful. And though the day had been long and part of Vayne was exhausted, resting was out of the question. Returning to Ordoch had stirred up emotions he thought never to feel again. He certainly didn't want to face them now.

Kayla made eye contact as they exited the shuttle Ariel had used to pick them up from the Tear. "More weapons reclamation?"

He grinned. "You read my mind." Physical exhaustion was the only cure for emotional turmoil. Well, when one was too broken to actually deal with one's emotions, anyway. Natali had taught him that, before he had betrayed her. He pushed that thought from his mind before Dolan's ghost could exploit it.

"We're already in our EMUs," he said, "it'd be a shame to waste the opportunity."

They partnered up with ship's physicist Tanet and the IDC

agent who called herself Rigger. Neither of whom would be Vayne's choice of allies in a fight, but they were competent enough to offload the weapons cases he and Kayla brought up from the unpowered decks below. The entire process was somewhat hampered by the fact that Kayla and Vayne had to ride the lift up with each load of weapons in order to thwart any attempt made by the *stepa at es* to steal them.

It was ironic that their attempts to protect the weapons by loading them onto hovercarts and moving them, was what had made it possible for the *stepa* to steal them at all.

Good times.

"At least we're almost done with this," Kayla said on yet another trip down to the zero-g levels. Tia'tan and the others had continued their work at other armories while they had been enjoying their 'homecoming.' "I bet we can collect the last of them if each team works through the night."

Fine by him. Otherwise he'd have no excuse for putting Tia'tan off. She'd asked how the visit to Ordoch had gone, and he'd said he would discuss it with her later. Well, later had come and gone and he still wasn't ready to discuss what it felt like to return home. He and Kayla hadn't even talked about it in all the hours since they'd been back on the *Yari*.

That didn't stop him from feeling like a jerk for not at least bringing Tia'tan up to speed on the details of the rebellion's progress. They'd become something of a team since escaping Falanar months ago, and dealing with the craziness on the ship since then. It was natural that he share with her what he learned. And he would. Just... later.

Kayla set the maglocks on the three hovercarts to lock them to the armory floor. He released the tie-downs on the nearest weapons crate before floating it over to start the loading process all over again. Kayla's voice caught his attention, but it was only her speaking in the guttural language of the imperials. The octet leader comming her again? Vayne hadn't bothered with one of their translator bots today, so he couldn't understand her reply. Considering she ended the conversation in about two seconds, it probably hadn't been what the guy wanted to hear.

"Still avoiding him?" Vayne asked her.

She kept her eyes locked on her task. "The octet was just checking in with status updates."

Maybe. But it hadn't escaped his notice that she hadn't taken even a minute to greet her IDC agent before getting to work.

"Besides, I'm not avoiding him. We're both busy."

"Right," he said, and this time she shot him a look before getting back to work.

"It's just that—" her growl of frustration sounded over their one-to-one helmet comms. "It's overwhelming. The reality of it all."

"The occupation?"

"That, but also the knowledge that we really can go home. I stood on *Ordoch* today. Only a few months ago that would have been impossible. It might not be quite the home I remember, but it's still home."

Vayne secured another crate to the cart. "That bunker felt like home to you?"

"A lot more than the slums of an imperial backworld did." She paused in her work of loading the small arms into their containers. "I can't get my head around it. The feeling in my chest when we were standing there, surrounded by our people. Natali..." Kayla looked up at him. "She was magnificent, wasn't she?"

He recognized the awe in her eyes; it was the same feeling harbored in his chest. "She was."

"I don't want to share that feeling, yet. Not with an outsider."

And Malkor certainly was that. Even Tia'tan, Wyrd though she was, couldn't be a part of this moment. It was too delicate, almost. As if sharing it with anyone besides the three siblings would somehow diminish its power.

* * *

They worked in silence for a while, perfectly at ease with each other, in tune.

Kayla refused to let her mind wander any farther than the next task at hand. Load crates. Secure them so they didn't float about in the zero-g environment. Guide the cart to the lift. Ride up. Ride back. Repeat.

As the armory cache dwindled and their task neared completion, though, the larger world crashed down on her. Her mind began churning over problems, worrying about all possible outcomes, following every line of enquiry and result. Her fervor of nationalism from Natali's rousing speech had a chance to cool, and the implications sank in hard. They loaded the last of the weapons into the maglift, weapons destined for rebel hands, and a future very different from the one she'd hoped for her people arose.

War.

Not just war, vengeance. Retribution.

Her people deserved it, her family deserved it. But the people of the galaxy, the TNV sufferers, demanded more than that of her.

She said as much to Malkor when they were finally back in his cabin sometime around "dawn" ship time.

"We both know that," he said. "If your people won't work in earnest to create a cure for the TNV, the entire empire will be eaten alive."

Tired as she was, she cocked a grin at him. "Aren't you being a bit dramatic?"

"Only in my wording. It's still true."

Her levity passed. It *was* true. And while those responsible for the coup on Ordoch deserved to be punished, whole planets of people didn't deserve to die for it.

Malkor sat on his narrow bunk, she in the lone chair in the cabin, its metal feet bolted to the floor. The thing was eerily new for being five hundred years old—and just as uncomfortable as it had been upon creation.

"We don't stand a chance of regaining our freedom if we

don't have a large enough military threat to force the imperials to the bargaining table," she said. "Especially once Vega arrives with her fleet of battleships."

"I don't disagree, but if Natali whips your people up into an all-or-nothing frenzy, they might refuse to bargain at all."

"I won't let that happen."

"You're not the one in charge," he said gently.

And that was fine with her... assuming all went according to plan.

"Tia'tan claims Ilmena will stand by whatever decision the Ordochians make, whether it be to help the imperials—sorry, your people—or not." It hadn't taken her long, once back with her family and fellow Wyrds, to fall back on using "the imperials" as a slur. "And after speaking with her, I gather Tia'tan's a little more influential on Ilmena than she let on."

"They feel no humanitarian urge to help us?"

"Malkor, the Ilmenans like you even less than my people do, if that's possible." She gave him an apologetic smile. "They did send one of their most decorated military officers to win the Empress Game and undermine your government from the inside, after all."

"She's military?"

"Ilmena has not been a peaceful place in a long time. And if Natali decided not only to reclaim Ordoch, but to start a war in Imperial Space, Ilmena would be right there with her."

"If," Malkor said, "they could ever finish rebuilding their intergalactic warships."

Kayla nodded ruefully. "We could really use those, with Vega coming."

"Speaking of fixing ancient battleships, Natali came to see me earlier." He watched her for a reaction, and considering how well he knew her, he probably expected some cursing.

She restricted herself to a frustrated sigh. "I had hoped she'd wait until I'd spoken to you about some of the octet traveling to Ordoch."

"I've only known your sister a little while, but that doesn't seem like her style."

Never was.

"Wetham's request seems logical to me," Malkor said.

"I just don't think it's safe—"

His chuckle interrupted her. "When have I ever been 'safe?'"

"Okay, fair point."

"This is what we do, Kayla, these kinds of missions. Honestly, we're probably better suited to breaking your scientists out of lockdown than any of the rebels. And not just because we look like the other imperials."

He was right, of course, but she didn't have to like it. "Who will you send?"

"Myself. And I'll ask Rigger, I think she'd be the most help, with her tech skills."

She shot to her feet. "You? Absolutely not."

He surged to his feet in response, his heavily muscled form eating up much of the available space in the room. She'd forgotten how he could loom over her, the way she'd thought him intimidating when they'd first met on Altair Tri.

"You wouldn't allow me to cast doubt on your ability to handle yourself in a tricky situation—not even for a second—so don't you dare do it to me."

They stared each other down, each breathing hard.

Finally, she said, "Damn you for being right," and he grinned.

She reached out and touched his face, heaviness inside. Was this what it felt like to love romantically, this fear? She thought that constant worry for another's safety was only present in the *ro'haar–il'haar* bond.

He laid his hand over hers. "I'll be fine."

"You've never fought psionics before."

He blinked, clearly surprised by her words. "We're infiltrating an imperial base—why would I start now?"

She stroked his cheek again. *You might not have a choice, my love.*

Late next afternoon, the rebel soldiers Wetham had promised arrived on the *Yari*.

Ida and Benny were on hand to greet them, as was the entire Reinumon family, including Corinth. The octet had been coolly disinvited by Natali.

For once Vayne would have preferred to be with the IDC agents. At least they didn't expect anything from him. The rebels, on the other hand, stared at him as if some kind of heroic sentiment might fall from his lips at any moment. Like he was guaranteed to lead them to victory. Vayne wanted to kick them all in the head for being so stupidly hopeful.

Instead, Natali ordered him to take point on getting the rebel soldiers settled, just before she secreted herself away with the head of the Ordochian contingent. He would have argued, but Corinth, near to bursting with the excitement of being around people from a homeland he barely remembered, announced to one and all that he would accompany Ida and Benny while they gave the rebels a tour. Kayla agreed, since Vayne would be there to keep an eye on him, and that sealed his fate.

Babysitting.

While being stared at.

While everyone else got back to serious business.

The next phase of their plan to secure the ship from the *stepa* was starving them out by retrieving any still viable calorie packs and dry goods available on the unpowered levels. Ida and her crew had done a good job of that on the powered levels, but that was before anyone knew just how mobile the *stepa* really were.

Vayne grumped along silently with the rebel tour group as they followed Ida through the rough molychromium corridors. No doubt his air of dissatisfaction could be sensed even by nontelepaths. At least it kept people from chatting him up.

On the plus side, the arrival of a new crop of Ordochians to marvel at her ship had Ida back to her old jolly self. He hadn't seen that happy slap-clap of her hands *whoooooshing* past each other, since before the imperials arrived. Before Gintoc had been killed. Her braid swung crazily in her energetic wake.

Ida spoke as much with her hands as with her voice, proudly extolling the wonders of her five-hundred-year-old ship. Vayne would have laughed at the wide-eyed stares of the rebels, only he'd been just as wide-eyed not too long ago. He'd reached out and touched the raw molychromium wall just as reverently, boggled at Ida, Benny, and the rest of the crew in wonderment as he tried to follow their archaic speech patterns.

They were living legends.

And he'd do well to remember that.

Had he become so accustomed to living free, to being in control of his own future, that he'd forgotten what a miracle having any future at all was? Three months ago he wasn't in control of his own mind, let alone his body. Six months ago he'd barked like a dog in front of Dolan's benefactors—thanks to the Influencer—and had been grateful, *grateful*, to lick each of their boots.

Without the Influencer controlling him he knew now how sick that was, but nonetheless, gratitude was the emotion stamped across that particular memory.

He felt instantly nauseated. Blindly he reached out, desperate for any concrete proof that he was here, now, and truly free. The rebel whose arm he latched on to turned her wide eyes to him, halting in her tracks. The flow of Ordochians on the tour broke around them as they clogged up the corridor.

Great, now everyone was looking at him strangely. Again.

The rebel smiled tentatively, and Vayne read pity in her gaze. Natali's words yesterday, her admission of their former POW status and the things that went along with it, rang in his head, shaming him once again. He released the woman like she was a poisonous snake and reared back.

Easy, he tried to tell himself, *easy. Act normal. You're weird enough to them as it is, having practically returned from the dead after five years.*

Her smile faltered. A question formed on her lips, he could hear it coming from kilometers away, but Corinth saved him. Corinth, who had been skipping along behind Ida, so

146

delighted to be included in such an exciting rebel moment, had fallen back to check on him.

::Excuse us,:: he heard Corinth voice to the rebel, ::I want to show my brother something.::

And just like that, Corinth had seized his hand and spurred him back to motion.

Who, exactly, was watching over whom?

::Are you all right?:: Corinth asked a second later.

How galling, to need rescuing from one's own demons by a child.

::I am hardly a *child*:: Corinth replied, giving him a frown. ::And Kay would lecture you on laying your inner emotions so bare in mind-speak.::

Even with the rebuke, Corinth didn't drop his hand. And Vayne, who loathed being touched by anyone without his express consent, clung to the connection.

::You're right, of course:: he said finally. ::Kayla does love to lecture.::

Even without a sound from the boy, Vayne felt Corinth snicker. Their connection quickly sobered, though, Corinth's thoughts and emotions cycling as rapidly as any teenage boy's. ::I saw you freeze up, is everything okay?::

How could everything be okay? How could anything, ever again, be okay? The Vayne that knew what "okay" meant had died a long time ago.

::I'm fine. Don't worry over me.:: They rejoined the tour just in time to hear Ida talk about the brilliantly—if chaotically—painted panels Ariel had used to line the corridor outside the officers' mess.

::I still can't believe Ariel painted all of these:: Corinth said. ::She's so—::

::Grumpy?::

::Exactly! And how did she have the time? Didn't the captain say that she and the others only came out of cryostasis recently? When the current Tear opened and contact with Ordoch was established?::

::That is a good point.:: A damned good point, one he hadn't considered before.

Corinth, either assured that he was fine, or teenage enough to be self-conscious about holding his big brother's hand, released his grasp.

::Fifteen Ordochians, straight from the planet:: Corinth continued. ::Rebel fighters, even, can you believe it? Well, of course *you* can, you got to go there yourself yesterday.::

Trinan and Vid might have some competition for Corinth's hero worship. In the old days, before the coup and the torture, Vayne would have reached out and ruffled Corinth's shaggy hair. Now he couldn't bring himself to summon that small familiarity. Corinth had usurped Vayne's place as Kayla's *il'haar*. And though the situation hadn't been voluntary on any of their parts, it was still the present reality.

Kayla said she considered both of them her *il'haars*, but a *ro'haar* had only one true *il'haar*. He hadn't survived the last five years to be replaced by a helpless boy.

Frutt.

Even in his broken state, that thought was beneath him.

He glanced at Corinth, but the boy skipped happily along once again, oblivious, his dazzled eyes on the rebels. At least Kayla's anticipated lecture on the necessity of control over one's emotions when speaking psionically had been effective—Corinth hadn't sensed a hint of his unworthy feelings.

Tia'tan's voice broke into his thoughts. ::We've got a situation.:: The controlled intensity of her tone sent him to high alert.

::A situation like the *stepa* stole more of our guns?::

::Okay, not quite that bad. Can you get down here?::

::Where's here?:: And how was he going to ditch babysitting duty? Corinth was probably safer here than anywhere else, on the move with the ship's captain and second in command, surrounded by a dozen armed psionics, but somehow he doubted Kayla would see it that way.

He pictured the ship layout. ::Do I need to suit up for this?::

::According to the *Yari*'s logs, yes, but....::

The hairs on the back of his neck rose up. ::But what?::

::But the people locked in these cells are doing just fine without suits.::

11

Vayne made an excuse to the group about needing the facilities, made Corinth promise to stay with the others, and beat it out of there.

Kayla's going to kill me. Ah well, he'd deal with that later. He certainly wasn't going to bring Corinth with him, and he couldn't pull Corinth from the tour and escort him to the engine room without a host of questions being asked.

Even if Tia'tan hadn't asked him to keep his activity a secret, he would have done so anyway. Prisoners kept on levels marked as off-limits due to a lack of life support was something to keep quiet about, at least until he knew what the frutt was going on.

The lift doors refused to open when he arrived, just as Tia'tan mentioned. The warning message was the same as those on the other blackout levels, mentioning a lack of breathable atmosphere, but when he entered his new passcode to override the warning and open the doors anyway, nothing happened. He did the same thing she had done, and rode the lift to the powered level above that one and climbed down a maintenance shaft.

::Which asshole forgot to weld this access door shut?:: he

asked Tia'tan as he made his way down. ::So much for 'level secured.':: He'd check the ship's datalog later and see who had reported finishing this level.

::No idea. Just hurry up.::

Vayne led with his plasma bullpup as he crawled out of the shaft and into the corridor where Tia'tan waited. It was dark except for the beam from his bullpup's light and the shoulder lamp on her EMU.

"What in the void made you try this?" he asked by way of greeting, scrambling to his feet.

She grinned briefly. "Good to see you, too." She'd pulled off her helmet, but otherwise was still fully suited up. "Let's talk and walk."

He fell into step with her as she started down the corridor. "And where's your sidekick? We're supposed to be two-by-two everywhere."

"Malkor's EMU malfunctioned. One of the seals started leaking even though the thing's brand new. I slapped a patch on it but alarms kept going off that he was about to die horribly so he's a couple levels up having Rigger run diagnostics on it."

"Let me guess, you told him you would be right behind him, but instead decided to have some fun crawling down maintenance shafts in an EMU." Vayne swept the beam of his light back and forth across the corridor as they walked, hunting for any threat. Tia'tan wasn't armed—plasma weapons were useless in the cold of space, so they hadn't brought any to the unpowered, unheated lower levels—and he felt pricklingly undergunned in the dark.

"We were pulling the calorie pack stores from one of the commissaries when the suit sprung a leak," she continued. "Neither of us felt safe leaving the cache out in the open so I told him I'd finish loading the cart and follow him up with it." Tia'tan's heavily booted steps echoed off the bare walls. It would be easy for anyone sneaking behind them to cloak their own footfalls in hers. "I punched in the wrong number on the lift without realizing it. When it wouldn't let me off, I got curious."

"Curious."

"Last time the crew told us a level was off limits, you found Itsy's cell."

They reached a branch in the corridor and she paused. Vayne held his breath as they listened. Nothing moved as their lights scanned over both options.

"This way." She headed down the offshoot, which was just as pitch-black as the main corridor. Panels were dead, running lights were off—someone had taken precautions to ensure that this floor drew as little power as possible.

Vayne continued to sweep ahead with his psi powers, only partly comforted when he didn't sense other minds nearby. There were ways to shield oneself from such detection, after all. "How much farther?"

She stopped in front of a door that looked identical to several they'd passed already. He reached his mind forward...

...and hit a wall.

It wasn't that he didn't sense anything in the room. He couldn't even *see* into the room. He looked to Tia'tan, brows raised.

She detached a grey module, no more than ten centimeters square, from the door's panel. "Try now."

This time when he reached out he encountered several minds, but only faintly. Their signatures were heavily muted, more than just a sleeping mind would be. In a coma? Some kind of stasis?

Tia'tan set the gray box—a mini psi field dampening device—on the floor.

Even knowing they were there, Vayne couldn't read much from the minds on the other side of the door. "What makes you think they're prisoners?" At this point, though, he could almost believe anything.

"I worked with Tanet this morning. The physicist can't remember his own security code, now that it changes so often. He had me memorize it, too."

A physicist with trouble memorizing numbers? That didn't bode well for Tanet's continued sanity.

The door's panel glowed to life as she tapped it to display

the SECURE LOCKDOWN message. "Apparently, Ida's crew, or the five that we thought of as 'the crew,' have access to this room." She entered the code twice, as prompted, and the door's locks disengaged with a *thunk*.

Vayne entered first since he was armed. Low lights revealed what looked like soldiers' barracks. Row after row of bunkbeds filled the long room. The officer cabin he was staying in sure beat the enlisted airmen's barracks.

Movement at the far end caught his eye. He swiveled his bullpup in the direction but Tia'tan laid her hand on the weapon and pushed it toward the floor.

::Gently.::

It pained him to walk slowly because the clock was ticking in his head, counting down the minutes until Corinth realized he'd been gone too long. Until Malkor worried that something had happened to Tia'tan. Until a callout was sent and everyone knew where they were and what they were up to. At this point, that was the last thing he wanted.

The light revealed six people occupying the last bunks of the room—all the other bunks were empty. Two of the people slept fitfully—eyelids twitching, a leg kicking, hands clenching and unclenching—as if they fought against sleep, or perhaps waking. A woman on the top bunk of another stack lay flat on her back, eyes wide and staring at the ceiling, lips moving as she muttered something to herself.

The three remaining crew members were conscious, thankfully. One, a woman, sat on a lower bunk. She held a picture of someone, the fingers of one hand tracing lovingly over the details of a face, over and over and over. A man stood near a wardrobe cubby, calmly pulling out folded uniforms, shaking them out, then refolding them. The third paced back and forth across the aisle. He held a datapad and seemed to be dictating something to it.

"Hello," Tia'tan said. "May we speak with you?"

The woman with the photo looked up and smiled. "Hello, have we met?"

"Yes. I'm Tia'tan, and this is my friend, Vayne."

The soldier folding clothes never looked their way, but the pacing man stopped, staring at Tia'tan intently.

"You have purple hair," he said, as if it were of great import. And for a soldier at war with Ilmena, identifying Tia'tan's race by her hair color would have been. Only, the man couldn't quite seem to piece that together. He pursed his lips, his brow furrowing as his brain worked the problem. Vayne held his breath, ready for an explosion of conflict, but the man only shook his head.

The woman spoke. "I am being Officer Kendrik, and this is Airman Gaar." Then she looked over her shoulder at the man refolding uniforms with precision. "Enska, leave off, now." Airman Enska showed no sign of having heard her.

"You are not crew of the *Yari*." Kendrik's statement had a bit of a question to it.

"We're visiting," Tia'tan said.

"In an EMU?" Gaar asked. "Others not having a need for one when arriving." His eyes scanned Tia'tan, then Vayne, then Tia again, as if he could almost decipher the puzzle they presented.

Vayne latched on to Gaar's statement. "Others? Who else visits?"

"The captain, of course," Kendrik said. "Prime Gunner Strokar is also to visit us. And sometimes it is a physicist that has the bringing of things."

Enska took another folded shirt from the wardrobe, snapped it open with a brisk shake, and proceeded to fold it tightly.

"When do they come?" Tia'tan asked.

Officer Kendrik started outlining a schedule of visits that Vayne couldn't quite follow, then Gaar broke in, confusing the issue, and a discussion ensued during which it became clear they had no strong concept of which day it was relative to any other day.

::What makes you think they're 'prisoners?':: he asked Tia'tan silently. ::Sure, the door's locked, but it's clearly for their own good. I wouldn't want these three wandering the ship alone.::

::Look at their ankles.:: She opened her mind to him, deepened her communication beyond mere speech. Vayne immediately felt her certainty that something wasn't right.

The right pant leg on each crew member was bunched, restricted from falling naturally by a tight metal band around the lower calf. When Gaar shifted his weight from his left to his right leg, Vayne caught sight of the skin below the metal band. The red-brown of burned tissue peeked from beneath.

Locator devices he could understand, in case any of these people got loose. But: ::Electric resistor bands?:: Prisoner restraints of that type had been deemed inhumane centuries ago. Tia'tan shared her thoughts and impressions instantly in a cascade of images. The thinness of the crew—clearly, they didn't eat as well as Ida and the others did—but most especially Officer Kendrik. The deep gouges in the metal of the band on Enska's ankle, along with a series of scratches across his skin, disappearing into his sock. Cyanosis of the lips and fingernails on the two sleeping men. The muttered words of the semiconscious woman on the top bunk: *It's not safe, need to hide. It's not safe, need to hide.*

And lastly, something he'd missed entirely: Kendrik's moment of acute alertness when they'd entered. Her gaze had flashed from them to the open door behind them, assessing the entire situation, before she'd dropped her head to study the picture she held.

"You are of Ilmena," Gaar said suddenly, staring hard at Tia'tan.

Vayne tensed. When Gintoc succumbed to madness and believed himself still at war with Ilmena, he had tried to kill Tia. Vayne expanded his shield to cover her without another thought—never mind that she held her own shield perfectly.

"Not being an enemy now, though," Gaar continued. "Memory is coming." His words gathered momentum, as if he rushed to speak before he lost his thought again. "We are in the future, and Ordoch still has the fighting but it is of a new enemy now. Ilmena is an ally?" This seemed a fact too impossible for the man to fully believe.

"That's right." Vayne didn't want to give him time to question it further. Kendrik seemed content to listen, not offering her own remembrances, if indeed she had any.

"We've been in the cryogenic long sleep," Gaar said. "And many things we find are changing when we are awakening. Awakening, hmm…" His energy seemed to be stalling out. "Awakening…" He turned to Kendrik. "The crew all, still having the long sleep?"

She nodded.

"Vittoria?" Gaar asked, but Kendrik didn't reply. "Vittoria still sleeps?" He reached out as if grasping for something that wasn't there. Kendrik met his questing hand and clasped it firmly with both of hers.

"Reanimation is not timing right of each crew member, Gaar," she said, her voice gentle.

"No!" Gaar shook his head. "Not true. Not my Vittoria."

Enska spoke without pausing in his folding or looking their way. "It being true, and you to cease the crying of forever. I am not to hear it again." He crumpled the shirt he had been folding. "We *all* have lost, not you alone."

"Enska," Kendrik said in reproof, but the man showed no reaction. Gaar, by contrast, began sobbing.

The voice of the semi-catatonic woman on the top bunk rose to match the din. "It's not safe, need to hide. It's not safe, need to hide."

"Now is time yours to depart," Kendrik said. "Quickly." Her gaze flashed past them once again, to the door, then she focused on their faces and Vayne would swear she was lucid. "When rescue attempt made is having the discovery, fog is increasing in here." She tapped her temple with one finger. "Gaar being in such state might alert them, when next they come, and I am tired of fog. Go." If Gaar wasn't clinging so tightly to her other hand, Vayne could imagine she'd be pushing Tia'tan and himself out the door.

::Vayne? Are you coming back?:: Corinth's voice sounded in his mind.

To Tia'tan he murmured, "Our time's up." If he didn't respond, Corinth's next question would be to Kayla, and then the whole ship would be alerted.

::I got waylaid by Tia'tan.:: He wouldn't have even told Corinth that much of the truth except the boy loved Tia'tan. She was second to Kayla in his eyes in terms of sheer badassery, ahead even of those two IDC agents who doted on him. ::I'm heading to you now.::

"We'll be back," Tia'tan said to Kendrik, but the woman shook her head.

"More attention we are not needing." Then she smoothed any expression from her face—or her moment of clarity was swallowed up by her insanity once again—and she dropped her eyes once more to the picture she held. Her fingers traced the outline of a child's face, stroked the teal hair.

Tia'tan sent a quick flash to him of her conviction that she had no intention of letting this drop.

"We *will* return," he reiterated, and then they were locking the crew back inside.

Late in the evening, Vayne stood in the doorway of the observation deck where he was supposed to meet with Tia'tan. The smaller of the two observation lounges felt almost cozy with the lights down, dominated by its immense viewports.

The middle of the room was filled with rows of metal benches bolted to the floor. Someone had long ago dragged in two of the more comfortable chairs from the officers' lounge and situated them in a corner. Pillows had been added, along with blankets, and the chairs had the look of well-used nests. He could imagine Ida and Benny passing many an evening in companionable silence as they stared out into the Mine Field that was their prison. Did they talk of their future? Or of the once glorious mission they'd had? Or was it a more intimate connection, shared without words?

Vayne froze in place when he spotted Tia nestled into one

of the chairs. Her hair was still damp from a shower. She had her legs drawn up under her, her chin resting on her knees as she contemplated space. She looked... restful. At peace. It was a look he hadn't seen for the entire duration of his captivity.

If he ever achieved such a state—which seemed unlikely— he would kill the person who broke into his reverie.

He turned to go, but her mind voice stopped him.

::Stay.::

Not just her voice, her essence. He felt her presence wrap around him even though she still sat across the room, a warm mixture of welcome, acceptance, pleasure at his company, and above all, a wish that he not turn away from her. That he not shield any part of himself.

It was so honest a sharing that he wondered if she realized what she revealed.

Her openness called to him. He walked toward her, unable to do otherwise. His family and the other POWs had guarded their psyches zealously, being under constant attack from Dolan. Locking himself in a mental vault was his new normal. The one person he'd imagined being able to let in was Kayla, but without her psi powers, their cherished connection was lost to him. *For now. She'll reconnect to her powers soon.*

He never expected to have an invitation to such personal communication from anyone other than Kayla, never mind a desire to reciprocate.

Tia's scent drifted to him, rising from the moist heat of her freshly showered skin: military-grade soap. Standard issue on the *Yari*. It was different from her previous, delicate scent, but whatever pleasing cosmetic she'd used before had been destroyed along with her ship.

Pleasing cosmetic?

Gods save him from such idiotic commentary.

Tia patted the chair beside her without looking at him, her gaze still on the stars. No demands, no questions.

He sank into the chair, growing more at ease with each quiet minute that passed. It was their first chance to talk since finding the imprisoned crew members that afternoon, but he was in no hurry to break the stillness of the evening. Bit by bit, the tension that strung him tight bled away into the softness of the chair. His eyes drifted shut.

Which was his mistake.

For a time he'd been able to forget their encounter in the bathroom. Now it all came back: the intensity of her lavender gaze, the burn of her touch against his bare skin, the impossibility of the idea that she touched him of her own volition...

...and Dolan's voice in his head, making him wonder if Tia'tan really used her own volition, or labored under his.

"Vayne?" Kayla called from behind him, and his eyes snapped open.

Tia'tan was looking beyond his shoulder, toward the doorway.

::I invited her:: he said to Tia. A fact he had forgotten.

She nodded. ::I assumed you would bring your *ro'haar*.:: There was no judgement in her tone. ::Just as I assumed she would bring Malkor.::

Vayne turned to look. Sure enough, Kayla strode into the room with her trademark "let's do this" stride, and the IDC agent followed.

"What did you find?" Kayla asked before she'd even reached them.

Vayne opened his mouth to argue against Malkor's inclusion—and Kayla clearly expected his opposition—but Tia stopped him.

::You can trust Malkor.:: She sent her surety along with the words, but trust in an imperial was too ill of a fit for him.

::How do you know for certain?::

::Simple. He's in love with Kayla. He's not going to choose any action which would endanger her or those she cares about.::

Vayne sent a flash of memory to her: IDC agents in their indigo and teal uniforms arriving in the palace, and then the bombs and destruction the day they left. ::He is an imperial.::

::Someday his words and his deeds will need to outweigh

that fact in your mind, Vayne.:: A hint of censure came across their link. ::We all want the same thing, now.::

Kayla arched a brow, watching them both, ready to defend Malkor's right to be there. Malkor's expression was so irritatingly neutral that Vayne wanted to argue, just to set him off.

::You had better be right about trusting him:: he said to Tia, then held his peace.

"Let's all sit," Tia'tan said. She rose from her comfortable chair, then padded over to the closest bench, inviting the others to join her.

Kayla sat across from her. "Tell me what you found this afternoon. The wait has been killing me."

Rather than explain in words, Tia saved time by expressing the pertinent moments with her mind, sending the three of them both her impressions and the gist of their conversation with Kendrik and the others.

Malkor blinked. Blinked again. "Well that's an expedient way to do things."

Vayne felt a petty pleasure at the knowledge that Kayla never communicated with Malkor on that level.

I am such an asshole.

"It's tough to tell from that impression alone," Kayla said, "how sane those crew members are."

Malkor nodded. "I agree. At times they seem lucid, but the preoccupation, the obsessive repetition of simple tasks, the woman half-catatonic in the top bunk…"

"You said the captain told you that as each crew member's sanity failed, they were forced to lock them up. That could be all this is."

"Ida also told us each of those had eventually succumbed to the brain damage," Vayne replied. "She led us to believe that Itsy was the last of them alive."

"Show us the room they kept Itsy in."

This time Vayne passed the impressions along, though it killed him to communicate with any imperial in that fashion. He showed them the walls of Itsy's cabin, words and mathematical equations scrawled up to the ceiling. The way the bed sheets were shredded and knotted into an archaic counting device, the different strands colored with urine and even feces. The rotting food piled up by the synthesizer, the broken desk, and over it all the terrible, terrible stench.

"People go crazy in different ways, though," Kayla said. "Itsy was sane enough in her own way to escape, avoid capture, and set the self-destruct on Tia'tan's ship."

"The restraints, though?" Malkor asked.

Vayne answered him. "Those would have been standard-issue restraints during a time of war five hundred years ago, I think."

"But these were used for more than just restraint, considering the severity of the burns we saw," Tia'tan argued.

"I can't imagine people with dementia stemming from brain damage learn a lesson very well the first time."

"The locked door should have made them unnecessary, if they truly were just for keeping the crew members corralled."

Kayla spoke up. "A locked door didn't stop Itsy, and from the footage I saw she was practically feral."

"Putting aside the issue of the sliding scale of their insanity for the moment," Malkor said, "if they were being held purely for their own safety, why would the captain go to such lengths to keep their existence from us? Changing the status of that level to unpowered in the ship's complink, restricting access via the lift, using a psionic screening device... She had to know, with all of us searching the ship, that they'd be found eventually."

"Maybe she thought it wasn't any of our business," Tia'tan postulated. "As captain, she intends to govern her crew as she sees fit, with no outside interference."

"Or to protect their dignity," Kayla said. "Let them go crazy in peace."

Vayne frowned. "She doesn't get to have that luxury. Not with other *stepa* running loose, stealing weapons. We're risking our lives, we deserve to know what's going on."

"I agree," Malkor said. "I'm not keeping my team in the dark." Even though he said it quietly, the man's voice had the same kind of certainty that Kayla always spoke with.

Vayne looked from him to Kayla. They wore the same focused, determined expression, had the same intelligent gleam in their eye. They even sat on the bench the same way: on the edge, back straight, feet shoulder-width apart with weight equally balanced—ready to spring into action.

Grudgingly, he could see how Malkor might appeal to a *ro'haar*.

"Do you think they're in contact with the other *stepa*?" Kayla asked. "What were Officer Kendrik's words? 'When a rescue attempt is discovered?'"

Vayne tapped his fingers on his thigh, uncertain. He'd been turning the strange conversation over and over in his head since this afternoon and he still wasn't sure if there was something sinister going on, or if they were trying too hard to make sense of the ramblings of a crazy person. "The supposed rescue could just be taking place in their minds."

"None of them made a rush for the door either time that I opened it," Tia'tan admitted. "Neither Gaar nor Enska showed any reaction to Kendrik's mention of rescue, and they spoke of the captain visiting as if she came for tea, not in a jailer capacity."

"Kendrik seemed pretty lucid when mentioning the rescue attempt," Kayla said, "and referencing a 'fog' in her head."

But no one really knew what was going on in the crew members' ancient brains, and that was the problem. Anything Kendrik and the others said or did could be analyzed any which way and produce a dozen different outcomes.

"We need to have Toble examine them," Malkor said, and Kayla nodded.

"Who?" Vayne asked, earning an immediate frown from Kayla.

"The octet has been on board for weeks now, and you still don't know their names?"

He shrugged. Kayla's look promised they'd "have words" later.

"Toble's our medic," Malkor said, neutral as before. "He's not a neuroscientist per se, but he'll know how to evaluate them."

"That's our next move, then," Tia'tan said. "Can you wake him?"

"Now?" Vayne asked.

"It's our best shot. I don't know when Tanet's code will change again, and we won't be able to open the door without a current one." Tia'tan looked at each of their faces. "Unless you want to confront Ida about it instead?"

They all shook their heads. It was possible Kendrik and the others had been quarantined in the same corridor as Itsy originally, and then moved once Vayne had stumbled upon her. If they confronted Ida before they had all the facts, where would she then move them to?

"Plus, no one will notice our absence tonight. Tomorrow we'll be all over the ship, working in teams on who knows what, with the new rebels in the mix—it'll be a lot harder to break away."

"Rigger and I are leaving for Ordoch in the morning," Malkor added. He turned his gaze to Kayla and gave her a half-smile. "I'd like to know what new sort of trouble you'll be in when I get back."

12

They made the trip to the lower deck mostly in silence, with only Toble asking questions about the crew's condition: things neither Tia'tan nor Vayne had known to look for, like pupil dilation or loss of coordination. Toble had his medical case in one hand, a datapad in the other. Malkor and Vayne both carried cases of medical equipment he had brought over from the *Lorius* as soon as he'd seen the rudimentary offerings of one of the *Yari*'s med stations. It seemed he now intended to set up a mobile lab inside the barracks.

Kayla, following behind, carried her plasma bullpup at the ready. Keeping alert and tuned to any possible disturbance wasn't a problem—she was still boiling from learning that her *il'haar* had walked into such a dangerous situation without calling for her first. She was no good to him as a *ro'haar* on the other side of the ship. And leaving Corinth's wellbeing to strangers? She didn't give a frutt how well trained those rebels were. If Corinth wasn't with an octet member, one of his siblings, or Noar and Tia'tan, he wasn't safe.

She and Vayne would most certainly be having words later.

They arrived at the barracks without incident. The lights were down, the bunks quiet. Hopefully, they were more sane than crazy, because the appearance of five strangers in their midst in the middle of the night would certainly set them off.

Kayla tapped the lights by the door, bringing them halfway up. The bunks at the near end were all made up and empty, so she followed Tia'tan to the near silent room. Beyond Tia'tan's shoulder she saw a woman pacing the narrow aisle that ran between the bunks. She wore a sleep shirt and nothing else, bare feet counting out seventeen steps in one direction before she turned and executed seventeen back toward them.

"Not safe. Have to hide. Not safe. Have to hide." The woman's shoulder-length hair curtained her face as she kept her head down, focused on each step.

"Hello," Tia'tan called softly. The woman ignored them completely.

"I haven't met her yet," Tia'tan murmured to Kayla. "She seemed semi-catatonic when I was here before."

"Well she's certainly mobile now." Kayla motioned for the others to keep back, then she approached the pacing woman. She stepped directly into the woman's path and waited.

Twelve steps, thirteen... Without even looking up, the woman sidestepped Kayla at a precise ninety-degree angle and continued on her way.

"Not safe. Have to hide."

"I'll wake Kendrik." Tia'tan searched out the woman on the bottom bunk farthest to the back.

Two men slept fitfully in bunks to Kayla's left. She damn near jumped a meter when one cried out and half sat up, eyes wide and unseeing.

His hand shot out, quicker than she could react, and clamped around her wrist. He pulled her with all his might and she stumbled down to one knee beside the bed, face to face with him. He had a sickly look, with blue lips, ashen skin, and clear fluid leaking from his nose.

"Don't let me sleep," he pleaded. "Help me to stay in the waking." His glazed eyes were wider than viewports and she wasn't sure who he saw when he stared at her. "Please." He squeezed her wrist as if she were his lifeline.

"Tell me how," she said, but already she was losing him. His eyelids fluttered, and he blinked mightily. "Stay with me." She shook his shoulder with her free hand, but his eyes rolled back into his head and he collapsed on the bed with a sigh that sounded like surrender. No amount of shaking could rouse him.

Kayla called for Toble to examine the unconscious man. "I'm not sure if he's heavily sedated," she said, "or if he passed out. Can you tell?"

Toble opened his medical kit and got to work.

Kayla rose and joined the others, but couldn't shake the eerie feeling the man's words had given her. What was happening here?

Thanks to the images Tia'tan had passed along earlier, she recognized Gaar, Enska, and Kendrik as they climbed out of their bunks. Officer Kendrik introduced the woman who continued to pace as Airman Lopez.

"Why this waking?" Gaar asked. Enska watched them with guarded eyes, saying nothing as he pulled a robe on over his sleeping tunic.

"We would like our medic to examine you, if that's all right," Tia'tan said.

Gaar gestured to the pacing woman. "Lopez being a medic of the *Yari*. Is not needed."

"I don't think Lopez is up to a more thorough examination of your symptoms," Kayla said.

Officer Kendrik considered this a moment. She looked to Gaar and Enska, likely in silent communication with them. It was hard for Kayla to be patient when so much was at stake. Clearly Officer Kendrik was the lynchpin. Whatever she decided, the others would go along with. Kayla struggled not to shake the woman and demand she comply.

"An examination again being acceptable to us," Kendrik said finally.

They all waited in awkward silence for Toble to finish examining the unconscious man. Once he did, he joined the group and organized Vayne and Malkor into setting up his mobile lab. He knelt in front of Officer Kendrik, who remained sitting on her bunk. With Tia'tan translating his Imperial Common for the woman, he asked a series of questions, some of which seemed to confuse her.

Toble must have felt every eye in the room on him because he stopped. He shot an annoyed look over his shoulder. "First, you're crowding me. Second, this is going to take a while so you might as well all get comfortable."

Not what she wanted to hear.

Nonetheless, she, Vayne, and Malkor cleared out and wandered to the other end of the room. Gaar and Enska reclaimed their bunks to wait their turn for inspection.

Minutes ticked by. More minutes. Kayla's earlier edginess was quickly being replaced by fatigue.

"What time is it, anyway?" she asked no one in particular.

"I don't know," Malkor said, "but I'm going to grab some shut-eye while I can. We have a big day scouring the lower levels for foodstuffs tomorrow." He selected a bunk close to the door and lay down.

Fingers interlaced, hands resting on his stomach, one booted foot crossed over the other, he looked pretty comfortable for a man who was too big for the bed. She hadn't realized the officer cabins were built more generously.

Vayne and Kayla sat side by side on another bunk by silent agreement. They were still in sync on some level even after five years apart. The knowledge relaxed her.

Vayne glanced at her from the corner of his eye. "Has the time of reckoning come? I can hear your lecture already."

He could probably predict every word of it, which made it all the worse, since he'd knowingly put himself in danger without her.

But the night was late, and for the moment things were peaceful. Sitting beside him, knowing her *il'haar* was safe, being close to the twin she'd thought she lost forever, her heart just wasn't in it. "I guess that saves me from having to say it."

"Consider me suitably chastised."

She snorted. "Unlikely."

They leaned together, arm to arm, and she tilted her head onto his shoulder. They had a clear view of Toble at work from where they sat.

Vayne's voice sounded in her head. ::Sleep. I'll keep watch on them, and wake you if necessary.::

With anyone else she might have argued it was her job to keep watch, but not with Vayne. The *ro'haar–il'haar* bond was an equal pairing, two pillars with different strengths, each supporting the other. She trusted him implicitly. And she sensed, more than ever before, that he needed her to trust in him and his abilities. He doubted himself in a way she never had, and he needed to know that someone believed in him.

So she merely murmured "thank you," and closed her eyes.

Sometime later—any hour in the middle of the night on a spaceship felt like any other hour of the night—Toble woke them to present his preliminary findings.

"I was only able to examine Kendrik, Enska, and Gaar. Lopez wouldn't leave off pacing, and Djittri and Windham remain unconscious." Toble wiped his brow, looking weary and frustrated. "Cranial scans of all three show a low level of damage, akin to sustaining one or more traumatic mechanical brain injury." His mouth twisted. "That, I'm afraid, is the good news."

Kayla rubbed her gritty eyes and sat up straighter, easing the kink in her neck. "What's worse than traumatic brain injury?"

"They're being poisoned."

That had everyone scrambling to their feet.

"They are being given an exotic cocktail of substances, some of which I can't identify—likely because they don't exist in the empire." Toble looked down at his datapad, scrolling through his findings. "The two substances in greatest abundance in each patient are heavy sedatives. At such high levels, I believe these tranquilizers are responsible for most of the symptoms we're seeing: the confusion, memory loss, inability to concentrate, impaired cognitive function, and of course, the heavy sleeping."

He consulted his notes again. "There is also a third drug with anti-anxiety properties, historically used to treat seizures. It was long ago identified as a carcinogen, though, and I believe that it is at least partly to blame for the brain tumors I'm seeing in each of them. Beyond that, they're being given a herb of some kind, and at least two other compounds that my database can't identify.

"Best-case scenario, someone is drugging these people with the sole intention of making them easy to deal with."

Not at all what she'd expected. "How are they being drugged?"

"It's in their food," Tia'tan said, and Toble nodded in agreement.

"Each reports feeling extremely drowsy a short while after eating. They lie down to sleep, sometimes for as much as eighteen hours at a time. None of them remember being handed medication to take, or given injections."

"If they're asleep that long," Vayne countered, "they could still be given injections."

"It's possible, but I didn't find any signs on their skin of repeated puncturing."

Kayla snapped her fingers, remembering. "That's why Kendrik's so thin, and also the most 'with it' of the bunch. She figured out a correlation between the food and her symptoms, so she's been eating as little as possible."

Toble nodded again. "Exactly. They have a food synthesizer, it would be as simple as someone dosing the calorie pack each time it was changed out."

"That's low," Vayne growled. He had one hand clenched in a fist. "We have to get them out of here."

Kayla laid her hand over his fist. "We don't know that someone is trying to harm them. None of the remaining crew are medics; someone might be trying to keep them from hurting themselves and just has the dose wrong."

Vayne gave her a look that said he doubted it.

"Since Tanet's code unlocks the barracks," Tia'tan said, "we can assume that Ida and the crew all have access. But considering how well the *stepa* get around the ship, it's possible that they have something to do with it."

"The way I see it," Malkor said, "we have four possibilities." He counted them off on his fingers. "One, Ida and her crew are jointly responsible for the overdose. Two, one of the five is poisoning these people in secret, and the rest of the 'sane' crew are unaware. Three, whoever is leading the *stepa* loose on the ship is overdosing them as part of a plan. Four, one of the crazy *stepa* is acting alone and no one on either side has any idea."

Kayla made a disgusted sound. "None of which we can determine with the information we currently have. How bad are the tumors?"

"They're small, for now. Still operable, at least in Enska, Kendrik, and Gaar's cases. Assuming we stopped the drugs immediately."

But that was impossible. They had no way of knowing when the calorie packs were changed out, and with the psionic field dampener on the door, none of the crew could get word to them when it happened.

And something else— "Tanet's security code will reset tomorrow. Without that, we won't be able to gain access to this room again."

"Then we take them with us tonight," Vayne said, clearly ready to do just that.

"No." A small voice came from behind Toble. "We are to stay. This room being our pen for now, until it is time." Barefooted, bare-legged Airman Lopez stood just beyond their circle, having snuck up without anyone noticing. Apparently she could stop pacing, but she still hopped from foot to foot, as if itching to get back to it.

"Until what time?" Tia'tan asked.

Lopez shook her head. "It's not safe, have to hide. Not safe. Hide in plain sight. Hide in here."

Kendrik approached as well. Lopez's chant grew in volume.

"She is not meaning what she says."

"Yes I am. Yes I *am*!" Lopez shouted.

Kendrik pulled Lopez aside, speaking in a low voice to her. It took some time, but eventually Lopez calmed down. She shot them one last look, suspicious this time, and then marched to the back of the room to resume her pacing.

"Who is doing this to you?" Kayla asked the officer.

Kendrik sighed. "It not being clear to me. I have a remembrance of time before, we were not in this room always." She looked around at the closely stacked bunk rows. "I had a cabin to my own. A command of my own."

"What happened?"

If she remembered, and it wasn't clear that she did, Kendrik wouldn't say. "You must needs talk to First Officer Zimmerman."

"Wait," Malkor said, "isn't Benny's last name Strokar?"

"Benny isn't actually Ida's first officer," Vayne replied. "Though he seems to act in that capacity now."

Kendrik nodded. "Zimmerman is First Officer, the only one who opposes the captain when it is becoming necessary."

"The First Officer is out of cryosleep?" Kayla asked. "You're certain?" She felt a little breathless—they might finally be getting somewhere on the *stepa* threat.

"Zim had control of my awakening, and I am here." She nodded at her own words. "I have spoken with him in this now time. It is to him that you should speak as well." With that she walked back to bed, lethargy showing in each dragging step.

"We can't just leave them here," Vayne insisted.

"I don't think they'll come willingly," Tia'tan replied. "Not if Kendrik orders them to stay. And we're not exactly equipped to drag off four unwilling hostages and two comatose people."

Toble seemed torn as well. "It kills me to leave their wounds untreated, to let them knowingly continue to ingest those drugs."

"If we want to help them," Kayla said, "we need to find Zimmerman." Wherever the frutt he was… "And hope that he's still sane."

* * *

It was far too early the next morning when Kayla stood in the shuttle bay watching Rigger and Malkor get suited up in EMUs. Ariel was huffing and puffing from inside the shuttle, doing her preflight checks and grumbling about the imperials not being ready yet.

"She really is kind of a bitch, huh?" Kayla said to Vayne, who had come to the shuttle bay, not to support the agents, but to support her.

He chuckled. "Ida likes to say, 'grumpy is her lot.'"

"Then she's sugar-coating it."

"After this much time in Ariel's company, I agree with you."

They waited in silence as Ariel grumbled and Malkor and Rigger donned the multiple layers of suit necessary for a spacewalk from the shuttle into the Tear.

Kayla couldn't stop the misgivings from running through her mind. Malkor would be half a galaxy away from her, out of any range of help she could give. He'd be at risk undercover, and likely considered an enemy by either side. The rebels wouldn't be any help if they were found out. Wetham still hadn't forwarded any concrete plan for the extraction of the scientists, and Malkor would be without the backup of the rest of the octet.

"Damnit," she muttered.

"You worry for him."

"Of course."

"You don't think he can complete the mission?"

Kayla cut Vayne an irritated glance. "I worry about you: does that make you incompetent?"

"You're my *ro'haar*, it's different."

She shook her head. "No, it's not." She turned to face him, meeting his brilliant gaze. "This has nothing to do with Malkor's abilities. The worry is for myself, for the pain I know I will feel if something happens to him. I worry because a piece of my heart will die if I lose him, the same as it would if something happened to you."

She continued, even though Vayne looked away. "Malkor is one of the most capable people I have ever met. There isn't a

172

mission I would hesitate to send him on—as long as psi powers weren't necessary for its success."

Vayne turned back to her. "That's my point. In our world, Kay, he'll always be a 'less than.'"

How dare he call Malkor a 'less than!' "I don't have my powers. Am I 'less than,' too?" she asked, the question a verbal snapping of teeth.

"That's only temporary—"

"Five. Full. Years."

"It's *temporary*," he stressed. "Now that you're back among your own kind, you'll find your powers again."

She let that go for the moment. She had the same hope, but was afraid to jinx things by saying it out loud. Across the room, Hekkar and Malkor were conferring, since Hekkar would be in charge of the remaining octet members in Malkor's absence.

"The only reason we have a shot at rescuing the hyperstream drive specialists from captivity is because of Malkor and Rigger. You or I could slap on a hologram and look like an imperial, but Malkor can act like an imperial. He doesn't need a translator bot to understand orders: he can actually read Imperial Common. He knows about life in the imperial army, frutt, he knows idiosyncrasies we couldn't begin to guess at."

Vayne crossed his arms over his chest. "Wetham said we have rebels embedded in the imperial strongholds who can do the same."

"Not as well, I assure you. Besides, those rebels have established imperial cover identities. They can't ditch all that hard work and disappear from the role they've been playing. We need those rebels where they are."

He didn't argue that point, instead turning a stony glare toward Malkor.

"Vayne, you need to stop underestimating him. I trust him, and every member of the octet, with my life." She willed him to listen. "With Corinth's life."

"But not with my life?"

She opened her mouth. Closed it.

He leaned in. "Exactly."

"That's not fair." Damn him. How could she trust Vayne's life to anyone but herself, when she'd only just recently gotten him back? "It's different, you're my *il'haar*."

He indicated Malkor with a lift of his chin. "And what is he to you?"

How to answer that? She loved Malkor, wanted a future with him, but what would that future look like? She thought of their time together, all they'd done since he'd found her on Altair Tri, and answered the only way she knew how. "He's my partner."

"*Ro'haar* and *il'haar* don't have 'partners,'" Vayne said in disgust. "They might each take a lover, they might have friends, but they don't have 'romantic partners.'"

She hated him for being right. Neither member of the twin bond felt the need to form a lasting partnership with anyone outside of it. They had family, friends, and might take a lover to satisfy those urges, but they didn't "fall in love," they didn't have children unless they were the head of the family and needed heirs. Even then the *il'haar* chose the mother of the children by psionic pedigree, not desire.

Nothing superseded the *ro'haar–il'haar* bond.

"Exactly," Vayne said again. Kayla felt like kicking him in the shin.

Malkor had finished speaking with Hekkar, she realized. He must have known she and Vayne were arguing and hung back, not wanting to come between them. She could tell from his expression, guarded though it was, that he was less than pleased with Vayne at the moment.

Great.

Was this what her future looked like? By trying to hold on to both of them, would she be stuck in an unsatisfactory relationship with each?

"It's too early in the morning for this shit," she told Vayne, and went to say goodbye to Malkor and Rigger.

13

"You're grinding your teeth, boss."

Rigger's voice rose above the roar of the shuttle's engine and snapped Malkor out of his thoughts.

"He's kind of an ass, huh?" Rigger continued. Malkor didn't have to ask who she meant. "I mean, I know he's been through an unbelievable nightmare and I should be sympathetic no matter what he does, but…" She shrugged the shoulders of her EMU. "He's putting the screws to Kayla every time I see him."

"He doesn't mean to," Malkor said, but it still pissed him off to see Vayne upsetting Kayla once again this morning. She never got mad at Vayne for anything the man did. She only got defensive, and that meant he had said something to make her doubt her worthiness as a *ro'haar*.

Which made Malkor feel like punching something.

"Grinding," Rigger pointed out again.

"So helpful."

She grinned. "I try. Here, pop your helmet on. We're almost to the Tear and I don't trust Ariel to warn us before she opens the doors."

"Do you know," Malkor said over comms, once they had both sealed their helmets. "The sad truth is the Wyrds on the ship like

175

us a whole lot more than anyone on Ordoch is going to."

"Just another beautiful day in the life of us IDC agents."

Malkor chuckled. "I guess we never were that popular back home, either, were we?"

"Speak for yourself. Gio was practically a superstar."

Mention of one of the two octet members who had stayed behind on Falanar brought the mood crashing down. They rode the rest of the way in silence, until it was time to jump out of the shuttle and soar through the Tear.

The breath caught in his chest as he floated, untethered, toward the anomaly. The Tear had no depth dimension, and its pulsing light made it hard to gauge its exact shape, so an image of him zooming right past and into the Mine Field to become a snack for the rooks filled his mind. He thought he heard Rigger praying to Falanar's three Divines, and then they were through.

At first everything was black. For a disorienting second he thought he'd slipped between realities or something, riding the Tear's time-space anomaly straight into no-man's-land.

Then his helmet's UV filter transitioned from shielding out the impossibly bright light from the Tear to managing the weak industrial lighting inside the cave. Rigger stood to his left, looking as dazed as he felt.

She popped her helmet off. "I *think* we survived that insanity?"

"You did indeed." The quiet male voice surprised them both, not least because it spoke Imperial Common. A diminutive Ordochian stepped out of the shadows at the mouth of the cave. He was slender and almost feminine by imperial gender reckoning, his age somewhere between that of Corinth and Vayne. "Welcome to Ordoch, agents."

This must be Mishe. "You speak Common?"

"I spend a great deal of time among your people," Mishe replied, unsmiling. His face showed neither welcome nor censure. It was a perfect mask of politeness, but Malkor had the feeling that if he and Rigger tried to walk back through the

Tear with their helmets off, Mishe wouldn't lift a finger to stop them. "Come, let me show you where you can change before meeting with Wetham."

Mishe started out of the cave without waiting. As she passed Malkor, Rigger murmured, "Told you I was popular."

They left the bulky EMUs in the cavern, grabbed their rucksacks, and followed after Mishe. Malkor had a sense, as he left the Tear behind, that he walked away from his last chance of ever seeing Kayla again.

At least he could finally make Vayne happy, he thought sarcastically.

Sometime later, Mishe left them cooling their heels, waiting for an audience with Wetham in a room that looked suspiciously like an emptied supply closet.

"Is Hekkar going to keep you apprised of the situation with the new *stepa* Tia'tan found yesterday?" Rigger asked. She was sitting on the floor, digging through the electronic equipment she'd brought with her.

"He's agreed to send messages through the Tear to this base." Malkor leaned against the bare shelves on one wall. "But I doubt we'll be in contact with the base once we go undercover."

"True." She had a datapad on each knee and was typing on both, one hand on each. "The good thing about this terrible plan is that at least I get to play with imperial tech again." She didn't look up from her fiddling as she spoke. "I feel next to useless on the *Yari*."

"We all do. And hey, you're not useless—you carry boxes like a champ."

This time she did look up, and her irrepressible grin was back in place. "Yeah, but not with my miiiind." She wiggled her fingers like a magician.

Malkor groaned. "You and your awful sense of humor should be right at home where we're going."

Not that he knew where that was, precisely. Or even generally. He'd had to argue against his own better judgement—not to mention with Kayla and Hekkar—to accept the assignment without knowing the details first.

It was worth the risk. He agreed with Natali and Kayla's assessment that in order to have the leverage to force the empire to the negotiating table, they *needed* to have the *Yari* and its superior weaponry in orbit around Ordoch. If sneaking three scientists off the planet was the only way to accomplish that, then Malkor would sneak three scientists out from under his fellow imperials' noses.

A knock sounded, and then an aide appeared in the doorway. She informed them immediately, "I don't speak your language," in a tone that would wither spring grass, and escorted them to Wetham's private study without another word. Well, apparently it used to be a storeroom, judging by the crates stacked in one corner still, but it now served as a study.

Wetham stood as they were announced. "Thank you for coming," he said in unaccented Imperial Common. "We appreciate your help."

"Of course." Malkor and Rigger seated themselves in two straight-backed chairs that had clearly been set out for them. They looked uncomfortable, and stood apart from the other chairs placed around the large table off to one side—definitely chairs for unwanted imperial "guests."

Wetham reseated himself at the head of the table and introduced two of his lieutenants. "Ygreda, my spymaster"—the woman with a headful of blue curls inclined her head—"and Aarush, my tactical genius." The tactical genius looked half dead. Bandages covered a portion of his face, wrapped tight around his head and spiraled over both arms and down his hands.

Malkor gave a seated bow to both rebels. "We are grateful to be able to help."

Aarush glared at him with one baleful eye. Malkor sensed that Ygreda was no more impressed by them, but she hid it better.

"I mean no insult," Malkor said, "but before we begin, who else here speaks Imperial Common?" He had no problem understanding them, but he wasn't sure about the reverse.

Both lieutenants raised their hand.

"Your kind have been here for five years, after all." And just like that, Aarush made him feel like a jackass for not learning Ordochian.

"That makes things easier," he said instead. "How many others in the base speak it? In the rebellion?"

Wetham answered. "Not many. Our spies of course, I and my lieutenants, and only a handful more. It's not exactly popular."

"A bit like choking," Ygreda added. "Crossed with hacking and a little barking."

Rigger gave her a sweet smile. "So we've been told."

Starting a meeting with insults seemed to be the Ordochians' style, at least around them. Malkor shrugged off his irritation and got down to business. "Tell us about your plans to free the scientists."

Aarush, after another second with the one-eyed stare, turned his attention to the map spread out across the table. "Your target will be Mesa. She's a prisoner at the detainment structure inside Vankir proper itself."

"Here? She's in the capital city?" Not entirely surprising. The empire would have made Vankir their main foothold on Ordoch, and Kayla had said the imperials—well, the other imperials—considered Mesa a top resource. She'd be held in their most secure location.

"We're a little outside of Vankir, but yes, she's close, relatively speaking." Aarush tapped a location on the map. "You'll need to free Mesa from the prison, then escort her through the city's several guard checkpoints, finally clearing the heavily fortified gate in the massive wall they've built around part of Vankir."

That much he'd assumed. "Natali told me one of the imperial base commanders had flipped?"

Aarush nodded. "A man by the name Brid Chen: have you heard of him?"

"Brid Chen?" Malkor leaned forward in his seat. "Are you sure?"

Aarush exchanged a glance with Ygreda. It was she who answered. "Several of my spies have had dealings with

179

Chen, I'm certain it is him. Why?"

"He's... Well, he's something of a friend." More like a gambling buddy, and that was years ago, back when they'd both been in their respective academies. The friendship had died a swift death once they'd sworn their allegiances to rival agencies, the IDC and the army.

"Friend or not," Ygreda said, "he's proven his dedication to our cause. I believe we can trust him with this mission."

Insane to think that someone so high up in the occupation command structure had changed sides and was now acting as a double agent. They would be shot on sight if anyone knew: no arrest, no trial.

Now that he knew Brid was the commander in question, though, Malkor was a little less surprised. The man always did have a strong moral center.

Ygreda met his eyes. "I have entrusted the lives of several of my spies to his keeping, if that convinces you."

"It does." And even if it didn't, he had no choice but to risk it if he ever wanted to see the *Yari* move its gigantic ass. "We need his cooperation to pull this off. My people can create a near perfect forgery of imperial army credentials, but they're useless if the commander who signs off on them is a fictional character."

Rigger agreed. "If we show up with orders to transport a high-profile prisoner, the officer in charge will follow up with the signing commander to confirm the orders are legit. Standard procedure."

Malkor waited, but nothing else was forthcoming. "That's it? That's the entirety of your plan?"

"What more do you need?"

"Where is Brid stationed?" He looked at the map. "Does he have some reason to request that Mesa be transferred to wherever we're supposedly transferring her?"

Ygreda looked at him suspiciously, as if he'd asked a trick question. "What does that matter?"

Malkor counseled himself to patience by remembering that Ordoch was a peaceful planet before they had arrived. It didn't have a military of any sort, and while the cities had a token police force, there was no career path that in any way resembled the training Malkor and his octet had received over their lifetimes. Even Kayla, for all her fighting prowess and bodyguard skills, knew little about running an op or designing a sting. Ygreda the spymaster had probably taught herself everything she knew, and that only in the last five years or less.

"Our phony transfer orders won't be approved if they aren't realistic, no matter who signs them," he said. "If Brid oversees a food depot, he doesn't need a hyperstream drive engineer. And if he doesn't have a prison under his command, then he's not going to be taking custody of a prisoner."

That seemed to make sense to them. Unfortunately, no one threw out brilliant ideas in the wake of his statement. Instead, all three members of the rebellion leaned forward in their chairs, waiting to see what brilliant plan *he* had.

And that, he thought to himself, *is why you Wyrds need us*.

Being devious was second nature to imperials—or for IDC agents, at least.

After hours of work, Vayne and Kayla sat in the commissary grabbing a quick lunch.

They weren't the only ones. Tanet sat by himself, speed reading something on a datapad while he ate. He still had a ventilation suit on; he must have been the half of a team on the unpowered levels, and was heading back to it after lunch. The captain sat with Uncle Ghirhad by the bank of windows. As usual they were smiling and laughing, cracking each other up. Benny sat at the captain's elbow, not joining in on the conversation.

::We need to change out the calorie pack in the prisoners' barracks.:: Vayne's voice sounded low in her mind, as if someone might overhear—which was impossible. He and Kayla were across the room from everyone else, situated in the corner by the door, but the physical distance wasn't necessary to keep a psi conversation quiet if Vayne only projected to her.

Kayla organized her thoughts quickly. Worry about her inadequacy as a *ro'haar* without psi powers in this box, concern for Malkor in that box... She tucked a few more things neatly away, then lowered her mental shields enough so that Vayne could slip into her mind.

I agree. There was no way she wanted Kendrik and the others to be continually overdosed if she could help it. *The effects will take some time to fade, so I don't think the switch will be noticeable for a while.*

::Hopefully we'll have figured out what the frutt is going on by then.::

Not that they'd had any luck in that area so far. Vayne and Tia'tan had been carefully using their psi powers as they worked, searching for the minds of the *stepa* or an area they couldn't penetrate with their skills. This had been done initially, after the discovery that someone had woken more crew members from cryo, but Ida and her crew had done most of the searching. They hadn't reported finding anyone. Was that because there was no one to find, or for other reasons?

Security codes changed this morning: we have no way to access the barracks.

::And Tanet wasn't paired with Tia'tan, so he didn't confide his code to her.::

Kayla ate another spoonful of the stew concoction she'd synthed up. The options on the *Yari*'s food synthesizer were truly hideous—the technology had come a long way in five hundred years.

You're not gonna like what I have to say.

She felt Vayne's hesitation. ::What?::

You have to read Tanet's mind so we can get his code.

Silence. Not just silence, he had pulled back from her. She waited him out.

::No.::

She waited.

::I'm not doing it.:: He was practically pushing her away.

She waited.

::We'll get it some other way. I refuse to violate him like that.::

Images spun out in her mind: Vayne sitting in a chair, Dolan standing over him, gleefully plucking thoughts from his head. Dolan was especially obsessed with Kayla, dragging memories from Vayne time and again. Another session, this time Vayne curled on the floor in a ball. A nasty event had just occurred thanks to the Influencer—she didn't know what exactly, he shielded that from her—and Dolan delighting in making Vayne relive it over and over. *Dolan was a sadistic bastard. This is nothing like that.*

::Invading someone's mind without their permission is exactly that.::

It's not for your own sick amusement. You're not looking for anything personal, it's just a number.

::I can't avoid personal things when I'm digging through his brain—I don't know what I'll find.::

I'll prompt him: the number will be right on the surface. She didn't wait for a reply, just set her mystery stew aside and rose.

Giant hands pushed on her shoulders and hit her in the backs of her knees, forcing her to sit down—hard. She tried to control her expression as the awkward landing caused people to glance her way, but her eyes must have been huge.

Did you just—

::Still not as bad as picking through someone's brain:: he snapped. ::At least you knew it was coming.::

I never expect *my il'haar* to manhandle me unless it's for my safety.

::What if it's for *my* safety?:: Vayne sucked in a breath as if shocked, as if he hadn't meant to say that. His anger at her roiled through her mind, but beneath it was something she hadn't recognized before: fear.

That fear killed her. Her heart welled with empathy for all her twin had gone through.

From the corner of her eye, though, she saw Tanet setting the datapad aside and finishing the remnants of his lunch. Her need to protect Vayne warred with her natural "let's get this done" drive, and for a split second, the tiniest moment, an image of the incarcerated Wyrds flashed in her mind's eye.

::Damnit, Kayla.::

I'm sorry, I didn't mean it. Shit. She was used to having Corinth in her head at times, but he wasn't so sensitive. He wouldn't have caught that thought.

We'll find another way. But she couldn't see one, at the moment. It was near impossible to imagine letting Kendrik and the others eat poisoned food, whether they were crazy or homicidal or not.

::Damnit.::

This time she didn't know who that was directed at.

::Go.:: The single word was bundled in so many layers of emotion that she couldn't make sense of it. ::Do it now, before I change my mind.::

A part of her wanted to forget the whole thing, but she had to trust her *il'haar* to make his own decisions of what he could and couldn't handle, or he wouldn't trust hers.

She rose from her seat again, this time without any resistance. She brought her cup to the synthesizer to refill, then sauntered over to Tanet's table and took a seat without asking.

The physicist gave her a friendly smile. "It being nice to see you."

She smiled back, it was hard not to. Tanet had been the friendliest of the crew from the start. She almost felt bad for what they were about to do.

"It's good to be around so many Ordochians." She sipped at the water. "Over the years, I lost hope that I'd ever be home again."

"I have feelings the same. Still, I have not traveled into the Tear, yet. I am not knowing if I have it in here," he tapped his chest, "to on Ordoch arrive in this new future."

They sat in silence a moment, each considering their strange future in Ordoch's new reality.

::Kayla…:: Vayne's voice was a warning growl.

Tanet sighed. "At least some of the future is on the ship here, the rebels making it easier to be gaining comfort of our new-old world."

Kayla nodded, trying to find an opening to bring up the lock codes. "There is certainly plenty to do on the *Yari*, no need to return to Ordoch yet."

"The days being full each now. So much excitement we are having after the long sleep and waiting." He leaned in. "I am enjoying much, do not tell the others."

She winked. "Your secret is safe with me." She glanced at the chronometer, groaned, and stretched. "I think I better get back to it. But first, speaking of secrets…" This time she leaned in in a faux conspiratorial fashion. "I'm glad we're working in pairs: I keep forgetting my security code."

"Yes! It did not change for five hundred years, now, every day changing." He closed his eyes as if concentrating. "I have to make a picture of it in mind's eye mine to hold on to it."

::Got it:: Vayne said, and withdrew from her mind so quickly that she mentally staggered. The commissary doors slid open behind her and she knew that Vayne had left her entirely.

"I'll try that, thanks, Tanet."

He smiled and she felt like a burglar. Ah well, she'd done worse things.

As she left the commissary, a rumble sounded deep in the belly of the ship. The vibrations shook the floor even at this level, the tremble shaking into the bones of her feet and rattling her teeth slightly.

Holy—

What the frutt was that? She hit the shipwide comm. "Are we under attack?" And where were the damn warning sirens?

"Today is having another stress test of the engine," Benny answered. "For many hours lasting."

How fun. The ship felt like it might shake apart.

Sort of like her damn life.

* * *

It was the end of the evening, and Kayla stood in front of the bank of mirrors inside the communal officer bathroom, brushing her hair. Vayne still hadn't communicated with her since she'd forced him to read Tanet's mind. He'd skipped out on working with her the rest of the day, choosing instead to pair with one of the rebels, forcing her to do the same.

Now it was late night and still no word. Crying on Tia'tan's shoulder?

The petty thought made her grumpy.

Vayne would speak to her in his own time, when he could forgive her. If he could forgive her.

Hey... He's a grown-up, he could have refused. Could he have, though? With his *ro'haar* asking it of him, and the drugged crew members counting on him?

There was no point in second-guessing herself all night... but she would, anyway.

Right now Kayla felt as useful as a candle in space. While she'd relaxed in a hot shower, Malkor and Rigger were on Ordoch, neck deep in an op. Noar, Larsa, and Corinth monitored the stress testing of the engine's structure, the rebels took turns keeping watch, and Toble tinkered away in one of the medical stations, formulating a series of tapers to step the sedatives down in the prisoners to avoid a catastrophic withdrawal. Since Tia'tan had been able to replace the calorie pack in their synthesizer without being detected, the prisoners would need the first of Toble's anti-anxiety/sedative concoction soon.

And here Kayla was, brushing her damp hair while she waited for reports from all the others who had actual useful things to do.

What she really wanted was to join Vayne and Tia'tan in continuing their search for First Officer Zimmerman and any of the *Yari*'s still unaccounted-for crew members. She was useless in that regard, too, however. Now that they knew the *Yari* had psionic shielding devices, Vayne and Tia'tan were slinking through the powered sections of the ship using their senses to look for psionic dead spots.

She could at least check up on Corinth. Kayla pulled her hair into a high ponytail, strapped a kris to each thigh over her leggings, and started toward the engine room. The walls of the corridor shook with the screeching vibrations rocketing through the hyperstream drive's chassis. Larsa said the series of stress tests would run for at least thirty hours—sleeping should be a treat.

She found Corinth, Larsa, and Noar in the control room overlooking the massive engine chamber. A dozen screens, each showing a different output, formed a bank of information. Each of them watched a different screen: it looked like they were cross-checking the readings against standardized charts.

The plascrystal window overlooking the engine room rattled in its frame, and the vidscreens bounced on their mounts. Kayla laid her palm flat against the bulkhead on one wall. It was like getting a massage. Quite nice, if her teeth hadn't also been rattling.

"How long will it be like this?" she asked, and all three jumped. Apparently they'd been even more focused than they looked.

::Kay!:: Corinth flashed her a big smile, then quickly turned back to the screen he'd been watching. ::I'm tracking any vaporization of metals from the engine scaffolding.::

"Have you found any?"

He didn't look up from the screen, just shook his head.

"And is that a good thing?"

::Yup!::

Similarly, after a brief glance in her direction, Noar and Larsa returned to their watches.

"This phase of test of stress being over soon," Larsa said. "Then the profile rests, rebuilds in intensity, and resets again."

"For thirty hours?"

"Already halfway done," Noar said, making it sound like the structure surviving this far into the testing was a success.

Kayla stood in the doorway, watching the back of three heads. Yup, she was sooo useful these days.

"Have you eaten today, Corinth?"

::Yup.::

"Recently?"

::I think so?::

He had an empty plate at his elbow, but that could have been from any number of days. She stepped closer behind him, leaned down, and sniffed. Someone might have brought him dinner, but no one had been making sure he'd bathed.

::Quit it, Kay.::

"You've got a date with a shower, mister."

::I will, I will, once these tests are done.::

"Promise?"

::Promise.::

She sighed. Somewhere along the way, during all the challenges of the last months, she'd let things drop. Who would have thought she'd be a better mother while they lived in a hovel in Fengar Swamp?

Kayla stood watching him a little while longer, since for once she had nothing she needed to be doing. She missed Corinth more than she realized. She'd been so busy since they arrived, every day working to keep the ship safe for him and the people she loved, that she hadn't spent much time with him. In fact, Vid and Trinan might even have had more contact than her. She put her arms around him, stinky teenage boy smell and all, and hugged him tight. He was no longer the frail waif he'd been on Altair Tri. The IDC agents had him eating for two, and he'd finally put some meat and muscle on his frame. He'd always be slim, but now he was healthy.

::Kay.:: He dragged her name out like it had two syllables. He finally squirmed and she let go.

"Sorry." *Sorry that you're growing up so fast all of a sudden, sorry that I'm gone all the time, sorry that five years of your life were stolen from you...*

Shrill beeping erupted from one of the many vidscreens Noar was monitoring. Kayla couldn't tell which one it was at first, since they all showed a profusion of charts and lines and oscillations and colors. Then one of the screens, previously

188

graphing a steadily rising line, shifted from orange to red-orange to red across the background. An endpoint appeared on the line all of a sudden, an inverted triangle with the words ESTIMATED CATASTROPHIC FAILURE POINT written inside.

Larsa cursed, a string of swear words so antiquated it would have been funny... if the entire engine room wasn't overheating like a spaceship on reentry.

"How bad is it?" Kayla asked.

"Not yet into the destruction phase, but the heat is not having the dissipation I hoped it would be having. Corinth?"

::The anodic film on the central shaft is beginning to vaporize:: he said to the room at large.

Noar swiveled his chair to double-check Corinth's readings. "He's right, I'm seeing cracking from the thermal stress."

Larsa was furiously making calculations. Noar brought up a schematic of the venting system for the engine. "I don't think it's a problem with the heat syphoning and exhausting pipes." He flipped through more schematics.

"Is possible the temperature will stabilize, being as how self-stabilizing the structure is. Calculations showing possibility." Larsa continued with more calculations.

Kayla stared down into the engine room, but nothing looked different to her. "Can't you just stop the test?"

Larsa shook her head. "This testing profile is a series of long stressed and shortness, being necessary for full drive function. Absolutely needing to surviving this, or hope of mine of flying is lost."

"Well you might not have a choice."

Noar had flipped through more schematics. Suddenly he pointed to one that looked suspiciously like the outside of the ship. "The problem's here. Where the outer pressure valve opens to cool the heat sink. It seems like something's... clogging it?"

"That is not making the sense." Larsa looked up from her calculation, double-checking the double checking that had been done so far. "We cleared debris of the Mine Field from our outside area, leaving the space open. Nothing of trash can be there."

"Do you have an outer camera there?" Kayla didn't like the sound of that warning beep, or Larsa's intention to keep the test running. What the frutt would a meltdown of the drive's structure do to the rest of the ship?

"This being a ship of five hundred years past. Cameras we are having of only the critical areas."

Ah, shit. And she was enjoying her few hours out of an EMU. "Someone needs to go out there and clear it, or jam it open, or whatever."

"That is responsibility mine."

Kayla was already heading toward the door. "No way. I'm not sending the only engineer we have on a spacewalk. I'm not sending any five-hundred-year-old crew member on a spacewalk either, so don't think of calling Benny or Tanet." Without her psi powers, Kayla really was the most expendable person onboard. She turned back to Larsa. "Let me do this. This is the best way I can help."

Larsa looked incapable of making the call, so Kayla just nodded. "Right, I'm glad you agree. Ariel is on guard duty in the control room with one of the rebels; I'll have her monitor me. And I'll wake one of the other rebels to spot me too." She pointed at Noar. "Get a schematic ready to load to my EMU infopad. Larsa, find the airlock closest to the vent and meet me there. I'm suiting up."

::Are you really doing this?:: Vayne asked her. She had no idea which level he was on now, trying to find the *stepa* hideout. She'd asked Noar to find him telepathically and give him the details.

She lowered her mental shields and Vayne slipped gently into her mind—so unlike Corinth's happy puppy rush that felt like a hammer between the eyes.

On my way right now. Her heavy boots clunked down the molychromium decking.

He was quiet for a moment, but she felt his worry.

I'll be perfectly fine. There's no better candidate.

::You couldn't send one of the imperials?::

I'm already awake and this has to be done now. And can you please *stop using the term "imperials" like a slur?*

::Sorry.::

Liar.

He chuckled in her mind. ::Tia and I haven't found anything yet, not so much as a shoe left behind, and certainly no people.::

Keep looking. We know they're there, on one of the powered levels. It's not like they're sleeping in EMUs on the lower decks.

There were a lot of powered levels to check through, sadly.

::Will do. Kayla— Be careful.::

I always *am.*

::Liar.::

14

Kayla met Larsa at an airlock she hadn't known about.

"This being the closest I can get you."

"Understood. One of the rebels, I think his name is Shimwell, is coming to spot me as soon as he's suited up." Kayla closed the screen on her helmet, ready to go.

"Wait for the spotting of Shimwell. Is protocol." Larsa looked adamant, but all Kayla could think about was the frantic beeping of the temperature sensors in the engine control room.

"I'll wait for him outside. You go back." The engineer was practically hopping from foot to foot in her rush to get back to the monitors.

"Spacewalking is not solo for anyone on board."

"Understood." Kayla picked up the toolkit, stepped past the first door of the airlock, and hit the mechanism to vent the atmosphere. "Ariel's monitoring me, and Noar will be guiding me," she said over the comm. "I'll be fine." She gave a thumbs up, activated the magmatism in her boots, and opened the airlock to space.

In moments she was out the second door and climbing onto the *Yari*'s outer surface. It was beautiful… and terrifying. She immediately hooked her tether to the link near the door. Space was so wide open all around her, it felt like she would be pulled into the emptiness at any moment.

Better to not consider it at all.

She kept her head down and started moving. Noar had told her to take a straight path "down" in relation to the "floor" of the airlock. He would lead her from there via comm.

It wasn't long before she heard Shimwell. "I'm at the airlock, coming out." He'd keep watch there, ready to come for her if she got into trouble.

Which she had better not.

Please let this be as easy as jamming a telescoping rod into the door to wedge it open.

As she approached, it quickly became apparent that things were not as simple as she'd hoped. The pewter gray of the ship's heat shielding was interrupted by some kind of black... blob. The closer she got, the stranger it looked. It wasn't a single blob; it was a mass of smaller blobs, which seemed to crawl over one another. Each had a delicate blue light twinkling on and off along its dark exterior.

What the frutt?

The vibrations from the stress testing rumbled through the ship's outer shell and into her boots. The exhaust shaft must be the perfect conduit. When she was within fifteen meters she could begin to discern the true shape of the blobs on the pile. They looked like a mass of... octopuses? Cephalopods in space? Each was no larger than her hand with fingers spread. Bulbous "heads" pointed up as tentacle appendages curled and crawled around each other. Occasionally one would break away from the pile and "swim" through space, circling until it found a spot that was more to its liking.

"Its?" Was she looking at critters? "Do you see this?" she asked Noar over the comms. The cam in her suit sent images down to the control room.

"I... have no idea what to make of that."

The life forms were completely unconcerned by her presence.

"Well, I'm not getting any closer until someone can tell me

193

what those creatures are." They better do it quickly because based on the schematics her suit's datapad listed, the things covered the vent.

"I'm checking the *Lorius*'s database against the image," Trinan said. Apparently the whole ship was awake and involved. "I doubt the *Yari* has any similar data in its complinks."

"No need," Ariel said. "That is having the shape and color patterns of a rook."

Kayla froze, not even daring to breathe.

Suddenly everyone was flashing mental pictures back and forth, rapidly comparing their own memories of the rooks against the image from her suitcam. The *Yari*'s crew had the most experience, and their memories flooded her mind with proof that despite the incredible disparity in size, she was definitely looking at rooks.

Her breath came back, shallow and loud in her eyes. Ice prickled across her skin.

"Get out of there, Kayla," Trinan said, at the same time she heard Shimwell say, "I'm coming to you." That's all she needed, more chances of something startling the miniature rooks.

Strident beeping filled the comms as Larsa spoke from the control room. "Needing to abort the test, captain." Natali then argued against it.

"Everyone shut up!" Though her mind was screaming for silence, Kayla's voice was no more than a hiss, terrified that the rooks—baby rooks?—would hear even that. "Shut up and stay where you are." She held still, watching to see if that startled them.

Not at all. They just kept piling on top of the heat vent, squirming to get under, over, and around each other for the best spot. Blue lights shimmered down the rooks' tentacles in hypnotic patterns. What drew them: the vibrations? The warmth?

Kayla pushed all other thoughts from her mind and cautiously, slowly, took her first step backward.

Nothing happened. She hadn't realized she'd been holding her breath in anticipation of a much deadlier outcome. She forced herself to breathe normally as she took another step backward, and another.

Just as she convinced herself she might survive the encounter, the entire heap of rooks dislodged from the ship in a flurry, like a startled flock of birds taking flight. Several of them winked out of existence entirely. Kayla ducked reflexively as the cloud launched toward her.

I can't believe I'm going to die out here, like this.

Instead of attacking, the creatures swirled around her, their black bodies gleaming. They tumbled and bumped into each other. Occasionally one would bounce off her EMU and ricochet back into the cloud. Apparently that was vastly entertaining, because they kept doing it.

::Don't move:: Corinth said. ::We're venting the engine room.::

The vent's three giant louvers, which protected the inner workings from ice, cranked open successfully. Her hope that the activity would draw the rooks' attention was dashed as they continued to investigate her. One rook landed on her forearm and wrapped its stubby tentacles around her suit like a wrist chronometer. Her mind screamed *Get it off!* but she couldn't have moved if she wanted to, her body locked in place by fear.

::It worked! Kay, it worked.::

This time. The test was only half over, though, and the rooks had looked plenty happy piling onto the vent and trapping it shut before.

Now what? She couldn't stay crouched out here forever, terrified to move. The creatures grew bolder, settling on her arm, shoulder, and even the helmet of her EMU for seconds at a time before flitting away. Maybe she could—

All rational thought ceased when, from nowhere, an utterly massive ebony form blinked into being no more than three hundred meters from her face. It was so large that she couldn't see around it to the other end. The breath caught in her throat. "Holy—"

Someone had hit comms, and all she could hear was the

proximity alert klaxons blaring.

No shit.

The babies spiraled up in a frenetic cloud of bodies that was either extremely happy or very, very upset. They zoomed over to the gigantic black form, winking out of sight, then appearing again many meters ahead.

People shouted in her ear to run back to the hatch, while in the background a debate raged about why they couldn't just shoot at the enormous life form when it was so close to the ship.

The shape of the blackness blotting out the stars shifted as the adult rook—for that's what it had to be—reared up. She could only stand there stupidly, watching as it rotated up up up, and its tentacles came into view. Beautiful blue lights lit patterns along its skin.

She flinched back when the tentacles flared wide, and then the rook settled on the ship's surface with the gentleness of an atomic bomb landing, its tentacles draping like a skirt in each direction. The force knocked the *Yari* out of its current position. A noise that must have been sub-hyperstream thrusters firing reached her as Ariel corrected for the impact.

Kayla waited for a terrible ripping sound or a wrenching crunch as the rook went to work destroying the ship. Instead…

…nothing.

Nothing happened. The rook seemed perfectly content to sit still, lights glowing almost peacefully, tentacles laying along the ship's hull with its bulbous… head? pointing out to space. The tiny rooks swooped and circled around the adult, brushing against the creature in apparent happiness.

Her first coherent thought since the adult's arrival was: *Run!*

She released the magnetic lock on her boots, and hit the retract mechanism on her tether almost simultaneously. She barely kept her grip on her toolkit as the tether yanked her back to the airlock.

"Has the vent been open long enough to combat the overheating?" she whispered over the comms. Would the arrival of the adult be enough to distract them from piling onto the vent again? Already one or two of the baby rooks seemed to have noticed her movement.

"For the time, yes," Larsa answered. "But the test has many hours of the lasting still, and heat build of major for the duration."

Of course it was.

Shimwell caught Kayla as she neared the airlock and pulled her in. "Then we'll handle it if a blocked vent becomes an issue again. For now, let us the frutt back into the ship."

ON BOARD THE IMPERIAL STEALTH SHIP *STEEL DOVE*, WYRD SPACE

Senior Commander of the IDC, and now Occupation Leader Jersain Vega, fought off an attack from Agira with all her might. They'd been sitting together on the loveseat in their tiny cabin aboard the stealth ship, when all of a sudden Agira had blasted her across the room with telekinetic punch to the chest. The force slammed Jersain into the wall and knocked the wind out of her. Another punch followed that before Jersain had got her shields up.

She would have been really pissed...

... if she hadn't asked for it, quite literally.

The trip from Falanar to Ordoch was a long one. With little else to do aboard the cramped *Steel Dove*, Jersain had been practicing with her psi powers every chance she got. She now had an excellent command of them, and felt confident in her ability to protect herself. Which would be essential, considering they were going to a planet populated by psionics who hated her and her kind. She'd ordered her thrall to spring sneak attacks on her, both telekinetic and telepathic, to see how quickly she could recognize them and react.

Not that the shot to the chest had been hard to recognize.

Jersain fought back, flinging a spear of psi force at Agira's head. Agira deflected the bolt even as she lifted Jersain off the floor, shield and all. Jersain winced as she collided with the ceiling.

"You have to think in three dimensions when it comes to fighting a psionic," Agira called, and let her fall to the floor.

Jersain glared at her thrall. She'd grown sick of that advice, mostly because she kept forgetting in the crucial moments. She opened her mind and let the full force of her power—Vayne's stolen power—rush through her. Vayne was a stronger psionic than Agira could hope to be: surely Jersain could best her, now that she could control her purloined powers.

The fight ranged back and forth in the small cabin. Agira finally burst through Jersain's shield. Instantly she had a telekinetic hand around Jersain's throat, lifting her off the ground and cutting off Jersain's oxygen. She pounded on Agira's shield, clobbering away with all her fading might. Spots appeared in her vision. *Wham, wham, wham*, she hammered desperately. She would *not* lose this fight, not when she was the superior psionic.

She took one last, gigantic swing at Agira's shield, which gave way with the feel of splintering glass. The constriction on her throat faltered. Jersain dragged in a breath and lashed out, knocking Agira to her knees.

Agira immediately withdrew her power from Jersain's throat and set her gently on her feet. Jersain coughed and fought to take a deep breath while Agira rubbed the shoulder Jersain had clobbered.

"Good job," Agira said, and smiled, looking like a proud momma bird gazing at her chick.

Jersain felt inordinately pleased. Well, pleased and annoyed. "I was almost asleep."

"I know." This time her thrall's smile was a little more devious. "But you said you wanted a challenge."

Jersain harrumphed, then relented. She smiled in between coughing and helped Agira to her feet. "I suppose I should thank you for being so devoted to me."

"Even when that devotion means knocking the snot out of you?" Agira blinked her eyes innocently, but Jersain wasn't fooled.

"Try not to enjoy it so much, next time."

Agira laughed, then quieted down as she took a close look at Jersain's throat. "Let me get a cooling cell on that welt. Sit back down."

Jersain was happy to comply. The fight had completely drained her. Now it was over and the adrenaline was starting to fade, she sank onto the sofa like a puddle of melting ice cream. She had enough pride to keep herself upright, but just barely.

Agira returned with a coolant cell in hand and sat beside her. Jersain let her fuss for a moment, twitching the coolant cell into the perfect position, then pulled Agira's hands down onto her lap.

"Enough, I'm fine." Better than fine. She'd beaten a natural-born psionic in a fight. Again. She felt like a warrior. A limp warrior, at the moment, but a warrior nonetheless.

"You did an excellent job keeping your focus, and it took me even longer to break through your shields this time."

Even though Agira said it in a glowing tone, it still irked Jersain to be reminded that she'd faltered her grasp on her shields. It was a strange thing to be trained by one's own thrall, and Jersain struggled with Agira's superiority in this arena. She liked it much better when the balance of power was tipped entirely in her favor.

"Your control has improved immensely in the past few weeks." Agira tilted her head to look at Jersain. "I think you need to continue working on the finer aspects, but—"

"But I'm an excellent blunt-force instrument?" Jersain quipped. Only… it was true. She still struggled to control the minute movements of writing with a stylus with her mind, but she realized only practice could perfect that.

"How does your head feel?" Agira asked, instead of answering the joke.

"Not even a hint of a headache."

"That's a great sign of how far you've come. Controlling your psi powers is much more natural, doesn't take as much mental energy." She gave Jersain's hands a little squeeze.

Jersain herself believed that. Well, she did in part. She really felt that things had become more natural for her, which was amazing considering she'd been psionic for less than a year. What gave her pause was the tremendous amount of success she'd had in recent weeks. Stunning, really, how easily she called the power up without feeling overwhelmed or likely to split at the seams, these days. In the last weeks she'd taken a leap forward, experiencing an almost exponential growth in her abilities when compared to all the months before that. She'd almost convinced herself she'd had a breakthrough.

"They're fading, aren't they." Jersain made it a statement rather than a question, because she already knew the answer. "Vayne's powers: they're starting to fade." Which explained why suddenly she was strong enough to control them.

"Don't say that."

Jersain dropped Agira's hands, unreasonably annoyed. She hadn't known how much she'd wanted to be wrong until her thrall's evasive answer set her off.

"It's true. I feel stronger than ever, as if I'm in control of my power instead of the other way around now, but..." And it was that "but" that made her grind her teeth in frustration.

Instead of pulling away or cringing in the face of Jersain's ill temper, Agira situated herself in the corner of the sofa and drew Jersain against her, so that Jersain's back rested against her chest.

Agira draped her arms around Jersain. "We don't know that for certain. Dolan seemed confident that the procedure would be permanent."

Jersain sighed, the temper bleeding from her body. It wasn't Agira's fault. Agira would give her own powers, and happily, if Jersain asked her to.

"Dolan could never find a permanent solution for himself. I was foolish to think he'd be any more successful with imperial physiology."

Agira didn't answer. There was nothing to say, really. She merely laid her cheek against Jersain's hair.

As far as doing something about the problem... Jersain had

handled that beautifully. The *Steel Dove* should reach Ordoch any day now, and then she'd have her pick from a planet full of psionics.

MAIN REBEL BASE, ORDOCH

Malkor ignored the nasty looks just about every rebel in the base threw their way. Even the presence of Wetham and Ygreda beside himself, and of Rigger, didn't stop Kayla's people from giving them the stink eye.

Same look, different part of the galaxy. Ah, the glorious life of an IDC agent.

On the bright side, he'd earned Ygreda and Aarush's respect on the last day as they thrashed out the details of the extraction plan. It was entirely possible they'd expected him and Rigger to have the combined intelligence of a rodent. Once that preconception had been shattered, they'd all gotten along quite well. Wetham was a bit of a cold fish, but Malkor liked the other two better than he'd expected to. Ygreda was sharp and decisive. She immediately grasped the basics of any plan they came up with and started fleshing it out on her own. Aarush had a real head for tactics and a quietly sarcastic wit. If he wasn't so injured, Malkor would have included him in their plans.

"I have great faith in you, agents," Wetham was saying as they strode along the corridor to the lift. "Rest assured that we'll be doing our part."

"You're certain your people will be able to place the charges at the prison under the cover of darkness tonight?" Malkor asked. "We only have one shot at getting Mesa out. I am hopeful we'll breeze right in, impress them all with our transfer orders, and breeze back out, but if something goes wrong, we're going to need a distraction. Once they know we want Mesa, they'll make sure she's never found."

Wetham nodded. "Aarush assures me his team can handle it."

"The IDs are as flawless as I've ever seen," Ygreda said. She returned the credentials to Malkor, credentials that Rigger had worked up last night after tapping into the imperial infolink network, and which Base Commander Chen had signed electronically this morning. They were dated for tomorrow to give time for the rebels to get the charges in place. They had a rare opportunity to gather intel directly from officers in the occupation forces, something the Wyrd rebels could never do, so they planned to make the most of an evening in the city. The rebels had pointed out which bars the officers frequented, so it would be easy to mingle.

The four stopped outside the lift. "I'll leave you here," Wetham said. "I wish you speed and success with your mission." He bowed, and was headed back the way they came as soon as he straightened.

Ygreda gestured into the lift. "Let's get you packed. Jahnni will take you to the nearest shuttle depot," she said as they rode the lift to the upper level. "You can take the shuttle into Vankir proper from there. The first real test of your IDs won't come until you hit the city gates."

"We won't have a problem," Malkor said. Rigger had been hacking networks and complinks since she was a baby, and forging the octet's needed documents since she was a teenager. There was no doubt in his mind that they'd make it through the outer gates. Things would become decidedly dicey after that.

"Your IDs are loaded with a small amount of credits: all we could spare."

At Ygreda's words, he cut a glance to Rigger, who winked. He cleared his throat to cover a laugh. "Funds won't be a problem."

The Wyrd caught on, and offered a quick smile. "Perhaps when you get back, you can see to our 'funds.'"

Rigger nodded. "I'd be happy to."

The lift opened and Ygreda showed them to a supply room filled floor to ceiling with every item you would need in order to fit in as an imperial, including weapons. He and Rigger were already dressed in imperial army uniforms with their officer rank designated at the collar.

"Once you've equipped yourselves, Jahnni will meet you on the ground level. Anything you need before I leave you?"

"We have everything, thank you." Malkor stepped forward to shake her hand, and Rigger did the same. "We'll contact you on the agreed channel when we're ready for extraction."

"Good luck, agents."

Rigger waited until Ygreda was out of earshot, then said, "We're going to need it."

"Let's at least get to the city before you consider us out of the game, okay?"

She grinned. "Sure thing, boss."

Despite her humor, it was a tense ride to the shuttle depot. Jahnni gave them terse, last-minute intel on the mood inside Vankir City. Apparently there had been a series of protests last night and now the army was on high alert. Admittance to the city had been restricted.

"Oh good," Rigger said, "I love a challenge."

Malkor was less than thrilled to hear about the whole thing. Still, their cover should hold up. What was one more log on the fire?

"Holograms," Jahnni reminded them, and then he set the hovercar down in the shuttle station's lot.

While it was highly unlikely that anyone would recognize Malkor or Rigger if they used their own faces for the IDs, facial recognition programs at the gate would flag them as among the empire's most wanted fugitives.

"You have a head like a bowling ball," Rigger told him as they left Jahnni behind and sauntered to the shuttle station platform.

"For which I have you to thank." Malkor gave her a once over. "I see you've managed to make yourself look a boar."

"You don't remember Ubeca Minstin?" She turned so that he could get a better look.

"Was Ubeca that Madame from Falanar's Pleasure District?" He laughed. "You nailed it."

The shuttle arrived then. He and Rigger surreptitiously checked their ion pistols in their holsters, grabbed their rucksacks, and boarded. They made it to Vankir City proper without incident. Most of the other passengers were Wyrds, and none made eye contact with him or Rigger.

They followed the flow of foot traffic leaving the station. Up ahead, huge flak towers rose out of the dirt, giant sentinels on either side of the gate. The towers were multiple stories tall and had armed sentries. The gate itself was closed. Cross-woven quadtanium panels made for an impressive structure that would be difficult to breach. The panels continued past the guard towers and formed a daunting wall that was interrupted regularly by more well-armed flak towers.

Malkor joined the queue of people wending their way up the hill. Apparently a different gate was used for vehicle traffic. Here, people were being checked one by one for security threats at a station in the base of the flak tower on the right. Judging by the length of the line outside, they had a long wait ahead of them. Thankfully they were inside the massive environmental dome that covered much of this continent's northern plain, so at least the weather outside was pleasant. They waited their turn, moving one slow meter at a time. An hour had passed before they finally entered the tower.

Each handed over their ID to the surly-looking soldier stationed behind a complink terminal, then laid their weapons and packs on the belt to be scanned and waited, albeit anxiously, for the go-ahead. The soldier at the complink certainly seemed to be giving the IDs a triple looking-over.

"Where have you come from?" he asked.

"Senfranco Base."

The soldier arched a brow. "And you arrived this morning? That must have been a rough trip."

"Nothing like flying in the middle of the night, am I right?" Malkor joked. "Our commander has a love affair with missions that need to be done 'yesterday!' I swear, he has ASAP tattooed on his ass."

The guard didn't join in the joke. "What's your business in Vankir?"

"Prisoner transport," Rigger said in her best "quit wasting my time" tone.

Tapping came from behind the desk as the guard's fingers flew over the projected keyboard. "You don't have a barracks designation. Every soldier from another command coming into the city needs to be stationed at a barracks."

"It's just one night: we figured we'd just take rooms wherever we found them."

The guard gave him a flat stare.

This was not going as smoothly as Malkor would like. Then again, most administrators seemed to get off on being officious assholes, so maybe things were par for the course.

"If you're coming into the city overnight," the guard finally said, "you need to be logged at a barracks."

"Fine." Malkor gave Rigger a look to keep her from saying anything else. "Then give us a barrack designation and we'll stay there overnight."

"Can't do that."

Would it hurt their chances of gaining entry to the city if Malkor reached over the desk, grabbed the guard by his lapels and shook the shit out of him?

"Who can?" he forced himself to ask calmly.

"I'll have to make a call. Whose command did you say you were from, again?"

It was practically lunchtime when they finally cleared the gate. But at least they *had* cleared the gate. One hurdle down, who knew how many left to go.

He stood with Rigger in the street on the other side, thoroughly saddened by the view in front of him. Trash littered the street from one end to the other, something that never would have happened before the occupation. A broken sanitation bot lay in a puddle of filth. Another spun in a crazy, ever-widening circle until a passing soldier kicked it back to the gutter. Squat buildings of dull organoplastic made up a shanty town of bars and prostitution and hid the Ordochian architecture behind.

"Let's get away from here," he said. The change his people had brought to the once great city angered him.

Away from the busy gate, the place looked more like he remembered—a confection of swirls and arches, loops and graceful turns. It was as if the buildings were having conversations with each other, one informed the other, and so on and so on down the street; as if the entire city had been built somewhere else and set in place exactly as it was now. It was amazing what architects and engineers could do when they didn't have to build the machinery to build the buildings. Amazing what the power of the mind could accomplish.

"Will we ever have a city such as this?" Rigger breathed, her voice softened with awe. "It's like riding through a cloud."

"We'd probably have to stop warring with each other, first." Which seemed unlikely. The blemishes on the city, the stains and dark spots existed anywhere an imperial installation had been built. That was less a commentary on imperial architecture, though, and more on necessity. Occupying armies only had time for one consideration: function.

And that explained why every imperial installation looked like a short stack of toddler blocks. No wonder they had commandeered so many of the original Wyrd buildings for their own use.

Both the prison and their barracks were located in the city center, not too far from the entrance to the massive Complex of Oligarchs. All the major ruling families on Ordoch had huge ancestral homes here, along with markets, restaurants, entertainment centers... The noble class—for lack of a better term—could live almost entirely within the Complex if it was so inclined, and this made the Complex more of a city within a city. The Reinumon palace, the home seat of Kayla's family and now center of the occupation government, was there as well. When he'd come to Ordoch as part of the IDC contingent five years ago, he'd spent most of his time within the massive area.

Their barracks had an excellent view of brilliant towers in all shapes and sizes rising over the verdant forest that formed the "wall" between the Complex and the rest of the city.

"Let's go check in," Malkor said. "I have a feeling it's going to be a long night of bar hopping before we get to the loose talk and valuable intel."

15

THE *YARI*

It was midday before Kayla woke up. She hadn't gotten to sleep until "sunrise" ship time. Now that she was awake and the events of last night came back to her, it seemed like she might still be dreaming.

Rooks? Seriously? And not just one, either. Once the first adult was happily settled, a second had blinked into place above it, looming like an enemy spacecraft. It hadn't made a threatening move, though. Instead, it gently—for a rook—rested its gargantuan body on the *Yari*'s hull beside the first, knocking the ship out of position once again and sending the crew into fits in Kayla's comm. Luckily Ariel had been at the helm, and had been able to reestablish their position. The last thing they needed was for the *Yari* to crash into the *Lorius*, or worse yet, pass through the Tear, leaving a second of the engine in a cave on Ordoch.

The two "parent" rooks then seemed to curl up together, the lights on their bodies making a gentle counterpoint to the vibrations of the ship caused by the stress test.

From their size alone, it was hard to imagine that they were living creatures. But to see how they had acted last night, and especially the "babies," they were so animal-like that it seemed unlikely another intelligence was using them as a mere vessel.

What did she know about xenobiology, though? The only wildlife she was familiar with was on Ordoch or in the Fengar Swamp. The only humanoid races she knew of were from the Wyrd Worlds or the empire, and that physiology was so similar that they had to have come from a single ancestor some time in their shared history.

One good thing about the rooks: her close encounter—and the fear of her demise—had broken the ice between her and Vayne. He'd rushed to see her as soon as she returned, berating her for her recklessness even while feelings of gratefulness that she was safe flowed into her mind.

On the downside, he'd reported that his search with Tia'tan for Zimmerman had turned up nothing.

Kayla levered herself out of her bunk and got to her feet. She changed into a tunic and leggings, then pulled on her boots and fastened her kris daggers to her thighs. The familiar weight of the knives was comforting. She'd spent so much time in her EMU lately that she hardly ever had them on.

I am so not cut out for life in space.

As she was getting dressed she commed the control room. "Are the rooks still out there?"

One of the rebels replied: "The stress test finished an hour ago, and they departed after that. Seems it really was the vibrations that had drawn them."

She didn't need to be told that. Fifteen minutes with the rooks had made it clear they loved the ship's vibrations. Or at least enjoyed them. The adult rooks undulated a sleepy light show with the pulses, the babies being a little more exuberant.

On her way out the door she checked with Hekkar via mobile comm to see if he'd heard anything from Ordoch. Nothing. Hopefully no news of Malkor was good news, at this point.

::Good, you're awake:: Vayne said in her mind. ::I'm meeting with Tia'tan and Toble in the commissary for lunch if you're up for it.::

Damn lack of psi powers. In answer, she kicked her steps

into a jog and reached the commissary in double time.

When the commissary doors slid open she heard Hekkar's voice: "Well, if it isn't the rook charmer."

"I thought we were going with rook babysitter?" Tia'tan called back.

Kayla rolled her eyes. "Very funny."

"Ooo! How 'bout, 'Kayla, queen of the rooks?'" That last one was from Toble.

"I'm glad you're all having so much fun at my expense." Kayla made her way to the food synthesizer in search of a hot, caffeinated beverage of any variety. Vayne met her there. "What, no snappy nickname for me?"

He smiled, but it seemed to have a shadow behind it. "I'll come up with something." In a lower, more serious voice he said, "I'm glad you're okay."

"Me too." She grabbed her steaming cup and followed Vayne back to the table where the others sat. She, Vayne, Tia'tan, Toble, and Hekkar had the commissary to themselves for a moment. Better get down to business before that changed. "What have I missed?"

Hekkar spoke up first. "As I said earlier, no word from the boss, but that's to be expected. Corinth is still sleeping. He was beside himself with worry for you, and finally crashed right before you did. Vid's keeping an eye on him."

"Good. He needs to sleep more, anyway."

Hekkar grimaced. "He thought you'd say something like that. You might want to dial back the overprotectiveness. Trust me when I say, young men hate that kind of thing."

Kayla blinked, her mug of tea suspended midair as she froze in the act of lifting it. The whole table paused, waiting for her reply. She fought the urge to snap back that she'd parent Corinth however she liked, and how dare he tell her how to handle her *il'haar*'s welfare.

Right away, she realized it for a knee-jerk reaction, her instant outrage fueled by her own fears that she was a poor substitute for a parent or his own *ro'haar*.

::Easy:: Vayne said. ::He's not wrong.:: He brushed against her mental shields and she lowered them without thinking, letting him in.

I know that, she practically snapped. She forced herself to take a sip of the red tea she'd synthed up. Conversation at the table returned to normal.

Images of Corinth came to the surface, how young he had been, how frail. How undernourished they'd both been for five years.

::Kayla... *This* is how he is now.:: Vayne sent an entirely different set of images of Corinth. He looked healthy and well fed. Taller. He wasn't so hesitant, and he actually smiled. ::*This* is Corinth. You need to let those outdated images of Corinth go.::

As if it were that easy. It wasn't something she was prepared to face at the moment. Focusing on the immediate tasks in front of her was much more appealing than self-examination.

When she didn't answer Vayne, he let the matter drop.

"Larsa said the stress test was a success," Hekkar continued. "She and Noar are also still sleeping, but Larsa said she plans to get back to work on drive construction as soon as she's up."

"Here's hoping Malkor and the rebels can get those three engineers Larsa needs," Tia'tan said. "Wetham said he's holding off on sending more parts for the drive until we know for sure that we'll be able to complete it."

Kayla could only imagine her sister's response. "That must have gone down well with Natali."

Tia'tan held out her hand and wobbled it side to side. "They're... still in discussions."

"She was being very politic about it," Vayne said, and Hekkar's eyes bugged.

"*That* was Natali being politic?"

Vayne gave him a strange look, like he couldn't tell if the agent was kidding or not. "You didn't think so?"

Hekkar cleared his throat awkwardly, and Kayla decided to take pity on him by changing the subject.

"What about the *stepa at es*?"

"Which ones?" Vayne asked.

Fair point. They had entirely too many unknowns running around loose on the ship, rooks included. "Officer Kendrik and the others?" Tia'tan made it a point to discuss the changing codes with Tanet every morning, offering to help remember his, which allowed them access to the prisoners. Thankfully, because there was no way Vayne would violate Tanet's mental shields again to read his mind.

"I visited them this morning," Toble said. "It's been less than a day since Vayne swapped out the calorie pack, so I didn't notice any improvement yet. I have them on a taper, stepping down the dose of sedatives they receive at a gradual pace. There's no telling how long they've been on such a high dose. We have to manage their withdrawal carefully. We should start seeing an increase in their alertness and cognitive function soon." He frowned. "They need real medical care for the brain damage they've received—it can't wait."

"We can't leave them there," Vayne said. "Nobody should be kept prisoner."

She heard her brother's unspoken, *like I was*. She sympathized with him, and knew seeing Kendrik and the others like that only reminded him of his own captivity, but Kayla wasn't about to let more people into the general mix if she wasn't certain that it was the right thing to do.

She looked at Tia'tan. "Have you had any luck locating the ship's first officer, or other crew members?"

Tia'tan shook her head. "None. We've been through all the powered sections. There are no souls to be found, and no shielded psionic dead spots." She tapped her fingers on the tabletop. "I'm starting to think Kendrik really is crazy, and Zimmerman is long dead."

"What about the unpowered levels?" Everyone turned to look at Hekkar as soon as he asked the question.

Vayne started to reply but Kayla kicked him under the table. He clearly had a nasty remark to make about Hekkar's intelligence, and she found it much more satisfying to cut him off than to argue about his attitude toward imperials.

"We know they're not living full time in EMUs," Tia'tan said, rolling with it. "But that doesn't mean they couldn't spend most of their time on one of the lower levels, coming back to the powered section to eat and change out of EMUs every so often."

"That sounds like a shitty way to live," Kayla said.

Hekkar shook his head. "That's not what I meant. What if one of the levels, or even a section of a level that we think is damaged, actually has power and life support? Think about it." He leaned forward, elbows on the table, working his hypothesis out as he spoke. "We all believe the lower levels are damaged or have compromised power relays because Ida told us that, right?"

Everyone nodded.

"And we can see the evidence on the ship's diagnostic," Toble pointed out.

"Right," Hekkar said, "the same diagnostic that shows us that Kendrik's level has no power." He let that sink in a moment. "I've been to a lot of the lower levels and they are definitely without power. But what if one level only *seems* like it has no power? Zimmerman, or whoever it was, had enough savvy and tech intelligence to wake crew members from cryosleep without Ida and her crew realizing it. What if they're hiding this, also?"

"And before now," Tia'tan said, "the captain had no reason to think they were capable of such a thing."

::Or that's what she claimed, at least.:: Vayne's mental voice had the same skepticism Kayla was beginning to feel when it came to the captain. She couldn't put her finger on any one thing, but...

::Same. She's certainly close-mouthed when it comes to the topic of her missing crew.::

And why they're missing in the first place, if they're not all insane.

Kayla thought about Hekkar's theory. "Seems at least

213

possible." More than possible. If it really was just a matter of walking around the powered sections with the psionic senses spread wide, Ida would have found the *stepa* long before now. "We've only been hitting the closed levels strategically, stopping at weapons depots and food stores—by no means searching the entire deck. If they hid in another part of the level, a small part, they could close the blast doors to that section and have their own environment."

Vayne looked skeptical. "That would have to be pretty lucky, them choosing a spot to hide that we never had reason to go near."

"What if they had help?" It was starting to seem more and more likely that they did. But from who? And more importantly, was that good or bad for Kayla and her *il'haars*?

"At this point," Tia'tan said, "we have nothing to lose by searching."

"We'll have plenty of time," Hekkar replied. "Ship's manifest shows that we've gotten all the food stores from the lower levels. Unless there's a different commodity that we should be collecting in bulk, we're out of work."

Vayne drawled, "You might as well go back home, then."

Too little, too late, but Kayla kicked his shin again for good measure.

"You do know that's not going to happen, right?" Hekkar asked. "At some point, you're just going to have to accept that we're here to help… and here to stay."

Kayla waited for Vayne's reply, not sure how well the direct approach was going to go over. He surprised her by simply shrugging. "We'll see."

"On a different topic," Tia'tan said, clearly not willing to let that exchange continue, "at what point do we bring all of this to Natali?"

Uneasy looks all around. Kayla disliked keeping secrets from her sister. Natali was her leader, after all, and a great ally. However, she was also completely autocratic—once Natali knew what was going on, Kayla and the others lost control of how to handle the situation. Natali might be inclined to take their advice... but then again, she might not be.

"Let's wait a little bit," Kayla finally said, trying not to feel like a traitor.

VANKIR CITY, ORDOCH

Malkor and Rigger spent the day touring the city. They did all sorts of things people of leisure did, such as checking the security measures at the armory—moderate, could be breached by a large group with adequate tactical support—running a tally on the various weaponry soldiers were equipped with on the city streets and on guard duty—ion pistols, blasters, and pulse rifles mostly, standard army fare with no plasma weapons in sight—counting assault vehicles—not many on the ground in the city, but they had the air space on lockdown—and even taking a transport to the outskirts of the city where the hydroelectric plant that supplied the bulk of the city's energy was working away—the plant was more of a fortress than the prison itself; there was no way a rebel incursion could take that over without heavy casualties.

Which was why they also visited the energy distribution center and took note of the location of the major transformer blocks.

Much easier to cripple or take control of Vankir's microgrid than destroy its power-generating capabilities for years to come, especially considering that they were hoping to retake the planet a lot sooner than that.

The sun was setting by the time they headed back to the barracks.

"I know the empire managed to take out Ordoch's entire state-run linkhub and set up their own," Malkor said as they walked. "Would the rebels be able to crash the new imperial linkhub?"

Rigger slowed a fraction to give more distance between them and a group of soldiers ahead before continuing. Luckily, the Wyrds on the streets gave them a wide berth. "Access to the linkhub and its code are the empire's best-guarded secret, according to Ygreda. I tell you, that cyber-attack five years ago was the single most brilliant move of the entire coup. Imperial hackers will be feeding off the glory of that hack for decades." She sounded a little wistful.

"Score one for the empire for putting our best criminals to work."

Rigger agreed. "Cyber-attacks were largely a thing of the past on Ordoch, so for once the empire was ahead, technologically speaking. The rebels just haven't caught up. It took time for the Wyrds to even get to grips with the idea of an occupation after the coup. Even longer still for there to be any concerted effort or organization of a rebellion. With little access to information or communications systems, it was damn near impossible for the rebels to get their shit together." She sighed. "I wish I'd been here years ago; I could have gotten them up and running with a darkhub much quicker than they did on their own."

He clapped her on the back. "Don't worry, you're still a legend to me."

"Yeah, I'd be famous... if all our missions weren't classified." She winked. Lights around the city came on as dusk settled. Their barracks came into view, bustling with soldiers during the post-shift, pre-carousing hour. "Come on," she said, "I'm sure you owe me a drink for some feat of tech genius or other."

He laughed. "Probably more than one."

Whether by accident or design, the guard had assigned Malkor and Rigger to the rowdy barracks. As the out-of-town "guests," they'd been treated to an honorary bar crawl. It seemed there was no shortage of ramshackle imperial bars to patronize, and the soldiers had a tab going at all of them. If the drinks were shit, at least the company was convivial.

There wasn't much else for an invading army to do with their evening, really.

As the enlisted soldiers got completely bombed, Malkor

and Rigger followed First Sergeant Toomalia Huds, Tooms to her friends, to a quieter establishment frequented by officers. It reminded Malkor of the time he and Hekkar had tracked down Carsov—the TNV specialists that broke Kayla out of the containment foam after TNV was released at Isonde's first attempted wedding—at an army bar. This time, however, the music didn't screech to a halt when they walked in, and no one sent them looks that said kindly drop dead.

Being incognito was a good thing, tonight.

It was easy to see that the Wyrd-run "bar" had been a cocktail lounge prior to the occupation. Various nooks for seated and standing conversation between small groups offered privacy while still giving the place an inclusive feel. The decor was probably edgy by Ordochian standards. Malkor merely found it tasteful and not overly obnoxious.

Of course, the imperials had classed down the joint, bringing in table games, loud music, and that perennial favorite: darts.

"Drinks are on us," Malkor said to Tooms.

She clapped him on the back and gave them a smile. "I knew I liked you guys. Come on, I'll introduce you around."

The bar served Ordochian instead of imperial liquors, which was a damn shame because they were delicious, and he and Rigger had too big of a day planned tomorrow to really enjoy them. Tooms introduced them to several staff officers who held various positions within the Complex of Oligarchs. Tooms got ragged on for being low man on the totem pole, but she shut them up handily after beating all comers at darts, even Rigger. The atmosphere was very genial and good natured. They were something of superstars, coming—supposedly—from Senfranco Base.

Thank the stars Base Commander Chen had brought him up to speed on the trials and tribulations of living in a tropical paradise.

"You know, we kind of hate you, right?" one of the officers said, after Malkor gave an enthusiastic tale about surfing at sunrise. Rigger ordered drinks all around, again, after that.

It was actually fun... too much fun. As the camaraderie

continued into the night, Malkor felt less and less comfortable in his borrowed uniform. In another life, he might have been friends with these people, Tooms especially. Instead, he was their enemy, using their willing friendship to steal secrets from them like the lowest kind of thief.

He was a traitor.

There. He'd finally acknowledged it. It wasn't just that Vega had branded him a traitor to the empire when she blamed her crimes on him and his octet. Deep down, in his heart, he was betraying the empire, using the skills they'd taught him. He was here to aid their greatest enemy, and undermine all these soldiers' hard work, day in and day out.

He looked at the faces of the officers gathered around the table, drinks in hand, laughing and swapping stories. If he had to, if it came right down to it in this very moment, would he kill these people for the cause of Ordoch's freedom?

Could he?

Shit. What the frutt had he gotten himself into, gotten the octet into?

Joining the rebellion was a lot easier in the abstract. Here in the concrete world, it really sucked. The look in her eyes as the evening wore on showed that Rigger felt the same.

"Did you hear the new head of the occupation is an IDC commander?" Tooms asked. "Can you frutting believe it?"

"Who frutted who to make that happen?"

"I saw that on the news vids this morning; no way that's real."

Malkor still couldn't believe it had happened, that Vega had mind-controlled her way to the head of what was purely an army operation.

"Frutting IDC," Rigger added to the conversation. "Gotta get their nose into everything."

"I'm telling you, it's not possible. The general wouldn't even piss on an IDC agent if they were on fire."

"I hear the Council of Seven intervened to make it happen."

That brought out a loud list of reasons why the council had failed the empire.

Tooms pounded the table to get their attention. "It's true about the IDC commander, Evie saw her."

Heads swiveled in unison until everyone was staring at the petite woman who drank sparingly and said even less. Tooms egged her on with an elbow. "Tell 'em, Evie."

"Gee thanks, Tooms." She rolled her eyes. "Fine, I saw her, she's here already."

What? Not possible. Isonde and Ardin hadn't even arrived yet, and they were flying in the fastest ship the IDC had. They hadn't even started discussions with Ordoch to revisit the idea of formulating a cure for the TNV.

"Evie's a staff sergeant for Base Commander Aretes," Tooms said as an aside, which meant Evie was exactly the person Malkor wanted to talk to. She was in a positon to see and hear the highest-level communications about the occupation.

"She's a real piece of work," Evie said. "First, she arrives in a fancy new stealth ship, parks it right on the lawn of the Reinumon palace. Then she marches straight off the bird and into Commander Aretes's office without a word to anyone. Like she already owned the place."

Apparently the army has something faster. Shit.

"I saw that," a guy named Heron said. "I was on watch at the time."

"She walks right in while we're planning the resupply of the outpost on Tera and orders everyone out." Evie chuckled, a chuckle that turned into a laugh as she remembered the moment. "You should have seen Aretes. She was like, 'Whoever you are, get the frutt out of my office, and close the door behind you.' She didn't even bother to stand. She knew damn well who the woman was, wearing that ridiculous IDC dress uniform, and Aretes ordered her out like she was a new recruit."

"How did she handle that?" Malkor asked. Probably tore someone's head off. At least she would have at IDC headquarters.

"Actually, it was kind of odd. She didn't say anything, just looked over at one of the people who came with her," Evie said. "It was definitely a Wyrd, the facial features gave her away."

Being on Ordoch so long, the soldiers would know how to tell friend from foe based on ethnicity, even if the difference was subtle.

"The Wyrd had this oversized conical bag with her. It was just that, that one look, and then we were all marching out of there." Evie looked up, making eye contact with him. "One second I'm standing there, waiting for Aretes to give her the business, next I'm out in the hall."

It was clear that she couldn't quite make sense of what had happened. Unfortunately the picture was becoming all too clear for him. He needed to talk to Isonde, stat.

Evie shrugged, putting the unsettling moment from her mind. "After that, she commandeered Aretes's office, and spent the rest of the day calling in soldiers from all over the city, demanding reports." Her humor returned. "Nobody looked pleased when they came out of a meeting with her."

Tooms made a sour face. "What does IDC know about military missions and running an occupation?"

"Nothing," Heron said, "that's what." In a less classy place, Malkor had the impression Heron would have spat on the floor with that statement.

"What a cluster frutt this is going to be," another of the officers said, setting off another round of head shaking and cursing.

Rigger lifted her half-empty drink. "Well, here's to the Council of Seven, for royally screwing us, yet again."

The next morning, Malkor woke up feeling like shit.

And not because he'd had too much to drink.

If something went wrong trying to get the scientist out of prison this morning and they had to use the charges the rebels had set, people were going to get hurt. Good people. Hard-working soldiers who, from what he'd heard last night, didn't want to be here. After the night-out vibe had faded and the alcohol-fueled melancholy had set in, he and Rigger had listened to story after story from people who missed their families back in the empire, who missed not being an invading army.

The occupation was never meant to last this long. And the overall feeling was that it shouldn't continue. When Rigger asked if they felt heartened by Operation Redouble and the incoming soldiers and resources, most said they hoped it meant they would be relieved of duty and sent back. Several questioned the mission and if they'd accomplished anything at all in five years. The overall feeling was one of futility.

Good for the rebels, at least.

He and Rigger got dressed, thanked Tooms for the evening, and then grabbed a transport to the prison.

"Well that sucked," Rigger said as they rode. He could only nod in perfect agreement.

"Focus on the mission," he said, as much to himself as to her. As an IDC agent, they'd both done plenty of distasteful things, things that didn't sit well. Focusing on the good they were doing was the only way to get through it.

"That ship had damn well better fly," Rigger replied, and gave him a half-smile as they exited the transport.

The prison lot had plenty of beat-up hovercars, service vehicles, and tactical vehicles, but what caught Malkor's eye were the two sleek luxury hovercars, with fresh indigo paint and the imperial seal on both sides, waiting out front. Some bigwig in the occupation must be visiting today, which was drawing a whole lot more attention to the place than he would like on a day he had to run an op.

Vega? The odds seemed impossible that she would be right here, right now. With the way their luck ran, though...

The guards on the prison steps looked edgy—not a good sign. But with eyes peeled for external threats, they only glanced at his and Rigger's IDs before waving them through the doors. Security inside was much tighter. A line of Wyrds, likely there for visiting hours, folded back and forth on itself, fitting as many people as they could into the space in front of the first security checkpoint.

Apparently an imperial uniform was a fast ticket to the

front, because the guards called them up immediately, ignoring the Wyrds who must have been there a while already. In this instance, though, he didn't mind abusing the system. Get in, get Mesa, get out. That's all he wanted to do.

They had their weapons catalogued and locked up, their bags searched, tagged, and hung on pegs for them to collect on their way out, and they had their mobile comms and datapads scanned before being returned. By then Malkor was thankful just to be able to keep his belt.

The guard buzzed them through the gate and waved them down a long corridor as if Malkor and Rigger knew where they were going. No doubt visitors would have been escorted through the prison. Hallways branched off in each direction, so they followed signs toward maximum security. The prison was as ugly inside as it was out. It had been built module-style, each section prefabbed in a factory, packed, brought to Ordoch, and popped up in place. Over the years, it had been expanded as the need to incarcerate Wyrds had increased. The organoplastic wore different colors determined by exposure to light, and they traveled into the newest—and thus darkest gray—section of the prison. It wasn't the most secure of facilities, but considering Ordoch didn't have *any* prisons, this was the best the army could do.

They showed their IDs at the interior checkpoint and got buzzed in to speak with the guard at the desk, the gatekeeper who knew where everyone was and what everyone was doing.

"Names?" The guard, whose tag said Lassar, held out a hand for their IDs.

Malkor and Rigger gave them, then waited while Lassar scanned their IDs. Malkor aimed for "casual" while Rigger stood stiff, going for "very official." It was a combo that usually played well on a mission—folks tended to dislike one type of personality, which gave them an instant sympathy for the other.

Lassar, it seemed, was all business. He scrutinized their faces, compared them first to the IDs in his hand, then to the image that came up on his complink, before finally returning the IDs. "What's your agenda here today?"

Malkor might outrank her, but Lassar had clearly related to Rigger's serious mien and directed the question to her, so she answered. "Prisoner transport. We're here to collect one Pipa Mesa and escort her to Senfranco Base, per Base Commander Chen's orders." Malkor held out his datapad as she spoke, showing the orders.

The guard at the desk frowned as he took the orders. "You're not on the schedule."

Shit. How crucial was that going to be?

Rigger took a polite approach. "I apologize for the inconvenience. Our orders came down at the last minute; things had to get shifted around."

Lassar's expression didn't change from his frown. Apparently he took his job seriously and actually followed schedules and read orders, instead of just waving people by. Just their luck.

Malkor looked back the way they'd come. The entire corridor was empty. Family members who came to visit were sent to a different series of checkpoints and waiting rooms. He and Rigger were the only people there on official business this morning. Time to be a little less polite. "I can see that the schedule is quite full at the moment." He nodded toward the datapad Lassar still held. "But as you can see, we will be taking prisoner 23-541 with us today, per Base Commander Brid Chen's orders. Flagged highest priority."

"Wait, prisoner 23-541?" The way Lassar asked for confirmation had the hairs standing up on the back of Malkor's neck. He set the orders down and typed something into his complink.

Then the whole op started to slide sideways. Malkor felt it like a physical shift in his footing. At the same time, Rigger slipped her hand into her pocket, the one that held her mobile comm and thus the detonation code for the charges set around the base of the prison. They were already inside the gates, it was just a matter of locating Mesa's cell...

Lassar reached for the phone on his desk. "I'm going to have to call my superior. If you'll just wait a moment..."

His superior? Not Chen, to confirm that the orders he signed were authentic?

Shit.

Lassar was turned away from them, speaking quietly into the phone, so Rigger leaned closer to Malkor and whispered, "Time to walk away from this one."

She was right, damnit.

Lassar glanced back over his shoulder at them, and Malkor gave him an encouraging smile. So close.

At that moment footsteps sounded at the end of one of the halls beyond. A voice he knew all too well could be heard as several people rounded the corner.

"I appreciate the constraints you're operating under," a woman said. "So far, however, your interrogation techniques have failed to produce results."

And there she was—Senior Commander Vega herself, talking to the general he assumed used to be in charge of the occupation.

"I'm placing Agent Schäffer in charge of interrogation, effective immediately. The IDC has some techniques that might prove more... effective."

It was the relish with which she said that last word that turned his stomach. Worse than that, though, he recognized the prisoner being led by a guard, following in Vega's wake: Mesa. No way would anyone believe General Chen had sent orders to retrieve Mesa to Senfranco Base when Vega was taking possession of the same prisoner.

"Our mistake," he said, but by now they were way past that. He felt the locked gate at his back, and Vega's curious stare as her party approached. His hologram better be flawless because if she recognized them, their lives were over.

"Wait a minute—" Lassar said, but Malkor ignored him.

"Now, Rigger!"

The insane *bang* of the charges detonating ripped through the air. Everyone covered their ears reflexively and hit the floor. Sirens blared into life; klaxons muted in the wake of the explosion's massive concussion of sound. A second explosion, much closer this time, rocked the prison, and the lights blacked out.

Inky darkness ruled, close and suffocating. Ringing sounded in his ears and the entire world felt muffled. *Holy shit—that was way too much explosive.*

Seconds later emergency lighting came up and he staggered to his feet. The dimly lit corridor filled with smoke.

"Get the gate," he shouted to Rigger. She seemed to understand, and lunged over the guard's station to access the controls while he sprinted to where Vega and the others lay sprawled on the floor, afraid of more blasts.

He jumped over Vega's prone form, on a laser-focused mission to retrieve the scientist and get the void out of there. Mesa glared at him with intense hatred when he grabbed her by the shoulder and hauled her to her feet.

Rigger shouted something about the power and the base being on full lockdown.

Perfect. Time for a plan B.

Mesa pushed off with both hands, intent on making her escape, but he caught her by her manacled wrists. Time enough later—like when they could hear clearly—to explain that he was a friend.

By this point Vega was starting to rise, so he kicked her in the head to keep her down and took off down an offshoot of the corridor, dragging Mesa behind.

"We need an alternate egress stat," Rigger said right beside him. They got maybe ten meters before something hit them from behind with the force of a transport, launching them through the air to land face first against the floor tiles. Rigger's mobile comm hit the tile with a bang and spun away from her.

Mesa shouted. Some unseen hand, some psionic, dragged her backward as Rigger scrambled on hands and knees for her comm. He made a grab at Mesa and missed. Beyond her shoulder Vega still lay on the ground, but she had one hand outstretched and her face contorted in intense focus.

Somewhere organoplastic shrieked as parts of the walls were sheared away.

"We gotta go, boss!"

If he lunged after Mesa and got any closer to Vega's orbit, they were done for. Shit shit shit.

"Abort," he shouted to Rigger, and followed her at a run away from Vega.

Once away from the central area, the prison lightened considerably despite the increasing smoke, as sunlight hit the few windows in what must be the visitation wing. Everywhere, people were crouched on the floor, screaming, uncertain of what to do. Malkor didn't spare them a glance.

He got a sense of déjà vu as they ran, looking for a way out. The same modular sections used to build the prison were used in temporary medical centers, supply depots, and housing units in disaster areas all over the empire, minus the cell doors. He recognized the layout: he'd been in too many temporary buildings all over the galaxy.

"What's the plan, boss? It's not like we can use the front door."

He spied the module he was looking for and banked a left at the next intersection. "This way." Should be offices or an administrative wing, based on the layout.

The acrid smell of melting organoplastic filled the air. He coughed on each breath, blinking the sting from his eyes. The fumes from organoplastic weren't supposed to be poisonous, but they weren't supposed to be inhaled, either.

"This module has the largest windows," he said. "Check that side."

They slowed to a jog, going room to room. One office offered a sizable window, but the glass was perfectly intact. They passed two, three more like it, and then came to the end of the line at a sitting area. Actually, it looked like a combination sitting area and kitchen. It had tables and benches...

... and a gap opening up between two wall sections. The strain on the rest of the building was putting everything out of whack. The separation in the sections caused the window casement to sag and warp, which in turn caused the glass to crack.

"Excellent," Rigger said. She rummaged through the drawers while he selected the best hammering weapon, which turned out to be a lamp perched on an end table.

"Ah ha!" Rigger held up her find—a metal soup ladle—and began stripping off her uniform shirt.

People cowering under a table in the corner looked at them like they were crazy, as Malkor ripped the shade off the lamp and tossed it aside. Crazy, maybe—just as long as they weren't crazy *and* captured.

He met Rigger at the window. She gripped the ladle in her wrapped hand and set the point of the handle to the crack in the window. The bell of the ladle rose up like a target.

"Ready?" he asked her. He gave the lamp—forty centimeters of molded steel—a practice swing to get a sense of its heft.

"Is that heavy enough for military-grade glass?"

"Maybe not the first time," he said truthfully.

Rigger gave her trademark grin. "What the void: I've got two hands. Let's do this." She turned her head away from the window and shut her eyes.

"That's my line." He drew back, fixed his aim, and swung with all his might.

Glass shattered as the force radiated outward from the tiny point of contact between the end of the ladle's handle and the window.

"*Frutt!*" Rigger had relinquished her grip at the last second, but not soon enough to avoid getting clipped by the bowl of the ladle as it went past. She clutched her hand, hopping around in pain as he knocked the remaining glass shards from the frame.

"Shit that hurts," she said. But since her hand hadn't been completely demolished and she didn't have the white look of someone about to pass out, triage could wait.

He stuck his head out the one-meter-square opening.

They'd gotten lucky—this side of the building didn't face the main street. It also didn't have any cover, though, and since it sounded like people were coming their way, they'd better move quickly. He gauged the drop to the ground—no more than four meters.

"Rigger?"

"Ready, boss." The lacerated shirt still wrapped around her arm and hand blossomed with spreading blood, but she ignored it. He helped her out feet first and she took the drop like the pro she was.

Smoke billowed into the room, drawn by the change in air pressure. Fire would no doubt follow. Indeed, he could distinguish screaming coming from inside the prison as well as without.

Frustration gripped him. So many innocent people trapped in here.

He pushed the thought from his mind and climbed out the window himself.

16

Malkor crept to the edge of the building and peeked around the corner. The front of the prison looked like a war zone, with fire and debris, injured people, and blown-up vehicles.

"Put your hand to your forehead and smear some of that blood on it," he said to Rigger.

"Might as well make it useful, if my hand is going to hurt so damn much," she quipped. Trust her to find some amusement in what was their worst blown op in a decade.

He put an arm around her like he was supporting her, she clutched her head and moaned for effect, and suddenly they were just two more casualties of the day, joining the panicked tide of people trying to get away from the disaster as they stepped out into the street. They blended in and were swallowed up in the shared anonymity of a mob.

Looking back on it an hour later, that really was the easiest part of the day.

The city was a mess in the wake of the attack, the streets jammed to a standstill with transports and people everywhere. Sirens wailed. Troop transports and emergency vehicles made grudging progress through the morass only by laying on their horns and shouting threats. Vidscreens on every corner carried news of the attack and the massive manhunt now underway for the few lucky prisoners who had escaped.

The city was going into lockdown, but Malkor would be damned before he got trapped here. They trudged kilometer after kilometer on foot, and still moved quicker than the traffic did.

Rumors swirled of protests in other parts of the city. Despite the planet-wide ban on using psi powers, a few Wyrds dared to levitate themselves above the crowd and zoom ahead. Three ion blasts from a soldier with a rifle and exceptional aim made short work of that nonsense. It also started a stampede.

Malkor and Rigger flattened themselves against a storefront as the crowd surged forward. Beside them a woman clung to a scrawny teenage girl to keep her from being dragged away by the storm of people. A man gripped an awning like it was his lifeline, and the store owner prayed.

The stampede wore itself out, no doubt passing the insanity to people farther down the line. They finally managed to catch a transport once the roads cleared up. The bulk of the vehicles were headed toward a different part of the city where a gate marked for civilian vehicles stood. Malkor lost track of how long it took to get to the gate, even with the reduced traffic. At least Rigger's wounds had coagulated.

Rather than wait in the interminable line that led to the gate, Malkor shouted loudly about official business and escaped prisoners. People practically jumped out of his path, desperate not to get singled out by a soldier even if he was cutting the line. He and Rigger, who had assumed the expression of a constipated drill sergeant, elbowed their way through. When at last they reached the checkpoint, Malkor slammed his credentials down on the counter and started shouting at the guard before the man had even opened his mouth.

"Do you know how long we've been waiting? Too damn long, that's how long. I've got orders to get to Senfranco Base ASAP. Orders from the new commander herself!"

"Sir—" the guard stammered.

"Don't you 'sir' me, boy. Just get that damn door open so I can move sometime this year."

"Can't you tell we just came from the prison?" Rigger barked. "Do you have any idea what it's like there right now? It's a frutting war zone." She shook her bandaged hand at the guard. "We're lucky we got out alive."

Apparently Rigger in full furor did the man in, because the guard handed over Malkor's ID and buzzed them through the gate.

Neither said a word until they had crossed through the flak tower and exited on the other side. They kept moving until they were well past the city walls and out of range of the weapons turrets. They needn't have hurried. All guards keeping watch from the towers were looking inward, focused on the chaos of the city down below. Nonetheless, they made it to the depot station in record time.

Rigger sent a message to the rebellion through secure channels. A reply came through almost immediately.

"What's the word?" he asked, and Rigger grinned.

"Our ride's on its way."

He smiled in return. "You know, those are the sweetest words you've ever said to me."

THE *YARI*

It was surprisingly hard to search an entire warship with only four people.

Especially when only two of those are psionics, Kayla mused at the end of another fruitless day.

"If I never see another EMU it will be too soon," she told Vayne, as they returned to the powered section of the ship.

"I second that." They hung their suits in the recharging bay, grabbed their plasma bullpups from a locker, and trekked back to the lift.

Kayla couldn't decide if she wanted a meal or a shower first. Maybe a meal in the shower. Then a nap. Then she'd get back in the EMU and start the cycle over again.

She kept her bullpup ready as they walked, though it was hard to imagine being surprised by a *stepa at es* when they'd been trying so hard to locate them for days. Frutt. At this point she'd almost welcome an ambush, just to get the whole thing over with. It certainly would save time.

And keep their movements on the ship from looking increasingly suspicious. Ostensibly they were searching the unpowered levels for any other supplies or parts they could salvage. Ida and Benny had argued against it, saying it would be a fruitless endeavor, but Natali had given them the go-ahead. End of discussion.

Kayla had visited Kendrik and the other prisoners with Vayne and Toble today. The medic was cautiously optimistic about their progress, but Kayla wasn't convinced they could be helped. Since the cessation of the tranquilizers and anti-anxiety medication, Enska and Gaar had become increasingly agitated, and Airman Lopez seemed just as obsessively focused on hiding as before. The one positive was that Kendrik seemed more lucid.

More lucid was relative in this case, though. All in all, it was a depressing and frustrating visit.

Kayla looked up as they passed a team of rebels in the corridor. Rebels working in teams had been tasked with rigging temporary grating across the entrances to the maintenance tunnels on each of the many powered levels. No one wanted the *stepa* to have free rein on the lower levels, but they couldn't afford to cut off all access to the maintenance shafts permanently, not on an aging ship. The rebels saluted as Kayla and Vayne passed.

"I wish they'd quit doing that," Vayne muttered.

"It would take an order from Natali to get them to stop, and I rather think she enjoys it."

"Well it's ridiculous," he countered, but as usual avoided talking about their older sister. The lift arrived and he almost dashed in, like getting away from that level would leave the subject behind them. She longed to ask him about it. The intention must have been clear in her expression because he said, "Don't."

Give him time, she counseled herself yet again. Stars knew, Natali was never going to speak of whatever had happened between them. She'd never been a sharer, not even before the incarceration, and she was only more closed off now. Whatever secrets she did share had died with her twin.

Corinth confirmed that they'd been like that ever since captivity, that nothing had happened between Vayne and Natali since then that he was aware of. Tia'tan concurred. Kayla had even tried to approach the subject obliquely with their uncle once or twice, but the usually talkative and jovial Ghirhad shut down when their time with Dolan was even hinted at. Not that she blamed them for wanting to pretend the last five years didn't exist; it was just that selfishly she wanted her twin back, and that could never happen until he began to heal.

"If you don't stop looking at me like that," Vayne said, "I'm locking you in this lift until morning."

She put her hands up. "I'm done, I promise." *For today. I'm never giving up on you.*

They arrived on their level. "I'm grabbing a shower," she said. "See you after for some dinner?"

He hesitated. Looked almost guilty. Or pained. Or both, maybe. "I... just need a break. I'm sorry."

"Hey, don't be sorry." Her heart broke for him that he thought he needed to apologize. That wanting alone time meant he was somehow damaged. "Even *ro'haar* and *il'haar* don't have to spend every waking minute together." She forced herself to grin. "I was actually looking for a nice way to say 'I can't stand the sight of you at this moment.'"

He laughed, relaxed, as she'd meant him to. She'd give him space, even if it killed her to be away from him, even if the fear that if she closed her eyes for a second he'd vanish, this time forever, chased her every day. He wasn't the babysitter of her paranoia.

"See you in the morning," she said, and used every bit of her willpower to turn and walk away.

Vayne watched Kayla go, wearing her slightly-too-bright smile, and hated himself a little more. He'd always assumed that the self-loathing would stop if he ever escaped from Dolan's machinations. Some days, it just seemed to get worse. Because now he had no excuse, and yet he still hurt the people that he loved.

Must you be melancholy all the time? the ghost of Dolan asked him, as it materialized in the corridor. *I remember you being a lot more fun.*

"And I remember you being a lot more dead," Vayne muttered. Yup, talking to a dead guy/himself in the middle of the corridor. He was halfway to being *stepa at es* even without the cryosleep brain damage.

Being alone with his thoughts—and his demon tormentor—probably wasn't healthy, but sometimes Vayne couldn't stand to be around other people while Dolan yammered away. And the bastard certainly liked to yammer when Kayla was around these days. Whatever reprieve Vayne had gotten from reuniting with his *ro'haar* was over. Dolan crept into his thoughts when he was too tired to guard against him, which was most nights lately. Sometimes it was just easier to give in and let Dolan say what he wanted. The *kin'shaa*'s voice was almost comfortable in its familiarity, and Vayne wondered if he would cease to exist without it. If their souls had somehow fused together.

Now you're getting the picture, Dolan said with a smile.

No, now he was getting one step closer to the edge.

He should fight it, for Kayla's sake. For his own. And he would… tomorrow. Tonight he stumbled to his cabin to lock himself inside with his ghost.

* * *

Kayla was halfway through her shower cycle when Natali's voice came over the ship's comm.

"Kayla, Malkor's calling in."

Thank the stars. She practically bolted from the shower to reply. "On my way. Hekkar?" The agent would have heard the ship-wide comm, but of course Natali hadn't invited him.

"Meet you there," Hekkar replied, and the channel clicked off.

In Natali's defense, she might not have noticed that Hekkar was in charge of the octet while Malkor was away. Kayla discarded that thought as too charitable, pulled on her clothes while still damp, and hurried to the control room.

Relief hit her as soon as she entered the bridge and saw Malkor's face front and center on the giant vidscreen. The other people in the room—Natali, Hekkar, Benny, and Ida on this side, Wetham and Rigger planet-side—didn't register for at least a solid minute.

Thank the stars he was alive.

He was alive, and he was frustrated, though he hid it well.

"What is it, what happened?" Kayla demanded. Rigger's and Malkor's faces were streaked with dirt and sweat and who knew what else. There was blood on both their uniforms, Rigger's eyes were glassy, and a bandage covered her entire left hand.

Wetham was the one who answered. "The mission was a failure due to the worst reason of all: sheer bad luck."

"Explain," Natali said, the word cutting like a laser beam through plascrete.

"Vega showed up," Malkor said. "She's there on the planet already. Hopped on a super-secret army plane probably the day the Imperial Army named her as the new head of the occupation."

"Did she identify you?" Kayla couldn't imagine he and Rigger would be walking around free, if that were the case.

Malkor shook his head. "No, but she was at the prison. She took command of Mesa *minutes* before we could. Minutes." He let out a sound of frustration. "If I hadn't made the call to wait one day and get charges put in place on the prison as a backup plan, we could have skated through with our IDs and Chen's orders."

"You couldn't have known that." And it was true, but she could tell he thought he somehow still should have known.

Natali got right to the point. "How do we extract Mesa now?"

"We don't," Wetham said. "The agents weren't identified, but their cover was blown. Now Vega knows *someone*—even if she doesn't know who, or why exactly—wants Mesa. She'll bury the woman underground, and we'll never see her again."

"What about the other scientists on the list?" Natali asked, but everyone in the room anticipated Wetham's answer.

"Mesa's world-renowned for her work on hyperstream drives and little else, so it's hard to imagine another reason why someone would go after her. Vega will have anyone who's anyone in the field of hyperstream technology rounded up and locked down."

"The only good bit of news," Malkor said, "is that we were able to notify General Chen in time. When the prison contacted him, he disavowed all knowledge of us and claimed the orders were forged, so at least we didn't lose that asset."

Natali said nothing. A less controlled person would probably be blistering the air with curses and kicked things. Kayla would have rather that than the icy calm Natali radiated. It chilled the air about ten degrees.

"So that's it, then," Hekkar said. "The *Yari*'s dead in the water."

Kayla winced. Natali gave him a venomous stare that had to have the agent wishing he hadn't opened his mouth.

"Putting that aside for the moment," Malkor said, "we have a big problem with Vega." He explained what he and Rigger had heard from the officers, and what had happened at the prison. "Hekkar's report months ago is correct, she does indeed have psi powers.

"Worse, though, our plan to infect Dolan's data with a complink virus before we handed it over to her obviously failed. She arrived on Ordoch with a Wyrd—an Ilmenan, judging by the look of her—and I'm convinced they brought the Influencer with them."

236

"Agira," Natali said. The name sounded like a curse. "Dolan's pet."

"You know her?" Kayla asked.

"She's a thrall. Somehow her mind conditioning is permanent. She helped him with his *experiments*."

Then Agira was lucky Natali hadn't been the one in the prison with her today, or the woman wouldn't have survived.

"Isonde has seen her in Vega's company; is it possible Dolan switched her loyalty to Vega somehow?"

Natali shrugged. "Who knows how that damn device works? I didn't think he'd ever be able to transfer powers to imperials."

"Is the process permanent?"

"Doesn't matter," Kayla said. "Now that she's got an entire planet of Wyrd batteries at her fingertips, she can suck the charge out of us whenever she wants. Plus she has a brainwashed Ilmenan who will complete the transfer process for her." She felt her rage beginning to build at the thought of the same process that had destroyed her family members being used on her people.

And on what scale? If Vega decided to give psi powers to other imperials, she could start a factory, churning them out, one after the other after the other. Hundreds of thousands of Wyrds used as fuel. Her hands curled into fists. She couldn't image what Natali, who had lived through the process time and again, must be feeling.

"If that is indeed what Vega intends and the various councils find out," Malkor said, "the empire will never release its grip on Ordoch." It took courage, but he met Natali's eyes as he said it. "We *have* to get the Influencer away from Vega, whatever it takes."

Natali finally nodded. "Thank you, agents. For your efforts. I'm sure you'll want to debrief with your team, and Wetham and I have much to discuss."

Ida spoke up for the first time. "Kayla, Hekkar, you can have the using of stateroom mine. The rest of us will be conversation for some time still."

Kayla couldn't be more thankful to escape what was sure to be a verbal power struggle, but she wasn't about to have a private conversation at Ida's desk, where it might be recorded. "It'll take a few minutes to round up the others," she said. "Just route the comm to my cabin and we'll convene there." She fled the control room before anyone could change their mind.

Trinan and Vid were waiting outside her cabin when she and Hekkar arrived.

"Toble?" she asked.

"Asleep," Vid said. "Wouldn't even wake when I rang his door."

Let him sleep; at least someone would be, and they could brief him in the morning. It's not like anything was going to change between now and then.

"Got word from the boss?" Trinan asked, and Kayla let them all into her cabin—which was entirely too small for one *ro'haar* and three burly male imperials.

"You two." She pointed at Trinan and Vid, then at her bunk. "Sit. You," she pointed to Hekkar, "take the chair. I can't breathe with the three of you crowding me."

"Yes, ma'am," they said in unison, Vid with a cheeky salute.

For her part, Kayla was still too edgy to sit. Now that she knew what could have happened, what almost did happen, her worry had kicked back in. Stupid response, that, being after the fact.

She flipped on her vidcomm, which was still waiting for a signal from the planet.

"So when are Malk and Rigger heading back?" Trinan asked. "They might not be able to sense psionic blank spots, but we could sure use their help searching for heat and energy signatures."

That they could. "They're not coming back, not yet anyway," she said, and explained what had happened in the prison.

Then Malkor appeared on the vidscreen. It looked like he'd stopped to swipe a clean rag over his face, but no more than that. Rigger wasn't with him.

"I had to order Rigger to rest," he said in response to her

question. "You Ordochians sure know how to party: she's high as shit right now."

Kayla winced. "Sorry about that. I think imperials require a smaller dose of pain blockers than Wyrds do."

"I don't know what the medics gave her, but she said she couldn't feel her face, never mind her injured hand, so I guess that's a good thing."

Kayla adjusted the vidscreen so everyone could see, then sat on the floor beside the bed. "Run it back for me. What, exactly, went down?"

By the time he finished briefing them on his day, no one was laughing any more.

"Rigger's hand will be fine," he finished up. "She has lacerations from flying glass shards, and a few of her fingers are fractured, but she'll heal quickly." He shook his head. "It could have easily been a lot worse."

Hekkar explained their progress—or lack thereof—with finding Zimmerman or any other *stepa*. "Without more people we can trust, I don't know if we'll find them."

"If they're even out there," Kayla said quietly. It was beginning to feel like they were chasing fumes.

"Well, someone stole those weapons," Trinan offered.

Vid punched him on the arm. "Potentially crazy people with plasma rifles—don't remind me."

"I've got some good news and some bad news about the search," Hekkar said. "Which do you want first?"

They all agreed on the good, because otherwise the highlight of the day was that Malkor and Rigger had only *kind of* been blown up.

"I was talking with ship's physicist Tanet earlier and quizzed him about the unpowered levels. We can rule some out entirely because those decks sustained massive damage and have pockets left open to space."

"What's the damage from?" Kayla asked. "I assumed the *Yari* just popped out of whatever void they'd been in and magically appeared in the Mine Field."

Hekkar shrugged. "I'm still having a hard time following the crew's speech, even with my translator, but I gather some of it happened at the time they disappeared. Tanet mentioned that when they tried to test the superweapon five hundred years ago there was a starbase nearby. The whole thing—and I mean the *whole thing*, including the asteroid it was built on—got pulled through the Tear with them. Things got bumpy somewhere along the way. The *Yari* sustained quite a bit of collision damage and the starbase got destroyed. Remnants of it are floating around in the Mine Field. Tanet's had a lot of time to speculate on how things happened, has created hundreds of predictive models, but there's just no way to know for certain. As for the other damage, that comes from collisions with present-day Mine Field debris, and of course, the rooks."

Kayla held up a hand. "Wait a minute. The rooks attacked the *Yari*? I thought they'd always kept their distance, until the stress test on the hyperstream drive."

"What do you mean 'until the stress test?'" Malkor demanded. "Rooks approached the ship? Explain."

Shit. Had all that happened since he'd left? She took a detour to catch him up.

"Anyway," Hekkar said once she'd finished and before Malkor could let them all know what he thought of Kayla doing a spacewalk with a family of rooks. "According to Tanet, the rooks would blink through the debris field, tear at the *Yari* like rats on a corpse, and blink out of existence again. That's what happened to the fuel for the hyperstream drive, as well as the parts in storage for completing it. It wasn't until the crew repaired the ion cannons that they could keep the rooks away."

"The rooks stole the hyperstream fuel?" Kayla asked, trying to picture it. "And how the frutt is any of this good news?"

Hekkar forced a hand through his flame-bright orange hair, looking sheepish. "Well, it's not exactly good per se, but I can cross several areas and a few whole levels off of our search pattern, considering they're exposed to hard vacuum. The other unpowered levels are structurally sound, it's just a matter of corrupted circuits et cetera."

Everyone else in the room looked as stupefied as she felt.

Malkor finally said, "That's the worst batch of 'good news' I've ever heard. How can there be any bad news left over?"

This time Hekkar definitely looked chagrined. "There's a whole lot more ship to search than we previously thought."

Kayla was quite certain she didn't want to hear this. What had started as a tricky search was rapidly spiraling to impossible heights. At what point did she kick them all out of her cabin, pull the covers over her head, and just give up?

"The Planetary Destroyer is still powered," Hekkar said.

"The superweapon?" Vid asked. "Isn't that a good thing for the rebellion?"

Kayla made a slashing motion with her hand. "Only if you want to destroy Ordoch, and possibly all of time and space along with it."

Hekkar clarified. "I'm not talking about firing the PD. So far in our search for Zimmerman, we've only considered the habitable section of the ship as a viable hiding place, powered or not."

Trinan sighed. "Isn't that enough? It's massive: bigger than some cities I've been to."

He wasn't kidding. The main cylindrical section of the *Yari* could fit a fleet of today's smaller, modern ships inside without feeling crowded. And that didn't include the long spindle structure jutting out from the center of the ship. The PD's housing channel was several times longer than the rest of the ship, but couldn't be more than a hundred meters in diameter. It looked more like an antenna than the conduit for a weapon capable of destroying entire planets.

Hekkar finished his story. "Tanet says the PD housing has its own power systems, and the crystals in those generators are still good. It doesn't have sleeping quarters or commissaries, but there are a few workstations and supply rooms down there, and it's conceivable that someone could turn the life support back on, if they wanted to."

"You're telling us Zimmerman and whichever crew members he has with him could be hiding *inside* a weapon of mass destruction?" Vid shook his head. "They really are all crazy."

17

It was late when Kayla finally kicked the octet out of her cabin.

She tried to sleep, but was plagued by dreams. She and Vayne were climbing this insane scaffolding in space, clinging to the metal rails while an impossible wind blew furiously all around them, trying to buffet them off. Vayne lost his grip, slipped, and was ripped away from her. She tried desperately to grab at him with her psi powers, but of course she had none, and was forced to cling there watching him get farther and farther away. The dream then repeated itself with Corinth instead of Vayne.

No wonder she never felt rested. Even in sleep, she worried about failing her *il'haars*. It was still the middle of the night, though, so she lay back down and somehow slept, only to be jolted awake minutes later by Benny on the ship's comms.

"Unknown ship approaching; captain and crew needed on the bridge."

"The void with that," Kayla said to herself, already out of bed and strapping her kris to her thighs. She might not be crew, but she damn well had a stake in whatever was about to happen.

She met Natali in the corridor and they double-timed it to the control room, entering just in time to hear Benny say,

"Ilmenan engine signature detected. Arm weapons, captain?"

"Negative. Stand down."

Unless of course, Kayla thought, *it was an Ilmenan ship from five hundred years ago. In that case, fire away.*

Tia'tan's voice sounded on the ship-wide comms just as the view screen switched to an image of the Mine Field. "It's the *Radiant*!"

Kayla sincerely doubted that. The Ilmenan tanker had been carrying the fuel needed to power the *Yari*'s hyperstream drive. It had jumped to the Mine Field in Imperial Space and barreled in, not knowing another way to get to the center directly. That was months ago, and no one had heard from them since. The odds of the *Radiant* surviving an encounter with the rooks or hiding for this long were beyond impossible.

A severely crippled ship came into view, a fuel tanker, by the looks of it. And something was... attached to it?

"Are those—" Kayla started to ask, but Tia'tan's voice sounded again.

"Don't shoot the rooks," she commanded, sounding breathless with excitement. "I'll be right there to explain."

"What's going on?" Kayla demanded.

Ida frowned at the image on the screen. "The *Radiant* was to be bringing our fuel. I am having the thinking that they failed."

The *Radiant* was in rough shape. What must have been its entire back quarter was gone, which meant there was a leak in their fuel storage tank. Oh... and their engines were missing. No engineer for the hyperstream drive, and now no fuel for certain... Maybe the *Yari* was never meant to leave the Mine Field. Maybe it should have died with the rest of the ancient battleships five hundred years ago.

The *Radiant* itself was only the first odd thing on screen. The second was the sight of two giant rooks, each with their tentacles wrapped around the ship like a living net. They dwarfed the *Radiant*, making it look like a child's toy in a sea monster's grip.

"Magnify," Ida said, and the automated systems complied.

The rooks' glossy black skin glowed with an almost metallic sheen. A crown of iridescent lights shimmered silver-white on the mantle of their bodies, and deepened to blue along the tentacles. They pulsed perfectly in time with each other in a dazzling, mesmerizing display.

It was beautiful, if completely alien.

Beautiful and frightening, because at any second the rooks could rip the *Radiant* to shreds, and it looked like they had already gotten a head start on that.

"Arm ion cannon," Ida said, and the system confirmed her order.

"Wait, Tia'tan said—"

"Is being precaution only."

Natali nodded. "Protecting the *Yari* is our top priority."

The doors to the control room opened and Tia'tan entered, a smile on her face. "I've spoken with Kazamel, they're safe, everything's all right. The rooks brought them here. They—"

She broke off on a gasp as something blinked into existence beside Kayla... and promptly dropped to the floor with a plop.

Everyone in the room froze.

The little black blob by her foot, a perfect miniature replica of the rooks outside, shook itself all over, lights pulsing wildly and tentacles flailing. It was in so much obvious distress that Kayla knelt down, anxious to help it in some way. Not that she knew what to do, and she certainly wasn't going to touch it.

::Kayla!:: Natali hissed in her mind. ::What the frutt are you doing, get away from it.::

It didn't seem to be in any position to harm anyone. Kayla ignored Natali, instead doing the only thing she could think of: cooing to the rook like it was a crying baby, making what she hoped were soothing sounds.

Who knows, maybe she sounded like an attacker to the rook. Hopefully it would blink out soon, traveling back to space.

"Kazamel says they're not used to gravity," Tia'tan said in a whisper, "and the adults don't know how to teach them about it, since it's a foreign concept to them."

Three more babies appeared in the control room, each plopping to the floor just as the first had done.

Ida and Benny cursed in ancient Ordochian, and Natali took a sharp step back from the one that landed on the console right next to her. Benny's hand crept toward the blaster on his hip.

"He swears they're safe," Tia'tan said quickly, sending out a mental wave that carried peace, calm, and even trust with it. The act would have been appalling on Ordoch, but if it meant the difference between starting a war with the rooks or not, Kayla was fine with it.

"They're friendly," Tia'tan insisted.

The baby in front of Kayla seemed to be calming, its lights settling to a less frenetic pulse. The mantle covering the body would fit in her hand if she held it. Even as she had that insane thought, the rook seemed to figure out the whole gravity thing. It lifted a few centimeters off of the floor and shook its tentacles out like a wet dog shedding water. Slowly, and a little unsteadily, it rose, checking itself along the way. The others in the room were rising as well, even as more babies blinked into existence from nowhere and fell like hapless idiots to the decking.

Kayla's rook quickly got the hang of it and began zooming around the control room. It looked like nothing so much as an octopus or a squid, swimming through the air as if it were water, its beautiful skin gleaming. Kayla slowly stood and the rook returned to her, spinning circles around her, high and low, dizzyingly fast. It disappeared, then reappeared on the other side of the room where its siblings were getting their bearings. It flitted with the others for a second, while all of the humans in the room stood perfectly immobile.

Kayla's rook hop-skip-blinked its way back across the room, materializing between her leg and her hand. It nudged her hand outward, but she needed no encouragement to move her hand the frutt out of there. The rook followed, though, spinning around her wrist to halt her movement, leaving her holding her arm straight out, palm up. Was it... playing with her?

Apparently the rook had her just where it wanted, because

it settled on her open palm with a plop. It sat splay-limbed on her hand, arms draped over the sides and lacing through her fingers. The rounded mantle covering its body pointed up toward her, and she hoped like the void that the thing didn't have a beak like the octopus it resembled and decide to take a chomp on her hand.

At least it hadn't electrocuted her with those blinking lights, or worse.

"Um... hello?" The lights on its mantle dimmed out, and all but the very tips of its fine limbs remained lit with a gentle blue.

Was that bad? She looked up at Tia'tan, who was as stupefied as Kayla by the whole thing.

Apparently that was as long as the rook wanted to sit still, because it blinked out again, reappearing by Tia'tan, then Natali. It and the others danced all over the room, alternately investigating the humans and just swimming around like fools.

"Incoming communication, on channel priority one. Answer with visual, audio, or dismiss?" the *Yari* asked.

Ida tore her gaze from the rook spinning above her head like a live tiara. "Display audiovisual on main screen."

The bizarre image of the giant adult rooks detangling themselves from the *Radiant* was replaced by a ship's bridge and a crew of smiling Ilmenans. A swarthy and slightly scruffy man stood front and center. He saluted, and his crew of four followed suit.

"Hail, Tengku Riab Tan Tia!" He made an elaborate bow that Kayla didn't think she could replicate, and the crew sank to the floor, dipping a knee before rising. "I didn't think I'd ever see you again. It is so good to lay eyes on you, Tia."

Tia'tan's smile was as big as the man's on screen. "You just came back from the dead, Kazamel, and I've known you for years—quit the formality. All of you."

Tengku Riab Tan Tia? If she remembered right, that salutation was sky high on Ilmena's list of political power players. Something like "grand vizier" to one of the planet's oligarchs. Kayla had known Tia'tan wasn't really a "princess," just like she wasn't. They'd both used the term to simplify their political systems for the imperials. But there was a lot more to Tengku Riab Tan Tia than just "Princess Tia'tan," apparently.

Tia'tan turned to Ida. "Captain, I present to you Dato' Sri Keong Kazamel. Kaz, meet the living legend, Captain Ida Janus, of the *Orichi Yari*."

"Pleasure to be met," Ida announced. "You will call Ida. And my first commander, Benny." She waved in his direction and Benny gave a stern nod. "We are being old too much for the using of formality, either."

"I see you've met the miniatures," Kazamel said, gesturing to the baby rooks flitting about. "They're harmless, most of the time." He smiled at a little rook zooming around on his bridge.

"How do you even know that?" Tia'tan asked. "Why didn't they tear your ship apart, and how did you survive all this time?"

Kazamel held up his hands. "It's a bit of a story. Permission to come aboard, Captain Janus?"

"My permission you have." The comm closed and Ida gave a happy slap-clap of excitement. "A mystery we have!"

The sharp sound startled the rooks, most of whom blinked out of the room entirely. Kayla's blinked out of her hand to hide behind her, tugging on her hair as it covered itself with her ponytail. If she wasn't still half afraid of receiving a painful death from the little creature, it would almost be humorous.

"I cannot believe this is happening," she muttered to Tia'tan.

Tia'tan stood on tiptoe and peeked over her. "I think you've made a friend. Let's go welcome Kazamel: this should be an interesting tale."

They met Kazamel and his small crew in the shuttle bay. Kazamel tried to bow again when he saw Tia'tan, but she barreled into him with a bear hug that could have snapped bone. He just laughed and hugged her back.

She finally released him, took a step back, and simply looked at him—really looking, as if to confirm with her own eyes that he truly stood before her. She blinked, then wiped almost angrily at her cheek.

"Damn you, Kaz, I thought you were dead."

"You and me both," he said quietly. "You and me both."

Their party grew as Ida escorted everyone through the ship and up to the larger observation deck. Several of the baby rooks had returned, and flitted about like black fairies, seemingly encouraged by the Wyrds' startled reactions.

"I am not liking the having of them on the ship, captain," Benny said to Ida as they walked.

The captain seemed to recover her famously sunny attitude. "I am of the idea that the choice is rooks only. We refuse in the negative, they are to stay anyway, perhaps."

"If I interpreted that correctly," Kazamel said, "you are right. The rooks are infinitely curious and go wherever it pleases them."

Noar joined them, along with Vayne.

Vayne grabbed Kayla's arm as soon as he caught her up, hauling her to a stop. ::Why the frutt are you walking around with these things as if it's no big deal?::

Kazamel says they won't hurt us. Kayla knew she sounded only half convinced herself.

::I am not risking my *ro'haar*'s life on a stranger's assurance.:: He turned on his heel without relinquishing his grip. Clearly, he meant to march her right back down the corridor like she was an errant child.

She twisted out of his hold. A rook materialized in the air between their faces, sending Vayne scrambling back with a curse.

It's fine— Even her thought broke off when the rook plopped itself on her shoulder, cuddled up to her neck, and wrapped a tentacle up and over her ear, as if in comfort.

The urge to knock it off her shoulder came instinctively, but she quashed that thought before Vayne could sense it. Otherwise her *il'haar* would be blasting the rook off with a telekinetic bolt strong enough to puncture the corridor wall.

His expression was somewhere between murderous rage and

horror, and she could relate to both. She didn't want her *il'haars* anywhere near these things either, not with so many unknowns.

I'm okay. Everything's fine.

::For the moment, maybe.::

Just go with it. There's nothing we can do, the things just fly wherever they want to anyway. She had to admit, they were kind of cute... in a slightly terrifying way. She could see the blue pulses of light shimmering along the rook's tentacles from the corner of her eye, and it was oddly soothing.

In fact very soothing. A warm, drowsy feeling of safety and calm came over her.

Vayne, still in her head, recoiled from the sensation, knocking her out of it. ::What is that?::

I think it's coming from the rook. Its lights flared, then the feeling of safety came back.

Vayne was quiet while he reached toward the feeling, tasting it, trying to identify its source, since he could tell Kayla wasn't summoning it. ::It has a different taste.::

The rest of the group had continued on without them, and Kayla was eager to catch up. *Kazamel will know.*

Vayne's reply was something of a pissed-off growl, whatever words he meant to say hidden in the grumble.

I'm going, stay if you want. She jogged down the corridor, the movement dislodging the rook.

::Not without me, you aren't.:: Vayne jogged beside her. ::Someone needs to save your reckless ass.::

She felt the undercurrent of grim humor in his voice, and she could only grin in response as they arrived at the observation deck.

A few rooks zoomed around as a pack in the wide open space, causing Vayne to halt.

It took her a moment to realize he wasn't looking at the rooks at all.

::So that's Kazamel:: he finally said. ::Tia'tan grieved his loss especially.:: He had the look of a man who was sizing the competition up.

Odd.

I guess so. She looked at Kazamel where he sat with the others, trying to see the man through Vayne's eyes. She saw nothing about the *Radiant*'s captain to put her off. Across the room, Ida and Tia'tan bracketed Kazamel, each looking thrilled to see him as they fired questions one after the other. Kazamel's crew members were talking to Noar.

Ida and her crew had been happy to meet Kayla and the rest of the Ordochian heirs, but they were ecstatic to meet the Ilmenans. Kayla had to jump out of the way when Ariel and Tanet came rushing in. The excitement caught the attention of the rooks, who left off circling and blinked out en masse, reappearing amidst everyone and causing a mild panic.

::Just what this ship needs... more insanity.:: Vayne was still frowning when they took seats on a bench near the others.

Kazamel and the others risked their lives coming to the Mine Field, jumping in blind, she reminded him. *They've probably been working for years for Ordoch's freedom.*

Which was more than Kayla could say for herself.

::I know:: was all he said, and she thought she felt a hint of shame coming from him. Not in his mind voice, but in *him*, as if they were connected on a deeper level and she had sensed it. The breath froze in her chest. Were her psi powers returning? She tried to reach out to him, struggling with a mind that couldn't move, couldn't feel, couldn't speak the way a Wyrd should.

Maybe it was just a reflection of her own shame that she put on him.

She wanted to know so badly. She wanted him to let her in, share his pain with her, his memories of their five years apart. She wanted to *know* him like she used to—she couldn't feel whole without that sense.

She remained a mute.

A wave of longing, of despair, threatened to drown her, but he was there, sensing her struggle and supporting her. Meeting her despair with hope.

::It'll happen soon, I know it.::

She nodded, pushing the failure aside to concentrate on the moment. It was the only way she knew how to deal with it.

Around them, the crew of the *Yari* had attached themselves to the *Radiant*'s crew, asking questions about life in modern Ilmena. They must love newcomers after five hundred years with the same people. Five hundred years of history were being discussed while tiny aliens traveled interdimensionally from one corner of the room to the other.

This is kinda frutted up, Kayla said, laughing despite herself.

::Exactly my point.::

Kayla focused her attention on Kazamel.

"We hid, mostly," he was saying. "It was clear as soon as we were pulled into the debris field from our hyperstream that we weren't flying a tanker anywhere. We clamped onto a huge metal wreck that could have been the remnants of an asteroid outpost, killed the engine, and sat down to wait."

His ship could be seen from the viewports. A half-ruined hulk with two rooks floating nearby. "The creatures didn't come around until later," he continued.

Kazamel's story of their time in the Mine Field was as odd as you'd expect from a captain arriving in a ship with no engine, traveling by rook.

"The squids—" He paused, glancing at Tia'tan. "Fine. The rooks, as you say, didn't know there were people inside the ships. They could tell the spaceships that entered their hunting grounds were artificial, but they didn't get the concept of a being riding inside a creation like that. Or so we think."

Kayla arched a brow in a nearly identical expression to Tia'tan's.

"Communicating with rooks"—he held out a hand and wobbled it side to side—"is an iffy thing. It's mostly images and the associated emotions being shared telepathically. There's no language that I can understand, beyond that."

So we're just guessing? Fantastic.

::And I'm supposed to believe this guy when he says the rooks are 'safe...'::

Kayla mentally shushed Vayne.

"If they thought spaceships were just constructs," Kayla asked Kazamel, "why did they tear them apart? Sport?"

"Yeah... About that." Kazamel gave Tia'tan an apologetic look. "I hope you're making progress on that hyperstream drive, but unfortunately... the rooks ate the fuel."

Tia'tan blinked. And blinked again. "Ate it? All of it?"

"I'm not sure if 'ate' is even the right word." He shrugged helplessly. "I don't claim to know how they work. I just got the impression that anything that fuels hyperstream and subhyperstream drives is like candy to them. Something about the fuel makes them happy, and they are ecstatic when they are chasing it down through space."

Kayla's head hurt. Badly.

"We were hunkered down, running as dark as possible, but apparently our hiding spot was near where one pack of the miniature rooks hang out. And when I say pack, I mean millions. They got curious and came to investigate without calling for the full-sized rooks."

"They certainly seem curious," Tia'tan said, cautiously watching a rook that had sidled into Kazamel's lap.

"Insanely so," he said. He placed his hand atop the mantle of the rook and it seemed to snuggle in deeper. Its light all but faded, the tentacles only distinguishable from the rest of its ebony body by the dim, slowly pulsing blue glow at the tips.

Kazamel gave a little laugh. "This one likes me: don't know why."

If Kayla or anyone aboard this ship ever lived through the fight for Ordoch's freedom, no one would believe the tales they told afterwards.

"Once a few of the miniatures blinked inside—and adapted their senses for our atmosphere and got used to gravity pulling them down—they were startled to discover living beings in the ship. They started communicating right away, in such a barrage of chaotic thoughts that we all thought we would go crazy from it.

"They were delighted that we were a ship specifically designed to carry not only its own fuel for propulsion, but an entire ship's hold's worth of fuel. They eventually communicated that they would like to have it—with some horrifying images of pulling other ships apart to feast on their fuel that I *think* they meant to be reassuring. We communicated—successfully, it would seem," he said, smiling at everyone in the room, "that we wanted to live and not be pulled apart by the rooks in their search for fuel.

"The miniatures' excitement brought the full-size rooks, and the whole 'conversation' began again." He shook his head, and Kayla could see he wasn't as sanguine about it all as he seemed. He looked at the rook in his lap, seemingly cuddled up like a kitten. He petted it, and the baby's tentacles wriggled slightly. Kazamel finally brought his wondering eyes back to Tia'tan. "They really aren't the mindless beasts they seemed to be initially: they just didn't know there was any intelligence in the ships.

"It took time... it took a long time... to get them to know and trust us."

Tia'tan patted his leg. "Seems like you've been gone forever."

Kayla felt like she'd left her old life behind and been trapped in a new, warped existence on this ship. What was it like for Corinth and Vayne, Tia'tan and Noar, having been here that much longer?

Kazamel continued: "We agreed to let them have our fuel, if they would try to get us to the *Yari*. They all knew what it was, as soon as we sent the image to them. Their response to the *Yari* translates to something like, 'Holy frutt, do not go near that stick of death! Pain! Pain and Burning! No like!'"

Ida laughed. "Good to know we are having that reputation now."

"They didn't believe us that the *Yari* could be friendly, no matter how many times we showed them images of people inside, made up stories of how nice you all were, how dear to us..." He trailed off, and it was quite clear that he was specifically *not* looking at Tia'tan. Past lovers? Unrequited love? Either way, the torch he was carrying seemed to irk the void out of Vayne.

The idea of Vayne being jealous of anyone over a woman was so foreign that it left Kayla uncomfortable, and uncomfortable with being uncomfortable.

Get over it, Kayla—she kept that thought to herself. Vayne had taken a lover before, just as she had. The affairs were always fleeting and didn't affect the *ro'haar–il'haar* bond. Plus, who was she to be jealous, with her love for Malkor?

She shook herself out of that ridiculousness. "That's why they came to the *Yari*, not because of the stress test on the engine." It made more sense now. "They were investigating us."

"Yeah," Kazamel said, "sorry about that. This field is so distorted, we had no way to get a message to you, to warn you. I told them to lay flat on the ship, guessing that you wouldn't be able to hit them with weapons that way."

He looked around the room at everyone. "Hey, what time is it, ship time? It's midday for us, but you all look like shit, to be honest. We can talk more in the 'morning.' Just show us to the food synthesizer for lunch and you guys should get some sleep."

Everyone protested, including Kayla. There was so much to know, still. Plans to make. Reports to Ordoch to be sent.

Kazamel held up a hand. "You all are a bit overwhelming, I could use a break." His eyes cut to Tia'tan. "And need to speak with Tengku Riab Tan Tia in private."

There was nothing to be done, not when he was so clearly evoking a protocol.

Ida stood. "I to get you RFID tags and security codes."

"And weapons," Kayla added. "Let's have a quick chat about the security situation we have going on, then we'll see you in a few hours."

18

THE *YARI*, THE MINE FIELD, IMPERIAL SPACE

Kayla grabbed an hour or two of sleep, then woke with a head full of crazy dreams. She lay there on her side, musing. Everything had been out of focus and strangely lit and colored, and at one point she was outside of her body looking up at herself. Then there was violence. Lots of it.

Wait— Had those been dreams? They felt more like things being sent to her.

::Kay, are you coming?:: Now she remembered what woke her up: Corinth mentally poking her, jolting her in his excitement. ::You're missing breakfast.::

She rolled onto her back and something bunched under her head.

"Hey!" She sat up and reached to rub her neck, but her hand bumped into something squishy. *Damn baby rooks.* It must have been tangled in her hair, because the weight of it pulled on her scalp when she stood up.

"Oh, just blink out of there, you tiny nincompoop." Not that it could understand her. She didn't even know if it could hear in the traditional sense. It figured out the solution quickly enough and blinked away, leaving her with tangles and the smell of singed hair. Lovely.

As she made her way from her cabin to the commissary, the rook returned, following alongside.

When Kayla walked in she found not just Corinth, but Noar and Larsa in the commissary as well, eating what looked like a leisurely breakfast. She'd become so accustomed to the trio taking their meals in the engine room while they worked that it was a shock to see them, not to mention Trinan and Vid. In fact, the commissary was packed with people: octet members, crew from the *Yari*, from the *Radiant*, and the rebels from Ordoch. It was kind of nice, actually. Or, it would have been, if she didn't recall that the reason Larsa, Noar, and Corinth could join them all for breakfast was because they had neither engine fuel nor a qualified engineer to help them build the *Yari*'s hyperstream drive. No point in tinkering with the thing, now.

Kayla stopped by the table where Trinan, Vid, Hekkar, Toble, and Corinth sat on her way to the food synthesizer. "Any word from Malkor this morning?" She hadn't caught up with him again last night before bed.

"He and Rigger are already planning intelligence-gathering missions with Ygreda and Aarush," Hekkar said. "We have zero intel to go on and we need to get the Influencer away from Vega ASAP." There was a pause while glances were shared between the octet members.

"When are you leaving to join him?" It was obvious that he had requested their presence. The octet could be of more use planning and executing ops against imperials than they could be guarding the ship against psionics.

Vid spoke up. "He asked for you, too, and anyone else who wanted to join us."

She glanced at Corinth. As much as he loved the octet he seemed uncertain about the idea, which was for the best at the moment. She wanted to go with the octet, wanted to be with Malkor, and most of all, she wanted to go *home*.

Her gaze searched out her sister. What Kayla wanted didn't matter as much as what the sovereign of Ordoch wanted from her. If Natali wanted her here, then she'd stay. It was her duty to support Natali, not just as the ruler, but as a sister and fellow *ro'haar* who had been through so much and was struggling to come back from it all.

The difficulty would come when Corinth and Vayne made their wishes known on the subject, but she'd cross that bridge when she came to it.

"I'll think on it. First things first, though—breakfast." She gave them a wave and went on her way to the food synthesizer. Her baby rook hopped, skipped, and interdimensionally jumped its way there to float by her head while she synthed up some coffee and hot cereal. Since both came out looking edible, she felt like she might finally be getting the hang of the *Yari*'s food selections.

Kayla carried her tray to the table where Vayne, Natali, Tia'tan, Kazamel, and Noar were eating breakfast—Vayne and Natali sitting at opposite ends of the table, of course.

"Morning." She set her tray down, and just as she threw her leg over the bench to sit beside Vayne, the rook blinked out of nowhere and flopped down on her seat. "Shoo, you!" She swatted at him, careful not to actually touch him. He swirled up into the air, lights blinking with his displeasure, and waited for her to sit.

"It likes you," Kazamel said with a grin.

"I'm not so sure about that." Even as she reached for her mug of coffee, the thing perched upright on her wrist and wrapped its tentacles around her arm to keep itself in place. "I had thought so, but then I woke up to find it had slept in my hair."

Vayne laughed, and she shot him a dark look. "Trust me, it sounds a lot cuter than it was. And I remember what I think were dreams, but they might be the rook talking to me with images instead."

"Were they weirdly colored, the positive and negative values reversed? And out of focus?" Kazamel asked.

She nodded. "It kept sending me images of rooks with tentacles getting torn off, rooks with burn scars, rooks with ship debris embedded in their skin..." Kayla shuddered. "The overwhelming emotion was one of concern, but now I'm starting to wonder if it was a death threat and he's warning me of my demise."

Two rooks appeared in the center of the table, skimmed around the one on her wrist, and flew off. Hers followed, leaving her to drink her coffee in peace.

"Nah, that's the way they say 'sick' or 'hurt.' They all think you're broken because you don't speak to them with your mind the way we do. It wants to fix you." He said it with a smile, but the words felt like a hard slap right across the mouth.

The word "broken" echoed in the silence.

"She's not broken, you asshole." Vayne's voice was a growl. No one said anything else.

"It's okay," Kayla finally said, even though that couldn't be further from the truth. It was what everyone needed her to say.

Kazamel, who clearly hadn't realized what a sensitive subject Kayla's lost powers were, looked abashed. He opened his mouth—probably to apologize—but she stopped him with a raised hand. An apology would only make it worse, and she just wanted this horrible moment over with.

"What did the folks on Ilmena say when you commed them to announce your spectacular arrival here?" she asked. She forced herself to take a bite of her cereal while she waited for the uncomfortable atmosphere to dissipate.

"That's what we were just discussing, actually," Kazamel said, then looked to Tia'tan as if to say, 'please get me out of the spotlight before I put my foot in my mouth yet again.'

Noar spoke up. "We got a report from the scientists working on a cure for the TNV. It's a mix of great and bad news."

"Give me the great news first," Kayla said. "I need a pick-me-up after a night of a rook's idea of 'sweet dreams.'"

"The great news is that they've developed a stable nanotechnology that can defeat a TNV virus one on one."

Kayla blinked. "What? How did you not shout that at me the second I walked in the door? That is amazing news!" A smile broke out on her face. "I don't care what the bad news is, that's amazing." She dropped her spoon in her bowl. "Did you tell the octet yet?" Despite thawing tension between the races, Vayne and the others had chosen a table as far away from the octet as possible, so Hekkar wouldn't overhear them. She had to comm Malkor. The number of lives that could be saved—

"Kayla, wait." Tia'tan's voice caught her. "There's more."

Wasn't there always? "What is it?"

Noar continued. "It's not a cure, really. What they've created is an inoculation against the TNV."

"I don't understand. If their nanobug can kill the TNV bugs…?"

"Honestly, I don't understood the full science of it, not being a virologist or a nanotech scientist." Noar shook his head. "It's complicated, but here's the gist of it. Our scientists created a biological organism that, when it senses the presence of the TNV, can hunt it down and destroy those cells, the same way antibodies present in our blood react to any virus we've been inoculated against. Not that the TNV is truly a virus. Or nanotechnology at all, really."

"We're getting farther afield," Tia'tan said. "Though, I do know how much you love science."

"Right," Noar said. "Right. So this organism, which they call 10-22R, will be an effective inoculation in people who do not already have the TNV, *assuming* they do not receive a massive infection of the TNV all at once."

That was decidedly less than great news. Her rook returned, materializing above her thigh. It instantly went to work investigating the kris she had strapped to her leg, wrapping its tentacles around the hilt and trying to draw the blade out. *Stop it, you little menace.* She gently untangled the thing's tentacles.

"The problem is the replication aspect of the TNV. It is able to break down a person's body to create more copies of itself, which it does at a fairly steady rate. 10-22R, in turn, can destroy those copies, again at a predictable rate. If the number of TNV organisms is large enough, it can replicate faster than 10-22R can destroy it."

Kayla nodded. It all made a sort of horrible sense. "And 10-22R can't replicate in situ without taking material from the host body, which is exactly what the TNV does and why we're trying to destroy it in the first place."

"So in theory," Natali said, leaning her elbows on the table, "you can 'cure' a person who is already infected as long as you have a large enough batch of 10-22R?"

"You could," Noar said. He made it sound like a terrible idea. "It comes down to resources, though. I have no idea what the actual number of infected people in the empire is—" He looked to Kayla and raised an eyebrow.

"There's no way of knowing exactly," she said. "Multiple planets, each with populations in the billions, are already infected. And millions of travelers are likely carrying it without knowing because the symptoms haven't shown up yet. Those millions are crossing paths with people in transit and arriving on other planets, moons, space stations, bringing the TNV with them." She shook her head at the enormity, the impossibility of it all. "The number is so large it defies the imagination."

"That's exactly my point," Noar said. "A large enough dose of 10-22R could inoculate a person for life against the TNV. It would require many, many times that dose to try to eradicate the TNV in an infected person.

"If the spread of the TNV were to stop now, it would still take us years to manufacture enough 10-22R to inoculate every uninfected person at this moment. With the way the TNV is spreading…"

Kayla finished the thought out loud: "They could all be dead before we can get them the inoculation." Shit. "Your people have done amazing work, Noar, but that's just not going to be good enough. The empire won't agree to withdraw from Ordoch with just a vaccine in hand."

"You're a fool if you ever thought the empire was going to withdraw voluntarily," Natali snapped. "The only way they're leaving is if we make them."

"People are dying by the millions, Natali, by the *millions*." Kayla caught and held her sister's ice-blue gaze. "They probably have as many dead as we have living on our entire planet right now." She willed her sister to understand, to see the empire as people, not just the enemy. "Almost all of those who are dead or dying are innocent of any wrongdoing against us."

Natali's jaw flexed. In her sister there was so much pain, so much trauma. Kayla saw it in the clench of her jaw, in the flash of almost rabid hatred in her eyes. After what she'd been through, was Natali capable of empathizing with the empire?

"We're talking about the future of our planet, not just what happens to Ordochians today," Natali finally said.

"No," Noar said, surprising everyone. "We're talking about the future of all the planets in the empire. I want the imperials out of Wyrd Space as much as you do, *en'shaar*, but I'm not willing to let an entire civilization vanish to see it happen."

Natali drew back slightly, as if his words had wounded her. She looked at everyone in turn, clearly trying to gauge how many at the table agreed with Noar's sentiment. Kayla did the same, but she couldn't tell. Tia'tan played things close to her chest always. Kazamel she didn't know well enough to interpret. And Vayne... well Vayne was filled with as much rage and pain and hate as Natali, so maybe at last they could be allies in something.

"What does Ilmena say to that?" Natali asked Tia'tan. Had she known of Tia'tan's high status on Ilmena before Kazamel arrived?

Tia'tan thought for a moment before answering. "The oligarchs are voting on it soon, but I anticipate they will approve the manufacture of a 10-22R vaccination for our own people." Tia'tan inclined her head to Natali. "We will of course offer this to Ordoch to use as a bargaining measure with the occupation. However, nothing will be given to the empire without discussions between both our worlds."

Natali looked displeased by Tia'tan's words and the shift in power it implied.

Vayne reached out to Kayla just then. ::Our family sure knows how to make breakfast fun.:: He brushed against her mind, asking permission, and she lowered her mental defenses to let him in so that he could hear her thoughts. He seeped into her mind, a little at a time, just the right fit.

Admit it. You wouldn't miss this for the world.

::Hey, I was the one who wanted to ditch this all for a farm in Ilmena's back country.::

Ilmena doesn't have any back country left. We're better off saving Ordoch, ditching the Reinumon palace, and moving to the Sanctuary.

::Wouldn't work: they only let previously extinct species live there.::

I feel dangerously close to extinction these days, don't you?

The tone of his mind voice changed, turning sad. ::I've been extinct for years.::

In the end, the discussion at breakfast boiled down to one thing: they *had* to have the *Yari*, with its vast bank of ship-to-ship weaponry, and the threat of the PD in their back pocket, if they wanted to accomplish any of their goals.

So of course it was dead in the water.

Perhaps not, Kayla thought once again, looking back on how the discussion had ended.

Kazamel had put the question to the rooks this morning of whether or not they might be able to move the *Yari* interdimensionally the way they had moved the *Radiant*. The two rooks had disappeared, presumably to discuss it with the others. Kayla had no idea what the risks to the creatures would be, but they all knew it would take an enormous effort, considering the size of the *Yari*.

It was their last hope for using the *Yari* in the fight against the imperials. Even Natali had conceded that if the rooks couldn't do this, it was time to abandon the ancient ship to a cold death in space.

The entire ship seemed to be holding its breath as they waited for the return of the rooks.

Kayla commed Malkor and told him about the possible inoculation against the TNV. It was too important to their joint goal of freeing Ordoch and eradicating the virus to keep it from him, as Natali had clearly wanted. This was what he had been working toward for years, why he'd tracked Kayla down and forced her to fight as Isonde in the Empress Game. This—the hope of a cure—was why he had given up his career and his life as an IDC agent, why he'd left the world he loved to come fight for her people's freedom.

They agreed that they would not inform Ardin or Isonde about 10-22R. That was up to Natali, as Ordoch's leader, when the time came for negotiations with the empire.

Sadly, that time had not come yet.

Malkor passed on the good news that Ardin and Isonde had arrived on Ordoch as the official negotiators for the empire. They had installed themselves at Senfranco Base with Base Commander Chin, rather than in Vankir City. Better to be well out of range of Vega and her Influencer.

Natali had closeted herself with Wetham via comms and he was no doubt giving her a very thorough account of the rebellion's progress, but Kayla had declined to be present for that.

Kazamel and his crew were busy stripping the *Radiant* of all useful parts and gear, since the ship would never be useful again. Ariel was shuttling Trinan and Vid to the Tear. It had been tough for Kayla and Corinth to say goodbye to them. The burly agents were like her family now, a part of the new life she was making for herself. But Malkor needed them more than she did, and their place would always be with their octet leader, no matter where he went.

Thankfully she hadn't had to say goodbye to Toble or Hekkar yet. Hekkar would pilot the *Lorius* if the rooks attempted to jump the *Yari*. Toble stayed aboard the *Yari* as he was the only medic on the entire ship and Ordoch had more technologically advanced medics at their disposal.

For now, all Vayne, Tia'tan, Kayla, and Noar could do was continue to search the ship for the elusive Zimmerman while they waited to hear back from the rooks.

Kayla was six levels down from the last powered level, breathing recycled air in her EMU and floating down another empty corridor in zero gravity beside Vayne when she finally made up her mind.

"We have to confront Ida about the prisoners," she said. "Whether the *Yari* makes it to Ordoch or not."

Vayne blew out a breath. "Finally. I've been saying that for days."

"I feel like we stumbled into some ancient feud between Ida and Zimmerman." Not that she had any actual proof to back that feeling up. "It's like there's two teams, and currently Ida's team has the upper hand, but Zimmerman's team is massing its forces, readying for a strike."

"And we're the ones who are going to get destroyed," Vayne finished for her, exactly in line with her thoughts.

"I don't know if Kendrik and the others are actually insane and locked up for a good reason, or if they're not insane but rather some kind of pawn in this conflict." Kayla corrected her flight down the corridor with a gentle push off the wall she'd been heading toward.

"And we will never know," Vayne said, "unless we confront Ida and the others."

It was dangerous, though. Depending on how the crew reacted to their questions, she might be touching off a war for control of the *Yari*. People would have to choose sides, and...

A black blob blinked into view and bounced off her face shield, halting her thoughts.

"The rooks are back," Kazamel said over ship-wide comms.

No kidding. Her pulse kicked up. All the waiting of the last few agonizing weeks would finally be over, one way or another.

Vayne, who floated beside her, sighed. "Let's see what fresh new insanity awaits us, shall we?"

It took some time, but finally they met up with the others on the large observation deck.

Kayla stared at the sight that awaited her beyond the portals. "Are those all…?" The Mine Field was almost entirely obscured by a sea of adult rooks. "There must be hundreds."

"If not more," Natali said. She was beaming. Not just a polite smile, but a full-on grin of excitement. Kayla wasn't sure she'd ever seen Natali smile like that since childhood. It was infectious. Natali pressed a hand to the portal as if she could touch the rooks.

They didn't cavort like the babies did, but the massive adults swam lazily around each other, skimming skin to skin as they passed, only to make a slow turn and do it again. Their inky black outlines were only distinguishable from one another by the lights dancing along their tentacles and across their mantles.

"They're willing to try jumping the *Yari* out of here," Kazamel said to the room at large. With the exception of those on guard duty, the observation deck was packed with rebel soldiers, Reinumons, and various crew members of both ships. "Actually, I think they're excited for the challenge. Apparently living in the Mine Field is a bit monotonous."

"What are the risks?" Kayla asked. With her only surviving family on board, including her two *il'haars*, she had to ask.

Kazamel tore his gaze from the sight of the rooks slowly swimming past the portals. "Honestly? I don't have the faintest idea, and I'm not sure they do either. They've never tried anything on this sort of scale before." He reached up and petted the baby rook who seemed happily settled on his shoulder. "I'm not sure their intelligence extends beyond day-to-day life. Or maybe it does and I just can't understand it. In either case, they don't seem too worried beyond the idea of it exhausting them."

Whereas Kayla couldn't help but worry, obsess over all possible outcomes and plan for every contingency.

::What about entering interdimensional space and never being able to leave?:: Corinth asked.

Kazamel closed his eyes as if concentrating. The room hushed, with the exception of Uncle Ghirhad and Ida chatting happily with each other at the back. When he finally opened his eyes again, he looked amused. "I'm pretty sure I just got the rook equivalent of 'we'll cross that bridge when we come to it.'"

"That doesn't exactly put my mind at ease," Kayla said.

Ida came to the front. "We are having no alternatives that come to mind mine. I, too, am excited for the trying."

Benny joined her, looking almost enthusiastic for once. "Five centuries is time long enough being stuck in place one."

"I stand with the captain," Tanet added, and Ariel and Larsa affirmed it as well.

One by one, everyone proclaimed their willingness to try the jump. Everyone except Vayne. Deep in her heart, Kayla knew Ordoch wouldn't win their freedom without the *Yari*'s firepower backing up the rebels on the ground. Things had gone too far for the promise of an inoculation and a "we'll keep trying for a cure" to move the imperials.

"Not everyone has to stay on board the *Yari* while the rooks attempt to move it," Natali said, not quite looking at Vayne. She was right. Several people could go through the Tear to Ordoch if they wanted, or even board Ardin's starcruiser, *Lorius*. Assuming they knew how to fly the thing, they could arrive in Ordoch perfectly safely, albeit a bit later than the rest.

::It's not too late to fly out of there and leave this nonsense behind:: Vayne said in her mind.

That was never going to happen, and you knew it.

::Did I? Maybe I always hoped this would fail.::

She turned to look at him, willing him to understand that he could do so much more than just retreat to a cave and lick his wounds. *Stopping Vega, freeing Ordoch—that's the ultimate defeat of Dolan and his plans. No more farming Wyrds for their psi powers, no more ruining lives with the Influencer. When we finish this, together, you will finally be free of him. Your captivity will finally be at an end.*

Please, brother, she wanted to add, but she couldn't put that on him. He needed to do this for himself, not because his *ro'haar* asked it of him.

::Even without your psi powers you still see too much.:: He sighed and hung his head. Giving up, at last, his dream of a quiet, peaceful, solitary life?

"What the void," he finally said out loud. "Count me in."

REBEL BASE, ORDOCH

Seated at a table in what had become the war room of the rebel base, Malkor focused on the mission in front of him.

The morning found him accompanied by Vid, Trinan, and Rigger, who looked remarkably cheery despite her bandaged hand. The first thing she'd said upon waking was that Kayla had always been right—imperial medical care was shit compared to what the Wyrds had developed. Ygreda, the rebellion spymaster, and Aarush, tactical lieutenant, were seated at the table as well. Aarush, too, was looking much better. He wore an eyepatch instead of bandages around his head now, and many of the wrappings around his burned arm had become unnecessary. He wouldn't be leading any tactical missions, not with his amputated foot, but he seemed sharp.

The topic of the war party was the mission to arrest Vega for crimes against humanity and steal the Influencer. Malkor pushed the schematics he'd been studying away and leaned back in his chair. "The plans for Reinumon palace are a mess."

"Sadly, yes," Aarush said. "They contradict each other, even these two," he indicated the sheets of paraffin paper in front of him. "They're filed in the same year, only by different architects. I'm not even sure which one was used in the actual expansion and which set was filed as a proposal."

"It's going to be tough to plan an op if we need backup plans for our backup plans," Vid said.

"At least we know which way we're going in," Rigger said with a smile.

That one had been easy. There was no way they'd be able to

both fight their way in *and* out, not with the sheer number of soldiers inside the palace. Then there were the soldiers in the palace grounds; in the other grand houses; in the Complex of Oligarchs; in the barracks just outside the Complex...

Their best bet for gaining access to Vega was to have a legitimate reason for appearing in her office. Being on "official business" would get them past all the security in the city, complex, and palace, provided the business was official enough.

"Are you working up new IDs for us?" Malkor asked her.

Rigger snapped the fingers on her good hand. "Already started. I've got several ready to go, and with a little more research in the army's files here on Ordoch, I'll be able to finish the others. I'm making extras, because we seem to go through those quickly." She winked.

"The holograms will be no trouble, either," Ygreda said. The spymaster would make a damn fine IDC agent, but Malkor didn't think she'd see that as a compliment, so he kept his mouth shut.

"I spoke to Commander Chen earlier," Malkor said. "He's willing to sign whatever orders we need. Since the prison... debacle... orders with his name on it are going to be studied more closely, but he'll stand by the orders if a soldier calls to verify them."

"Which I'm sure they'll do if we're trying to see Vega," Trinan said. "Now all we have to do is invent some business official enough to get us seen by the head of the occupation herself, and not some underling."

They looked at each other. Waited. No brilliant ideas sprang forth.

Malkor chuckled. "Let's talk egress instead, and come back to that." He'd just have to hope for inspiration. Which meant it might be time for more coffee. He grabbed the carafe and poured out another cup full of the weak substance that passed for coffee on Ordoch. Rigger would definitely have to recalibrate one of the food synthesizers down here if they were going to make this their new home.

The thought gave him pause. In fact, it made him distinctly

uncomfortable. Could he make a life on a planet where he'd always be an interloper? He looked at the others, imagining what the Wyrds would see: an invading army; soldiers who had subjugated their people for years on end—who had murdered and raped them. He pushed that to the back of his mind. He'd rather plan this near impossible op than think about a future on Ordoch, even if it included Kayla and Corinth. And Vayne, he forced himself to add after a second.

He took a swig of his coffee and focused on the debate raging around the table.

"Sounds like you IDC agents spend a lot of time crawling through sewers," Ygreda was saying. If she wasn't quite smiling, she was at least at ease with them enough to make jokes. "There was a time in our recent history when we Ordochians became almost entirely reliant on bots. We had bots for everything, and I mean *everything*." She shook her head. "I think we were on the verge of creating an AI to even run the day-to-day functioning of the planet, but luckily, woke up to our insanity in time."

Aarush said, "Well, the Bot Revolt woke us up. In either case, even though we've come back from that dystopia, the result is that a lot of our infrastructure is still completely controlled by bots." He slid another sheet from the pile and laid it in the center of the table. "The sewage and water systems aren't traversable, thanks to the various sanitation bots who run them and the guides that keep them on track."

"We could use Vega and her thrall as hostages to get out," Trinan ventured. "Except, then the army would have eyes on us and could follow our movements wherever we went. We wouldn't want to lead them to a rebel base or safehouse."

Vid jumped in on the theorizing. "Could we apply for asylum with Ardin and Isonde? They're in Commander Chen's territory, so it's at least partially neutral."

Malkor shook his head. "I'm not willing to risk anything tainting Isonde and Ardin's political position right now. When we can finally force the empire to the negotiating table, we need them to be rock solid as negotiators for the empire. We don't want the treaty and their loyalty questioned."

"Not to mention their votes on the Council of Seven," Rigger added. "They need to be seen as acting in the best interests of the empire at all times."

"We do have access to a few aerial vehicles with stealth technology," Ygreda said. "If we need to expose ourselves and take hostages, someone could pick you up, then fly away stealthed."

Malkor considered it. "That's one option. I'd still rather get Vega out of there with less fuss if possible. What about the roof?" He leaned over the building plans in front of him. "There's a place large enough to land the shuttle here." He indicated the position, clearly designed for such a purpose. "Since the army controls the air lanes and a stealth craft won't be seen flying in, they would not anticipate that we'd run up instead of down. Check out the plans for roof access: let's see if we can pin down a few possibilities, in case one of these plans is wrong."

Aarush excused himself from the room for a moment, making smooth progress on his crutches. They'd located two roof access points Malkor felt reasonably certain of by the time he returned. He looked pleased, in that reserved Wyrd way.

"What is it?" Malkor asked once Aarush had seated himself again.

"I know how we can get into the palace *and* guarantee an audience with Vega. Mishe, one of our contacts inside"—he nodded at the spymaster and she inclined her head in turn—"just reported that Vega has a massive manhunt underway. That's our ticket in."

"Well?" Malkor tried to keep his impatience out of his tone. "Out with it."

"All we have to do is bring her who she wants… Vayne Reinumon."

* * *

271

"The PD can be using as a ship-to-ship weapon, if we were to narrow the cone of fire," Ida said, clearly frustrated. "Tanet and Benny have already assured us all, you time and again, Kayla, that it has the makings of safe."

She, Natali, and Kayla were on the bridge discussing the plan of attack once the rooks jumped them into Wyrd Space. What happened in those first few minutes after their arrival at Ordoch could decide the fate of their planet.

"I don't want to murder every single imperial soldier orbiting Ordoch if it's not absolutely necessary," Kayla argued back, but she was losing, and she knew it. Ida and Natali's plan was sound—if indeed Tanet and Benny had recalibrated everything about the PD. Nearly everything.

"We won't open with it," Natali said. "Of course, we'll offer them a chance to surrender, first." A chance the empire would never take, not when it came from a single ship, one that had clearly seen better days.

"But this has to happen quickly, Kayla, and you know that," Natali said. "As soon as we arrive we'll be vulnerable to attack. If we threaten them with the weapon and *don't* actually use it, then they'll know we're toothless and attack anyway."

Damn her for being right.

"You're *certain* Tanet has made this safe?" Kayla asked Ida for the hundredth time. "It's not going to actually hit the atmosphere, or worse, the planet itself?"

Ida nodded, looking exasperated.

"And it's not going to fail catastrophically again, sending us to the void like it did to you five hundred years ago?"

Ida seemed to be gritting her teeth. "He has had the years of five hundred to fix it."

"You've heard his explanation," Natali said, looking annoyed as well. "We're dialing it way back, using a fraction of the energy used the first time." She touched Kayla's shoulder.

"Look. This is war. If we want to free Ordoch, this is how we're going to have to do it. And once the ships have been destroyed, the rebel forces will move in and retake strategic points throughout the continent."

It all seemed so simple, but could it really work?

"I don't need your permission," Natali said. "But... I would prefer it."

At last Kayla nodded, touched that Natali would even consult her on this. "You have it."

As she was heading for the door, she heard a comm come in from the planet: Malkor asking for Vayne.

What the— Can it be true, they're actually on speaking terms now?

Her heart longed to believe it, but she knew both men too well. It would take at least a decade for their relationship to thaw, if not more.

So why was Malkor comming Vayne?

The question of Malkor's comm quickly took a backseat to all her more pressing issues. The *stepa* were her primary concern as she strode down the corridor toward her cabin. She'd meant what she said to Vayne about confronting Ida and freeing the prisoners, but right now couldn't possibly be a worse time to do it. What if everyone just sat tight for another few days? Whatever was brewing on this damn ship had been simmering for five hundred years; it could simmer a few more days. Just until they made it to Ordoch... Or they didn't.

After that, all the void could break loose on the ship and it would be fine with her. She just needed a few more days.

Speaking of time... Kayla glanced at her wrist chronometer as a different concern pushed its way to the front of her brain. Thankfully she was already close to Hekkar's room. She felt almost as comfortable working with him as she did with Malkor, and with Malkor on Ordoch, Hekkar was her go-to guy for the octet.

He opened the door as soon as she rang, so she ducked inside before asking: "How long ago did Toble say he was going to check on Kendrik and the others?"

Hekkar glanced at the chronometer, but Kayla already knew: too long ago.

"Maybe an hour," Hekkar said, realizing exactly what she had. "Toble should have reported back by now."

"He didn't go alone, did he?"

"I think Tia'tan or Noar accompanied him." Hekkar paged Toble on their shared IDC comms. No answer.

"Damnit," Kayla said. "Something's wrong." She wasn't ready to alert the entire ship yet, though. What she really needed was her frutting psi powers right frutting now. Instead, like an asshole, she had to use the ship-wide comm and ask Vayne to contact her privately.

::What's wrong?:: He swirled inside her head.

Kayla and Hekkar grabbed their bullpups and headed out the door.

I can't reach Toble, and he went down to assess Kendrik and her crew over an hour ago. Did Tia'tan or Noar go with him?

::One moment.::

If something *was* wrong, she needed to get down there ASAP. But if that were true, then she also needed a psionic with her, and that meant waiting until one of the three could get away. Damnit, damnit, damnit!

::Noar's working with Corinth and some others on the shield generators, but I can't reach Tia.:: Worry flowed into her. Her need to move now was echoed by Vayne. ::I'm coming to you, where are you?::

It was agony to walk calmly down the corridor on the command level and carry her bullpup casually, when she wanted to sprint dead out to the nearest lift. Instead, she had to walk, greeting anyone they passed as if she had time for that. Vayne met her and Hekkar at the lift, and the three of them boarded while talking about dinner in the commissary. As soon as the doors closed they were double-checking their weapon charges, the seating of her kris daggers in their sheaths, Hekkar's spare ion pistol in his ankle holster...

"We can't keep this up," Kayla said. "All these secrets and charades... It's bullshit. There's too much going on to continue doing this."

"Agreed," Hekkar said. "We need to confront the captain with what we know."

"What we *know*," Vayne said, "is exactly nothing. And all I care about right now is finding Toble and Tia'tan safe."

Nothing more was said as they arrived and the lift doors opened.

No threats awaited them, and no sounds were heard. They cleared the corridor quickly and cautiously, sweeping for any sign of activity, but saw no one. Even so, Kayla's senses were tingling with the certainty that something had gone wrong. Vayne must have picked that up, because he started running, heedless of any threat, forcing her and Hekkar to do the same.

Her fears were confirmed moments later when the stench of burnt flesh reached them. They arrived to find the door to the barracks wide open. Her mind couldn't quite register what she was seeing when she entered, because it was so far from what she expected to find.

Bunks had been ripped from their moorings and the twisted wrecks thrown about the room as if a tornado had come through. Bedding was torn and flung everywhere. One of the bunks had crashed into the diagnostic imaging equipment Toble had brought in to examine the crew, smashing it to pieces. Based on the tangle of metal and blood and body parts, at least two of the crew had been in their bunks when they'd been crumpled into a ball as if by some giant fist.

It only took a glance to confirm that Toble was in fact dead. He was propped up against a bunk, his body burned by multiple plasma blasts. His head had been torn from his body and placed in his lap, the face a charred mass of white bone and melted skin. Both of his arms were missing entirely.

Kayla swallowed hard to keep the nausea at bay. She

spotted Toble's medkit hidden under what used to be a bunk and focused desperately on that one thing. If anyone had miraculously survived this, she was going to need it.

"Vayne, call for Natali," she said, even as she spotted Tia'tan on the floor. "And tell Corinth to lock himself in his cabin and not open the door for anyone." Kayla's anxiety kicked up another notch. *Please let Tia'tan still be alive.* Blood formed a halo around the Ilmenan's head, and she lay unmoving on her back, pinned under another bunk.

Her chest moved the slightest bit, rising as she struggled to take a breath. "I've got Tia'tan!" Kayla shouted.

"I'll check the others," Hekkar answered, already in motion.

Kayla dove for the medkit, crawling past a severed limb to squeeze under the destroyed bunk. She wedged herself under the twisted metal, fingers outstretched and grasping. "How many are dead? Are all of the others accounted for?"

She finally got a purchase on the kit and shimmied backward out from under the bunk. *Focus on Tia'tan. One task at a time.* Luckily, all her field medical training was fresh, thanks to fighting in the Blood Pit and living life in hiding.

Focus, Kayla. Assess first, then treat. Right.

Kayla forced herself to take an objective look at Tia'tan. Blood from a wound on her head coated her forehead and her eyes, dripping down by her ears. Her hair was so matted with it that Kayla couldn't locate the injury at first. Tia'tan's skin was pale, her breathing shallow, and her heartbeat was racing. Shock, most likely; her body shutting down from the trauma.

Kayla dropped to the floor beside her, tearing the medkit open and dumping the contents. She registered a sound of pain coming from Vayne and pushed it aside, grabbing a monitor strip from the medkit and wrapping it around Tia'tan's uninjured left wrist to keep track of her vital signs. Apparently the strip was set to give audible report because it spoke immediately, confirming Kayla's fears about shock setting in. Kayla stripped off her shirt and pressed it to Tia'tan's head. *Where was the wound?*

"This one's dead," Hekkar called. "These two as well."

Natali burst into the room. "How could you not tell me any of this?" she demanded.

"Later," Kayla snapped. "For now, alert Noar—I'll need supplies from the ship's med station. Splints for sure, and we'll need gurneys to transport Tia'tan and whoever else." They'd need something to cover the bodies up with, but that could wait.

Natali joined Hekkar in his gruesome task while Vayne conveyed Kayla's orders telepathically.

Tia'tan's right forearm was bent at an unnatural angle, and one of the arm bones had sliced through the skin. It was hard to gauge much else with the collapsed bed frame on top of her. She was hesitant to move it, as it might make things worse, but things couldn't really get much worse, at this point. The bunk could have crushed her spine or ruptured her organs. Either way, it had to come off, and who knew where else Tia'tan would start bleeding once circulation was restored. Kayla pulled a stack of dermalplasts from the kit and called to no one in particular. "Get this bunk off of her, now." She didn't dare take her eyes off Tia'tan, afraid the woman would slip into death if she so much as blinked.

The twisted metal wreck flew off of Tia'tan and crashed somewhere farther in the room. Tia'tan moaned and came to, her eyes fluttering, the fingers of her good arm twitching. The monitor strip calmly detailed her wildly erratic and crashing vital signs, causing Vayne to come running.

"Only one of them is alive," Natali called. "The rest are gone."

With the wreck of the bunk removed, Tia'tan's mangled and bloody left side came into view. It must have taken the brunt of whatever had happened. Two long lacerations opened up on her thigh, each pumping with fresh blood now that circulation was returning to her lower body.

Kayla shoved the stack of dermalplasts at Vayne. "Here. Slice open her pant leg and apply these: the adhesion will stem the bleeding. Vayne!" She had to shout a second time to get his attention. "Damnit, Vayne, I need your help to save her, so get it the frutt together!" That snapped him to focus. "Cut the rest of her clothes, too, so I can see the full extent of her injuries."

Tia'tan's clothes fell apart as Vayne sliced through the fabric with his mind.

"Tachycardia detected," the monitoring strip reported.

Fantastic.

"Someone come put pressure on this!" Kayla released her hold on the makeshift bandage she'd been holding to Tia'tan's head without waiting to see if anyone heard her. She scrambled for the defib electric pack, sending half the contents of the medkit flying as she pulled it out. She had the electrodes extended and was trying to decide where to affix them on Tia'tan's chest when the monitor called, "Ventricular fibrillation detected. Heart failure imminent."

Kayla jammed the electrodes down. "Vayne, get clear."

"Cardiac arrest detected. Recommend biphasic defibrillation."

"Whatever you say," Kayla muttered, and punched the button. Tia'tan arched off the floor as the pulse shot through her body, probably doing even more damage to herself. Kayla held her breath for a result.

"Cardiac arrest in progress. Attempting defibrillation again," the monitor reported, having synched with the defib pack.

Tia'tan arched again in a gruesome contortion. She lay motionless for a second, looking like death, then she dragged in a breath and started gasping and coughing at the same time. The monitor reported a resumed sinus rhythm.

That's not going to last long, Kayla thought to herself. Tia'tan's abdomen was swollen. Trauma to the liver or spleen? Ruptured arteries? She had no way of knowing. Other than the lacerations on one thigh, her legs looked relatively intact, thankfully.

Natali knelt at Tia'tan's head, holding Kayla's shirt to the bloodiest area once again. "The living crew member is Benny, actually, and in surprisingly good shape considering the state of everyone else."

Tia'tan struggled to breathe. Kayla grabbed the stethoscope from the floor, set the ear pieces, and listened to Tia'tan's chest on each side. She wasn't a pro at diagnosing, but she couldn't detect any sounds on Tia'tan's left. A collapsed lung seemed very possible, considering the blunt-force trauma to that side of her body. Not to mention the head wound. How bad was that? Mild concussion, or something more concerning like intracranial bleeding?

This was way beyond Kayla's capabilities.

At least Vayne had the dermalplasts applied to Tia'tan's thigh, hopefully saving her from bleeding out. Kayla spoke to Natali, even as she sorted through the medkit's contents for a plasma packet. "She needs a trauma surgeon. Probably more than one. I need you to contact Wetham and have him send medics immediately."

This second, or she's not going to make it.

Kayla found the blood construction apparatus and the packet of blank plasma. The machine would type Tia'tan's blood, then recreate it by transforming the blank plasma into a compatible blood synthesis. Judging by the wounds, Tia'tan was going to need more than one transfusion.

"I don't care what you have to promise," Kayla continued, "just get surgeons here. Tell them to bring as much equipment as they can, the *Yari*'s is beyond out of date." She hooked the blood construction apparatus to Tia'tan's left arm and ran the sequence.

Natali nodded. "I'll make it happen. Tell me how many guards you want for securing the medical station and I'll have them waiting by the time you get there." Then she was gone, calling out orders on the ship's comm, summoning the captain and crew and getting everyone gathered into the control room for a lockdown—one or more mad men were definitely on the loose. Noar arrived with supplies at that moment, accompanied by two rebels ready to help.

"Mother of All—" someone swore in Ordochian. Someone else ran back into the hallway and retched.

Noar, thank the stars, was a professional in the face of a catastrophe, bringing over the supplies and asking immediately, "What do you need?"

"Can you stop the bleeding on her head wound? If it's not immediately life-threatening, just wrap a bandage around it and we'll deal with it later."

Assuming there was a later.

Kayla was flipping through info on the medical datapad, looking for the best place to insert a syringe into Tia'tan's chest cavity to draw out some air and hopefully reinflate her lung. At this point, it was all Kayla knew how to do for her in terms of life-saving measures.

Vayne sat almost as pale as Tia'tan, minus the blue tinge to the lips. He wasn't moving, not even blinking, as he started at the reformatted blood pumping into Tia'tan's arm. He was stressing Kayla right the frutt out.

"Vayne, prep a splint, we need to set her arm," she said, mostly to give herself enough breathing room to attempt the lung reinflation procedure.

Noar must have handled the head wound, because he murmured that he was going to check on Benny.

Tia'tan's monitoring strip warned of critically low blood oxygen levels. Her abdomen was definitely filling with some sort of fluid. Kayla felt for the location of the ribs, said a prayer that she didn't hit any nerves, veins, or arteries, and inserted the needle into Tia'tan's chest cavity. The syringe filled with air as she drew back on the plunger.

That was right, wasn't it? Man, she hoped so. She stuck Tia'tan a second time, drawing off another fifty ccs of air, but that was all she dared do. She was already introducing a possible infection to the lungs, and if she'd done the wrong thing... No time to think about that now. She hushed everyone and listened to Tia'tan's left lung again. Better. Not perfect by any means, but she was breathing easier. *Thank the stars.*

"I need to examine Tia'tan's head wound, then clean and treat as many of the external wounds as I can, but that's going to have to wait until we get her upstairs."

"Are you sure we should move her?" Vayne asked. He looked terrified by the idea.

"We have to. She needs to be on a ventilator, and she's lost a lot of blood." A lot. She was going to go into cardiac arrest again if they didn't move quickly. "Plus I need to get antibiotics into her, among other things."

Kayla could see the mutilated body of Toble from the corner of her eye and it was killing her. "Can someone cover Toble, for the love of the void?" A rebel rushed in to help.

They worked quickly to stabilize Tia'tan for the move. Hekkar and the rebels cleared wreckage from around her and laid down the backboard. They'd already set up a gurney. Noar held her down by the shoulders as Kayla directed Vayne how best to set her broken arm bone. He could do it with much greater accuracy using his psi powers. Tia'tan thrashed weakly at the movement, startled to a greater level of consciousness by the new pain. Her eyelids fluttered and she gasped something out. A word? A name?

"Benny," Noar said, "she's worried for Benny, I can feel it." He bent closer to her, whispering something soothing, which Kayla promptly tuned out. She didn't give a damn about Benny right now, or any of the crew. It was *their* fault this had happened, that Toble had been mutilated and Tia'tan lay near death.

Vayne held Tia'tan's straightened arm immobile and Kayla applied a dermalplast to the skin where her bone had broken through. She quickly wrapped it in a coolant cuff to help reduce the swelling. Tia'tan passed out as Kayla splinted it, which was another worry, since Tia'tan likely had a massive concussion and shouldn't be allowed to sleep.

How the frutt would she know?

Noar immobilized her neck and head with the braces the rebels had brought, Vayne tied her legs together, and Kayla gingerly laid her broken arm on her chest before covering it with the other.

"We're going to treat her like she has spinal damage, since we have no idea if that's the case or not." Kayla looked up at Vayne. "Shift her onto the backboard, then lift her onto the gurney. I know you want to be gentle with her, but believe me, fast is better." She tried to convey the extreme importance of what she'd just said. "The best way you can help Tia'tan right now is to get this over with."

When Vayne nodded, Kayla scrambled to stuff medical supplies back in Toble's case. "Make sure the lift is waiting," she said to a rebel. All around them the crews' comms chattered as people called back and forth where they were and where they were headed. Natali had ordered several rebels to the medical station that Kayla was headed for, and it sounded like Ida was going there with another stretcher.

"Can you be my eyes and ears for this?" Kayla asked Shimwell, one of the rebels who had accompanied Noar. She would rather have Hekkar, but he was in no fit state at the moment, not with Toble's ruined body only paces away. "We need to figure it all out, and the next few hours could be telling, but I can only focus on Tia'tan right now."

"I've got it," Shimwell said. "And I'll send the injured crew up after you."

With that, she abdicated any and all responsibility for handling the massive shit storm they'd entered, leaving it up to Natali and everyone else to manage the details and keep her loved ones safe.

Kayla arranged the defib device and the blood charger on Tia'tan's chest, then gave Vayne the go-ahead to lift her telekinetically. Hekkar and Shimwell slid the backboard under her, strapped her on, and then Vayne lifted her onto the gurney. The monitoring strip warned of worsening vital signs and Kayla's chest constricted.

"Hurry," she said, and took one last look at Toble's lifeless form. *I still need you.*

19

Vayne covered Tia'tan's body with his mind, laying psionic pressure on her like a smothering blanket in order to keep her perfectly still as he rushed the gurney along. Every instinct screamed for him to slow down, be cautious, handle her like glass, but the fear coming off of Kayla in waves had him flying down the corridor.

She mentally chanted *Don't stop, don't stop, don't stop*, and while he didn't know if she meant him or Tia'tan's heartbeat, the end result was the same: Vayne kept running, Kayla beside him.

They arrived at the nearest medical station without incident, and were met by several well-armed rebels. No one spoke except Kayla. She ordered everyone around relentlessly, getting things ready and in place before moving Tia'tan into a bed. He watched his sister's nimble fingers flying over consoles and doing up tubes, none of which he had the first clue about. Her face was screwed up with frustration and intense concentration as she worked. Being in the dark was killing him. Every twitch and moan from Tia'tan had him holding his breath. He had to know what was going on as it happened, or he would lose it. He brushed at Kayla's mental shields, promising without words that he would only listen, not disrupt her at all, and begging her to open to him. If she wouldn't...

He shut that dark line of thought down instantly. Kayla saved him by letting him into her mind.

While Kayla looked so capable outwardly, inwardly her thoughts were a mess. She didn't know where anything was in the room, or even what half of what she needed should even look like, considering it was five hundred years old. She cursed her limited medical knowledge, the *Yari*'s refusal to accept input from Toble's modern-day devices, and the person or persons who had done this to them all. She was convinced she was going to accidentally kill Tia'tan with her ineptness, and just as convinced Tia'tan would die if she did nothing. She hated this ship and every crew member on it quite vehemently in this precise moment, and she wished desperately that there was someone—anyone—on board who could just tell her the right thing to do. She hesitated, becoming stymied in all the choices and what ifs.

"You're doing great, Kayla," he said aloud. "Keep going." Please keep going. She had to, because who else was there?

She blinked, her eyes refocusing, and gave him a grateful smile. "Thanks," she said, then, back to it, shouted, "Where the frutt is my hot water?"

By now she had Tia'tan breathing oxygen from a mask, hooked up to lines bringing in blood and fluids, and being treated with antibiotics. She set Vayne to washing the blood from Tia'tan's left side so they could assess the injuries more fully. She unwound the bandage from Tia'tan's head, examining the gash across her forehead that had bled so profusely. When she didn't freak out or send everyone scrambling with another set of orders, Vayne realized that, like most cuts to the scalp, it probably looked worse than it was.

Ida arrived with Noar, two rebels, and Benny on a gurney. The captain immediately took charge of Benny's treatment, leaving Kayla free to focus on Tia'tan.

"Thank you," Kayla said to the captain, then switched her focus immediately. "Noar, I need you, since you're the only other person in the room who knows how to operate imperial medsticks." She gestured to the open kit on the table beside her. "Can you start on those cuts on her thigh while I run some diagnostics?" She didn't even wait for a reply.

Vayne withdrew from Kayla's mind. When had he become so useless? He wanted to help, knew he should do *something*, but he was paralyzed. The scene was so familiar. His mother had lain in that bed, wracked by horrible agony after Dolan had used his machine to rip the psi powers from her mind... again. She hadn't been bloody like Tia'tan, but she'd been just as close to death.

Natali lay there.

Erebus, the night he died.

Jinto, who had been his favorite aunt.

Kerryn, who was his lover at the time of the coup.

Vayne had lain in the same prone position, suffering from yet another bout with Dolan's machine, Natali watching over him, Uncle Ghirhad keeping vigil.

They died, one by one, bodies finally giving out.

He'd died there, at least in part.

And it was happening again. Had Tia suffered brain damage? Would she emerge from this the same, or had she been irrevocably changed, the way each of Dolan's prisoners had been?

Had he already lost her when he was just starting to know her?

Kayla swung the antiquated diagnostic equipment from its cradle in the wall and studied it. "I need the manual. It's over there, by the lab bench."

This he could do. Vayne whisked it from its slot and floated it over to her, holding it open so she could flip through the pages without moving away from Tia'tan. It took a lot of hmming, button pressing, and page flipping, but she was finally satisfied with the settings and hit the start button. The machine hummed to life and started some kind of calibration sequence, if the readout was accurate.

Kayla finally had a chance to examine the damage to Tia'tan's left side. She had a series of scratches and lacerations from her chest to her hip, but nothing serious. A massive hematoma was forming over her ribcage, though, and the swelling in her abdomen wasn't decreasing.

"Let's let the scanner do its thing," Kayla said to everyone. Noar had closed the deeper tissue on Tia'tan's thigh wounds, and would repair the dermis once the scan was complete.

While they washed up, Vayne reached out gingerly with his mind, brushing against Tia'tan's. He was met immediately with a great deal of pain, which seemed to be the only thing she was aware of at the moment, and even that was being reported on an instinctive level. Her consciousness, if it was even still there, was buried so deeply within that he couldn't reach her.

Ida joined the others. "Benny is being of sound body, mostly, but blood vessels having popped in his eyes is to lead me on a belief of strangling. Also, marks on his neck have appeared to the shape of hands." She shook her head. "I am not knowing who has the making of all this. It seems possible not, and he is still unconscious."

"But you *did* know about Officer Kendrik and the others, correct?" Kayla pressed. "They'd been locked up on your orders?"

"Locked up and drugged," Vayne spat, furious over the whole thing. They should have freed the prisoners as soon as they found them, then none of this would have happened. Toble wouldn't have been compelled to check on them once again, and he wouldn't have asked Tia'tan for an escort.

"I had my crew to be quarantined, yes," Ida confirmed. "For health and safety being theirs. But I would *never* harm them, not in any way of your thinking." She drew herself up. "I am captain of this ship, their wellbeing of responsibility mine."

Vayne turned to face her, unable to keep quiet. "Those sedatives you used were killing them. Only four people had access to their cell, which one of you was it?"

"You having the access too, apparently." Ida looked just as furious as he felt. "How am I to know or to know not whether this is one of your doing?" She turned on Kayla. "What was *your* medic doing there? He could have the knowing of how to drug a body."

"He was trying to help them," Kayla shot back. "And he died for it. He was trying to help *your* crew, which you should have been doing."

"Why was their presence kept from us?" Vayne asked. "You told me and Tia that none of the other quarantined *stepa* had survived."

"It not being your business."

"Everything that happens on this ship," a cold voice said from the doorway, "is my business." Natali had arrived. "Captain, we will discuss this later."

Ida's lips tightened a fraction, but she inclined her head. "Yes, *en'shaar*." The perfect Ordochian soldier, bowing to the wishes of the planet's proclaimed leader.

How long would that last?

The diagnostic machine beeped, drawing everyone's attention. Images started scrolling on the complink at the lab bench.

"At least we know it's working," Kayla said, sounding hopeful for the first time.

"The surgeons are on their way," Natali reported. "They're packing equipment now. Do you have any special recommendations for them?"

Kayla sighed. "She'll definitely need surgery on her arm, has a seriously collapsed lung, probably punctured by a fractured rib, so they'll need a machine to suck the air out at the very least, and most likely surgery there, as well." Kayla squinted her eyes closed for a second, as if trying to keep a million minute details inside her skull. "I assume she has a concussion, considering how everything was beat to shit in that room. As soon as the scan is finished I should be able to gauge if she has swelling in her brain. For now they should act as if she does and plan accordingly."

She looked up at Natali. "Tell them to bring any possible medications they think she'll need. I have no idea if the freshlock on the *Yari*'s medications works as well as it's supposed to. I could be pumping expired saline into her right now." She kicked a cabinet in frustration. "I wish we could transport her to their medical facilities, but that's obviously impossible."

"Good work, Kayla. Honestly." Natali held her gaze, and something passed between the two *ro'haars*, a message of support and solidarity that only another *ro'haar* would understand. "I'll leave you to it and update Wetham. Let me know what you learn from the scans." She turned to go, but paused on the med unit's threshold. "I've asked Wetham to notify Malkor and Rigger about Toble's death. I am truly sorry for you all."

It was all over but for the waiting.

Kayla sat on a stool beside Tia'tan's bed, one eye on the monitor, one eye half closed in sleep. The adrenaline had passed, leaving her depleted. Only the fear that Tia'tan might die at any moment kept her awake.

"You should rest," Vayne said. "I can watch her for a bit."

Kayla just shook her head. She'd been too late for Toble: she wasn't going to fail Tia'tan.

The surgeons had yet to arrive, but Ariel reported that they would dock at any moment. They'd better frutting hurry up. She'd only been able to determine any of Tia'tan's injuries by having Toble's medical datapad scan the diagnostic images that the *Yari*'s equipment had taken, and then spit out a diagnosis, which Kayla had passed on to the Ordochian medical team. She certainly didn't know which way was up when looking at the abdominal scans.

Even though the equipment was monitoring Tia'tan's vitals, Kayla felt the pulse at her wrist herself. Still thready. "For the love of—"

"Shuttle has returned," Ida announced over the comms.

"We're standing by to offload the equipment," Natali replied.

"About time," Vayne muttered, never pausing in his pacing.

"There's still so much to do. The bodies, Toble..." Kayla trailed off, unable to fully grasp the reality that Toble was now dead. The medic had saved her life, had preserved the use of her arm after first Janeen's attack with the muscle-stiffening drug, then again after the biocybe's attack during Malkor's rescue. He'd patched them all up, so many times.

Grief rose up to choke her. She cleared her throat, pushing the feelings down, trying to lock them away so she could stay functional for as long as necessary. "We have to get to the bottom of everything. Who attacked the prisoners? Why? Where have they gone? Or is it one of the dead crew members we found in the room?"

A little while later they heard boots running down the corridor, orders being called back and forth, and then a small army burst into the med station armed to the teeth with life-saving equipment. She gave a report of all actions she had taken to an efficient man who seemed to be in charge. She ran down the diagnoses she'd made, with caveats, and which medications she'd administered. Then she was politely, but forcefully, urged from the room so that they could take over.

Benny woke and reported his story to Ida. He said he had gone to the room to change the calorie pack in the food synthesizer and check on the prisoners' health and wellbeing. Everything had seemed a little off to him. The inmates appeared agitated instead of peaceful, and everyone was eyeing everyone else with suspicion. Then Tia'tan and Toble had arrived, setting off Enska, and the chaos had begun. Others in the room might have attacked each other, or fought against Enska, but Enska was the one who had done the most damage, including killing Toble and injuring Benny and Tia'tan before fleeing.

20

THE *YARI*

Finally relieved of the duty of keeping Tia'tan alive, Kayla knew she should probably take the chance to rest. No doubt a fresh disaster would wake her in a few hours.

Instead, she turned to Vayne. "I want to find Zimmerman, Enska, and whoever else now. *First.* I want to question them without Ida and her crew around."

"I like how you think, but with so futile a search to date, where do you suggest we start this time?"

She told him about Hekkar's discussion with Tanet and the possibility that Zimmerman and the others could be hiding in the PD itself.

"That is the most outrageous thing I have ever heard," Vayne said. "It's amazing the crew of the *Yari* survived as long as it did, huh?"

"So, are you in? I hope so, but I'm going whether you're with me or not." No one could stop her now. She was already making plans. She'd need an energy cell strong enough to power one of the lifts through the unpowered section, an EMU—there was no guarantee that Zimmerman had turned the life support on there, even if she suspected he had—and a bullpup, as hers was left in the barracks where they'd found Tia'tan.

"Are you kidding? You couldn't leave me behind if you wanted to. Let's go."

They were armed and ready with bullpups in minutes, jogging down the corridor to save time on their way to retrieve a power pack and their EMUs. Vayne hoped the PD housing was powered and atmosphere-controlled, as Hekkar had speculated. That way, his bullpup would function and he could shoot every last one of the *stepa* hiding out down there.

Then again, the weapons they'd stolen would function as well...

Fair enough: he was in the mood for a fight.

So bloodthirsty, my dear Vayne. I like it, Dolan purred in the back of his mind.

"Shut up," he muttered.

Kayla gave him a funny look. "I didn't say anything."

"No, I know, it's just... Never mind." It's just that he was crazy, that's all. Maybe he should stay on this ship with all the rest of the insane people when this was over. At least then, when Dolan finally succeeded in either taking over his mind completely or convincing him to kill himself, no one would think it was odd.

"Sense anything?" Kayla asked as they jogged. Somehow, she managed to run with her bullpup semi-aimed at the same time.

He shook his head. Not a person nor a psionic blocker either. He'd had zero experience with those blockers in his previous life—they'd fallen out of use on Ordoch as espionage became a lost art—but he was adapt at sensing them now, thanks to the one on the barracks. Or previously on the barracks, he should say, as that one had since been destroyed.

As they neared the lift, the doors opened and a man Vayne recognized only from a military ID stepped out. "I hear you're looking for me," he said.

Zimmerman.

It was tempting to shoot him in the head right there and call it done, but Vayne needed answers, not more corpses.

Kayla looked decidedly less likely to hold her fire.

"Woah!" Zimmerman spread his empty hands out at his sides. "Let's take it down a notch, shall we? I'm First Officer Oliver Zimmerman, presently of the *Yari*." He was tall for a male Wyrd from five centuries previous. His teal hair was cut military short, his skin was as pale as any spacer's, and he looked completely sane. At that moment, at least. "And you're going to have to come with me if you want answers." He stepped backward into the still waiting lift even though neither Vayne nor Kayla had lowered their weapons.

"I haven't kept hidden all this time by having conversations with strangers in the middle of corridors," he called.

Vayne took a cautious step, but then the lift doors started closing and Kayla sprinted, so he held the doors open and raced in after her. No one spoke until the doors closed and the lift started moving.

"Where are we going?" Kayla asked. Zimmerman merely shrugged.

"I didn't sense you," Vayne said, confused. "Not until you came into sight."

"We're soldiers trained for war. We're skilled in stealth, in the technique of cloaking our minds." He looked Vayne up and down, assessing him. "Even from someone as strong as you, it would seem." He lowered his hands to his sides. "We're overdue a chat. Why don't you put your weapons down and I'll try to answer your questions."

Vayne hesitated. He was so full of rage and fear for Tia'tan that he wanted to shoot *something*. Kayla pointed hers at the floor but held on to it, ready to shoot Zimmerman if he so much as breathed suspiciously. Vayne had to follow suit.

"To answer your first question: no, we did not kill Officer Kendrik and the others. We did not murder your friends."

Something was off about the man's speech, but Vayne couldn't quite put his finger on it. "Who did?" he demanded.

"You'll have to ask the captain about that."

"Are you saying Ida did it?" Kayla asked.

"I'm saying she knows who did."

The lift opened on a powered level that looked just like any other powered level. No one else waited for them, no sign saying "secret base this way" came into view. Even knowing it was risky, but with no other choice present, Vayne and Kayla followed Zimmerman down the corridor until they came to a commissary. No one waited inside there, either. It was merely the three of them in the long, empty soldiers' commissary. No trap, no ambush, no firefight.

"What are we doing here?"

"Chatting," Zimmerman said. "You didn't think I was going to take you to my secret lair, did you? This is just as good a place as any."

The discrepancy came to Vayne then. "You speak clearly, without the archaic dialect."

Zimmerman laughed. "That? That was easy enough to shed. We've listened to every transmission that's ever come through the Tear from Ordoch, spoken to modern-day Ordochians on the other side. It took little effort to learn the necessary adjustments.

"The captain and the others could do it if they wanted to," Zimmerman said disparagingly. "I think they like being antiques."

"Why did you learn it, then?" Kayla asked.

"Why else? To join the future. We want off of this ship. We want to start a new life on Ordoch, a second life. We want to see our homeworld again, live among our people."

"You keep saying 'we,'" Vayne said. "How many 'we' are we talking about?"

"Enough," Zimmerman answered. Vayne couldn't tell if he intended that as a threat or not, but it didn't exactly comfort him.

"Why are you hiding?" Vayne asked instead. "You seem sane enough to me—so far. Why are you not with the rest of the crew?"

"Is that what she told you?" Zimmerman asked. "That we're hiding out because we're insane?"

"Brain damaged and insane, technically." So far, though, he

found Zimmerman to be the most normal of the ancient crew. "Are you mutineers? Is this some personal battle between you and the captain that we've stumbled on?"

"You could say that. Ida and I are at war because I know she's a traitor and she wants to keep me quiet."

Interesting… "A traitor to who?"

"Ordoch." Zimmerman looked at them as if they should have known that.

Kayla looked skeptical, and Vayne agreed. Ida might be up to something, but she was the most loyal commander he knew, sticking by her commission even five hundred years later. Staying on point and on mission to protect Ordoch from its enemies.

"You have to be joking," Vayne said. "Is this a five-hundred-years-ago thing?"

"When you have frontal lobe damage from shoddy cryosleep pods, five hundred years ago is now, and vice versa." Zimmerman looked almost sad for a moment. "You have to remember, we haven't 'lived' for five hundred years, not really. We were asleep for almost the entirety of it.

"War is still our reality." Zimmerman seemed to be remembering a different time as he spoke. "While other officers were woken from cryosleep periodically by the system in order to check on the ship and everyone else, I wasn't woken. Ida had me declared a traitor and locked in a pod the moment she realized I had discovered her secret."

Okay, now Zimmerman wasn't sounding quite as sane as they had hoped for.

"Get to the point," Vayne said. "People are dead, or nearly dead, and all of this goes back to you and Ida, each declaring the other and their followers insane." The hand holding his bullpup twitched as he spoke. "Tell us what happened, exactly, and do it quickly."

Kayla added, "Why shouldn't we comm Ida and tell her exactly where we are?"

"If you didn't doubt the captain, at least on some level, you would have already told her," Zimmerman countered.

Score one point for Zimmerman.

"Ida isn't Ordochian, not really. I mean, she's genetically Ordochian, but she was raised on Ilmena. She and several others on board were raised by crazy fundamentalists with an intense hatred for all things Ordochian." He paused, clearly ordering his thoughts, trying to decide where to start. "Bah. There's so little time. Already your absence has been noted and deemed suspicious." He gave the ghost of a grin. "The manhunt is on. Again. Or still. Whatever."

Vayne hadn't heard a thing. Then, for one brief second, he heard everything, a dozen mind voices calling to each other, tracking whereabouts and clearing levels. Corinth searching for Kayla's mind, terrified beyond words to find nothing when he reached out. Before he could reply to any of it, the sounds all disappeared.

"You've been blocking us," Vayne growled, though he should have expected it. Zimmerman had been keeping him or Kayla from contacting anyone psionically and vice versa.

Zimmerman held up a hand. "I can tell you're both ready to murder me, but there's something I need to show you first."

Vayne kept his weapon trained on the man as he went to the defunct food synthesizer to retrieve something.

"This—"

The commissary doors suddenly slid open behind them. "Watch out!" someone shouted from the entrance, and a shot streaked over Vayne's shoulder, white-hot plasma cutting a ribbon through his own shield before it headed toward Zimmerman.

"Get down!" Zimmerman called, and he dodged out of the way, but not quickly enough. The blast hit him in the thigh and knocked him sideways. Benny came sprinting past, followed by Ariel, who jumped on the struggling Zimmerman.

"Which ones do we shoot?" Kayla shouted without looking away from the combatants. Suddenly Zimmerman had a plasma pistol in his hand, and Ariel was wrestling to keep it pointed away from her.

Benny turned to Vayne. "Get out of here for safety being yours! Go!"

Another bolt of plasma lit up the room, this time launched from the pistol upward to the ceiling. Benny, Kayla, and Vayne hit the floor simultaneously.

We are so getting shot. Vayne strengthened the psi shield he surrounded Kayla with, even while she scuttled to cover his body with her own.

Neither of which would do a damn bit of good if that pistol got turned their way.

"We need him alive," Kayla yelled. "Don't kill him."

Vayne sent a blast of telekinetic energy toward the weapon, intending to knock it from both Ariel's and Zimmerman's grip. Instead, it ricocheted off the tangle of physical and psionic forces the two were using against each other. At least now he knew where to get in. He struck out a second time and the gun went flying across the room, landing against a bulkhead where Vayne trapped it, making it impossible for any of the others to reclaim it.

Benny rose to his knees, still clasping his bullpup, but Kayla was quicker. She drew the imperial weapon she wore at her hip and unloaded the complete charge at Zimmerman and Ariel.

Holy—

"What have you done?" Benny screeched.

Kayla sat back on her haunches. "Relax. That was stun level." She sighed, looking at the now unconscious crew members. "That happened so quickly..."

"You were fools to being trust of him," Benny snapped, his voice hoarse from the attack he'd suffered last night. "Fools to of his talk be listening." He shook his head in disgust. "Could have been killed, and then where would Ordoch be? Come. You help to get to the brig now."

Benny stood and strode to the comm system. "Calling off of the search, we are having possession of Zimmerman."

21

Vayne stood in the corridor in front of the medical station, looking through the glass at Tia's still form. The medics from Ordoch had completed a second surgery on her abdomen and now she lay peacefully, undisturbed. The blanket covered most of the bandaging, but her forearm had a skin patch where they'd entered to put pins into the broken bones, and her brow had tiny dermal regenerators on it to heal the scar from where she'd been struck. As long as she hadn't received any brain damage—and it was still too early to tell—she'd be as good as new in a little while.

All in all, she looked remarkable, considering she'd looked like a corpse less than a day ago.

He saw it perfectly, as if for the first time: Tia on the floor, bloodied and mangled. Tia on the bed, alarms beeping and the surgeons shouting, "we're losing her."

And he, locked on the other side, frozen, useless. Just as he was now.

I could have lost her.

The pain hit like a kick to the chest, so hard and unexpected that his shoulders hunched in response and he couldn't draw breath.

::I'm sorry.:: He couldn't stop his emotions from accompanying his voice, they were too big to hold in. Shame. Failure. Fear. Longing—futile longing, for something that would never be. A desire to be known. Truly known. Not as the person he was before Dolan, as the person he could become.

Thankfully, Tia'tan was too far gone in unconsciousness to hear him.

Would she have *seen* him, in a different universe? In a lifetime where he could actually escape Dolan's ghost?

Which brought him to why he was here, now, saying a pitiful goodbye like an idiot while everyone else on the ship made final preparations for the rooks' jump.

Vayne's brief conversation with Malkor earlier—not even half a day ago—had convinced him of what he needed to do. The best way to keep his *ro'haar* safe, to keep Corinth, Natali, Tia, and Noar safe, to help his people and his world, was to stop Vega. And if he had to play the bait in Malkor's scheme to steal the Influencer, he was more than ready for that.

Kayla's words from earlier came back to him: "Stopping Vega, freeing Ordoch—that's the ultimate defeat of Dolan and his plans. You will finally be free of him. Your captivity will finally be at an end."

He wasn't sure he believed that, but... He glanced at Tia one last time... It sure would be nice if it were true.

Inside his head, he could hear Dolan's ghost laughing.

We both know what you are after, my dear Vayne, and it isn't freedom. The Influencer is the ultimate prize. With your strength and my knowledge, we could rule the galaxy.

"I'd rather die."

You forget how well I know you, how well I made you.

"You know nothing," he snapped. Void, was he really arguing with a dead man, standing in the corridor where anyone could hear him? At what point would he concede that he'd finally gone over the edge?

We'll see shortly, won't we?

Time to go.

In a perfect world, Vayne thought as he rushed to meet with the rebel Shimwell, he wouldn't be leaving the *Yari* just yet. In a perfect world he'd have the luxury of tearing the entire ship apart in search of the murderer who'd nearly killed Tia'tan.

Most on board the *Yari* believed Zimmerman to be the killer who had torn through the prisoners' barracks. With him now in the brig, they considered the ship relatively secure.

But Kayla didn't, Natali didn't, and Vayne sure as the void didn't. It didn't make sense. Zimmerman had been perfectly hidden for so long, why come out now to kill Kendrik and the others? And why would Kendrik trust him if she were aware he could do something like that?

Zimmerman was probably the root of most of the danger on the ship, but he wasn't guilty of this crime. Not that they'd ever know for sure, since Zimmerman refused to speak to any of his interrogators.

Vayne hustled to the maglift, anxious to rendezvous with Shimwell—the rebel Kayla seemed to trust—before the man changed his mind. Shimwell was extremely loyal to the rebellion, Vayne learned, which worked in Vayne's favor. The man readily agreed to commandeer one of the *Yari*'s shuttles and fly him out to the Tear. He looked doubly excited when Vayne explained it was for a mission vital to regaining Ordoch's freedom.

They were almost to the shuttle bay when Shimwell mentioned he needed to confirm the transport order with Natali first, since she was his superior on board. Vayne spouted off three different reasons why even Natali couldn't know about the mission, and that was when his plan hit a snag: Shimwell had seen Natali in action.

And once a person had seen Natali at her haughtiest, iciest, most authoritative, they never wanted to cross her.

Luckily invoking Wetham's name saved the day. Shimwell's ultimate loyalty belonged to Wetham, not Natali. After that it was as simple as claiming that Vayne's orders came directly from Ordoch's de facto leader, especially considering they couldn't contact Ordoch to confirm the orders with Wetham and still keep it secret from those on the *Yari*.

And if, after they'd launched the shuttle, the entire ship, including his *ro'haar*, were shouting on the comms at them to turn around and return to the ship for the jump, well, Vayne could make up for that later. After all, he'd left Kayla a note explaining his reasoning. That would serve to blunt her wrath a little bit, right?

Definitely not.

Poor Shimwell was going to get the dressing down of his life once he returned to the *Yari* without Vayne.

The trip through the Tear was as terrifying as it was brief. Luckily it hadn't decided to close and send him to oblivion— this time—and he arrived at the cavern in one piece. Vayne doffed his EMU and followed an overawed rebel to the main level of the base, where Wetham and others waited to greet him. The rebel leader ushered him forward. Vayne made himself nod and acknowledge people as he walked down the plascrete corridors of the subterranean levels, all the while thinking, *If any of you come near me, I'm going to lose it.*

Luckily no one demanded a speech, and Wetham brought him to the room where Malkor, the remains of the octet, and several of Wetham's lieutenants were meeting.

Once greetings were finished, Malkor pulled Vayne aside. "How did it go with Kayla? I admit, I'm a little surprised to see you at all."

Vayne arched a brow. "Isn't that why you commed me in private, to avoid having the discussion with Kayla at all?"

"I commed you in private because despite being an *il'haar*, you're still your own man and have a right to consider a proposal on your own, before your overprotective *ro'haar* declares it out of the question." He frowned. "I never meant for you to keep it from her."

Vayne gave him a bland stare. "You don't know Kayla as

well as you think you do if you imagined she'd agree to stay on the ship while her *il'haar* confronted Vega."

"Maybe you're not giving her enough credit to make the wisest choice. She's safest on the ship, out from under the occupation's thumb."

The others in the room were doing an excellent job of not looking their way. Still, Vayne lowered his voice.

"She doesn't give a damn about her own safety, not where you or I are concerned, which is precisely why neither of us told her."

Malkor stared at him a moment, then nodded. "At least you and I can agree on something."

And curse the man, Vayne liked him a little more for it.

Malkor felt just a *little* bit guilty about not having told Kayla about the plan.

Okay, enormously guilty. He also wasn't certain she'd forgive him for endangering her twin's life in such a way. He'd done it out of love for her, though, and he'd make the same decision again.

The truth was, he needed Vayne. Not only was he their best ticket to a meeting with Vega, but as one of the strongest psionics alive, he was also their best weapon. Malkor didn't know what kind of psionic strength Vega had, he only knew she had taken Vayne's own powers from him and somehow made them her own. Add to that the fact that she would be accompanied by at least one other psionic, and Malkor knew he needed the best. Since they couldn't sneak a dozen psionics into the palace with them, Vayne was their only hope.

Despite what Vayne had said, Malkor did know Kayla. Perhaps even better than Vayne did in some ways. He knew what it meant to Kayla to keep her twin safe. He also knew that she wanted above all things for her people to be free. He couldn't bear the thought of her having to choose between her *il'haar* and her people. Was he wrong to take the choice from her? Possibly. But he wasn't perfect, and there were no perfect choices in this war. The best he could hope for was that she understand he had done it out of love for her, and one day, maybe, forgive him for it.

There would be plenty of tough choices ahead for all of them, no matter the outcome of today's events.

Malkor joined the others at the table to hammer out the last of the mission's details.

"I assume you don't have any devices that block psionic energy," Vayne said to Wetham.

"Right. The imperials took control of the few blockers our minimal police force possessed when they took over the planet. If there are others in existence, we don't have access to them."

"And Vega certainly won't have any of them active near her, not when her stolen psi powers are her best weapon," Aarush added.

Ygreda spoke up. "My spies confirm that the case we suspect of carrying the Influencer is in Agira or Vega's possession at all times. They haven't been able to search their rooms, but whenever Vega and Agira leave, they have the case with them."

"It would be better if they didn't," Vayne said, "because then we wouldn't have to worry about one of them using the Influencer on us."

Malkor had to agree. "If we get lucky and they don't have it in Vega's office with her, then we'll break into their rooms."

Ygreda pulled one set of blueprints off of the stack and indicated what used to be Kayla's parents' apartments. "Which are here."

The fact wasn't lost on Vayne, judging by his sour expression.

"We'll want to go in with as few people as possible," Vayne said. He looked at Malkor. "No offense, but your mental shields are terrible, and certainly no match for the Influencer."

"Are yours?" Malkor asked, not to be a jerk, but because, as mission leader, he needed to know his team's strengths and weaknesses.

Vayne considered it a moment. "Possibly. Not if Dolan were the one using it, but I think I can handle Agira."

"What makes you think she'll be the one using the Influencer?" Vid asked. "I thought Vega was the stronger psionic of the two?"

"She is, but Agira's had a lifetime of psionic training. Compared to her, Vega's a child, stronger or not. If I were Vega, I'd want Agira behind the Influencer's controls."

He turned his attention to Malkor. "Is there anything preventing this from being as easy as using me to gain an audience, shooting through their psi shields with plasma weapons, and walking out? I hope there isn't, because I really like the sound of that."

Malkor chuckled. "That does sound fantastic, but sadly, no, it won't be that easy. As IDC we're not privy to the details of all the army's military-grade tech, but I do know they possess several different gun-jamming device types."

"We can confirm that," Aarush said. "I've seen them employed here on Ordoch."

"All right," Vayne said, "then we'll go with plan B. My 'guards' will deposit me in Vega's office. You'll then turn around and walk out, whether she dismisses you or not."

"Is that wise, you facing them alone?" Rigger asked. Malkor could tell the rest of his team was wondering the same thing, but none of the Wyrds looked concerned. Actually, Wetham, Ygreda, and Aarush looked slightly offended by the question.

Wetham answered her. "He can't fight Vega, Agira, and the Influencer if he has to worry about shielding you too."

"You forgot about shielding the room as well," Aarush said, "to keep Vega or Agira from alerting the guards and calling for reinforcements."

A damn good point. They'd never get out alive if Vega called the whole palace down around their heads. Malkor said, "Since we're hiding our faces under holograms, we can bring an Ordochian with us, provided they understand Imperial Common. They can stay outside the office and handle the telepathic shielding, and you can handle Vega and Agira."

Vayne was nodding. "That will work."

Malkor cleared his throat. With all Vayne had been through, some of it at the hands of Vega herself from the sound of things, Malkor wouldn't blame him if he were out for blood. However... "We need Vega taken alive."

Vayne arched a brow, and the entire room quieted to a hush. Was this the part where Vayne told him to frutt off? Because that moment had been coming since the day they met.

"We need her to stand trial on Falanar as an enemy of the state," Malkor continued. "She needs to be publically discredited, so that the true extent of her crimes can be discovered."

Vayne continued to stare at him, and he began to feel just a little uncomfortable. Was he reading his mind right now? Kayla had said that if they practiced mentally reinforcing their shields over and over, that at least he and the octet would know if someone was trying to mess with their minds. But she'd also added, "As long as the psionic isn't super strong."

"I'm not going to kill her," Vayne finally said, but his tone didn't reassure Malkor.

"You're not?" He almost added, "Then what are you going to do?" because it was clear Vayne was planning something.

Vayne answered the unspoken question. "She stole my powers from me. I'm merely going to take them back, and if she doesn't survive..." Vayne shrugged, and though he didn't exactly smile, the look in his eyes chilled Malkor's blood.

And so it was, finally, at long last, that the *Yari* was ready to shake five hundred years of dust from its bones and fly once again among the stars.

Kayla was ready to shake the shit out of her *il'haar* and Malkor simultaneously, but sadly, they were both out of reach at the moment.

A note, Vayne? Seriously? She couldn't begin to process her emotions, not when so many other things needed her attention. There would be time enough to skin him alive later. For now, it was time to free Ordoch.

Kayla stood on the bridge next to Hekkar, holding Corinth's hand while everyone else arrived. Corinth clearly had his own feelings about Vayne leaving them behind, but he hadn't shared them. Kayla didn't know whether Corinth gripped her hand because the coming jump was so momentous, or to stop her from following Vayne and leaving him behind, too.

Natali stood front and center, next to Ida. Ida's crew were stationed at various consoles, ready with comms, weapons, and navigation. Kayla didn't trust any of them, but as the Ordochian rebels filed in, then Kazamel and his small crew followed by Noar, she became more certain that with these loyal people, Natali could take command of the ship in a second if it became necessary.

Her one nagging worry was the absence of Science Officer Fengrathen. She was the *stepa* who'd touched everything off by appearing in the corridor when she should have been in cryo. Presumably she was loyal to Zimmerman, but hadn't appeared when he was captured. Her body had not been found, which meant she was a loose end when they could ill afford to have one.

"Vidscreen to activate," Ida ordered, recalling Kayla to the present.

One look at the screen reminded her that her problems were so much greater than a single woman on a gargantuan ship.

The fleet of rooks covered the *Yari* like a shiny black skin, lights flashing and rippling wildly as they readied themselves to attempt the jump. The baby rooks, and it seemed like there were millions of them, clung to the hull like so many stickers, though how much help they would be, she couldn't say.

Kazamel, who had been standing with his eyes closed near the portals, finally opened them. "Ready?" he called, his voice sounding confident. He was in contact with the rooks, and would be the one to give the actual order to attempt the jump.

"You may be proceeding," Ida answered.

Kazamel nodded, closed his eyes, and then…

…nothing.

Nothing at all.

There had been no feeling of movement, no time had passed, but Ida let out a happy "Whoop!" anyway.

What…?

And then Kayla saw it. Or rather, didn't see it. The Mine Field was gone. The horizon of debris she'd become so accustomed to seeing was absent from the view, and in its place was a new arrangement of stars.

Holy—

::It worked!:: Corinth grabbed her arm, as if he needed something concrete to grasp and prove he wasn't dreaming. ::I can't believe it, it worked!::

All around her people were cheering and hugging each other, but inexplicably, all she could do was cry. Fat tears rolled down her cheeks as emotion overwhelmed her for a moment. Even more than stepping through the Tear, *this* felt like coming home.

Which meant she had a war to join, so she had better get her shit together.

They'd had the rooks blink them near Ordoch, but not too near, as no one was sure what the creatures' accuracy rating was. They also wanted to be out of weapons range of the imperial ships in orbit while they got their bearings. The sub-hyperstream drives on the *Yari* worked fine and could take them the rest of the way.

Beyond the viewport, Kayla could see the adult rooks frolicking in a dance as exuberant as any the babies had done. Blue, silver, and white lights flashed in a dizzying display. They had a moment of sheer enjoyment, all of them, and then:

"The imperial ship is hailing us, *en'shaar*," Ariel said, breaking into the revelry.

Kayla glanced around. The bridge was packed, giving the illusion of a battleship filled to the airlocks with people.

Natali nodded at Ariel to accept the comm.

The vidscreen switched images and Senior Commander Jersain Vega of the IDC greeted them from the throne room of Ordoch.

Thank the void Natali was the one in charge; she had the

icy aplomb to handle Vega. Kayla had too much history with the woman to be anything but hostile and aggressive.

"Natali," Vega said. "So good to see you again." She wore a formal IDC dress uniform and sat in the chair Kayla's father used to occupy.

Kayla didn't realize how hard she was gripping the pommels of her kris daggers until her palms started to hurt.

"Vega. I cannot say the same." Natali's voice was as fine and sharp as laser-cut crystal.

"There are rumors here," Vega continued, "that the Reinumon heir has returned. I thought they might mean you, but now that I see you're on that derelict ship, I wonder if they meant Vayne. Did you send him to the planet ahead of you?"

Natali ignored the question and asked one of her own. "How soon can I expect your ships to leave Wyrd Space?"

Vega didn't miss a beat. "Just as soon as you provide me with a cure to the TNV."

"What I will provide you with is a chance to withdraw from my planet with your lives."

"Is that so?" Vega didn't seem impressed. "Perhaps—"

"Captain," Benny said, interrupting. "The PD is having the primed and ready for firing, on your command."

Natali whipped around. "What? No, stand down!"

Ida smiled a cold smile, one Kayla had never seen from her before, and a terrible foreboding settled over her.

"She's the traitor!" Kayla shouted, realizing too late that they had put the wrong ship's officer in the brig. She drew her kris and sprinted toward Ida, but she couldn't move as quickly as sound.

"Fire at will, Benny." Ida's voice rose above the chaos that erupted on the bridge as the rebel soldiers scrambled to stop her and her crew from reaching any controls whatsoever.

"Firing," Benny confirmed, his words sucking all the air from the room and freezing Kayla in place. What had he just done?

"For Ilmena!" Ida crowed, her eyes shining with triumph as Ariel, Benny, and Larsa echoed her. "Mission of ours is complete."

The rebels descended on the crew and yanked them away from their stations. Natali cut the comm to the planet, and they all watched in horror, waiting for one or all of the imperial battleships on the screen to be obliterated.

They waited.

And waited.

"Natali," Kayla said, getting her sister's attention as Ida continued her victory speech despite nothing happening.

"Now all of Ordochians having the taste of their own weapon," Ida went on.

Kayla could only speak in a whisper as dread rose up inside her. "I don't think the PD is at all what we thought it was…"

22

The way into the city was blissfully uneventful.

They rode in a doubly stolen vehicle—stolen once by the army, then retaken by the rebels—Trinan and Malkor up front, Vayne and Mai in the back. Mai had been Aarush's choice as the strongest psionic in the rebel base, and Vayne concurred. Thankfully, he was well trained in fighting and tactics by Aarush himself, too. Malkor would still rather have his octet with him than another psionic, but he agreed with the plan.

Their IDs held up without issue at the city's vehicle gate, not that the guard gave them a second look. The sight of Vayne in the backseat took all of his wide-eyed attention. Not every day you see the military's most wanted man. After being assured that Vayne had been properly dosed with the anesthetizing agent that would block him from using his psi powers, the guard waved them through the gate.

The same thing happened outside the Complex of Oligarchs, and at the palace gates themselves. Vayne was a star attraction.

"We're taking you on every op from now on," Trinan said. "No one looks at us twice with you around."

"I'm wondering if Vega told them I drink imperial blood or something. I've never seen people so frightened."

As they walked up the palace steps, Malkor felt the eyes of everyone on them. He led the way, head high, eyes front, wearing an expression that did not invite questions or conversation. Trinan and Mai followed behind with Vayne between them. Vayne, with hands cuffed and head bowed, did a passible impression of a disgraced prisoner.

Malkor presented everyone's IDs in the lobby and demanded an immediate audience with Vega. The lobby, which had been bustling with soldiers and functionaries, suddenly emptied of all non-essential personnel. The guards held their weapons a little tighter as the soldier at the security station made the call.

Minutes later, a contingent of three soldiers arrived, clearly having been summoned. Malkor expected an argument over being allowed to escort the prisoner all the way to meet Vega. Typically with such a high-value prisoner, everyone wanted to take some credit for the capture, no matter how small. If not that, then at least have the glory moment of being the one to present the prisoner to their commanding officer.

Not so in this case. The soldiers merely asked that Malkor and the others follow them. No one, it seemed, wanted to take possession of Vayne.

Instead of putting him at ease, the lack of problems was winding Malkor tighter. It always seemed that the longer it took for the shoe to drop, the harder it fell. Not that their plan allowed any room for error in the first place. So he kept his mouth shut and followed the soldiers through the palace. Walking through the halls was surreal after five years. He never thought he'd be back here, and certainly he hadn't thought he'd be back here fighting against his own people. As with the rest of the city, the soldiers had made some changes—the Reinumon banners had been taken down and some statuary removed—but it was in large part unchanged from when he'd been here the first time.

And when he was gone? What would it look like in another five years?

Hopefully they would all have a chance to find out.

* * *

It was probably best, Vayne mused, that his part required keeping his head lowered and acting drugged to oblivion. Otherwise, he'd be tempted to murder every last soldier they came across, mission or no mission. It was still a struggle to remain impassive as he followed Malkor through the halls of his childhood home, his memories forever tainted by the overlay of imperial occupation.

He gritted his teeth as they walked, counting the seconds until he stood before Vega and could finally unleash five years of rage. They'd be lucky if he didn't burn down the entire palace.

"Senior Commander Vega will see you now," someone said.

Trinan and Mai released his arms and dropped back. Malkor, as the highest ranking of the three fake soldiers, would bring in the prize alone.

As the guard posted outside Vega's office opened the door for them, Vayne heard Mai's voice in his mind.

::Beginning the shield now, sir. Good luck.::

At least the man hadn't saluted this time.

Vayne and Malkor entered the office and stopped just inside the door. It was crucial that Malkor escape the room before the fighting started, otherwise he probably wouldn't survive and Kayla would never forgive either of them for that.

"Well this is a pleasant surprise," Vega said, and rose from her chair behind Vayne's aunt's desk. Agira was present, as expected, and seated where his father had sat. The Influencer was out of its case and resting on the front corner of this desk, like it was a prized trophy.

Part of her daily decor, or had they broken it out just for him?

Vega was saying something to Malkor, congratulating him maybe, but Vayne couldn't make out the words over the sudden roaring in his head. A million emotions, each painful and distinct, ripped through him, threatened to send him to his knees with their intensity. For a minute he thought he would

311

lose all control, and then someone spoke.

Don't blow it, Vayne, and don't damage my machine.

Vayne was rocketed into crystal-clear focus, everything so sharp that when Malkor left and the door clicked shut behind him, he actually felt the sound.

"I admit," Vega said, "I hadn't thought to see you again."

"Pleased?" Vayne asked, trying to decide when to attack. He would have loved to catch them both undefended, but they weren't so foolish as to be unshielded in his presence, drugged or not. Agira was also shielding the Influencer.

"I am more pleased than you could ever know." Vega smiled at him, a smug smile that he recognized from his time with Dolan.

"You enjoyed watching, didn't you?" His mind raced with images, times he ran around in Dolan's emotional labyrinth while Vega looked on, a voyeur of the worst sort.

Vega's brow puckered with confusion. "Excuse me?" She looked to Agira for context.

"Dolan. You enjoyed watching him work."

She lifted one shoulder in a shrug. "He did love to have an audience for the things he could make you all do. I was merely there to appease him."

Liar. She planned several of those games we played, Vayne. Dolan's dislike of the woman came through loud and clear.

"Not everyone's a sadist," she said with a look of feigned distaste. "Some of us just want power."

Look at her. Standing there, judging us as if she were some kind of superior creature.

The fingers of Vayne's left hand curled into a fist, and suddenly he wasn't certain that the action had been his own.

"For instance, I desire your power." Vega's smile returned. "And now it is mine, for however long I wish."

Dolan chuckled. Did the sound come from Vayne's lips? "You think you can replace me?"

Vega looked at Agira again, and the thrall seemed uncertain. They'd expected him drugged, they hadn't expected him half out of his mind, in the grips of a phantom takeover, had they?

Vayne clung to sanity, to his purpose. Incapacitate Vega, collect the Influencer.

We should take her now.

::I want to wait until Agira makes her first move with the Influencer:: Vayne answered Dolan. ::I'd rather I'm undistracted by combat, so I can recognize the feel of her using it.::

The longer we wait, the better coordinated they'll be. Dolan's voice was derisive. *Not that these two fools have any chance against me.*

Vayne hesitated. This wasn't at all how he'd expected this moment to go, under mental assault before he'd even begun.

::Will you be frutting quiet and let me fight?:: For the love— He just needed the monster quiet for a few more minutes. He needed control of his body to do this.

Without warning, Vayne struck. He sent a spike of kinetic energy straight to the center of Vega's shield, when he was certain he'd meant to hit Agira.

Her eyes widened as she realized her mistake in assuming him drugged without confirming it for herself, but she absorbed the blow without a hitch, letting it flow around her shield and dissipate.

Damn. She was stronger than he'd anticipated. And better trained.

You're stronger than you realize, Vayne. And now I am as well.

Vega answered back with a clobbering force that lacked finesse but packed a serious punch. Vayne responded, testing her shields, sending hits here and there while she did the same, looking for any weaknesses.

Would she find his?

Agira made the mistake of not throwing at least a cursory blow his way, so he was prepared for the Influencer's opening salvo when it came.

She had a soft touch, he'd give her that. She knew how to ease the Influencer's impulse into the mind gently. But the command to stop attacking Vega was so contrary to his driving need that Vayne could ignore it outright. Or he would, in just a moment, once he tightened his shields a bit.

Close your mind to her. I could do this in my sleep.

::Kindly shut up.::

Vega stepped up her attacks, whipping slashes across his barrier. He responded with an upward push that should have plastered her to the ceiling, but she only rose a meter off the ground before she centered herself again.

Agira was doubling down, and Dolan was straining to get loose, to grip the reins of Vayne's powers and fight.

::I would rather see us lose to this upstart imperial than give you control over me ever again.::

We're going to lose if you don't get your shit together this instant. Must I do everything for you?

Agira tried a different compulsion with the Influencer, imploring him to trust her, to let her in.

As the feeling of safety crept in, Vayne imagined he heard his mother's voice. "Rest, Vayne. You've been so tired for so long." It was an effort to turn away from her, to push her out of his mind. "I can help you," she said. "Just lower your shields."

Vega helped him by battering his shields and drawing all of his attention. At least the idiots were working against each other. He sent a thousand stinging needles at her, piercing pressure at too many places to count in her shields, forcing her to split her focus in a way few others but he had ever mastered.

"You might have my powers, but you'll never be me," he snarled at Vega, hitting her again and again. Draining his energy, but she'd falter first—he knew it. He drove her to her knees with his attacks as she focused all her power on shielding.

An amateur mistake. She should have lashed out at his weakening shields, as he transferred more power from his defense to his offensive efforts.

Agira, seeing Vega's weakness, stretched her own shield to cover her commander's kneeling form.

Dolan snorted. *Once a fool, always a fool.*

Suddenly a gigantic *boom* hit the palace, a deep bass

concussion that shook the walls. Then another, and another. Beyond the confines of their battle, people could be heard shouting, then sirens kicked in, warning of an air raid. More concussions, these closer, like the crack of massive pyrotechnics. The cacophony of sound broke Vayne's concentration and his shields faltered, as did everyone's.

The Influencer pumped into his mind, stripping away his defenses, calling him to lie down and rest.

Vega slumped on her knees, chest heaving, and Agira gripped the table to stay upright as each grasped the reprieve from the other's onslaughts to recover.

The floor was so inviting, so soft, and going to sleep was such a good idea.

If you don't get yourself up off that floor this very instant, I will kill you myself!

Vayne fought back. Fought against the control like he'd never fought before, struggling up. He winced at the pain in his head as his will sheared against the will of the Influencer.

"Don't damage him," Vega gasped, "I need him whole and unharmed."

"I'm trying." Agira poured her efforts into the machine again, and Vayne thought his head would split in two.

He lashed out, striking at Agira over and over. "Never... Again..." He choked the words out through clenched teeth. Never again would someone control him.

"Never!" He flung Agira back against the wall, smashing through her shields as she struggled to retain her connection to the Influencer. At this point, weak as she was, the Influencer had a better chance of defeating him than she did alone and she knew it.

She poured on a new compulsion, one that said he was weak, that he couldn't defeat her, that he wasn't strong enough.

Vayne recognized it. Dolan had used that very same compulsion on Natali the day he finally broke through her mental shields to reach her innermost self. He had used it when Vayne—driven by Dolan and the Influencer—had raped Natali, violating her in every way. The machine had twisted events for Vayne, so that while Natali experienced pain, he believed himself to be having the most blissful experience of his life.

The memory couldn't be undone just because he now knew the truth of what had happened. Whenever the moment invaded his consciousness, his body still responded with lust, even as his mind sickened and everything good in him died all over again.

Vayne roared aloud. Cried out with rage and pain and shame and hatred and utter devastation. Roared for what he had done to Natali and what had been done to him. He wrapped a fist of psi power around Agira and squeezed until her ribs cracked. Her body crumpled like tissue paper and he dropped her to the floor.

"Agira!" Vega cried. Still on her knees, she looked up at him in horror, and he felt like the monster he was. Reveled in it.

"I could kill you before you knew it had happened," Vayne said, his voice raw. For once, Dolan was blissfully silent.

"I—"

"Shut up. If you say. One. Frutting. Word. I *will* finish you." He gasped air, couldn't draw in enough, felt lightheaded. His power, drained before, surged anew. It clamored for release, begged to be unloaded into Vega until he had nothing left.

All around them the sound was rending the air. More bursts hit with a force that resounded in his chest. Everything was shouting and running and sirens and panic, but inside this office, inside his head, was silence.

No Influencer in his mind.

No memories.

No Dolan.

Only Vayne and a choice to make.

The Influencer sat idle on the desk, powered up and awaiting commands. His commands, if he wanted. He could drive Vega around like a puppet. Lift her to her feet and parade her through the palace grounds like a doll—and make her enjoy it all the while.

He could make her his thrall.

He could make them all his thralls.

Anything and everything he ever wanted, could ever desire, sat waiting for him on his father's desk.

Vayne calmly, one step at a time, walked to the Influencer. He reached out, hand shaking with anticipation of what could be, and powered it down.

He turned back to Vega, who had been eyeing the door—as if she could ever escape him.

"You have something of mine. I want it back."

Malkor held his ground in front of Vega's office door.

Amid shouting. Amid air-raid sirens. Amid sonic booms both near and far, he, Trinan, and Mai held their ground and gave Vayne the time he needed to fight his demons.

Their first opponents had been the guards stationed outside Vega's office. As soon as the attack started—whatever the attack was—they tried to reach Vega. Because of Vega's paranoia of being attacked by even her own army allies, weapon-jamming frequencies were engaged in the hallway; but although Malkor's ion pistol and standard army-issue sidearm might well be useless too, he and Trinan were much better at hand-to-hand combat than the soldiers were, thanks in part to Kayla's instruction over the past months. They dropped the two guards easily and left them unconscious on the floor, while Mai held the shield around the room. Vega would not easily escape, even if she somehow managed to defeat Vayne.

More soldiers had come, looking to evacuate Vega from the palace, and still more, seeking orders and guidance. Trinan and Malkor handled those as well, with aid here and there from Mai.

"I sure hope that's the sound of the *Yari* obliterating the occupation bases," Trinan said, wiping blood from a split lip.

"Either that or the rebels' coordinated attacks on the city," Malkor agreed.

Considering the panic in the palace, it seemed unlikely this was a planned offensive by the imperial army. Or maybe that's exactly what it was, designed to remove the upstart IDC senior commander from power…

He heard the door behind him open and spun, ready to do battle again if need be.

Vayne stood in the doorway. He had a case slung over his shoulder and a tight grip on Vega's upper arm. Both looked like death—ashen skin, sunken cheeks, sagging like they couldn't stand—but Vega was definitely the worse for wear.

Vayne handed a sullen commander over to Mai. "If she so much as looks at you crossly, don't hesitate—kill her." The Wyrd nodded, and looked pleased at the prospect.

"Agira?" Malkor asked.

"Dead and good riddance." Vayne looked around the corridor, at the pile of groaning and unconscious soldiers piled there. "By the way, what the frutt is going on out here?"

"Hopefully the *Yari*'s travel-by-rook plan worked, and this is the sound of them kicking ass." Malkor liked that possibility best, because it meant Kayla was still alive and the occupation was finally at an end. "At least getting out of here should be a snap. I'd wager the palace is empty by now."

Trinan took off his hologram and slapped it on Vega. At this point no one was going to look at them twice, but it never hurt to be careful. They jogged through the Reinumon palace, Mai prodding Vega when she tried to get the attention of a soldier hurrying in the opposite direction.

Malkor kept a close eye on Vayne, ready should the man collapse, but he seemed mentally strong despite his physical exhaustion. Most of all, there was a clarity in his gaze, a sense of peace that Malkor had never, ever witnessed in him before, not even when he'd reunited with Kayla.

It eased Malkor's worry about the future somewhat. Maybe everything really would be okay. Maybe now Vayne and Kayla could finally reconnect fully, and if that left no room in her life for Malkor anymore, well—he glanced at Vayne once again—that might almost be worth it.

He commed ahead to Vid and Rigger, and made it to the top level to find they had neatly locked down both ends of the corridor and had the roof access open and ready to go.

"You're not going to like what you see up there, boss, no matter which side is doing it," Rigger said, her lips tight with worry.

Trinan took the ladder first, then reached down for Vega as Mai prodded her up.

Before he ascended he heard Vid say softly, "I fear the damage is already done."

It was a bizarre scene that awaited them on the rooftop. Canisters floated in midair, perched atop the stealth flyer. More canisters littered the roof, some empty and spent, some quietly releasing an aerosol of some kind. Fluttering bits of debris rained down like snow.

All Malkor could do was cover his mouth with his sleeve and urge his team to sprint to the dubious safety of the flyer.

As they ran, though, he feared Vid was right—the damage had already been done.

23

ON BOARD THE *YARI*

Kayla flew down the *Yari*'s corridors so quickly that her feet never even touched the molychromium decking. If she'd had her psi powers, she would bear down on the lift, sending it screaming down the chute faster than the maglift mechanism allowed for. She was already calling for the rebels on guard outside Zimmerman's door to open the cell and wake the prisoner before the lift doors opened.

"Get him up!" she shouted. "Grab a syringe full of stims if you need to."

Somehow the rebels heard her over the blare of the ship's klaxon calling all crew to battle stations. Apparently the imperial ships had taken issue with whatever the *Yari* had just fired at the planet and had decided to fight back. Natali had taken command of the ship and was welcome to it.

Kayla couldn't worry about that now. Thankfully the guards didn't question her authority, and had the cell unlocked and opened by the time she reached them.

Zimmerman, who looked like he might have been sleeping, was sitting up.

"Tell me what the frutt is going on," she demanded.

"I have no idea," he said, gesturing to the flashing lights in the hallway.

"Not that, we're under attack." Funny that that was a secondary concern right now. "I mean with you and Ida and your little war. Ida just spouted off some crazy nonsense about Ordochians getting everything they deserved, her crew mutinied against Natali, and apparently the amazing planetary destroyer has just been fired at Ordoch instead of the nearest imperial ship."

She stepped into his cell, unafraid of anything at all right now except what had just been done to Malkor and Vayne. She got right in his face.

"What did Ida just fire at my planet, and how the void do we fix it?"

"There's almost too much to tell," he said. "And if she really did fire the weapon, you're going to want to start at the cure and work backward—trust me." He got to his feet. "There isn't a lot of time."

Kayla heard people filing into the corridor behind her, but she ignored them and stared Zimmerman down. "Start talking."

"You recall I warned you that Ida was an Ilmenan sympathizer."

It was inconceivable that one of Ordoch's greatest military heroes was actually a double-agent. Or, it would have been, if Ida hadn't just fired on her own planet.

Zimmerman blew out a breath. "By now you know the so-called PD isn't a beam weapon at all, and your history books are full of military propaganda."

She was beginning to suspect that. "Well, there is a beam weapon," Zimmerman corrected himself, "or at least, there was, but it was nowhere near as powerful as they claimed."

"The reality of the weapon is much more complicated than that. Even at the height of the Nanotech Wars with Ilmena, none of us wanted a holocaust. The idea of destroying an entire planet, making it unlivable for millennia, killing billions of people and making refugees of a civilization, wasn't something even our military dictatorship could stomach. Honestly, I'm surprised the populace ever bought into the propaganda, with that being the outcome the government was selling them."

"Why would the government need to lie about the type of superweapon it had designed?" she asked. "Ordoch was rabid to end the Nanotech Wars by then: people would have cheered the military on."

He smiled grimly. "You forget, I was there. Believe me when I tell you this technology would never have been approved. The military developed a nanovirus designed for one purpose: to attack and destroy a person's cartaid arch. The superweapon is the carrier of enough copies of the virus to infect everyone living on Ilmena and destroy their ability to use psi powers."

Kayla felt horrified. The imagined PD would have inflicted damage on a scale so massive she couldn't quite wrap her mind around it. But this, this she could imagine. She had lived through losing her own psi powers. It was worse than losing one's sight or hearing. Psi powers weren't a single sense; they infused everything a Wyrd did, every part of who they were.

To imagine an entire planet maimed, crippled in that way...

"Without psi powers," she said, "they wouldn't be able to use their shields, their telekinetic weapons."

"Their communications systems would break down," Zimmerman continued, "they'd be much more susceptible to mind control and mind reading. There are more traditional forms of warfare, of course, but they didn't have any in place at the time."

And why would they? Everyone had psi powers: it was a way of life. It would be like building war machines for the blind, just in case everyone stopped being able to see.

"It was ingenious. We would have taken control of the planet within days," Zimmerman said.

"That's why this ship is so full of soldiers, because it's an invasion, not the crew necessary to man a ship. So what happened?" Kayla asked. "A biotech weapon didn't cause a tear in time and space that swallowed an entire ship and one

Ilmenan science station on an asteroid."

Zimmerman's gaze turned hard. "Captain Janus happened. That science station? It was a top secret military research center Ilmena had recently built, sparsely populated, so classified that no one there knew what anyone else was working on. It was the perfect test site for the virus.

"Once we were in range, we prepared the virus for launch. Everything was good, orange lights across the board. The virus samples were stable and viable, the aerosolization sequence had been tested a million times. We released the payload at the asteroid, and when we did…" Zimmerman made a motion with both hands like a bomb going off between his palms. "I think your history, written by the military, by the way, claims that we were destroyed as we valiantly attempted a test-firing of the PD?"

Kayla nodded.

"Clearly that's not what happened," Zimmerman said. "Tanet still doesn't know for sure what happened.

"What we do know," he continued, "from reading the ship's datalogs before they were destroyed, is that someone accessed the beam weapon's complink and set it to charge. They overrode the buffer capacity safety settings and looped the command, causing the buffer to be overloaded with excess energy. The whole thing imploded. That it happened so soon after we fired the virus delivery system makes me think it was meant to stop the test from ever happening.

"Beyond that, I'm not sure, but that's where the energy that flung us through time and space came from. There was no test firing of a magical PD beam."

Kayla waved her hand to keep him moving. This might be a fascinating historical discovery for a later date, but she needed to help her people *now*, if she even could. She zeroed in on the only thing that mattered: "How do you stop the virus? Once it has run its course, I mean. You wouldn't send Ordochians down to the surface while the virus was still active."

He opened his mouth to speak but she interrupted him.

"And don't you dare tell me the soldiers were inoculated against it, and that Ordoch is screwed because it's too late to use a vaccine."

"There is a way to shut it down. Or at least, there was." He paused, looking sad.

"Spit it out."

"We use the controllers—and the children."

Kayla caught her breath. The three teenagers in cryosleep, all three past the point of surviving reanimation.

He nodded. "You saw them in the cryochamber. They're the ones who were supposed to interface with the nanovirus using a master-code version of the virus. You see, the virus has psionic receptors." He seemed to be struggling with the words to describe it all. "It doesn't have a consciousness or anything, but it can receive and react to certain basic commands, given to it by the master-code virus, what we call the queen bug."

Kayla tried to follow what was being said, but it was hard when all she could hear was that the three children with the solution were the three children dead in cryopods.

"So," she said, working it over, "the queen bug has a consciousness?"

"From what I understand—and you have to remember, I'm the first officer, a military man, not a man of hard science—it has something approaching a consciousness. It's a biomechanical interface, part complink, part nanovirus. It attaches to the host's cartaid arch and links its awareness of the individual nanovirus cells with the host's awareness. The host can then pass a command to the nanovirus to deactivate it."

Zimmerman shrugged. "I'm sorry, that's about what I know of it. Fengrathen can tell you more, she's the lead science officer on board."

"Why children? Why not have an adult interface with the virus?" And who the void would attach a biomechanical nanovirus thing to a child's brain, even in a time of war?

"Their connection to their cartaid arch is not completely solidified, so there's room for the queen bug to attach. Also, their brains are more flexible than an adult's. They can grow and evolve with the queen bug, hopefully surviving the experience."

Kayla held up a hand. "I'm sorry, what? *Hopefully survive?* You mean these kids only had a *chance* of surviving the procedure, even before five hundred years of faulty cryosleep?"

Her heart started pounding in her chest: not because the hope of a cure was dead, but because, in the face of it all, one possibility presented itself to her. One horrifying, unacceptable possibility.

::I'll do it.:: Corinth's voice. He must have come with the rest of the people to hear what Zimmerman would say and she hadn't even realized it. She'd been too focused on Zimmerman to realize where her younger *il'haar* was.

Corinth pushed his way to the front of the crowd. He drew himself up to his full height—when had he gotten past her ribcage?—and squared to face them both. He was serious but unafraid. ::Do you have more copies of the queen bug on board? If so, I volunteer to interface with one.::

"Corinth—" her voice was a whisper. "You can't." She was shaking her head, but she didn't know against what. Against him, or against the truth that if Corinth didn't try, they had no one else?

He tilted his head. ::Why not, Kay? Because I'm not strong enough?::

She realized then she'd already lost. Any answer here other than her utmost faith in him would hurt him deeper than even the loss of his twin had.

"He doesn't have to be a strong psionic," Zimmerman said. "This section of the *Yari* acts as an amplifier, allowing the queen bug's signal to reach planet-wide, more than any psionic could do on their own, no matter how strong."

"He is strong." Kayla couldn't look away from Corinth. His bright blue eyes, so like Vayne's. "You're one of the strongest people I know, Corinth," she said quietly. And it was true. "All you've been through, all you've lost. Your struggles in the last five years…"

She looked at him, really looked at him, and saw beyond

the child he'd always been. She saw the young adult he was, and the man he could become. He'd not only survived, he'd thrived in this last year.

"I know you're capable of this," she said gently. "I know how much you want to help, but I—" She what? Didn't want him to? Couldn't bear to lose him? Could she be that selfish, with their world in the balance?

Corinth lifted his chin. ::I'm not a child anymore, Kayla, and you don't get to make this decision for me.::

He turned to face Zimmerman completely. ::When do we start?::

"Wait," Kayla said, and held up her hand when Corinth started to argue. "I'm not going to stop you, but I have to ask—will the queen bug destroy his arch the same way the nanovirus does: will he lose his psi powers?" And if he did, would he ever speak again?

"It shouldn't. Not in a child." Zimmerman hesitated, then said, "There's one last thing you should know. I suspected it right away, but I had Fengrathen run tests to confirm it. The nanovirus we created? It's the basis for the one the imperials call the TNV."

VANKIR CITY, ORDOCH

It would have been impossible to leave the city if they hadn't had a flyer. As they traveled over Vankir from the palace, Malkor looked down to see utter chaos in the streets. His and Rigger's trip from the prison earlier looked like a military march compared to this.

The shuttle was quiet all the way back to the rebel base. A subdued Vega sat between Trinan and Vid. Vayne, with the Influencer on his lap, lay with his head back against the seat, eyes closed, but Malkor doubted he slept. Mai had his eyes on Vega, alert for trouble, and another Wyrd drove. With nothing else to do, Malkor returned to watching the world go insane outside.

Canisters continued to drift down, carried gently by paper parachutes. No doubt they'd been transmitted through the atmosphere via rocket and then let loose as the rocket disgorged its payload. Even if the army had an effective anti-air missile system in place, there wasn't enough ordnance on the planet to take out every one of the canisters before they landed. And with an aerosol delivery system, who knew if shooting them out of the sky would even be an effective defense?

It was hard to wait until they reached the base for answers, but every frequency was jammed full, so wait they did.

The flyer touched down as close as possible to the abandoned manufacturing facility, and they all sprinted from the plane to the cover of the building. Canisters littered the ground here, too, though, and the air had a metallic bite to it when Malkor breathed in. For once he was thankful to get underground. They stripped out of everything they were wearing and left it in a pile, along with the rest of their gear. Rebels in hazmat gear hosed them down, but there was a feeling of "too little, too late."

Vayne unpacked the Influencer and left the case with the rest of the contaminated things as they entered another room and got dressed. It was only then that they were allowed any deeper into the base. They were shown immediately to the situation room—the one room in the base that was full of high-tech electronic equipment—and greeted by Wetham and his lieutenants.

"Success," Malkor said without preamble. Vayne hoisted the thing he'd carried with him since leaving Vega's office, and Malkor got his first look at the dreaded Influencer. Truly, it resembled nothing so much as an ancient typewriter, from the days before complinks, and fitted neatly tucked under his arm. He deposited it in front of Wetham like the head of a slain beast, then crossed the room to stand as far away from it as he could.

They'd already deposited Vega with her jailers before joining the senior leaders of the rebellion in the situation room.

"So?" Malkor asked, looking at the myriad vidscreens and

trying to make some sense out of the insanity he saw. "What is it?" His skin felt itchy. Was it his imagination?

"Well, the good news first, I suppose," Wetham said. People were calling in reports, tracking data, passing paper around, and doing the million and one things you might expect to be happening in the middle of a war. He was like an island of calm in the midst of it, never seeming uncertain or unequal to the task, just steady and perennial.

"We heard from the *Yari*. The jump was successful, the ship is in orbit around Ordoch."

"Did they end up firing the PD?"

Wetham nodded. "They did. At the planet. What you undoubtedly walked through on your way here is the result of Captain Janus betraying us. Apparently she and several of her remaining crew members are deep-cover Ilmenan operatives, though born Ordochians. Captain Janus executed a five-hundred-year-old directive to destroy the Ordochian people by firing the *Yari*'s superweapon at the planet itself."

Which made absolutely no sense, but Malkor set that aside for the moment. "What was the empire's response?"

"A brief, and I mean very brief, skirmish broke out between the imperial ships and the *Yari*. When the imperials fired on the *Yari* for what they saw as an attack against their forces on the ground, they hit several of the rooks that had disentangled themselves from the ship." Wetham gave Malkor a somber look. "We did hope to avoid mass casualties, and I regret to inform you that the rooks tore apart one of the battleships before we could stop them."

At this point, concern over enemy casualties was so far down his list of worries that he filed that under "to think about in my free time."

"The other two battleships surrendered to Natali immediately and were spared. We expect to receive a surrender from the imperial army forces on the ground momentarily. Though that's really just a formality at this point."

Wetham was quiet then, pensive, and Malkor sensed they

had come to the end of the good news. He hadn't expected to find the commander of the rebellion in a somber mood upon news of a victory—but then, today was not your average day.

Finally, Wetham took a deep breath, settled something within himself, and spoke. "The end result of Ida's actions, unfortunately, is that Ordoch has been infected with a nanovirus originally designed to destroy psi powers in Wyrds. And while only the main continent has been hit so far, it's only a matter of time before the prevailing winds spread it across the entire globe."

Wetham's particular phrasing caught Malkor's attention. "You said, 'originally designed.' What is it capable of now?" He had a million and one questions beyond that, but this seemed to be the one that truly mattered in this moment. "What else does it do?"

"Apparently our five-hundred-year-old virus was the blueprint for the empire's TNV. It might be fitting, actually," Wetham said. "Our refusal to help you five years ago will now prove to be our downfall."

24

THE *YARI*

It was a strange procession that filed its way down through the unpowered sections of the ship, covered as everyone was in spacesuits. Kayla and Corinth led the way, followed closely by Zimmerman, who floated one of the *Lorius*'s stasis pods beside him, and last came Noar.

Kayla felt most keenly the absence of their other loved ones: Trinan, Vid, and the other members of the octet, Toble, Vayne, Tia'tan, and especially Malkor. All people who cared for Corinth, all people who would be here supporting them if they could. Natali was split by her desire to be with her family for such a personal moment, and her need to be with her people for such a crucial one. Privately, she thought Ordoch could have waited one more day for its *en'shaar*, but maybe she and Natali were not as alike as she'd always thought.

They had to leave the lift on the bottom level of the habitable section, as the narrow spindle section jutting out from the center of that part of the ship wasn't in line with any lift tracks. Noar sped them down the zero-gravity hall with his mind, getting them to the hatch access for the PD housing in record time. It had an airlock, which boded well for Zimmerman's insistence that the housing was on its own power and atmosphere entirely.

Kayla knew that every second counted now for the people infected with the nanovirus, but once Corinth bonded with the "queen bug," he would never be the same again—if he lived. She hesitated at the airlock.

::There's no time, Kay:: Corinth said, reaching for the mechanism. He was eager to do this, eager to prove his worth to himself, to their family. He rushed ahead without fear, so sure of the outcome. In his mind, the hardest part—convincing Kayla to finally let him be an adult—was behind him. He probably saw nothing but smooth sailing ahead.

She saw what she always saw: the pitfalls, the snares. The overwhelming odds and the terrible stakes.

She forced herself to smile just a little. "I'm coming."

They entered the airlock, cycled it, and stepped through into the most powerful weapon system the galaxy had ever seen.

It looked a lot like a locker room.

In fact, it looked just like a locker room. The ship was finished here, and instead of the molychromium bones, the floor was covered in an industrial gray rubber mat, easily washable and probably fungal resistant. There were benches to sit on while donning or doffing gear, storage lockers of various sizes, a pressure chute for laundry, showers, a bathroom... It was so eerily normal that Kayla wasn't certain they'd come to the right place.

Several vending machines were attached to the wall side by side, dispensing things like protective eyewear, sterilized clean suits, and shoe covers. It felt like the anteroom for a super-secret laboratory.

"Disappointed?" Zimmerman asked.

"A little. I was expecting something straight out of a sci-fi vid." At least it had lights and gravity and atmosphere. She opened her face shield and breathed the stale air.

The circular room wasn't large at all. In the center was a ring of protective railing guarding a hole in the floor several meters wide. A ladder descended into the hole on one side, leaving the rest of the space for a lift platform.

A lift platform that, judging by the sound of it, was rising to meet them.

A woman came into view, toe to chin in sterilized lab gear. She was reading from a datapad even as she worked the lift controls. It was Officer Fengrathen, whose appearance had touched off the discovery of Zimmerman and his contingent of not-crazy *stepa at es*.

She looked up from her notes just as the lift stopped. "Let's go: she's almost awake and we have to get this thing started."

They piled on, and as the platform started to descend, she finally noticed the stasis pod. "What's that for?"

::It's for me:: Corinth said, ::in case things don't go so well.::

Zimmerman said the best way to halt the queen bug from taking over his mind entirely—or simply destroying him—was to put Corinth into cryosleep the second they noticed something going wrong. There was no way Kayla was trusting him to one of the *Yari*'s pods, not when the image of those three dead teenagers was still so stark in her mind. She'd had Hekkar yank this one out of the *Lorius*'s much more modern med bay and fly it over. That had taken the longest of all the prep.

The platform descended through what began to look like a laboratory. Each level they went down was hermetically sealed, with its own small airlock needed to enter from the lift or ladder. Kayla could see beyond the plascrystal windows into what looked like small medical labs, or maybe research labs. There were benches and instruments and complinks and microscopes and racks and racks of storage. Fengrathen stopped the lift at one the labs, eyes once again on the datapad, and ushered everyone off. Her lips moved as she read, like a baker reading a cookbook and trying to memorize which spices the recipe called for, and she entered the lab last, sealing them in.

Not that it mattered, at this point.

"Okay, on the table," Fengrathen said. "Well, first, off with the EMU, then onto the table." She went to check on a machine that seemed to be beeping out a countdown while Kayla and Noar helped Corinth out of his suit and Zimmerman got the stasis pod plugged in near the quadtanium table that looked more ready for a dissection than a medical procedure.

She steadied Corinth as he stepped out of the heavy outer suit. "Don't be afraid," she said.

He looked up, surprised. ::I'm not.::

"I meant me." She said it as a joke and he smiled, but she was terrified. Even as he climbed up onto the table and lay back, she wanted to snatch him to her and run off.

But there was nowhere to run, and he wouldn't want her to take this moment from him, no matter what it might cost both of them.

Fengrathen wheeled over a cart that had a few innocent-looking, everyday medical devices on it. "Hold up your arm," she said brusquely, mind clearly on the task and not the patient. Or host, or whatever Corinth was about to be. She took some blood samples, hooked up some sensors, and walked back to the gently humming machine.

A minute passed.

Two.

Three.

Corinth's smile faded. Given time to think about what he was doing, doubts were surely starting to creep in.

"Here," Kayla said, taking his hand and giving it a squeeze. "*Speak* with me."

She lowered her mental shields, not bothering to pack away all of the worries she'd always hidden from him before. He entered her mind in a rush, too quickly, filling all the open space and causing a spike of minor pain between her eyes.

This time she laughed instead of admonishing. It was so like him, in his puppy dog excitement to know another person. Maybe a lifetime of training still wouldn't cure him of it.

You are doing a very brave thing.

He squeezed her hand in return. ::It doesn't feel brave. It feels… easy. Like it wasn't a question at all. Just… 'Yes. I want to do this thing.':: He paused for a moment, then asked, ::Is this how you always feel?::

What, certain of what I'm doing?

::No.:: His eyes narrowed as he concentrated. ::Worried. Do you always have all this…:: she felt him turning over the boxes of fear in her mind, peeking into closets of doubt. ::All of this clutter in here? This unnecessary junk.:: He kicked at a pile of leftover worries from their time on Altair Tri. ::Stars, Kay, no wonder you're so overprotective.::

I am not. I am just right protective.

His mental eye-roll came through loud and clear.

In the background a machine beeped with a result and Fengrathen uttered a "hmm."

"What's 'hmm?'" Noar asked, when Fengrathen said no more than that. Corinth valued Noar as a friend and a teacher, maybe more so than Vayne, and when Noar, who was usually so unflappable, asked his question in that tone, Corinth's anxiety began to climb.

"An aberrant result. Don't worry, I'm rerunning. The queen bug will keep for a few more minutes."

Kayla didn't think *she'd* keep for another few more minutes of this not-knowing.

Fengrathen came over to the table to explain the procedure. All Kayla really heard were two things: "can't be done under anesthesia" and "going in through the ocular cavity." That was way more than she wanted to know. Corinth squeezed her hand again, and they both clung to each other for strength.

Something on her wall of machines beeped again and Fengrathen excused herself to check it. Zimmerman went over as well. Kayla was dying to see whatever they were looking at, but was just as certain that she didn't want to know.

Once you have the superbug, she said to him instead, *will you still be my* il'haar?

::Only if your feelings won't be hurt once I'm more powerful than you.:: She felt his humor, reflected it back at him. He turned serious, then, and held her gaze. ::I will always be your *il'haar*, no matter what.::

Her heart swelled in her chest almost painfully. *Then I am the luckiest* ro'haar *in the entire galaxy.*

::You're damn right you are:: he said, and laughed out loud at the surprised look that must be on her face.

"Corinth Reinumon, who taught you to talk like—"

He laughed again, his voice scratchy and soft, but it was *his voice.* Out loud, not in her mind.

He coughed, laughed again, then said, in the faintest croak, "Vid."

Kayla leaned over him and gripped him in a fierce hug. She laughed. She cried. She held him until he squirmed and she felt embarrassment roll off of him.

::Quit it, Kay.::

She wiped at her wet cheek as she pulled back. He'd laughed. She'd heard it. Life was good. Precious.

"That's not right, is it?" Zimmerman asked.

"I ran it twice," Fengrathen answered. "I mean, we always knew it was theoretically possible..."

Instruments went flying as Noar stole the datapad from her hand and tossed it across the room. When he had everyone's undivided attention he calmly, very politely asked, "What are the findings?"

Kayla held her breath.

"Well, according to that—" Fengrathen pointed to her scattered data, "Corinth is immune to the nanovirus."

She heard the words, but couldn't quite... "What does that mean? For him? For the planet?" Elation soared through her at the thought that Corinth wouldn't have to be infected after all, but fear came just as hard on its heels. "Malkor? Vayne?"

Fengrathen shook her head. "His body will just destroy the queen bug as soon as we implant it. It won't have a chance to establish a connection." She shook her head again. "I'm sorry."

Kayla rose up. "You're sorry? You're *sorry*? Everyone we have ever loved, will ever love, is down there on the planet, infected, *dying*, and you're saying you're sorry?" She was incredulous. "You *created* this frutting thing, for frutt's sake. There has to be another way to stop it."

::Kay...:: Corinth sat up on the table, his dejection complete. ::It's not her fault.::

"Like frutt it's not her fault. It's all of their faults." She jabbed a finger at Zimmerman. "You, Ida, the whole damn ship. How could you make something like this?" She was coming unhinged, she could feel it. The pain was just... so great. In her chest. She couldn't breathe.

Oh, gods! Malkor, her Malkor.

And Vayne...

"Try me," she said suddenly, grasping at anything. "I'm not immune, am I? Test me." She was fumbling with her suit, fingers numb and not working. "Noar, help me." She looked at him, imploring. He had to help, someone had to help. She was drowning and she couldn't breathe.

Then Noar and Corinth were there, stripping the suit off, moving her limbs with their minds to get her head and arms clear in a flash.

Kayla thrust back the sleeve of her ventilation suit and held out her bare arm. "Do it."

Fengrathen looked at Zimmerman. Finally Zimmerman just shrugged and nodded, so Fengrathen took her samples.

::It won't work, Kay. You're too...::

"Old?" She chuckled, but she wasn't as insane as she feared. "It's not the age that matters, right, Zimmerman? Or it is, but only if you're worried about your psi powers growing correctly afterward. You said it's the state of the cartaid arch. Children are used because part of the arch is still bare and there's room for the master nanovirus interface whatever to attach itself. Right?"

"Right," he said slowly, studying her, trying to figure out where she was going.

"Well, my cartaid arch is in perfect condition, pristine, even. I should know, I had it checked out by a sadomasochist." She laughed, and now she knew she had really lost it. Who would have thought that having Dolan inside her brain would ever turn out to be a good thing? "That queen bug of yours will love it."

"But..." Zimmerman hesitated, and Fengrathen's machine

beeped away. "I hate to state the obvious, but, it takes psi powers to interface with the queen, and you don't have any."

"No," she agreed. "But I will."

Dolan, you asshole, you might save us all yet.

::I heard that.::

Get out of my head, Corinth.

REBEL BASE, VANKIR CITY, ORDOCH

"She wants to do what?" Malkor shouted the question at Vayne, even though he stood no more than a meter from him. "Absolutely not. How could she— And she was going to let *Corinth* try this?" Somehow Malkor found himself stuffing his gear into his rucksack while he shouted, pulling on his jacket, which was still damp from being hosed down.

"Apparently it would have been safer for Corinth, but he's immune." Vayne didn't stop packing to listen to Malkor shout, he just kept stuffing that damn Influencer into its damn case. Malkor felt like grabbing the Influencer and smashing it to a billion pieces.

"We are *not* doing this." Malkor half-jogged to follow Vayne out of the decontamination room. Somehow his gear bag was in one hand, his weapon in the other, and he was trotting.

Vayne just kept moving. "If we're not doing this, then why are you all packed, and why are Trinan, Vid, and Rigger right behind us?"

"They're not." But they were. He and his team were following after Vayne, through the plascrete corridors of the rebel base, and up to the surface where death awaited on a single inhale. "Kayla is not injecting the queen of all superviruses into her brain and wiring herself to the ship. No way."

"If she's not, then why is Hekkar touching down in a shuttle?" Vayne slung the Influencer, case and all, over his shoulder and strode out of the building to where Hekkar had landed.

"Vayne, wait." Malkor grabbed the man's arm, pulling him to a stop as Hekkar opened the doors. "We can't bring this up there." Malkor gestured to his face, to where the skin was getting blotchy with hives, to where the nanovirus was cannibalizing his tissue in order to replicate. "So far Kayla and the others are infection-free."

Vayne turned so he was looking at Malkor head on, eye to eye, staring right into him. "If we do not bring this Influencer up to the ship right now and let Kayla try this, then I promise you my crazy sister is coming down here to get it." He gripped Malkor's shoulder. "*Hear me*. She is either going to save us, or die with us, but she is never going to sit safe and sound up there while we suffer on the ground. So get that thought right out of your head."

Vayne turned away and climbed into the shuttle.

Then he was buckling in, and somehow Malkor was beside him, and Trinan and Vid and Rigger beside them. Hekkar was grinning like a mad fool—maybe they all were—and then they were off, bringing death or salvation to the *Yari*...

Or maybe a little bit of both.

Damn you, Kayla, this had better work.

Kayla received the "good" news that she was not, in fact, immune to the superbug with a mixture of excitement and hope. She could end this.

She sat on the lab bench-turned-medical table in Fengrathen's mad scientist lab, Corinth beside her, both of them strung so tightly the vibration from a tuning fork could make them snap. It was a good kind of tight, though, the tense of action, of things about to happen. An energy that hummed through them.

Even though they weren't still linked mind to mind, she could feel the emotions rolling through him. Disappointment. Relief. Even a little jealousy that she got to be the one to try to save everyone.

Fengrathen was talking, trying to prepare Kayla for what

she might experience and what it might all mean. The more she spoke, the less Kayla wanted to try this. What in the void had she been thinking?

"This *will* damage your cartaid arch," the scientist stressed. "Our brains were designed to be linked to biomechanical interfaces like this."

Fengrathen's voice was dry, factual, and Kayla appreciated that. Her own emotions were out of control in a way she'd never felt. "We've never had a test subject with your particular situation: a fully developed and functioning cartaid arch without psi powers connected to it. I honestly don't know what to expect."

"Well then, it'll be fun for all involved, won't it?" Kayla smiled—what else could she do?

Fengrathen paused, studied her as if unsure Kayla's state of mind was conducive to this sort of thing. Kayla smiled harder.

"You *might* feel something like... a sensation that the interface is trying to take over your consciousness. This was reported by two of our test subjects."

"And did it?"

"Did it what?"

"Did it take over their minds? Am I going to become possessed by this thing?"

Fengrathen looked to Zimmerman, then back at Kayla. It was clear the scientist still took every cue from the first officer, no matter that their war had been over for five hundred years. "In both cases, the subjects suffered massive brain hemorrhaging and died before the phenomenon could be explored."

Holy—

::Don't tell Vayne that last part:: Corinth said. ::Or Malkor. Actually, don't tell them any of it.::

He looked up at her. ::Right, Kay? We'll keep our worries in little boxes to ourselves.::

"What terrible things have I been teaching you?" She shook her head. "We're not going to hold onto this worry. We'll tell them, just... after. How 'bout that?"

The vidcomm on the wall came to life showing Natali's face. "Vayne's on his way with the Influencer. Are you sure about this?"

Kayla looked at her younger brother. "Just as sure as Corinth was, when he volunteered first." He ducked his head as if her words embarrassed him, but she saw his small, proud smile.

"We're all here," Natali said, and backed up so that Kayla could see everyone gathered on the *Yari*'s observation deck. There was Kazamel and his crew of Ilmenans, Noar, Natali, Uncle Ghirhad, Tanet, Shimwell, and all of the rebel Ordochians who had come through the Tear to help. There were the Ordochian medics and surgeons who had saved Tia'tan's life, as well as half a dozen *Yari* crew members that Kayla had never met before—Zimmerman's crew. The sane *stepa*.

It was weird not to see Ida, Benny, and Ariel as part of the group, but those three were being held in the cells, hopefully eating the same drugged food Ida had no doubt served to Kendrik and the other members of her own crew.

"Thank you all for gathering," Kayla said. "And thank you for all that you've done. You've put your lives on the line for our mission, the freeing of Ordoch, and now we've almost achieved it. I say 'almost,' because we're not yet free of the plague that started it all. The TNV that brought the empire to its knees is the same virus we created during the Nanotech Wars. The *Yari* unleashed the virus in Ilmenan space centuries ago, unbeknownst to us all, and then the virus was carried along with the *Yari* through a tear and into the Imperial Mine Field. From there it came into contact with imperials, mutated, and evolved. The imperials found their own way to weaponize it as we once had, despite our different genetics, calling their designer version the Tetrotock nanovirus.

"They brought our own plague back to us, and perhaps we deserve to die for creating this terrible, terrible weapon in the first place."

She shook her head. "I don't intend to die. I intend to fight. I will fight until the galaxy is rid of this plague once and for all. But to do that, I need help. I must ask a horrible favor of one of you. No, not a favor. A gift, for I can never return it." She studied the faces of the people she'd come to know, fought beside. She searched them all, hoping there might be just one...

"I am not able to access my psi powers, as many of you know. However, I can use the controller to neutralize the TNV *if* one of you will volunteer your psi powers to me. They would be cut from your mind. The process, I'm told, is excruciating." She saw Natali wince and look away. "There's no guarantee that your powers will ever return. And... you might die from the procedure."

"Wow," someone said, as the comm split and another stream merged with it. "You really sold that, Kayla." It was Vid. "Sign me up."

She couldn't help it, she laughed. "Vidious Con Vandaren, have you been teaching Corinth some sass? You should have heard him earlier!"

Vid grinned. "That was all Trinan, I swear!" It looked like they were on board a shuttle.

Hekkar pushed Vid's head out of view. "Permission to dock, Captain Reinumon."

Natali's lips quirked. "Don't you dare make me captain of this boat. As soon as we're done here, I'm going planetside and never coming back. But, permission granted."

Hekkar closed the comm line, and Kayla was left staring at a group of people, each with hands raised. Even the *Yari*'s survivors raised their hands. Everyone on the observation deck, with the exception of Natali, stood ready to offer their powers for the chance to stop the plague.

"Well, aren't we all just a pack of sorry fools," Kayla said.

Uncle Ghirhad spoke. "I'll do it." He looked at those gathered around him and motioned for them to lower their hands. "This is my task: let me do this for my niece." A few of the rebels protested, arguing that they were younger and stronger, that they would hold up better under the processes, but Ghirhad just waved them off.

"I have done this before and I have survived. I can do so again."

Kayla bowed her head. "Thank you, uncle." She would never have asked him to submit to that torture again, but she could see in his eyes that he needed to do this for their people as much as she needed to volunteer her perfect arch. "Thank you."

25

One of the many blessings of Corinth being immune to the TNV, Kayla thought, was that he could stay by her side for the procedure. She didn't need to banish him to another part of the ship when Vayne arrived, TNV and all, with the Influencer.

Uncle Ghirhad was nestled in the stasis pod, wide awake but sealed inside, safe from the nanovirus Vayne was about to bring onboard.

Zimmerman looked at Fengrathen, she at him, and then they collided in the most passionate kiss Kayla had ever witnessed. She would have covered Corinth's eyes if she wasn't too stunned to move.

"I've been wanting to do that for five hundred years," Fengrathen said when she finally came up for air. Then added, "Sir."

They weren't concerned about infection. They were Ordochians and they were going home, no matter what.

Kayla closed her eyes. Vayne was on the way down through the ship, but the person she wanted most in the universe, the person she *needed* by her side, now and forever, wasn't there.

"Kayla?" It was Malkor's voice coming from the comm. He and the infected octet were quarantined to the shuttle. If this failed and there was no cure to be had, some people aboard the *Yari* might make a life for themselves somewhere else. It only made sense to minimize the risk of infection, but it physically hurt to see Malkor so far away.

"I'm here," she said, and waved from her perch on the metal slab of a table. "We're getting ready to do this, all in one shot." She held up her fingers. "Superbug? *Boom*." She counted them out. "Uncle Ghirhad's psi powers? *Boom*. Rig me up to the psionic amplifier at the center of this death machine? *Boom*. Put the TNV to bed? *Boom* and done. Just like that."

"Just like that, eh?"

"Yup."

They were both silent a moment, simply looking at each other. There were tears in her eyes and she blinked them away, not because they embarrassed her, but because they made it harder to see how absolutely perfect he was in this moment.

"I can't have this conversation right now," she said.

He nodded. "That's why we're not having it."

And Fengrathen's machine was beeping and Vayne had arrived and Malkor's face was so dear and it was time to go.

"I'll see you soon, my love," she said.

"You better. You still owe me a sparring rematch."

"You're wrong about her, Fengrathen," Kayla said a half-hour later. She could only see out of one eye and her head hurt like a hovercar had fallen on it, but somehow she was still alive.

"Her?" Fengrathen asked, and her voice was far away in one ear.

"The superbug, it, whatever, she absolutely does have a consciousness, albeit a minute one." Currently that consciousness was crawling upside through her mind, squiggling, squirming, and wriggling its little tendrils any and everywhere. Spiderlike its fingers crept, feather-light and whisper-thin, threading through everything Kayla had ever been.

It found its perch somewhere Kayla couldn't follow. She saw it from beyond an invisible barrier, the glass in her mind that kept her psi powers forever from her. She watched as that little spider wound its web and spun its nest, right and tight and out of reach.

At last, when it felt safe and ready, that little queen came looking for Kayla.

And *boom*. Superbug. Just like that.

Kayla's eyes opened as wide as they could go and she gasped for breath as the controller interface connected with her and she became instantly aware of... Every. Single. TNV. Cell. In the entire world.

Her brain felt like it would burst. How could there be this many? Luckily they did nothing more than just exist in her consciousness or else her brain really would explode. And as she reached out, looked here and there at different cells, she realized that she wasn't connected to every bit of the virus in the galaxy. She could sense by the shape, the pattern of those cells, that she was connected only to the TNV on the ship and the planet. The others, the controller was somehow telling her, were too far away to connect to. They'd have to travel...

The controller started thinking about traveling, and where it might like to make Kayla take it, and Kayla knew.

"It's time," she said, blinking away the awareness of the virus for a minute so that she could see in front of her. "Vayne, we have to do this quick. I think the controller is realizing that I'm defenseless against it right now."

She levered herself up on her elbows, even though her head screamed in pain with the movement, and looked at Vayne.

He stood next to Dolan's hated device, a frown so severe on his face that she thought of withdrawing her request that he use the thing to transfer Ghirhad's powers to her.

"If you can't do this—"

He shook his head. "That frown wasn't for you." He scrubbed a hand over his face. "That frown was for the past, and the past is dead. Finally."

She lay back down, unable to stand even the littlest effort to hold herself up. "Are you ready, Ghirhad?"

His voice came out muffled through the stasis box. "As ever, my dear. Do not worry about me: it doesn't hurt if you give in."

With that cryptic statement between them, Vayne brought the Influencer to life.

Kayla closed her eyes. Breathed. And waited.

Then she felt it—fingers in her mind, tiptoeing between the threads the superbug had laid out. A spark of power, a gem that glowed like a sun, a tiny bead sewn inside her head. Then another. And another. A glittering trail laid out, crisscrossing the landscape of her mind, lighting the way to a path she'd lost long ago.

Each spark she passed filled her a little more, giving her a boost as she climbed up and over, hunting out the next one, and the next. Until her hands were full with them, and her pockets full, and her heart full.

Tiny gems lighting a path, marbles glowing in her hands, suns forming in her mind...

Power blooming out of nothing. Glass shattering.

Freedom.

She breathed and stretched and *flew*.

This wasn't someone else's power: this was hers. Vayne had showed her the way back to it; Ghirhad had given her the boost she needed to reconnect.

Something shrilled in her ear, a desperate alarm that demanded attention.

"We're losing him!" Fengrathen shouted.

The others didn't know that Ghirhad was already gone. That he had given everything he had left to the cause. *Thank you for your last gift, uncle.*

Kayla laid there for a minute afterward, feeling her strength return, remembering what it was like to have another sense. She was almost afraid to test it.

Someone squeezed her hand. ::Come on, Kay.:: Corinth. She squeezed back.

Vayne's face came into view, smiling in a way she hadn't seen in five too long years.

"See? I told you you weren't broken."

She smiled, or at least she tried to. Mostly she couldn't feel her body.

"Not broken, just lost."

::And now you're home:: he said in her mind.

::And now I'm home.:: But first... "Hook me up to the damn ship and let's get this over with."

It was all sorts of excruciating to get up off the table and onto her feet. After she proved to herself that she could do that, she gave in and let Vayne carry her telekinetically out of the airlock and to the waiting lift platform. The amplifier was several levels down, apparently.

Kayla closed her eyes as they descended. She ran through parts of her mind she hadn't been able to access since before the coup. Places she had forgotten. Skills and strengths she hadn't been able to use. Stars, so many of them...

But virus cells clamored at her from all over. Demanding nothing, just so loud in their existence that she couldn't stand it. They blotted out her mind. That's when she felt the controller stretching its grasp, trying to wriggle tendrils back into and across the path Vayne and Ghirhad had cut for her in her mind. Kayla stamped them out. Every one. It was easier as she became more accustomed to it, but that damn noise...

She might have passed out because the next thing she knew someone was shaking her by the shoulders, calling her name.

"Kayla, you have to wake up. Kayla!"

"Quit it, Vayne, I'm awake."

He didn't look like he believed her. She didn't quite believe her. She was sitting in a very comfortable chair in a tiny round room that was as boring as a cubbyhole.

"If you're sure you're ready, I'm going to plug you in, now," Fengrathen said. Without another warning, she did just that.

Kayla's world expanded. Her psi powers magnified a thousand times. More. A million times. More, even. She could reach out and move a grain of sand on Ordoch's surface with her mind. The things she could do with this much power...

But there was only one thing she wanted.

Malkor's face came into her mind.

"This is for us, my love," she murmured. Then she closed her eyes and sang a lullaby with her will. Wove a blanket of sleep, and laid it over every clamoring voice until each little existence, one by one, dimmed and finally winked out.

EPILOGUE

THREE WEEKS LATER ON ORDOCH

Three weeks later, Kayla stood amongst her family and friends in the center of Vankir City, surrounded by thousands of citizens who had gathered in what used to be downtown, to observe the *Yari*'s final flight. Every vidscreen on every building and scaffolding broadcast the footage of the ship being towed to Ordoch's closer sun.

First Officer Zimmerman stood in a place of honor in the front, along with Officer Fengrathen, Tanet, Larsa, and the few other crew members who had been rescued. While Zimmerman's plan to stop Ida by preventing the *Yari* from traveling to Ordoch had failed, he was still a hero of the people of Ordoch. They all were.

And Ordoch needed heroes right now.

Kayla felt a blunted optimism when she looked at the survivors. Each was receiving proper medical treatment now, and while some brain damage couldn't be reversed, other damage might heal. She hoped so, at least.

On the vidscreens, the *Yari* entered into a steep orbit around the sun. The ship was more than a legend and a weapon, it was the casket for hundreds of ancient Ordochians who would never survive reanimation. They would burn with the ship, along with Captain Janus, who chose death over imprisonment. The punishment for Ida's remaining allies, Benny and Ariel, had yet to be decided.

It was late, the celebration long over. Vayne roamed the Reinumon palace by moonlight, stalking through its halls, noting every wound the imperials had inflicted. For now, it was abandoned. He hoped it stayed that way. Something about the grand house just felt... violated. But that didn't stop him from pacing here at night whenever he couldn't sleep. It was like a sore he kept picking at, returning to over and over.

It wasn't healthy. He knew that. *I won't come back tomorrow*. He just needed to remember tonight, to remember the before, the person he'd been before Dolan had ever come into his world.

Vayne paused his footsteps, waiting...

... but the voice never came. He was well and truly free of Dolan.

So why am I still waiting?

His wandering brought him where it always did: the *en'shaar*'s study, where his father and aunt had worked in tandem. More importantly, it was where he had defeated Dolan for a second time.

Something rustled in the dark as he entered, bringing Vayne's senses to attention. He tightened the shields protecting him and reached out with his mind.

He collided with a consciousness so chaotic and full of rage that he recoiled from the strength of it.

"Natali."

He could barely make her out by the bookshelf, the moonlight pouring in from the window making the shadows deeper next to it. He held perfectly still, willing her not to flee. For years now they'd run from the sight of each other. It was instinctual.

Only... it didn't have to be. He could change things. He'd rather eat glass than face her, but there was no other way.

"We'll never move on if we don't acknowledge what happened." The words were easier said in the dark. For a long time he thought she wouldn't answer.

At last she said, "Perhaps you're right, brother." He heard her coming toward him and he didn't know whether to force the issue by staying in the doorway or to let her pass. She simplified things by gently pushing him aside without touching him.

"Perhaps," Natali said again, and then she was gone.

It was a start.

The next morning Kayla sat outside on a bench, in what used to be the workers' picnic area of the old manufacturing plant. The weathered building that had shielded the heart of the rebellion was at her back, the grass at her feet, and the sun on her face. She tilted her head to catch the most of Ordoch's sunbeams and, eyes closed, smiled.

It was treaty signing day, and all she wanted to do was take her boots off and walk barefoot, toes touching soil.

"You know what I miss?" she said to Malkor, who sat beside her on the bench, soaking up his own dose of sun. "Those damn baby rooks." Who would have thought? "One of those guys would be sitting in our laps right now, a gaggle would be bumbling along ridiculously in the tree branches..." She could picture it, even though the rooks had only stayed at Ordoch for a few days.

Malkor chuckled. "You are alone in that one. They were always underfoot."

"But they were so fun." She cracked one eye open to see him shaking his head.

The rooks had left within days of jumping the *Yari* to Ordoch. If Kazamel interpreted their combination image–emotion language correctly, normal space made them ill. Or hurt them. Some equivalent thereof. The Mine Field, with its broken physics, was the only area in this dimension that they enjoyed. And now that they knew they were killing living creatures when they tore open ships to get at the fuel, the fun had gone out of things.

"I think," Malkor said, "they are returning to their home dimension. Or their interdimensional home. I'm not quite sure."

"I am never returning to space for as long as I live," Kayla said. Leave interdimensional beings to someone else. The grass in the courtyard, the open air, the sunshine, it was all glorious.

"Never?" Malkor asked. "Does that mean I should tell Hekkar to unpack our bags?"

She sighed and opened her eyes. "Is it really time to leave?"

"Sad but true."

Kayla had been so busy these last few weeks, helping her people begin the long and arduous process of reclaiming their world, that she hadn't paid attention to the preparations being made for the trip back to Imperial Space.

More importantly, for the queen bug's trip to Imperial Space.

The thin, impossibly long arm of the *Yari* that housed the PD had been dismantled prior to the *Yari*'s demise. Engineers had extracted the only two parts Kayla needed: the psionic amplifier and the drive that powered it.

Those had been fitted to a modern Ordochian ship, which would carry Kayla on a journey through the Protectorate and Sovereign Planets until each cell of the TNV she could find had been obliterated.

Ironically, the ancient virus Ida had released on Ordoch wasn't harmful to the imperial forces stationed there. It only attacked the cartaid arch. Once the arch was destroyed, or if you didn't have one, as imperials did not, then the virus would simply become dormant. Thankfully, the empire was not privy to that information, or treaty negotiations would have gone a lot differently.

It had taken the imperials' own scientists to adapt the virus to their brains, and in the process they had unknowingly unlocked the runaway replication—the real danger from the TNV. But no matter who was responsible for unleashing what,

Kayla felt the ultimate responsibility for stopping all of it.

It didn't make leaving Ordoch any easier.

"We'll make it as quick as possible," Malkor said. He gave her hand a squeeze. "Don't worry, there will be plenty left to do when we return."

"Corinth will be excited it's time to travel," she said.

"He's still determined to come with us?"

"He told me he's ready for another adventure. Apparently three weeks of litter picking and debris hauling have not been exciting enough for him." And life on Ordoch was going to be like that for some time. There was so much to be done. "Besides, I don't think he wants to be away from Trinan and Vid."

"Those two spoil him too much. I told them that."

Rigger, Hekkar, Tanet, and Vid still hadn't decided what they would do next, now that they had all been pardoned and given honors as heroes of the empire for their roles in everything. For now, they intended to accompany Kayla and Malkor on their journey, and she was glad for it.

Secretly she hoped they'd decide to live on Ordoch afterward, but she wouldn't push it. Not yet, anyway…

Malkor rose from the bench and pulled her to her feet by their entwined fingers. "Come on, we'll be late."

A crowd had been forming all morning. Today was the big day—the formal treaty signing day—and Natali and Wetham decided the momentous event should take place here, at the rebel base, rather than in the Complex of the Oligarchs or at the Reinumon palace. This was where the hope of the Ordochian people was kept alive, and this was where its future would begin.

Isonde, Ardin, the generals of the army, Wetham, and Natali had been closeted for long hours drawing the treaty up. The Council of Seven had ratified it immediately. Ilmena had added its stamp of approval as well, committing to supplying the empire with the plans for the 10-22R inoculation. Kayla wouldn't live forever, and no one wanted to take chances.

* * *

Kayla tucked her arm through Malkor's as they approached where her family had gathered with the others. Natali and Wetham were of course discussing state business. Thankfully they'd both seen the wisdom of becoming joint rulers as they took Ordoch into a new era. Watching their leaders argue, the poor lieutenants of the rebellion looked pained, as if they couldn't decide if they should side with their rebel leader or their hereditary leader. Hopefully the contentious period between Natali and Wetham would end soon. They would rule well together, Kayla could already tell—once they finally accepted that neither's commands outweighed the other.

Vayne was talking in a group with Tia'tan and Noar, among others, and he actually looked somewhat at ease. He might even have smiled at something Tia'tan said to him.

Kayla pulled Malkor to a stop, wanting to drink in this rare moment, savor the image of her brother coming back to life. It filled her heart.

Malkor leaned down and whispered in her ear. "You know he can feel it when you stare at him like that." There was a gentle tease in his voice. "He said it was like having a chaperone."

"Do I do it that much?"

He chuckled. "All the time, my love."

Vayne broke away from the group when he saw them, and came over to say hi. He greeted Malkor, if not warmly, then at least in a friendly fashion. It was a start. Malkor left the two of them alone to talk for a moment.

::Are you still determined to leave?:: Vayne asked.

::Must you say it like that?:: She'd never grow tired of this, being able to speak mind to mind, as they ought to have been able to this entire time. ::It's only for a short while, and then I'll be home again.::

He looked past her shoulder to where Corinth was excitedly telling Malkor something. ::And will it be their home as well?::

::Certainly, should the octet want that. Should Malkor.::

Vayne made a sound of exasperation and returned his gaze to her. ::Of course that's what he wants, you idiot. You just haven't asked him yet. Both of you are too worried about the other feeling obligated that neither wants to say anything.:: He grinned. ::It makes me want to strangle both of you.::

::Admit it, you've wanted to strangle Malkor for longer than that.::

::True.:: He paused. ::Just promise me you'll come back.::

::Of course I will. What kind of thing is that to say?:: She whacked him on the shoulder, because that was the kind of affection *ro'haars* gave their brothers, when their hearts were too full with leave-taking and hope for the future that they couldn't speak, psionically or otherwise.

::Are you still determined to stay?:: she asked him finally.

::I think so. What other place is there for me? This is our home.::

It was the first time he'd said it, and something in her eased to hear it. She'd know where to find him when this was all over, when her work for the people of the empire was finally done. And she'd be with her *il'haars* once again.

Kayla sensed the shift in his mood, the darkness that always lurked in him these days coming closer to the surface.

::You know:: he said, and she braced herself. ::If you bring him back here, things won't be the same.::

Him always referred to Malkor.

Through their link, Kayla saw memories of their life together on Ordoch, in the time Vayne only ever referenced as *before*. *Before*, he was happy. Before, he was whole. There was laughter and triumph and joy in those memories.

::Oh Vayne.:: He was close enough that she could feel his struggle. ::Things were never going to be the same.::

He nodded, expecting the answer.

::But they can be better:: Kayla countered, stopping him from walking away. ::Before, we had only each other. The single *il'haar–ro'haar* system was so rigid that it kept us isolated, even among our family. Now we have so much more.:: She summoned images of Corinth, of Natali, of Tia'tan and Malkor and even Tanet, *Yari*'s sole surviving physicist, who had been found innocent of any collusion with Captain Janus.

::We have all these people now, and we know them deeper and better than we ever could have if things continued on as they'd always been.::

"I love you," she said aloud, needing him to hear it. She pulled him close in a fierce hug. "You will always be my *il'haar*, and I will always be your *ro'haar*." She leaned back, looking at him eye to eye without letting go. "We will just have more people to look after than we did when it was only you and I."

His lips quirked. The corner of his mouth kicked up, and he almost grinned when he said, "I have a hard enough time looking out for you as it is."

There were a million more things to say, emotions to share, healing to do… But it could all wait for another day. After all, they had the rest of their lives.

Kayla stepped back. The shadow in Vayne's eyes passed, the set of his shoulders relaxed slightly.

Good.

The chatter of the gathered crowd came back to her, and Kayla caught sight of Tia'tan looking their way, concern in her eyes. Vayne saw her, too, and even without eavesdropping Kayla knew they were speaking to each other. In fact, she'd noticed it quite a bit these last few weeks.

"You know," Kayla drawled, unable to resist poking him verbally. "If Tia'tan stays here, things are never going to be the same."

He shook his head. "Ilmena has recalled her, now that the occupation is at an end. Besides, Tia wouldn't want to stay on Ordoch."

"To quote someone I love very dearly, 'Of course that's what she wants, you idiot. You just haven't asked her yet.'"

He looked distinctly uncomfortable at the entire conversation, and Kayla suspected she had hit close to the truth.

Vayne nudged her. "Go find Malkor before he puts his foot in his mouth… again."

ACKNOWLEDGEMENTS

Thanks go first to my agent, Richard Curtis, for being my advisor and advocate. I had a difficult time during the writing of this novel and he was supportive throughout. Thanks to my editors, Cat Camacho and Joanna Harwood, who gave me excellent notes for improving the book. A big thanks to Titan Books for being flexible with my deadlines.

Thanks to my husband James for being the wonderful, supportive, and all-round fun partner that he is. I wouldn't have gotten this book done without his pep talks and cheerleading, not to mention the insane number of times he walked the dog when it was really my turn to walk her.

I receive a lot of help from my two critique partners, Diana Botsford and Jen Brooks, but I have to say an extra special thank-you to Jen, who went above and beyond the call of duty by turning around critiques at a blistering pace at the eleventh hour when I desperately needed her help—even when she was on vacation. I can only hope to be half the friend/crit partner she has been to me.

Most of all, thank you to my mum and sisters. It would take too long to list the many ways they are wonderful, so, ladies, let me just say, "I know you know."

ABOUT THE AUTHOR

Rhonda Mason divides her time between writing, editing, bulldogs, and beaching. Her writing spans the gamut of speculative fiction, from space opera to epic fantasy to urban paranormal and back again. The only thing limiting her energy for fantastical worlds is the space-time continuum. When not creating worlds, she edits for a living, and follows her marine biologist husband to the nearest beach. In between preserving sea grass and deterring invasive species, she snorkels every chance she gets. Her rescue bulldog, Grace, is her baby and faithful companion. Grace follows her everywhere, as long as she's within distance of a couch she can sleep on. Rhonda is a graduate of the Writing Popular Fiction masters program at Seton Hill University, and recommends it to all genre writers interested in furthering their craft at graduate level.

You can find Rhonda at
www.RhondaMason.com

THE EMPRESS GAME
RHONDA MASON

The Empress Game, the tournament that decides who fills the final seat on the intergalactic Sakien Empire's supreme ruling body, has been called. The seat isn't won by votes, but in a tournament of ritualized combat. Kayla Reinumon, a supreme fighter, is called to the arena. With the empire wracked by a rising nanovirus plague and stretched thin by an ill-advised planet-wide occupation of Ordoch, everything rests on the woman who rises to the top.

CLOAK OF WAR
EMPRESS GAME BOOK 2

The bloody tournament to determine the new empress of the intergalactic empire may be over, but for exiled princess Kayla Reinumon, the battle is just beginning. To free her home planet from occupation, Kayla must infiltrate the highest reaches of imperial power. But when a deadly nanovirus threatens to ravage the empire, it will take more than diplomacy to protect her homeworld from all-out war.

THE HIGH GROUND

MELINDA SNODGRASS

Emperor's daughter Mercedes is the first woman ever admitted to the High Ground, the elite training academy of the Solar League's Star Command, and she must graduate if she is to have any hope of taking the throne. Her classmate Tracy has more modest goals—to rise to the rank of captain, and win fame and honor. But a civil war is coming and the political machinations of those who yearn for power threaten the young cadets. In a time of intrigue and alien invasion, they will be tested as they never thought possible.

"Melinda Snodgrass just keeps getting better and better."
George R.R. Martin

"Space opera with a social conscience as well as lots of sprawling action." David Drake, bestselling author of *With the Lightnings*

"Written with an easy elegance. The opening salvo of what promises to be a grand space opera." Bennet R. Coles, author of *Virtues of War*

OFF ROCK

KIERAN SHEA

In the year 2778, Jimmy Vik is feeling dissatisfied. After busting his ass for assorted interstellar mining outfits for close to two decades, downsizing is in the wind and his ex-girlfriend/ supervisor is climbing up his back. So when Jimmy stumbles upon a significant gold pocket during a routine procedure on Kardashev 7-A, he believes his luck may have changed— larcenously so. But smuggling the gold "off rock" won't be easy...

"Get the casts of *Firefly* and *The Expanse* good and hammered, then say something about their mothers. The ensuing brawl looks a lot like *Off Rock*."
Robert Brockway, senior editor at Cracked.com

"A sci-fi caper with wit, style and imagination to burn."
Chris Holm, author of *The Killing Kind*

"*Off Rock* is a joy from cover to cover."
Marcus Sakey, author of *The Brilliance* trilogy